THE WORLD'S REVOLUTION
· BOOK TWO ·

NATURE ERUPTS

A CLIMATE CRISIS ANTHOLOGY
EDITED BY C.D. TAVENOR

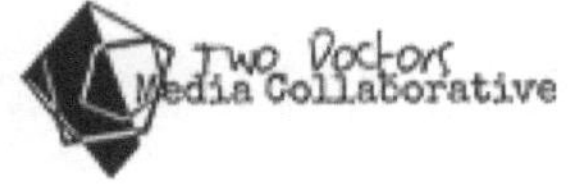

Published by Two Doctors Media Collaborative LLC

www.twodoctorsmedia.com

Cover design by S.E. MacCready

https://semaccready.com

This is a work of fiction. Names, characters, businesses, places, events, locales, and incidents are either the products of the authors' imagination or used in a fictitious manner. Any resemblance to actual persons, living or dead, or actual events is purely coincidental.

ISBN (E-Book): 978-1-952706-37-0

ISBN (Paperback): 978-1-952706-36-3

ISBN (Hardcover: 978-1-952706-38-7

CONTENTS

AN INTRODUCTION TO NATURE ERUPTS

Welcome to the second anthology of the World's Revolution.

I'm incredibly honored to have had the opportunity to work with the authors of *Nature Erupts*. Their stories inspire every day, even after I've completed editing and compiling the anthology. Their words continually shift the way I think about the climate crisis, and I hope they'll do the same for you.

Just like *Gaia Awakens*, the second anthology of the World's Revolution features stories all entangled in one narrative. *Nature Erupts* builds off the stories you've likely already read in a variety of ways, some more explicit than others. Our returning authors often decided to continue narratives of the characters they developed two years ago, but others went in entirely different directions. Our new authors brought fresh perspective to the World's Revolution, injecting a new take on the spirituality of the fight against the climate crisis or rejecting the fantastical elements of the story entirely.

Some stories stand on their own within the overarching narrative, illustrating a thematic point complicating the other stories of the World's

Revolution. Others connect with one or two others. Quite a few tell a larger, overarching story building off the events of *Gaia Awakens*. Together, they weave a complex tapestry of climate fiction.

All around, *Nature Erupts* pushes the narrative of the World's Revolution toward an ending—though it may not be the ending you expect. You'll need to read to see how it all plays out.

The stories contained herein reflect the worldviews, narratives, and hopes of these authors. They are one small part of the infinite multiplicity of stories continually being told about humanity's relationship to the climate crisis. Maybe you have a story inside yourself—write it! Read these stories as reflections of these authors—and use them to find more stories of climate fiction. Use them to inspire your own tale. Use them to shift your perspective slightly, understanding the worldviews of a few writers spread across the world.

I want this introduction to be brief, so I'll end it with a brief reminder: climate fiction acquires its power from the reader sitting with a story's themes and considering how it impacts their world in the here and now. The climate crisis is upon us; it surrounds us every day. Whether you live in Columbus, Ohio like me, where a once-in-a-life time derecho/heat wave knocked out the power of 200,000 people in 2022, or you live in the regions experiencing continuous drought (here in the US or worldwide), or your community is facing the impending threat of sea level rise, climate change is not a future event.

It has arrived.

So when you read these stories—or any climate fiction—let it inspire you to hope for a better world. Let it move you to take action. Let it give you the strength to stand up against the oppressive forces creating the climate crisis in the first place.

In solidarity,

C.D. Tavenor

A MOMENT TO BREATHE

ADAM BASSETT

Town of Chatteris, United Kingdom
2055 C.E.

The drive home from London took about two hours. It shouldn't have, but the car was so old he could practically smell the petrol. Under better circumstances, he might have welcomed it. Two hours to do nothing but drift off, avoid the odd bird, and listen to music. The speakers' bass didn't do Gale Zee's new album justice. He tried to focus on her music, but his mind kept drifting back to London.

Fitz had tried to make it work in the city. He really did. But every day he went to that little office, listening to jackhammers and cement trucks continually raise floodwalls around the Thames while he sat alone in his cubicle reading shit that the big-shot barristers didn't want to. Software could only get you so far. So much had to be sifted through manually. Interpreted. Fitz knew paperwork came with a career in law, but at uni he used to be able to break that kind of work up with other things: lacrosse, anthropological studies, the odd concert. No time for that after graduation. He didn't fully grasp what his chosen career would be like until his two years at CC. It must be a problem with them, he thought, and found a new job at Dunn, Weiss, & Falburg. Nothing changed.

He was already thinking about putting in his two weeks when his mother called. His father was getting worse. She wasn't sure how much longer he would be around. He wasn't on death's door, but things were getting harder. His memory was slipping, his breathing more strained. "He's not about to keel over, you know," his mother said. Fitz could imagine her sitting on the edge of her gaudy corduroy chair—just as he was at his desk—whispering so his father couldn't hear her. "I didn't think about these things before. Now it's all that's on my mind. I don't know what shape he'll be in the next time you see him."

"What are you doing?" Jacob Dunn asked, his frosted tips poking above the cubicle walls. He didn't need to explain his meaning, but he glared at Fitz and mimed putting a phone down all the same.

Fitz wrote his letter of resignation on his work computer. That night, he updated his employment status on his social accounts. Maybe it was a bit early, but who would really care? Two weeks later, he was on the road, headed toward the town of Chatteris: home.

There was no plan. He just knew he was sick of work—sick of London—and that his father was sick. He wanted to see him before he got worse. He wanted to think about something other than soliciting. He wanted his father to stay alive and his mother to relax and to feel like he hadn't wasted his youth getting a degree he didn't want. Fitz sucked on his lips, wishing he could think of just one way to achieve any of that. Should have gone into med school like his father suggested. Then at least he might be able to help people. Or maybe he should throw himself into the English Channel to see if he could *awaken* like one of those delusional wanna-be superheroes trying to save the Earth from these rising tides. At least that would be interesting, right?

•••••••••••

A142 would have been underwater if not for the temporary barriers erected along each side. The road marked the end of Fitz's trip north. When he visited from university, the land was farmlands and forests like something out of a storybook—but most of that was flooded now. Soham and Ely were just above the water, but the roads between them were either barricaded or flooded. Even on the A142, he sometimes drove through puddles where the barriers leaked. It got worse as he neared Chatteris. Rust lingered on some of the barriers. Graffiti revealed itself on those beside the old Trinity Farm Fishery, which was rotting in the still water licking its foundations.

· · · ● · ● · ● · · ·

The old house was mostly as Fitz remembered it: small, brick, just like the rest. His mother's little garden had seen better days, though. A large bush remained, but he remembered there being more flowers and ferns around its base last time he visited. Even the birdhouse that used to be posted above it was gone.

A child left his old house. He wore a blue shirt and jeans, his backpack bouncing as he sprinted down the street. Fitz didn't recognize him.

He took out the keys. The music, the engine, all went silent at once. The town was quiet. A sign hung above the streetlight that read: *This is a Neighbourhood Watch area.*

His mother came out of the house and waved, beaming. Fitz got out of the car and gave her a hug. She said, "Your music is too loud."

She insisted on helping bring Fitz's things inside, even though he didn't have that much. Fitz's London flat was furnished when he arrived. He never felt much of a need to get a wider table (it was just him, after all) or a different color couch, so everything he owned fit into a single suitcase and an old messenger bag.

"That was your father's bag, you know," she reminded Fitz.

"Who's the kid?" Fitz asked, nodding down the way he ran.

"Oh, Paul? That's Mary and Melissa's boy. Smart kid. He brings in our mail on his way home from school, sometimes sticks around to help out."

"Nice of him."

"The girls are happy about it. Whenever he's with us, he's not taking apart anything. Oh, right. He loves to take apart things. Sometimes it gets the better of him. He disassembled Mary's watch entirely. He did put it back together *after* he was caught, but apparently it didn't work quite right after that." His mother picked up the messenger bag, grunting under its weight. "Let's go inside and get you settled. Your father will be so happy to see you."

· · • • • • · · ·

"How's London?" his father asked. It was always the first thing he asked, ever since Fitz left for uni. *How's London.* The answer was always the same: busy, loud, tiresome, but the food was excellent. On one street he could find Indian takeout, American fast food, Italian pizza, a Thai restaurant, Turkish café, a French bakery, some kind of sushi place, and no fewer than two pubs.

"Great," Fitz said, joining his father at the kitchen table.

"Your mother told me you quit your job."

Of course she did.

"It was time to move on," Fitz shrugged.

"You have another firm lined up?"

"I'm not sure if I'll go to another firm," Fitz said. Then, before his father could argue: "Not in the city anyway. Maybe a smaller town. Like Chatteris."

"I thought you liked London."

His mother set a cup of coffee in front of him. She smiled sadly at him. She knew. He didn't see a point in hiding anything from her. The day Fitz told her he was coming to visit, the day he quit, he told her about all that. She never judged him (openly) about that stuff. His father . . .

"I like London," Fitz lied. "The firms there are just rough. Always plowing forward, never putting much care into the case. It's like working at a butcher's. I feel like I could help better at a smaller place. Besides, the construction was giving me migraines on the daily."

"Is Mary-Anne still practicing?" his father asked.

Fitz shrugged. He wasn't even sure he knew who that was.

His mother leaned back in her chair. "She retired and moved to Paris, after she met that Franco fellow, remember?"

"Right." He furrowed his brow.

"We can talk about this later," she said. "I'm sure Fitz didn't come all this way to talk about work. And you have that meeting tonight."

"Meeting?" Fitz asked.

"Your father's been attending Mr. Weber's town meetings."

"He moved in earlier this year for some job. A very bright young man," Fitz's father said, his eyes suddenly alight. Suddenly he was talking with his mouth *and* hands. "He's trying to raise money to improve the flood control around here. Barriers are starting to leak, and the permanent barriers we were promised when the fens began to flood years ago never came. He figures if we're loud enough we can raise a bit of money—a bit of awareness—that the fens are in trouble." A pause. "You should come."

"You're going tonight?" Fitz asked, looking up at his mother, willing her to get the implied message: *is he well enough to go out tonight—to a gathering like this?*

"That would be lovely," she said. Either his silent message went over her head, or she was telling him it would be fine. Fitz couldn't tell which.

· · · • · • · · ·

The meeting was at the café just down the street, near enough to walk. Fitz stayed close to his father. He could hear the old man's breath strain as they neared the café, though he refused to show it.

Once they were inside, he led Fitz toward a group of people gathering on one side of the café. He was introduced to nearly two dozen people. He recognized most of them but couldn't place any names without help. They were all busy with their careers or uni when he was trying to learn BMX tricks with his friends down West Street. He'd never really thought to pay any attention to them back then. They all knew him though. They welcomed him like a prodigal son returning home.

The ones who didn't know him from back then shook his hand and called him "the barrister," which was a hell of a stretch, but he didn't bother correcting anyone.

Thomas Weber showed up a minute later. He wore a collared shirt and jeans, all ironed and bright. Even his smile shone when he shook Fitz's hand and said, "It's great to finally meet you." As if they'd already been friends long before this.

"Tell Fitz what you're working on now," his father encouraged the man.

"It's nothing, really. In the grand scheme of things our efforts often go unnoticed—and not for no reason. There's terrible things happening across the world—but they matter to the locals. You saw the flooding on the way up, right? Of course you did. Can't miss the sound of your wheels plowing through the leakpools. We've been able to replace some of the worst barriers, but it's not enough. Thankfully, a lot of these old towns were built up on hills—however small they may be—but a few places have already succumbed to the rising waters. Wiggenhall, Nordelph, half of Thorney and Crowland are good as gone now. Whole towns just wiped off the map, ruins for future generations to wonder how anyone ever lived there. It's no Tuvalu, and there aren't as many people at risk here as there are in the big cities, but this is where the farms are. Where lives are, you know?"

Fitz opened his mouth to agree, but Thomas didn't seem to notice.

"Of course," he pressed on, pacing around them, "I don't need to tell you—you get it. You grew up here. Your father's very proud of you, by the way. But that's why we're all here—to protect what's left. The barriers we have won't last forever, and nobody in Parliament seems to care. You vote conservative, labour, green? Doesn't matter. That's why we've got to take action ourselves. Raise money. Raise hell. Within reason, of course. Listen, if you're going to stick around for a while, we could use your help. A big-shot London barrister could really make some positive changes here."

"I don't—"

"I'm not saying you're going to change the world." Thomas raised his hands. One found their way onto Fitz's shoulder. "Small steps forward are still *steps forward*. Just put a bug in somebody's ear. Get your firm to donate to our cause. Tell them it will be good for public approval or something—they love that stuff. You know. We do what we can here, but I'll bet you could really rustle some feathers. Okay, good talk, I have to go see Mary though and best to do that early on—she'll talk your ear off so if I don't go now we'll start the meeting late again!"

And then he was off, gliding to another corner of the café where a pair of women hugged him.

"That was . . ."

"I know." Fitz's father laughed. "He gets excited. Come on, I'll get you a coffee."

· · · • · • · · ·

Thomas Weber didn't appear to have many talking points, because much of the meeting sounded extremely similar to what he'd talked to Fitz and his father beforehand. Still, they were important points. When he called on Fitz and asked "what's the scene like in London?" he thought about it for a moment and realized how different things were. All the construction he hated listening to from dawn to dusk outside his flat was on floodwalls and those new drainage channels, and in the distance the drone of an always growing wind farm.

When Fitz described that to the nearly two dozen attendees, they didn't focus on his complaint about the noise. Even the barista scoffed. He hadn't realized she'd been listening until then.

"This is what I'm talking about." Thomas grinned, his eyes wild. "They can totally reshape London, but when it comes to the fens, it's too expensive or too *low-impact* to bother with! I don't want to be in Cambridge a few years from now shouting 'remember the fens' because those arseholes in Westminster decided to put our calls on hold!"

Everyone in the café—his father included—performed some mixture of shouting or raising their fists. The air in the café had changed. Fitz had expected a meeting about local matters, where the old folk who attended were more concerned about how each others' kids were doing. Even after he met Thomas, he figured it would just be a fundraiser. This was something different.

Fitz raised a fist with them, just to fit in. It felt good.

· · · ● · ● · · ·

Fitz had been in his hometown for a few weeks when he decided to call an old friend in London about Thomas' fundraiser.

He met Olivia at CC, his first big employer post-university. They were both paper jockeys, and both quit around the same time. When he went to another firm, she joined London Solutions—a green power company that needed somebody to handle their legal and paperwork. They'd hardly spoken since, but she frequently updated her social media with selfies in front of people she met or sheets of solar panels. By the look of her public feed, she seemed more involved in things than her title suggested.

She was still on Fitz's contact list from that one time they'd gotten Thai food three years ago (it hadn't worked out, clearly). He tapped her name and brought his phone to his ear.

The dial tone lasted centuries. The pauses between them were monumental.

Olivia's voice came through, suggesting he leave a message after the beep.

Fitz hung up. It was ridiculous to think she would help. They hardly knew each other anymore.

He searched through his contact list again. Most of the people there were former co-workers. He wasn't on bad terms with any of them, but he hadn't exactly become friends with any either. Olivia had been the closest thing he had to that—for a time. How, Fitz wondered, had he spent so many years in London, but made so few actual connections? He tried to think back, and there was really no good reason for any of the early nights to bed or turning down Peter's invitations to the pub. When did they stop inviting him, again? Was Chatteris going to drown because he didn't feel like getting a beer with his co-workers?

Fitz laughed. How could he not? The only other option was to acknowledge how ridiculous and fucked things were.

For a moment, he even considered reaching out to one of those international environmental groups always in the news talking about fighting for "Gaia" or whatever. The groups supposedly hiding secret superheroes. They often made a spectacle of their barristers. Maybe even barrister superheroes. But no. Even if one of those groups wanted to help, they'd probably only make things worse for Chatteris. Chaos and destruction always followed well-meaning international activist organizations. He'd seen what happened on the news in Michigan over in the Midwestern Federation. Those moose. *Robot* moose. And the protests. And subsequent mass arrests.

His phone vibrated in his hands. Olivia's name appeared on the screen. It took a moment to realize what was happening. On the second vibration, he pressed the large green call button and raised the phone to his ear.

"Hello?"

"Hey, you called?" Olivia sounded different than he remembered. Her voice seemed brighter. Maybe it was just the phone.

"Yeah, I'm glad you called back. How have you been?"

"Fine, you?"

"Good, yeah."

A pause.

"I heard you quit DWF?" she asked.

"Yeah." Fitz stared up at the ceiling. "I've just been helping my folks back home for a bit."

"Oh, good. I always love going back to Cardiff to see my family there."

"Right, yeah."

Fitz took a deep breath.

"So what's actually going on, you?"

"What do you mean?"

"You drop off the face of the Earth for three years then call all of a sudden? I don't mind, but you're not just calling to catch up. You don't do that." She laughed. "You need a job or something? I'm not sure we're hiring but—"

"No," he stopped her. "It's nice of you to offer, but no, I think I'm done with all that. I don't think CC was the problem—I think I just don't like the job."

"CC was definitely a problem." She laughed again. "You heard about the lawsuit against them right?"

"No?"

"Yeah, we got out before things *really* got bad. They're in hot water right now. Something about under the table deals, bribing officials, it's a whole thing. I hear the UN might be dropping some climate bounties on key execs."

"Christ. Can't say I'm surprised, though."

"Yeah. But if you don't need me for a job, what's actually up?"

"Well . . . the hometown's in hot water too, Liv."

She was silent.

"Listen." Fitz stalled, trying to find the right words. He hadn't actually planned this far ahead. "Things are basically underwater. A lot of the old towns out here in the fens are up on hills, but they're not that high up. On my way north, I saw barriers leaking and farms rotting in a couple inches of water. Wiggenhall, Crowland, all submerged. Future generations are going to grow up on *islands* out where there used to be vast farmlands and cattle fields. Long enough and these places are just going to be wiped off the map. But there's some people here trying to prevent it from getting any worse. We just don't have the money—"

"I could donate a couple of pounds," Olivia said. It felt like a knife in Fitz's heart.

"No, I mean, your company does environmental work, right?"

"We help set up solar panels and maintain one of the wind farms around *London*," she said. "The smallest wind farm."

"Could you talk to your boss for us?"

"Us?"

"I just mean—"

"Fitz, I admire that you've found something you care about. Really, I do. But LoSo isn't a charity. We've only got a dozen people here. We can't send the money you need, and our people can't drive three hours north to set anything up in a swamp. It sounds like things are already too far gone anyway. Green power doesn't do a lot of good for people who are already underwater."

Fitz bit his lip. He could taste blood.

"Have you tried contacting the green financing people in Westminster? I think they're the ones funding all the construction around the Thames."

"Yeah," he said. Thomas had, at least. They didn't answer or return his calls.

"Maybe the Red Cross, or something?"

"They're busy," Fitz said.

She was quiet for a while, until finally Olivia said: "You should just bring your family to London. They'll be safe here. We can actually help them here."

"We?"

"Look, you know what I mean. Out there, it's just too hard to do anything. We have to focus on where people actually live. Besides, the coast there is so low. It's too complicated, too expensive. Do you know what it costs to install just one drainage channel? I saw an article on it the other day—"

"Thanks, Liv," Fitz said. He ended the call.

· · · ● · ● · · · ·

Fitz went out seeking donations with his father—the exercise was good for him anyway, and it gave them a chance to talk. They knocked on doors in Ely and Huntingdon. A few other people from the weekly meetings joined in as well. Mary and her wife went as far as Cambridge—though they had little luck.

Despite no help from Liv or any other group outside the fens, they raised enough money to replace a large section of floodwall along the A142. Thomas said the town council of Chatteris and the city council of Ely were both on board and adding to the donations with what they could. So much of the coastline was already lost, but they could at least protect some of what remained.

The sum total was a good chunk of cash. Enough to change somebody's life. But in terms of flood prevention, it wasn't nearly enough. Still, Thomas was talking about how they could prevent Chatteris' islandification. That alone would have ripple effects. Somersham, Colne, and Earith (the most enthusiastic donors to their cause by far) would be protected by the new walls too. The new wetland that formed between Chatteris and those towns might dry up and become usable again.

That night's meeting was more like a party. Thomas convinced the local pub to donate some of their beer and the café played all the music the volunteers liked—mostly old pop and punk from the turn of the century. It didn't strike Fitz quite right, but it wasn't awful. He got to see his father happier than he'd ever seen the man in his life. He was flirting with Mary, which Fitz recognized was probably not an excellent choice, but the man was in his eighties and ill. Fitz decided not to raise a fuss, and Mary eventually got distracted by Thomas anyway.

His father sat next to Fitz after that, a dumb grin on his face. "We did good," he said, taking in the room, taking in deep breaths.

"I think so," Fitz said.

"I'm glad you're here."

Fitz put a hand on his old man's back. "You better not cause problems for Ma when we get home after this."

He stared back at Fitz for a moment longer than seemed right, his eyes glazed over, until finally they weren't. Like a light switched on somewhere inside his head, he nodded his head so quickly, he almost fell out of his chair.

"How many beers did you have?" Fitz asked as he got him upright again.

"Just one, I think." He giggled.

"Well, you're cut off, you damn drunk." Fitz laughed. "Stay there, I'm getting you some water."

· · · ● · ● · · · ·

Thomas wasn't at the next meeting. They held it without him after waiting nearly an hour, but there wasn't a lot to discuss. Nobody had an agenda, not even an idea about what to do next. Mary suggested they should start thinking about the next fundraiser, insisting there was more that could be done. Nobody disagreed, but Fitz wondered aloud how often they could ask for money before they were turned away. Only the small towns in the fens were listening to them, and they had the most finite resources.

Nobody disagreed.

That week, as things calmed down, Fitz found work at the café. The owner recognized him from Thomas' meetings, and one of her baristas had just flown to London for university. It didn't pay much, but the hours were flexible, and since the café was where Thomas held his meetings, he could work and keep an eye on his father when he attended them. His father insisted he should set higher goals for himself, but Fitz just told him he'd figure that out later. For the time being, he was glad to be home and help them out around the house.

Thomas was absent the next meeting too, and when Mary went snooping around his house she saw his car was gone. The lights were off. She was in tears when she told everyone. Nobody wanted to say what they all were thinking. They contacted the police station to see if any calls had come in from or about that address. They asked Thomas' neighbors if they'd seen anything. Finally, it was Fitz's father who said it: "We got conned."

"It's criminal," Fitz's mother said over the dinner table. Her face was beet red.

His father had that blank stare again.

"Isn't there anything you can do?" she asked.

"What's done is done," Fitz said. "Even if we found him, we can't even go after him. Everything was a handshake agreement. Nobody signed anything when they donated to us. Legally, the group is no more valid than a church choir or secondary school clique. Best to just move on."

Fitz took a drink of coffee from his mother's yellow Kim Possible mug. One of the many perks of his new job. He hadn't been able to afford this much coffee since before university. It was weak, though. He was only allowed to take home coffee made with reused beans, but at least it was something.

"It's disgraceful," his mother said. "You all did such good work and it's just gone."

His father said something, too quiet to catch.

"You think somebody will pick up where Thomas left off?" Fitz asked. "Once Mary gets over this, I could see her doing it. She and Melissa were always there."

"Mary likes to talk," his mother said, "but she would be a mess running a thing like that. She can't even stop Paul from tearing apart their devices. She's got no understanding of how to run a group like that. How to make contact with benefactors, how to handle money like that," she said. "She might give it a shot but I don't think she could manage it all. Despite how it ended up, Thomas was doing a lot."

Fitz took another drink. "That's all it is, isn't it?"

"What?"

"Talking to people. Moving money around. A couple of smart invest-ments. Being at the meetings and, you know, just giving a shit." Fitz swirled the half-cup of coffee he had left, watching it lap up against the walls of his mug. "I could do that."

SINK OR SWIM

ISHA G.K.

Mumbai, India
2055 C.E.

The ghost of Mumbai first came to Anu in the middle of a committee chamber in the Municipal Corporation building. She dressed irreverently as a local Koli fisherwoman, short coloured saree flashing stark in high-definition 4K while the rest of the room faded to suits and skirts to accommodate her.

Anu furrowed her eyebrows. *What?*

Her eleven years in international business development had not prepared her for a woman floating, *literally floating*, around a faceless pack of corporators.

The corporators, of course, appeared unfazed. While the . . . *thing . . .* laid hands on their shoulders, looked into their notes, or patted their heads, the men and women of the City Affairs committee went about their, well, affairs.

I must be dreaming, Anu thought, diverting her eyes to the domed ceiling. *This city does not allow me to sleep, and then sends me a floating Koli as a wake-up call.*

She heard an oddly dainty laugh radiating from the centre of the room. "Little do you know, child," came a sing-song voice.

What, what, what?

Anu's eyes shot to the committee Chair's desk. No ghost. The Chair, a Borivali corporator, furiously typed into an Xplorer holoboard. Around the Chair, the other corporators—both physical and virtual attendees—whispered unperturbed. Their echoes rang against the concrete of the Indo-Saracenic walls, impossible to miss. Yet Anu could have sworn that moments before, their deliberation had been dimmed in favour of a golden-skinned ghost.

I'm really dreaming.

She shook her head, turning back to the corporators. She needed to get her head back to the real world. There was no ghost. There were only the committee chambers and these corrupt corporators, starkly reluctant and uncertain about her.

Anu found it laughable. *This is it, then. Sink or swim.*

The committee Chair cleared her throat then. "We appreciate you for recognising Mumbai's prowess in transforming cities and indeed, our world," she said in crisp Marathi. Nodding, she switched rapidly to English. "However, we cannot arrive at a consensus at this time. We apologise—but opening our systems so radically to SustainAble and ReCity is not a minor decision. Our constituents owe it to us to make it in good conscience."

Good conscience. A teenaged Anu might have bristled at the hypocrisy. Now, past thirty, she had both the training to retain a smile and the experience to give the Chair the benefit of doubt.

Perhaps this woman, insignificant as the city ward she had been plucked from, truly cared about the dying remains of Mumbai. Unfortunately, she lacked the acumen to recognise that her home finally had a golden ticket to regaining significance, and that it would not find one again.

This is the oldest story in the world, Anu thought. *Or at least in this decade.*

The truth had never been clearer. The acquisition of ReCity by SustainAble had transformed urban areas across the globe, despite resistance from tech-fearing de-growthers and not-in-my-backyarders. Anu had developed a knack for countering these individuals—typically millennials with a warped sense of justice and privacy. This had, in turn, helped her catapult quickly into international business development—at the highest levels of corporate, paid to shuttle across borders at ReCity's expense.

The truth is, our tech deserves better than this sorry city, Anu thought.

"Is *that* what you think?" she heard then, soft at first, then loud, and soft again. Singing.

Anu's breath caught. *What on earth?*

She nevertheless ignored the nagging voice. *Never mind our tech, I deserve better than this sorry city*, she thought. *Nightmares in the middle of a working day, what's next? God forbid someone in this slumworld of a city thinks they recognise me.*

Anu once again shook her head. *Never mind that.*

Once the formalities were over, she spoke her rehearsed gratitude to the corporators and exited the committee's chambers. *They think sinking a ReCity transformation will help them swim. They don't realise that they're halfway to the Indian Ocean floor already, gasping for air.*

Even as the thought formed in her head, though, Anu found herself reflecting on her bias. It especially stood out later when her associate, Matt, questioned her approach.

"Well, how did you feel about that?" she asked him on the footpath outside as their autonomous Tata hissed to life. Anu started softly massaging her shoulders after sitting down, glad for the comfort of the car. The exorbitant rental and parking expense was more than worth it—she could not imagine how the packed metros and buses would have felt after this harrowing of a day.

Matteo, or Matt, thought for a few seconds. He was a Spanish economics graduate a year into his rotations at SustainAble, currently placed with her at ReCity. "Perhaps I missed something," he ventured. "This one felt different, not just from Kuala Lumpur and HCMC, but also from Hyderabad. I wonder . . . if we could have pressed more."

Matt wasn't wondering if they could have pressed more; he was imploring Anu why she had chosen not to. Their previous pitch at Hyderabad, not too far from Mumbai, had been a success in part because she had been at her persuasive best with local council members. She had cajoled a good portion during closed-door meetings, too. No one could doubt her ability to lobby politicians.

Mumbai, though . . .

She had loved Mumbai once. Mumbai, with its beaches and street food and unmistakable waft of chai. Mumbai, with its gleaming metros and trusty old local trains. Mumbai, with its diversity and its resilience. Like many a Mumbaikar, she had joked that the pull of the city had been instilled while she was still in her mother's womb. Even when the slums started sprawling, the rivers rotting, and so many took to the streets for sleep, she insisted on staying, believing Mumbai could never be wiped away.

Mumbai, Bombay, the maximum city of dreams—she had lived through so many of its ups and downs. The super-cyclone Prarambh had ultimately proven her right: even the most extreme weather event this side of the peninsula had not managed to wipe Mumbai away.

But it wiped me *away.*

In her head, the sequence of events blurred often, and her outlook in the aftermath of Prarambh changed frequently. *No, I swam away,* Anu corrected herself. *I had lived in ignorance, and Prarambh was my awakening. All that it wiped away, it did for a reason.*

"There we both can agree," sang the ghost-voice in response.

No, come on, Anu thought. *Not again.*

The ghost's saree was gone: in its place, a bright orange salwar-kameez clung to her glowing body. She sat in front of Anu next to an entirely oblivious Matt, an elbow resting on the car window. The ghost's slight form did little to hide the cityscape rushing beyond the window. Anu could glimpse a coastal road almost entirely deprived of cars.

A quiet road to the past.

"It's funny, isn't it?" The ghost chuckled, sounding childlike and ancient at the same time. "Only yesterday, your parents broke Covid-curfew to protest construction on this road. Today, in a way, you see their vision of its abandonment come to fruition."

Anu ignored her. Matt was still awaiting a response, after all.

"I recognise your concerns," she acquiesced to him. "We still have a few days before Pune. Let's press the corporators behind the scenes. Do you want to look at other persons of interest we can pursue?"

She was wholly uninterested in bribing unworthy corporators, but she would not have Matt on her case if she could help it. Predictably, her colleague slipped on his Xplorers right away. Anu watched him for a few seconds. His slim ReCity-sponsored glasses rested easily on his nose. He moved his hands around, navigating virtually. *That should keep him busy.*

By then, the ghost of the wretched city, too, seemed to have left her alone.

At the hotel, the Auton parked itself next to its siblings, and Anu made a beeline for the Irani café-bar on the ground floor. The corporators' stuffy countenance, her runaway imaginary ghost, and Mumbai's sweltering heat were pushing her to the edge. A cold beer would help.

She sighed. *District cooling would make all of this better, but Mumbaikars aren't built to recognise what's good for them.*

Her pitch had included it as one of their proposed interventions. In the 2020s, when net-zero energy buildings had taken India by storm, district cooling had still been impractical. Cities still had underground spaces unmapped, with no telling where a clogged sewer ended or utility cables began. The technology itself had been far too expensive, too nascent, too *western*—not enough of a workforce trained to develop it in an increasingly isolationist nation.

What a delusion, she thought. *Had the underground been mapped and cleared, had sustainable design been more than jargon, had India bothered reflecting the world . . .*

Anu accepted these alternate history scenarios as unrealistic. India had been struggling to feed its poor while contending with the worst impacts of warming. Healthcare and governance systems had been overwhelmed. Those privileged enough to comprehend climate diplomacy had bristled with anger at the western world, eager to grow differently.

Even now, not much had changed. The Singapore Alliance and the Unification of the Global South at least offered India and other low-emitting countries the capital to invest in solutions.

Anu had been fifteen when the Alliance was inked; raucous, rowdy, and rebellious. She had lived through her parents' climate anxiety and activism, loving them for it but swearing to chart her own path. Working in a SustainAble-ReCity partnership was perhaps the ultimate defiance; joining a conglomerate very like those her parents had campaigned against their entire life.

Even before the super-cyclone forced her to move away, she knew ReCity offered better growth and travel credits, both hard to come by. Besides, ReCity was truly a revolution, bringing cities the cohesive transformation they needed. There was no better company to sell her time, energy, and soul to.

And that brings me back to how blind the corporators are. Anu slipped into a high table at the café-bar. The passively ventilated room was adorned in tribal Warli art and proudly declared itself to be a Corporation-designated Cooling Pavilion on days above a preordained wet-bulb temperature. Another plaque proclaimed the hotel's status as a Mumbai University living lab and library. Chennai indie played in the distance while a unique mix of alphonso mango and jamun plum hit Anu's nostrils. She nearly lost herself in its Indianness.

I shouldn't go down that lane, she told herself. *I need to remember that I swam.* Instead of the bar, then, she decided to lose herself in ReCity.

Her Xplorer glasses still placed her amid the demo. She glanced again at the tailored portfolio put together for Mumbai.

Their vision of the city was beautiful, robust, efficient; entirely unlike the dirty alleyways and ineffective infrastructure Anu recollected. This was ReCity's genius: demonstrating the potential of otherwise unremarkable places. A flood-protection solution in action; algae-based carbon-capture; multiple small modular reactors; hydrogen refuelling… the interventions struck out of virtual Mumbai in bubbles.

How could the corporators say no to this?

"Well, why not?"

Again the sing-song voice!

Anu sighed audibly. *I really need sleep, don't I?* Turning the translucency on the Xplorers down, she saw the apparition of her exhaustion, her Koli ghost-woman, this time wearing a lehenga. It seemed fashioned out of the same bright orange as the earlier salwar-kameez, as though the ghost had brought the wrong outfit to a wedding and altered it in the final minute to fit in.

Anu rubbed her eyes. *I'm really losing it,* she thought.

The ghost, younger this time but perceptive as always, cackled in response. "Oh, *I'm losing it! I need sleep! I'm Anu, I'm so tired and I hate the corporators and I hate Mumbai! What I'm seeing before me can never be real!*"

Oh Ram, Sita, Jesus Christ, and all the Gods above. Anu was lost for words. Even a figment of her imagination was choosing to mock her! What a day.

Just as she started wondering if her bed might do her more good than a beer, the bartender finally arrived. "Sorry to keep you waiting." The woman sighed. "It's far too full for a Wednesday. How can I help you?"

Her accent threw Anu off. *Why does this state have to be so low-tech?* She wished she could have poured herself a pint or had one of those barbots do it rather than engage with another human being.

Noticing Anu hadn't responded, the bartender continued. "We have our reccer here." A tablet on the counter flashed for Anu to tap her WatchXplorer and receive personalised recommendations. "If you're feeling wine, we have a good Sula on offer paired with spicy Khandeshi food. All ingredients grown on our terrace, of course. For beer, the Vet-ale from Pune is my go-to; just the right hints of cinnamon."

The woman pronounced Vet-ale like Vetal, the namesake mythical vampire. Way-tahl. Anu measured how simply *Marathi* the pronunciation was and wondered how it would sound off her tongue. It wasn't just its harsh intonation that had hit her; it was the exact lilt that the bartender spoke with, rolling the L in Vetal as a native speaker would.

Hearing English spoken in the harsh Indian tongue was commonplace. But between her two trips to India and countless Indian techies worldwide, Anu had never been in close proximity with someone who . . .

Talked so much like aai.

Her mother . . . Anu frowned. It had been so long since . . .

And she did something that surprised her. "A . . . A pint of Vet-ale, please," said a voice, but it was no longer the English accent she was used to hearing herself speak in.

For only a few moments, she was no longer Anu the ReCity biz dev exec, but instead Anushka, a lost twenty-two-year-old unknowingly suffocated by the three-block radius she had spent all her life in. For a few moments, she had never swum away from the city, and instead, she had sunk, sunk, *sunk*—

No. Anu steadied herself. *What is happening to me? First the ghost, and now this.*

If the bartender noticed any oddities, she did not mention them. "A pint of Vet-ale, coming right up!" she beamed, and disappeared from the vision of Anu's Xplorer glasses, now on standby with inactivity.

I need to leave this city, she thought, feeling old and heavy and young and light-headed at the same time.

"So soon, Tai?" teased the ghost, now sitting at the empty stool next to Anu.

You're not my sister, Anu scoffed wearily in her head.

"There!" The ghost threw her fist childishly in the air. "I knew I'd get you to acknowledge me!"

No, no, that's not what I was doing. God, I need sleep.

"Pshht. Look at me! Don't you know yourself? Do you think you could have dreamt *me* up? Do you think *you* have the imagination needed to make *me*?"

Hmm.

Despite herself, Anu glanced back at the ghost. And despite herself, she had to admit, the ghost-woman was . . . not wrong. How could she have possibly dreamt up this perfectly semi-corporeal in-between of an entity and imagined the melodies she talked in, the assortment of common yet unforgettable clothes she draped herself in? How was she suddenly capable of this? *Perhaps it's time to book an appointment with the therapist again.*

Or . . .

For a second, Anu entertained the possibility of this ghost being, well, *real*. Then she shook her head. *No, I need to be rational. Therapy it is.*

Beside her, the ghost rolled her eyes again. Startled, Anu realised her imagined companion was suddenly a teenager wearing denim shorts and a crop-top screaming of a Prateek Kuhad tour.

"You know," sang the Prateek Kuhad fangirl of a ghost. "It's funny. Indians, well, we don't always think about therapy the moment the spirit of an entire city appears to us."

Anu pursed her lips. Well, it wasn't like she had anything better to do, so why not humour her newly imagined spectral companion?

What do Indians typically think about when a 'spirit of an entire city' appears to them, then? Anu asked in her head.

The ghost—no, the spirit—shrugged. Even cosplaying a teenaged concert-goer, she had an otherworldly light about her.

"Well, they think about the gods, of course. Durga, Parvati Maa, Mother Mary . . . Oh, Gaia is another one, though that one mostly comes from your lot, the foreign-returned. There was one who called me Jijabai—Shivaji's mother, you know, founded this state and all that."

Vaguely aware she was engaging with a personification of her madness, Anu snorted. "Well, who *are* you then?"

The ghost straightened suddenly, tilting her head curiously at Anu. "Why, haven't you guessed yet, Anushka?"

Anushka.

Anushka.

As the name repeated itself over and over in her head, Anu found her-self aching with a sudden vulnerability she had forgotten she possessed. She felt unfamiliar and untethered, watching from elsewhere in the Irani café-bar as her heart sank to the floor and a hammer softly knocked her back through her memories. *Anushka. Anushka. Anushka.*

Anushka.

She did not know how much time had passed when a pint of beer slid before her on the counter. Her spirit-companion was gone, but there were others trickling in now. Anu felt the strong urge to dash, but a knot in her stomach weighed her down, fixing her in place. She somehow found it in herself to thank the bartender.

"Hope you enjoy it!" The woman winked. Then, her eyebrows fur-rowed. "If you don't mind me saying, you look very much like someone I used to know. I've been thinking this entire time. I asked my broth-er"—she pointed to a man leaning by the other side of the bar—"and he said you reminded him of someone we went to school with, Anushka—"

The rest of the bartender's words were drowned out by the thumping of a heart Anu belatedly realised was her own. Her eyes were dry, her breath hitched. Dusk seemed to choose those seconds to arrive, transi-tioning the lighting of the room. Anu's legs limped. She needed to run, but half of her was immobile, holding an invisible hand out to a past life.

Everything connected. The café-bar she sat in. The hotel housing it. The bartender, and her brother, entirely at home. It had been over a decade and the city was unrecognisable from the late 2030s, but Anu knew. *Anushka* knew.

"I . . . I . . ."

I need to leave.

I need to stay.

The bartender—no, the owner of the hotel—stood expectantly. A cur-sory glance at her nametag confirmed it. She was co-owner, at least, with her brother Tanmay. Anu had been in the same class as him for . . . seven years? Anu had been invited to the launch of their largest venture years ago, the very hotel she was in now. A converted neo-gothic prop-erty inherited from a Parsi gentleman's club of yesteryears. Prarambh had arrived before the launch and Anu had forgotten the siblings in the following eleven years.

Until now. And that brought her a choice, she realised.

Stay or leave.
Sink or swim.

She remembered the water then, blasting through their flat with corrugated shutters and stray branches blowing far with the wind. Booming in the skies and bashing past the streets, unprecedented and uncanny. Rising and rising and rising till there was so much her mother could not breathe.

The other kind of water, too: her father's tears, unexpected and inevitable as an Arabian Sea Category 5 cyclone. Her parents had lived their entire lives dedicated to saving this city from its fate, but they had been unable to save themselves. Anushka had been the daughter they had never desired but had been blessed with nonetheless: a burden to the world but especially to her father, who died that day, even if his body did not pass for weeks after.

She was sick of this place, or she had been. Sick of the yearly floods; sick of the urban decline; sick of how nothing changed. Least of all the people—complacent in their existence, complicit in decay, and content with inequalities they perpetuated.

Tens of thousands had died at the hands of Prarambh and the Tarapur Nuclear Leak immediately after. Many more had been stranded, screaming to the heavens, trying to stay afloat. The rich had not been spared, either. The actors and industrialists who had not already deserted Mumbai had done so soon enough, fearing property blight, and took their wealth along with them.

Anu had watched the spectacle unfold from afar after digging into her inheritance for a one-way ticket to London. She had been one of the first few Indians claiming a climate refugee status in the UK, something she was certain had hinged on said inheritance. The vast majority of Mumbaikars had not been quite as lucky. Cushioned in Caledonian Road's cheap co-op housing, name shortened to Anu, she recognised how she sounded in her grief as millions less fortunate than her had nothing left at all.

Yet she had walked around London, from gleaming, glistening Canary Wharf to peaceful, placid Richmond, wondering what it would have been like to grow up in that city so teeming with excess, flirting even more closely with the sky than Mumbai. Would it have saved her parents?

After all that, perhaps, it shook Anu to see remnants of her past life still here, in Mumbai, so . . . thriving.

I always thought these people were too inert to leave, she told herself. *I never imagined I'd be here to see what became of them.*

Now, I can decide if I want to. The hotel owner, Kari, was still standing expectantly before Anu, unaware of her dilemma.

Sink or swim. Stay or leave.

In the corner of her eye, her spirit reappeared, still in the Prateek Kuhad crop-top, downing imaginary shot-glasses on another side of the bar counter. In between vodka and a murky lime chaser, the spirit looked up at Anu and blew her a kiss.

"I believe in you!" she shouted. "You can do it!"

Sink or swim. Stay or leave.

And even if this teenager of a spirit was a figment of her imagination, even if she was an annoyance to her day, Anu chose to stay.

"Kari," she mouthed, sounding less like herself and more like her mother with every word. "You're Kari, from school. Wow."

In that moment of madness, Anu felt herself reshape, melding into the flooded fabric of Mumbai. Kari squealed joyfully, hugging Anu as a long-lost friend, and her brother Tanmay came by soon after to express his own awe at serendipity.

"This is incredible," Tanmay exclaimed, looking Anu up and down. "I'd been thinking about you a few months ago, wondering where you disappeared to. Surreal."

Anu let out a small laugh. *Actually, my spirit-companion is surreal enough for both of us*, she thought.

"Well, I sure hope I am real," she said out loud.

"You don't look like you've aged a day," Kari said. "So, what have you been up to? You haven't been hiding in Mumbai, I'm guessing?"

"Or Pune," Tanmay chimed in. "Or Nashik. I asked everyone from school, and no one knew. It's like you poofed into thin air." He frowned sympathetically. "I . . . was sorry to hear about kaki and kaka, by the way. I wish I could have supported you."

The familiarity surprised Anu. How many times had Tanmay even met her parents, to refer to them as an aunt and an uncle? *Just this local love for viewing everyone you grew up around as extended family.* She remembered how communal her childhood had been, but now it was more a distant dream, hard to piece together. Clearly, that aspect of Mumbai remained unchanged.

"Thank you," Anu managed. "I appreciate it."

"It's good to see you're better now." Kari reached out and squeezed Anu's arm. She thought about withdrawing away, but her body remained frozen. She was watching herself interact with Kari and Tanmay, dissociated and unable to pilot the conversation.

"Thank you," Anu repeated, a numbness passing her feet.

"Well, don't be shy," Tanmay smiled. "Where have you been all this time? What brings you back?"

"Oh, you know." *London, and Columbus, and Shenzhen, and—* "Here and there. Visiting for work now." She kept it short. Less detail offered, less questions asked.

But nothing was ever that easy. "Oh," Kari recognised. "Are you here with SustainAble? We had a number of bookings, but most rooms are unoccupied. I'm just glad they paid."

Whoops. That had been Anu's doing. Thinking the Mumbai trip would be fruitless, she had asked her solutions engineers to not accompany her. Before she could reply, though, their conversation was interrupted.

"Kari!" a voice called.

A new group had walked in, brightly dressed, loud in conversation and laughter. They were not the most beautiful set of people, but they commanded attention: other sounds in the bar suddenly lulled as everyone turned to look.

It struck her that as Tanmay and Kari's attention was diverted, Anu could disappear. She was curious too, though, and she did not have to wait long for an introduction.

As Kari's staff set about taking orders, the hotel owner hugged the head of the group—a small woman about their age who had called out before.

"How's it going?" Tanmay asked the new arrival. "We were wondering if you would come today." He gestured to Anu then. "Oh, this is Anushka, we went to school with her. She's visiting for work. Anushka, this is Sunidhi. She is a corporator, and a good friend."

"Nice to meet you." Anu smiled, even as her insides swirled. *Anushka. I need to swim. I need to swim.*

Why did a corporator have to arrive at the bar? *I wanted to slip away from the corporators, but I swerved, and I ran right into one of them.*

I thought I slipped away from the city, but I swerved, and I ran right into it.

"Nice to meet you, too, and sorry about all the ruckus," Sunidhi apologised. "We got out of a day-long deliberation, and I invited the rest of the Protocol committee for a drink. We really deserve it."

At least Sunidhi and her posse were not in the same committee that had hosted ReCity's proposal.

"That sounds painful." Kari groaned. "What can I get you?"

So they were off. Sunidhi asked for mint masala chai and Tanmay asked about a mutual friend and Anu asked herself out of the discussion.

When did the corporators become so powerful? she wondered instead. Other patrons were approaching the members of the Protocol committee around her. The corporators were men and women and hijras, young and old and middle-aged, speaking a host of languages—clearly diverse. Suddenly, they did not seem quite as faceless to her as before.

They were radically different from pre-cyclone days, at least. Corporators then had failed their voters time and again, turnouts falling every election until *Prarambh*. Influence had been limited to a small number of unelected administrators. *What changed, then?*

Anu had dismissed most of the research briefing her colleague Matt had prepared on Mumbai. Maybe she could find an answer there. However it had happened, the corporators had suddenly evolved.

And if the corporators were different, how different was Mumbai? Did she even care to know?

However different they are from the past, they're still blocking progress, still not grasping the good of the city and the planet, she reasoned. *Their rejection of ReCity proved that.*

Wanting a change of scenery then, she decided to move outdoors. The café-bar's patio overlooked Girgaon Chowpatty, all sun and sand and sea. At this hour, the water gleamed a shade of blue-orange tides silently knocking against the beachfront. Along it was a walkway narrowed to its extremes by sea-level rise, but even then rife with activity—evening walkers, a photography club, even a couple of hawkers. Anu chose a high table in the corner, settling into the light serenity of the evening.

"There's no harm in admitting you missed it, you know," came the singing. Anu was less surprised to hear it this time. The spirit was again a little older, again in her bright orange lehenga.

Anu ignored her. Instead, she asked—aloud, this time, because clearly all her common sense had left her—"Who *are* you? I mean, I know you're only visible to me, and I know I need to see a psychiatrist ASAP, but what the hell?"

Surprisingly, the spirit smiled. And when Anu blinked, once again her companion changed form, now far older, but ageless all the same. The spirit now wore a snow-white nine-yard nauvari saree, her hair tied up in a slick bun.

"Why, I am all that you see around yourself, Anushka, and so much that you do not. I am all that was once here, all that still stays, all that will come to be. I am the dreams this city is built on; the sweat that is given to it; the ideas that come out of it and go forth into the world beyond. I am Mumbai's mangroves, its canals, its streets, its skyscrapers, its slums, its roads, its animals, and yes, its people. All their spirits, all their lives, they all live within me."

For a by and large articulate person, Anu found herself once again seeking the right words. This . . . could not be happening, could it? *The spirit of Mumbai . . .*

As though spoken to, the spirit laughed. "Yes, precisely! That's what I'm known best as. The Spirit of Mumbai, undying, resilient, and so on. Many names, but that one sticks best through all these centuries I've seen. Aside from Mumbadevi, perhaps."

Anu felt herself rub her eyes. *Mumbadevi. The goddess of Mumbai.*

O—kay. Okay. Okay.

How in the world was she imagining all this? *Things have been moving just a tad too fast lately*, she thought.

Clearly, she needed a breather.

The spirit—Mumbadevi—smiled, uncharacteristically sympathetic. "You can take your time processing it. I understand, it *is* a bit to take in. But I'm here. Whenever you need me, even when you don't know you need me, I'll be there."

Anu stayed there for close to an eternity, staring out into the Chowpatty and Arabian Sea, hit by a small breeze that smelt of bun-maska with a hint of bhutta—not the American corn-on-the-cob sort, but real bhutta of the old, made with Indian maize. Her stomach called out in hunger, and Anu remembered all the years before, when her aai and baba would accompany her to Dadar Chowpatty. Maybe if she was well-behaved that day, maybe if she asked sweetly enough, they'd buy bhutta for her. Those had been better times.

Better days.

It took a mention of her company to kick her to reality, uttered indignantly by a man on the next patio high table. A Municipal Corporation lanyard hung on his unbuttoned neck, but he was far enough away that Anu could not make out any of the details even if she squinted. *Corporator? Staffer? Administrator?* It was unclear. There was a woman sitting with him, but unhelpfully, there was no lanyard on her at all.

". . . don't know what they hope to accomplish," the man was saying. "ReCity, SustainAble, whatever they call themselves, they're exploitative and neo-colonial. We all know it. How can they pretend to know *our* city better than we do?"

The woman agreed. "You know, they think they're changing the world, but they're just Big Tech. This isn't the twenties; we're not our parents. Did you see what happened in Lagos? They think they're transforming cities, but it's really a soft takeover of our data and our government. This Gaia thing going on, though, that's more the right idea. What those Awakened people did to SustainAble in Ohio and that Bent Greens place—that should be happening everywhere."

Anu rolled her eyes. *You're all blind. You would be dead without our knowledge and tech. Lagos didn't know what was good for them. And your 'Awakened' people are a hoax.*

The disgruntled man went on, though. "If we allowed ReCity in, they'd shut down all our urban farming, and they'd shut down the recyclers to make us reliant on imports again. Or give us nuclear, as if we want more of it after Tarapur!"

"Hmm." The woman took a swig from her wine glass. "Well, there is an argument to be made to decarbonise faster through density, industrialisation, and so on. But then we risk becoming *exactly like the West!* None of the rotten systems change. We become like these SustainAble folks—sad, and lonely, and so separate from nature. And crippled by technology, letting AI rule, leeching away our humanity. No, thank you."

You're wrong, Anu thought. *Technology builds in efficiency and resiliency. Leeching humanity never factors in.*

The man shuddered. "Prarambh brought in pralay for us," he recited. "They think we want to go back to how things used to be. What do they know about us or what we want? These westerners, they think they can come here and tell us what to do. It sickens me. We don't need them."

Prarambh brought in pralay. Anu had seen the slogan graffitied around Mumbai, referring to pralay, the mythical deluge after which the world recreated and cleansed itself.

What do you know about cleansing? she wanted to demand of the two strangers. *I had to cleanse myself of all the garbage this city threw at me. I had to cleanse my parents of it, and I failed, so I had to swim away.*

Her shoulders felt heavy, her eyes red. *I want to cry*, she thought. *Why am I here; why am I so cursed as to be exposed to this city again?* Everything around her seemed dim and dusty even as she discerned fireflies welcoming the night. Her breathing sped up. Time . . . slowed down.

I hate this.

Again, she stayed there. Eventually, when her WatchXplorer confirmed her heart rate had normalised, she flashed it at a pay-station by the exit and walked out without a second glance.

In the days that followed, she chastised herself endlessly, questioning what had passed through her when she confirmed her identity to Kari. Or when she washed away her English persona while talking to the siblings. Or when she stayed on the bar patio, overhearing strangers.

And in those days, she wondered about Mumbadevi, the Spirit of Mumbai, the ghost of all that the city was and would be. Somehow, since that fateful day, the deity—if she was one—had chosen to stay away. If she was to be believed, she was giving Anu the time to "process."

To hell with processing this . . . incident. Mumbai had committed an assault on all her senses that day, but now she was past it, and Anu knew she could not afford any slip-ups. She was unable to rail in her curiosity fully, though, and cursed herself for it. The background research briefing she'd never read enticed her more now. It took all her strength to continue to reject reading it.

Instead, Anu humoured her curiosity in another unhealthy way. Mumbai's data protection laws were stringent, but SustainAble and ReCity had enough nonetheless. Sequestered in her hotel room one day, she looked for Kari and Tanmay on the Xplorer first. Subsequently, she found herself looking up their corporator friend, Sunidhi, a lawyer in office for four years. The Protocol committee led her to the man who had incited her near-anxiety attack—another lawyer-turned-corporator, it turned out—who had surprisingly attended the same school as Anu, or Anushka then.

She also learned that the schoolmates that had not run from Mumbai were either in public service of some form or somehow involved with the community. A solar engineer she'd played football with married a classmate leading a Tribal Art Council. The head girl from the year above was now in microfinance at a credit union that had gained prominence after the World Water War and the Multi-Market Collapse; her wife was a circular consultant for the Mumbai Metro.

A 360-capture of them on their Xplorer feeds placed them at a town hall led by Sunidhi, their ward's corporator. Anu wondered if she would have been a part of it had she chosen to stay. They looked confident and earnest, doing their part for Mumbai.

Anu recognised in herself an unexpected yearning then. She absent-mindedly moved her fingers over the 360-capture, envious of how comfortably they belonged to each other and to their city.

She had assumed that belonging to SustainAble and ReCity would be enough for her, but now, she was uncertain.

No, I swam, she chastised herself again. *The city was going to sink me, and I swam.*

And still, despite the swimming, so many years from it . . . here she was, in the city of her dreams and nightmares, alone but so full of memory.

It was the small things that disquieted Anu: her aai's hearty smiles, her baba's wordless embraces, her cousins with the pranks and protests planned with equal precision. Her kakas and kakis, ever disapproving and ever supportive all the same. Their family dog, Monsoon, a fat ball of soft fur and chaotic energy. Her best and perhaps only friend, Amrita, who loved everyone and who everyone loved back. Mumbai, a map upon which all these stories unfolded together, intersecting often, but taking off and charting their own paths otherwise.

Anu had only ever been a pin on the map—never a string that travelled all its secret streets and speakeasies. She had only ever been a point her favourite characters travelled through sometimes. And then the characters had scattered, or perished, and it had only left her, choosing to swim away.

She did not realise when she slid down one wall of the hotel room. Her fingers trembled.

And then, the singing.

"I'm sorry for what happened to you," said her spirit-friend then, appearing at the edge of her bed.

It had been three days since Anu had last seen her, but the spirit had kept her mid-sixties look, wearing the same white nauvari saree. Anu was alarmed suddenly by how there almost seemed to be no passage of time in those three days—she felt exactly the same as in the café-bar patio, and Mumbadevi's unchanged appearance hit home. Her emotions were in as much of a grinder as that evening. She ruefully wondered how it could possibly have taken so few days in Mumbai to crumble into a nostalgic, anxiety-ridden, spirit-seeing mess.

"I really am sorry," Mumbadevi said again. "You did not deserve it. No one does. It was a horrifying day, and you should never have lost so many people so close to you."

Anu looked back to the floor. *But I did lose them*, she thought. *Amrita, whose body was never found; Monsoon, his poor lungs so full of water he could not breathe. Aai, lost to the floods; baba, lost to heartbreak. My surviving kakas and kakis and cousins, too shaken to talk to each other and too horrified to stay together.*

Aloud, she whispered, "I hated you. Spirit of Mumbai, didn't you say? I hated you. I hated that everyone believed in you so much we stopped believing we needed to do something ourselves. And—and when push came to shove, when shit hit the fan, your *spirit* was gone. There was only us, and there was the water. And I had to swim away, you know, *I had to swim away. I had to swim away.*"

Anu did not realise when she started crying. She also did not realise that the tears had been lying in wait all this time, desperately wanting to break through. Now they came in full force, and she sobbed as though she never had before and never would again. Her nose filled with snot and with her blurry vision she tried reaching for tissue, but it was *so far away*, she just wanted to get all the tears out first, for wouldn't it be easy to cry a river and then swim away from it, away from all this pain? Maybe away from all the hurt and all the memories, she could be stoic again. Better than this city that had wronged her, taken so much away from her that she could never get back.

Mumbadevi moved down to the floor next to her. Within moments, Anu found herself resting her head on the spirit's shoulder. The spirit's body was somehow more real and tangible than Anu had thought it would be, and wrapped in Mumbadevi's arms, Anu's tears slowed, her eyes clearing.

The spirit had stayed quiet through Anu's monologue, but once she'd grabbed a tissue Anu felt a little more whole, Mumbadevi gave her a sad smile.

"I am the Spirit of Mumbai, yes, but I've never been different from all of you," she murmured. "See, that's what no one pays attention to when I introduce myself. I am the Spirit of Mumbai, which makes me the Spirit of *all of you*. All of you, all of me, we've always been one and the same. Believing in me, believing in Mumbai—it's always been the same as believing in *yourself*."

And in an instant, Anu was hit by perspective.

"Did . . . did you plan all of it?" she asked the spirit. "What happened that day—with Kari and Tanmay, those corporators—it all happened after I first saw you in the Corporation. Was all of it you?"

"It was, and wasn't," Mumbadevi answered. "It was me in that I am Kari, and Tanmay, and each of those corporators, and yes, even you. It was me in that I am a manifestation of Mumbai wanting to survive an extinction it created for itself. But it also wasn't me, in that I did not plan how it would play out. I only knew that you needed me, and I was there for you when you did. Like I am now."

"But why me? What did I need?"

Mumbadevi was still smiling. "Well, I can't answer that for you, can I?"

There was a silence between them once again. Then, Anu shook her head.

"Well, none of this makes sense. I thought I had moved on, you know?" she mused. "I thought I was over all of this. But I still feel twenty-two, angry, and so, *so* alone. And I . . . I feel a sorrow, not only at what I lost, but what I was unable to gain. Does that make sense?"

Mumbadevi nodded, so Anu continued. "I saw the corporators and I thought about how they were actually *doing* something for the city, right here, on the ground. How they were trying to be good to it as so few had been before. I saw Kari and Tanmay and their friends, and I thought about how I would have been one of them had I never left, part of a . . . community.

"I saw Mumbai these last few days, and I thought about how I gave up on this common ground shared with my family and my friends. I could have honoured it in their memory, used my privilege to help those that needed it, sunk into my roots and deepened them. But I swam away, chasing . . . what? I don't know what I am anymore, beyond some flimsy success. It scares me."

Anu was shocked at her confession, at this barrage of thoughts she had not even known she could put into full sentences, even broken, run-on ones. As though to check she really had spoken so much out loud, she looked to Mumbadevi beside her. The spirit held up her palm to Anu's cheek. Anu savoured its warmth.

No imaginary companion could feel like this, could they?

"It is okay to be scared, Anu," said Mumbadevi. She was younger again now, in a bottle-green kurti, tiny sequins sparkling in the light that leaked through the room window. Absent-mindedly, Anu thought, *my god, she is beautiful.* There was no way she could have dreamed up so much unearthly grace.

They spent the rest of the day holding each other. They spoke sparsely, and when they did, it was in soft whispers meant only for the room, not to be uttered outside it. Anu had never pictured being consoled so delicately and tenderly; being caressed so carefully that every muscle in her simultaneously relaxed. The spirit of the city somehow knew every ache and every scar covering Anu's body, and with every passing minute, the anguish, bottled up for eleven years, dimmed until there was nothing there at all.

At the end of the night, when Mumbadevi was gone, Anu wondered if this was what it meant to be born again.

In the morning, for the first time since the incidents at the café-bar, she chose to step out of the hotel room. She rented an electric bike from a station just outside the hotel and decided to ride it until she no longer could. *Work be damned.*

Instead of the billboards she remembered, Anu breezed past trees of all shapes and sizes. Hundreds of Mumbaikars walked and cycled on the streets or waited in shade for buses. Some filled up microbatteries at energy stations that doubled up as workspaces, making hay while the sun shined with cheap electricity. Under overhead monorail lines, a group of college students staged street performances about politics of the decades past. A few meters away, a troupe of dancers practiced for Garba season, providing a performance for passers-by.

Anu heard delighted yelps of children dashing after dogs and adored sighs of mothers dashing after them. She zoomed past commuters walking into Mumbai Local stations toward work, and those walking out toward home. At delivery points, electric tempos picked up parcels, carrying them to Mumbaikars everywhere. An old couple walked quietly in the cool breeze; a young couple relaxed at a park café, in love with each other and with the moment they found themselves in.

Anu found herself in love with the moment, too. This gust of happiness . . . she remembered taking it in once before. Paris, where they had failed to get a sign-off for ReCity. In hindsight, the French had been a bad target. Their governance was too conservative, their local talent too progressive, and their ego too immense.

Was it ego, though?

Or just attachment to their city, and trust in their structures?

When she deposited the bike back at the rental station at the end of the day, Anu recalled what she had overheard in the bar patio.

Mumbaikars may just be as prickly as Parisians, with just as much attachment to their city; just as much love for its spirit.

Anu had remembered the slums and the homeless and labelled them as Mumbai. And sure, Mumbai wasn't perfect, but she had seen so much to the contrary already. Despite everything she wanted to believe, Mumbai was alive. Perhaps not by ReCity's indicators, but Anu only saw Mumbaikars content and fulfilled, so did any other metric even matter? Mumbai was more prosperous, and more magical, than ever. Mumbadevi was proof of it.

Meanwhile, Matt ably accomplished the task Anu had set him, chasing after a corporator sympathetic to ReCity's case. Said sympathetic corporator managed to slate them in to pitch to the Improvements committee. The day after her bike ride, the two of them made their way to the Corporation building once again, and on the way, Anu asked Matt for his research briefing on Mumbai.

And as the briefing lit up her Xplorers, the past decade unfolded before her eyes. Mass outrage on the streets after Prarambh. Citizens supervising the reconstruction of Mumbai. Protests and civil unrest across India, rehauling Indian administrative systems. A new governance system working earnestly to realign the city. There was turbulence, and crisis after crisis, yet Mumbai rose again, and again. It redefined community-centric leadership, rehabilitating mangroves and informal settlements alike. Employment opportunities improved every year. The city represented inherent climate risk, but it was building resilience.

It was so close to succeeding.

No wonder the corporators think they can do better than ReCity, she thought. *They nearly have.*

Or perhaps they truly have *done better, and it is ReCity who ought to learn from Mumbai rather than the vice versa.*

Anu remembered what Mumbadevi had said: the spirit of Mumbai was the spirit of all of them. This Mumbai she now found herself in, this new Mumbai, was more its people than a monolith of the past she remembered.

She saw merit in so much of the portfolio her solutions engineers had put together; so many areas where efficiency and technology could improve Mumbai's climate performance. The reasons for the corporators' caution dawned on her just as swiftly. She had seen them as a faceless pack, indistinguishable from each other, but her bias had clouded her perspective.

The corporators represented Mumbai more than ReCity ever could. How could solutions engineers sitting in Berlin or Bangalore read the nuances needed to transform a city they had never mingled in? ReCity was more faceless than the corporators ever would be.

As for her . . .

It was easy to make decisions about places you were disconnected from. Mumbai had been home for Anu, but she had pushed its existence away, seeing only Prarambh.

Leaving a sinking city is the easiest thing in the world. But coming back to see how it swam while you were away . . .

Inside her head was a battle: ten years at ReCity clashing with twenty-two as a Mumbaikar. Her faith in ReCity's tech clashing with everything she knew Mumbaikars wanted.

It didn't have to be one way or the other, though.

Maybe . . . maybe it was possible for Mumbai to be both citizen-centric *and* efficient. Maybe it was possible for *Anu* to be both—a ReCitizen *and* a Mumbaikar.

Anu's Xplorers turned off, and she frowned at Matt. She wondered how the company would feel if she radically rehashed their strategy for a city they had never seen.

When the committee secretary later indicated ReCity's turn to pitch, she considered the meaning of Prarambh. *A new beginning.*

Mumbai had its Prarambh in the wake of the eponymous super-cyclone, and Anu could choose to have hers now. *Who am I?* she wondered.

And then Anu remembered all the confessions that had spooled out of her, all the hours spent in the comfort of the Spirit of Mumbai, and all the good she still wanted to believe she possessed. *What am I capable of doing for my city?*

What will I do?

This time, instead of swimming away from Mumbai, Anu swam into its depths.

LOVING ALGAE

C. D. TAVENOR

Northwest Ohio, the Midwest Federation
2055 C.E.

For some reason, I always regret going home. Not visiting my family, of course. But the *act* of going home itself. It always comes with baggage.

I certainly love my parents, they're wonderful people, but I always get roped into solving problems I simply do not want to solve. They send me to meet their neighbors to chat about a random legal issue. It doesn't matter that I'm an attorney for the state legislature, advising politicians as they fight tit-for-tat with their partisan opponents.

When you're a lawyer, everyone assumes you know every law. That you can solve every legal problem. This might be the Midwest Federation now, but Ohio never changed, both in Columbus and in its small towns.

So as I drive up to my parent's early twenty-first century farmhouse, its rooftop turbine majestically spinning in the wind, I wonder what problem they'll present to me today. Sure, they invited me home because "I hadn't visited in a few months" and "your father's birthday is next week, so come for the weekend." But the "request" will come shortly after I walk in the door.

As I park my electrobike, the Toledo talk radio show fades toward silence. I'd been listening to it on my way up 23 from Columbus. It had been a fascinating overview of recent social movements nationwide, contextualizing a few recent protests along Lake Erie's shores as they continue the decades-long fight to stop the toxic algae blooms and mitigate water pollution's relationship to the climate crisis.

When you work for politicians, it helps to stay up-to-date on the most recent "hot-button" issues. Inevitably, even though reps *think* they knew everything about anything, they usually know very little at all. The support staff, like me, pull them back down into reality. The Midwest Federation might be water-rich, unlike the western nations of the good ol' former United States, but it still has its own problems to solve. And the politicians constantly debate what obligations they have, under their treaty with Canada, to share the water-wealth. Geopolitics surrounding Lake Erie havn't really shifted in a half-century—the words are just ordered differently.

My mother walks out the front door, interrupting my inner monologue. She appears so suddenly, it's as if she'd been waiting by the window since I sent the DM letting her know I left Columbus. Her graying blonde hair compliments her farm-tanned, wrinkled cheeks. "Jordan, hello! It's so good to see you!"

She looks a little older every time I come home. But her welcoming speech is the same as always, like a scripted auto-responding message.

"Hey mom," I say. I skip up the steps and sweep her into a hug. "Dad out of the fields already?"

"He just finished showering. Biosolid application day today, but he got the smell off him well enough."

I chuckle. "Momma always says, don't bring pig shit in the house!"

"I have *never* said it like that!" But she smiles, and we go inside.

We enter the kitchen, and the scents of chili spice, onions, and cinnamon waft through the air. Glass mason jars, scooped free of an orange goop, litter the island. Pumpkin chili is my favorite, and it signaled a big ask coming. Still, at least it'll come with a good meal. I go toward the cabinets to sneak a spoon and try a taste, but my mom grabs my sleeve and pulls me away.

"Still a predictable greedy eater," she says, guiding me into the streaming room. "I swear I taught you better."

"You taught me to like your cooking."

"Oh hush. Vick!"

"No need to yell, Meredith. I'm right here."

My father sits in his chair, his balding, pale head barely peeking over the beige cushions. "Welcome home, Jordo."

"Hey dad." I plop on the couch.

"That's right," Mom says. "Both of you stay there while I finish dinner."

I know it's all part of their plan. She'll keep cooking, the scent of pumpkin chili enticing me, while he tells me of the new problem I should solve.

"We need your help, Jordo," my dad says.

Ha! I hate to be right, but even this surprises me. They didn't even wait. They're asking right out the gate.

"I just got in," I reply. "Can't it wait?"

He raises his hand and swipes left, the wall screen activating a stream he'd apparently paused. "I'd rather we get right to it. Just watch, then tell me your thoughts."

On the screen, a ToledoLive reporter stands beside a farmer. The headline reads "local Waterville farmer's crops attacked; seventh incident this week." The man looks exasperated, face red with fury.

"So tell me, Richie, what do you think caused the attack?" The reporter shifts a mic to beneath the man's chin.

"It's those damned greenies down the road." He waves in away from the camera. "I know they're anti-farm, anti-meat, and they're after our crops, after our livelihood. I've seen the docu-streams where they dump manure on the steps of the statehouse. This is just like them. I've got evidence!"

The shot shifts to an image of land along the banks of the Maumee River. It's too early in the year for anything to be sprouting, but I recognize the telltale signs of recent biosolid injection. But there's something else, too. The ground, scarred, looks like a series of giant plows angrily ran through it. Dirt and fertilizer sits on the field in haphazard humps, and a trail of muddy sludge trickles into the irrigation ditch separating the field from Route 24.

"More on this developing story tonight at 11 on our YouStream account. You won't want to miss it."

The video pauses. Dad glances from his seat, an eyebrow raised.

"Goddamnit," I whisper.

"You're intrigued, yeah?"

"Yes, of course!" I can't deny it. It's weird. Seems out of character for environmental activists, but you never *really* know. "I'm not sure what I'm supposed to do to help."

"Talk to Richie. He's a good friend. Always has been. Might have a few . . . crazy ideas, but he's a good man. I'd rather you help him than someone egg him into doing something stupid."

Now that, that's a good point. If the wrong person talks with Richie, they'll encourage him to take action against someone who's probably innocent. I shake my head. "Fine."

"Dinner won't be ready for a few hours!" shouts my mother from the kitchen.

"Y'all always do this to me."

"I'll drive you," my dad says, already rising from the couch.

· · · **·** **·** **·** · · ·

The field is just as it appeared on the stream—broken, torn up, and muddied. A biosolid slurry slowly pours into the irrigation ditch away from the river itself, its nitrogen-rich stench wafting to invade my nostrils.

My senses always love it when I return home.

"Jordan and Vick, I appreciate y'all stoppin' in," Richie says. His pale-white hands tremble in the late winter wind, their color contrasting with the sleeve of freckles peeking out on his wrists from beneath his sleeves. "This is the spot. It's those terrorists up the street."

"You really shouldn't call them that," I say before I can bite my tongue.

"Why? That's what they are."

I shake my head, trying to think of a way to dig myself out of this conflict. "Where are they staying?"

"There's a whole crew of 'em at Brenette's, just squatting around her old barn."

I nod. "And you've known her for what, forty years? I think you can trust her not to harbor . . . saboteurs." The word terrorist is incredibly loaded, especially given its historical context. One of the Muslim reps I work closely with rails against its use at least once a year. I know I probably can't shift Richie's entire view on its use, but I might be able to pivot its use today.

"But I got proof. The news station refuses to air it, says it's not high quality enough, but I know what it shows. Vick, I showed you. Ya saw it."

My father crosses his arms. "It definitely shows something happening the other night." he tilts his head gently toward me. "You should take a look."

Without another word, Richie extends his fingers, and his watch's feed reveals a miniature screen in the air, visible through my Lenses. A dark, grainy video shows Richie's driveway extending toward Route 24. Beyond, the darkness of the Maumee envelops most of the shot, though I spot the large pine tree at the right edge of the shot, the same tree a few dozen meters from where we're presently standing.

"Watch." Richie points near the highway on the screen.

For a moment, nothing happens. The camera's mic captures the buzz of fuzzy static; a tree blows in the night wind.

A shadowy mass ripples along the river.

A few moments later, the edge of a similar shadow resides beneath the pine tree, its features indistinct.

"See. That. That right there."

I frown. Something definitely happened on the recording, but I can't say it's the cause of the destruction at our feet. "Is this the only recording you have? Have you enhanced its quality?"

"It's an old system," he replies. "Zear helped out, they tried messing around on some fancy app, but this is the best they could do."

I resist the urge to ask what Zear thinks about the cause of the attack. Richie's kid is a bundle full of contradictions, and probably agrees with their father. Instead, I say, "I think the simplest way I can help is for me to go talk to Brenette."

"Now I wouldn't want to put you in any dan—"

Shaking my head, I lightly chuckle. "I think I'll be okay. Brenette was practically my second mother."

My father joins my laughter. "Ain't that the truth."

· · · · ● · ● · · · ·

We leave Richie at his house, still frustrated but ready to wait to do anything until we give him a call. Brenette lives on the northside of Waterville, almost halfway up the highway to the town of Maumee. When I was in middle and high school, I was best friends with Shanya, Brenette's oldest daughter. We lost touch after college, and it's been a few years since we talked. Even longer since I stopped in to say hello to Brenette herself. The reunion would be interesting, to say the least.

As we roll up to her private lane, the evidence of the "green" encampment abounds on her property. Groups of three or four young adults, possibly even high school age, walk down the lane, holding signs and wearing masks. Banners sway on flag poles distributed between trees, and tents dot the empty adjacent field. As we drive by, the kids smile and wave.

"Dad, you know they can't be the culprits," I say.

"Yeah, I think you're right." He snorts.

"And you've told Richie you feel that way, right?"

"He should know."

"You've got be explicit!"

"I don't *affirm* his beliefs."

I shake my head. Sometimes, my father's generation can be so terrified of confrontation. To be fair, they grew up in a time when a different extremist political event happened every other day. Their reticence to return to the hyperpolarization of their youth makes sense.

As we reach the end of the lane, Brenette's high tunnels reveal themselves, spreading in a consistent grid to the north. I remember helping build them years ago, and it warms my heart to see their glory today. Her farm is thriving, from the looks of it.

Other activists mill about, congregating in small groups. It reminds me of my days in undergrad and law school, when I participated in my fair share of marches. There's a power in collective action that can't be ignored. While they rarely bring about change solely on their own, their consciousness-raising impact can't be denied. They pushed me into a life of politics, that's for sure. I have a theory that my father once marched in a protest back in the early part of the century. I've never managed to get the story out of him, though.

"When was the last time you saw Brenette?" I ask my father as we exit his truck. As we step away, its solar roof tilts westward to catch a few final rays of late afternoon light.

"Last week at poker," he says.

"Oh." I shake my head. "Oh! Wow, didn't realize you all stayed in contact."

"Your mother and I hang close to our friends."

"I didn't—"

"I think everyone knows you and Shanya moved past your time as friends. Doesn't mean it don't make us sad."

I don't really know how to respond, and it doesn't really matter. There's nothing to say. He's right. See, I often think the reason I dislike returning home to my parents is because they ask me to help with things. And that's part of it, of course. But it's also out of shame. I left too many relationships behind when I disappeared for undergrad and law school and beyond. It's hard to rebuild a relationship when you know you're the one who destroyed it in the first place.

"Well welcome home," says a soft voice from the porch as we approach.

I suppose I shouldn't have expected anything less than a warm welcome from Brenette, however.

She rises from her porch-couch as we ascend the steps, her obsidian hands tightly grasping the armrest for balance. Her thick hair has streaks of white in it, showing her age. When she establishes her footing, arms spread wide, and she pulls me into a hug before I can even contemplate escaping.

"It's taken you long enough," Brenette whispers as she pulls away. "Too bad Shanya ain't here either."

"Indeed," I say. "It's been far too long."

"And yet I think I know why you're here." She eyes my father. "Vick, this about what I think it's about? I already told you my thoughts over a direct M."

I scratch my head. "Honestly Brenette, I'm just here to warn you. Richie seems really pissed."

She smirks. "He's always pissed."

"He's got a recording," Dad says. "There's something weird on it."

"I'm aware," she replies. "And these kids got nothing to do with it. They're registered with the Midwest Water Protectors, got their permits and everything. Good kids. Just marching back and forth down the bike lanes. Richie tell you what I told him?"

"No," my father and I say simultaneously.

"Of course he didn't." She shakes her head. "Look, Jordo, Vick, I love ya both. It's always good to see your faces. But Richie's gone off the deep end with this one. Making up nonsense. Whatever's causing these strange attacks, it ain't these kids, and it's pretty easy to prove it too."

It's my turn to shake my head. "I don't doubt you that it isn't these kids, but what makes you so vehemently certain?"

Brenette laughs, its sharp pitch ringing in my ears. "Simple logic." Without saying another word, she motions with her hand and ushers us inside.

At the kitchen table, two water protectors draw on cardboard. As we walked by, I notice the words—NO PEACE TILL NO PFAS, CLIMATE CRISIS IS WATER CRISIS, and CLEAN WATER NOW. It's like I'm stepping into the public radio piece I heard on my ride up from Columbus earlier today. The kids simply smile as we walk by and enter Brenette's office. A digital map of the Maumee River Basin, displayed on the back wall, contrasts against the room's off-white paint.

"Okay, so first off, it's pretty simple why it can't be these kids," she retorts. "First attack happened a week ago from yesterday. The water protectors started setting up their camp on my land only two days ago."

"Well, that's fair enough," says my Dad. "Why didn't you say so earlier?"

"Because I shouldn't have to figure this shit out for you, or for Richie, or for you, Jordo." She crosses her arms. "Y'all show up to my house and accuse my guests of wrongdoing, it smells like prejudice against the people who be trying to do their best. To do right by the river. Least we can all do. You still farming right up to the bank?"

My father absently looks away, and Brenette gives me one of her looks I know all too well. It's that "Count the chickens in your own hen house before looking in mine" look. After all these years, I still recognize it on sight.

"We'll set Richie straight," I say.

"Yes you will." She approaches the map. "And you'll actually fix this problem, too. If the answer comes from me, Richie won't trust it. " In the air, she taps a few virtual buttons and sends me a zipped folder of files, my stream giving me a notification immediately. "But I think you'll see the same pattern I see."

····•··•····

Late that night, well after we've eaten my mother's delicious meal, I find myself pacing back and forth in the basement. On the wall, I've projected the same map of the Maumee Basin, featuring the data points provided by Brenette. They highlight each of the "attacks," complete with drone footage showcasing a similar scene to what happened to Richie's fields. All along the Maumee, from the first farms south of Perrysburg down to a few miles past Waterville to Richie's farm, almost to my parents' land. Seven attacks, with the land dug out and scattered in mounds.

All in just over a week.

"Make it make sense," I whisper.

For a moment, an odd thought sneaks into my head. *I should call Shanya.* This is the exact type of puzzle we would have loved solving together as kids. But no. Imagine me, calling Shanya up and saying "Hey, I know we haven't spoken in a few years, but you want to help me figure out who is attacking farms all around town while your mom's being accused of harboring civil disobedients?"

It wouldn't be a great look.

I needed to solve this on my own.

"You really should sleep." My mother, standing on the stairs.

"I'm going to figure this out."

"I know you will, but you can figure it out in the morning."

I try to crack my fingers, but instead I just stretch my joints until they scream in pain. "I feel like I'm missing something pretty simple. Why'd you have to give me a project that I actually like for once?"

She chuckles and sips the whiskey she's favoring in one hand. "Everyone was getting restless with these strange occurrences. It was Vick's idea, not mine. He said, 'Meredith, everyone's at each other's throats on the voice channels, and I'm going to lose it. Jordan can figure this out. He always does.' So I messaged you."

"Why me? Why am I the one to solve this? I'm not a farmer. I barely understand the data I'm looking at. I write laws, not spreadsheets."

"Sometimes, it takes an outside eye to spot the wound festering in plain sight that everyone else should easily see yet simply doesn't." She turns off the overhead light, plunging the room into darkness. "Now sleep! Or I won't roast portabellas in the morning."

· · • • • • • • · ·

My stream's incessant vibrations pull me from restless dreams. I groggily check my watch, seeing that it's 9am and—

Police, at Brenette's.

It takes me less than three minutes to throw on jeans, grab a tumbler of coffee, and rush outside to my bike. I shout something to my mother about being back shortly, even if I have no idea how long this will take.

These kids don't deserve whatever it is Richie's trying to have the police do. The police are still the police, even after the law enforcement-union cracking legislation from a few years ago, and a multiracial crew of kids hanging out on a Black woman's farm present a recipe for disaster. As I ride my bike up 24, I try calling Richie, but it goes straight to voicemail.

Because I realize my mistake.

Last night, after Dad and I met with Brenette.

We never gave Richie a call. Never told him our thoughts.

And now he went and did something stupid.

Sure, I don't *know* it's his fault. But it's *definitely* his fault.

As I arrive at Brenette's place about fifteen minutes later, it's without a doubt the fault of Richie. He's standing there beneath a powerline, chatting up a cop. A crowd of the water protectors stands at the end of Brenette's drive, holding their signs high, chanting, "No water, no peace." A half-dozen swat officers block the road with shields.

Without thinking, I whip out my green legal observer cap from the storage compartment of my e-bike. I don't play the role very often anymore, but I'm still an active member of the Midwest Lawyers Guild. It's an easy way for me to support free speech rights and associated causes.

And the hat always sends the more aggressive cops a simple signal. *You're being watched.*

Of course, Richie doesn't know what my hat means. He waves as I approach, oblivious. "Jordan, good, you're here. Officer, this is—"

"I'm Jordan Warnick, Deputy Director of the Midwest Federation Legislative Service Commission." I nod, trying to pull off "official" swagger.

Not sure if it works, but the cop holds out a hand, and I reluctantly shake it. "Richie's a friend, as is Brenette, the owner of the farm up ahead."

"Pleasure to meet you. Officer Franks."

"Why're you all here?"

"Richie here gave us a tip about trespass—"

"I'm going to stop you right there." I shake my head. "How long have you known Brenette? You think she'd let these kids here without a free speech permit? Y'all know her style. Y'all remember her time on City Council." I did not, in fact, know if they remembered, but they should. They were Waterville police. "Anyway, I'm good friends with County Commissioner Fields." It's true—we went to law school together. "She approved their free speech permit. Did y'all even check?"

Officer Franks's eyes widen as my tirade finishes. He barks an order to a fellow cop who rushes over.

"Look," I say, not waiting for them to conference with each other. "I can hang out, observe y'all, make sure you don't violate any rights. Or you can just go home and let the kids do their thing."

"You've made yourself clear," Franks says. "We'll head out."

"Good."

Richie just stands there, fuming. "But they're guilty!"

I shake my head. "Richie. Seriously. I need you to go home. I should have called last night. They're not guilty. It's someone else."

"There's no other explanation. Unless you have one?"

"Not yet."

"Then how do you know?"

"It's because he listens!" Brenette strides out of the throng of protesters as the cops pull away in their cars. "Richie, you need to start using your ears. These kids arrived nearly a week after the first attack on the Burns's biosolid swell. *How could it possibly be them?*"

"Well then, maybe it's you."

The scene shifts into deathly silence. I can't believe his accusation. The man has known Brenette probably longer than I've been alive, and here he is, accusing her of attacking his crops because he simply has no explanation for what's happening. She glances at me, anger in her eyes. "Jordo, you better solve this problem and get him off my land, or Richie's gonna wish he never learned what it meant to accuse a Black woman on her own property."

"See officers, she's threat—"

I walk up to Richie and held a finger in front of his mouth, pointing him toward his car. "You heard her. Get."

There's a split-second where I think he might hit me. For a moment, I consider what it would mean if I pushed him away. But instead, he huffs and stomps toward his vehicle. I turn to face Brenette.

"I'm so—"

"Don't you dare apologize to me. It ain't your fault he never fully unlearned the racism of his ancestors. Just do what you said you'd do and figure out what's causing this."

· · · ● · ● · · · ·

I'm in my parents' basement again, staring at the data. I've started pulling in MF Ag and EPA shapefiles, overlaying heat maps over the locations of the attacks. There are plenty of possible trends, but predicting the *right* trend will be a problem.

There hasn't been an attack every day, but there's been an attack almost every day. Enough to assume an attack will come tonight, since we didn't hear about an attack last night. The consistency feels methodical, as if whoever is assaulting the crops has a particular motivation behind everything. I scroll through heat maps showing crop type, tile irrigation density, no-till usage, and river setbacks. Nothing seems to line up. Almost all the farms along the river are using some combination of the state's endorsed best practices.

I'm missing something.

Something that should be absolutely obvious.

I pull up the footage recorded by my Lens when standing before Richie's attacked acres. The video showcases the scarred ground, dirt pulled up in piles with sludge pooling away from the river. Having property along the river bank is an obvious enough connection; I put those pieces together hours ago. It must have something to do with water pollution, given the connection to the river. But what?

The website for the Midwest Water Protectors finds its way onto my wall screen. I'm not even sure when I navigated to it, but there it is, the mission and policy declaration of the organization, right in front of my face. *With direct action and policy expertise, we pursue the fundamental right to safe drinking water for all people through recognizing the rights of waterbodies to exist as natural entities, devoid of harmful pollution.*

I scroll further down the page.

Phosphorus from agricultural land is the primary cause of deadly algae blooms in the Great Lakes. Thus, we DEMAND the immediate cessation of all biosolid use within one-hundred meters of any water feature.

I squint.

Could it be that simple?

One data-layer sat idly on my GIS dashboard, untouched. It seemed too personal. Too individual. But I overlay it upon the map of the attacks.

A perfect match.

Precisely two days before each attack, the "victim" filed their biosolid application confirmation paperwork. And—

Shit.

I look at the spreadsheet, disbelieving what I am seeing.

I close the apps, slip on my shoes, and sprint upstairs. I'm barely registering the texts I'm sending—one to Brenette and one to Richie. "Mom? Dad? Where are you?" But I needn't have asked. I stumble into the kitchen, and they're both sitting there sipping a beer.

"Can we help you?" my father asks.

"Outside with me, now." I say. "To the river."

"It's thirty degrees outside and 11 at night. Can it—"

"No! Now."

My feet have a mind of their own, and I don't wait for them to respond. I grab my coat from the rack and step outside, walking down the drive toward 24 and the fields across the way. Before I feel like a second has passed, I'm standing on the other edge of the ditch, my parents' field smelling of freshly applied manure.

It doesn't take long for my parents to catch up, though they're out of breath. "What the hell is this about?" says my mother.

"You wanted me to solve Richie's problem," I say. "Well, I think it's your problem too. And everyone who lives along this river. As for the cause of the attacks . . ." That still remains a mystery to me. "I think we just need to wait and see."

"We're next?" asks my father. "Should I call the cops?"

I shake my head. "I have a feeling the cops won't be of much help."

A few minutes later, two cars park near us. Brenette and Richie, both bundled in winter coats, step into the below-freezing air.

I wave.

"What, you bring us out here to settle our differences?" Brenette says as she sees Richie. "I ain't about that life."

"Sorry I couldn't explain more," I reply. "But it's almost time."

Richie, for his part, says nothing, instead taking a spot beside my father.

For a few more minutes, the night air remains silent, the only noise coming from a train in the distance.

Then, from beyond my parents' field, in the murky depths of the Maumee River, a wave rises.

Ebbs.

Overflows.

It seems impossible, seeing the river acting as if it had a tide. It flows into the Great Lakes, a bodies of water nowhere near the size to have fully-fledged waves, let alone up its tributaries.

But there was no other way to describe what accosted the river bank.

A dark green wave rushes onto shore, taking form above the field. Towering nearly a dozen feet in the air, the blob coalesces into a murky, swampy thing. It slurps forward, and before long, it moves into the glow of the street light above our heads.

Needless to say, we all remain completely motionless as the creature approaches.

The illumination of its body reveals the truth. It's murky river water, but it's almost exclusively river water overwhelmed by the green algae of the Lake. It is the personification of the blooms we've known to expect and loathe our entire lives. It is the monster, the boogeyman taunting everyone across the region, reminding them how easily a single bloom can overwhelm their drinking water.

And it's speaking.

lugmehlugmehlugmeh

I glance down the line of gawkers beside me. None of us know what to say.

lugmehlugmehlugmeh

"What do we do?" I whisper.

Lug meh. Lug meh.

"I think it's speaking to us," says Brenette.

LUG MEH.

And then everything clicks into place.

"It's saying 'love me.' It wants love." I don't actually know if its sounds mean anything at all. They could be just sounds. Not words. But if giving them meaning would help the people around me solve their conflict, I would use my interpretation to achieve that end. "It wants affection. It wants to be treated with respect." I look up at its formless, gaping face. "Is that what you want?"

LUG MEH.

Richie softly yelps.

"Brenette, is that the evidence you were looking for?" I inquire.

"Not precisely, but I think it gets the point across," she says. "Y'all wanted to pin it on me and the kids. Well look at yourself in the mirror. Am I right, Jordo?"

"No more pig shit," I say. "Richie. Dad. Y'all been told long enough. It's time to stop doing what you're used to and love the river."

Lug meh.

Richie looks at Brenette, glances at my father, then back at Brenette. "I'm sorry. Truly sorry. I should have known better—*you* deserved better."

With that, the creature slumped back into the river, disappearing beneath its surface.

· · ● ● · ● · · · ·

I'm about to head back to Columbus. It's Tuesday afternoon, after the long weekend. I don't really know what to do with the truth; the visage of the lake, the algae monster, it replays over and over again in my head, especially its words. My parents have promised; as has Richie. What we witnessed . . . it's shook me. How can I return to my job in Columbus with that image in my head? Nature, personified, emerging from the river to rear its angry head at us.

It's terrifying.

Just as I hit the power button on my electrobike, I receive a message from Brenette, asking me to stop by on my way out of town. Not wanting to face the reality of a day of work tomorrow just yet, I shoot back a "yes." A few minutes later, I'm parking beneath her porch. The protesters are gone, back to college or wherever home base might be.

But there are two electrobikes parked next to mine, and I know Brenette doesn't ride one.

I don't knock—I walk right through the front door, entering the living room. Brenette sits in her preferred loveseat; to her left, on the couch, sits a woman with gently tanned skin, likely middle-aged, wearing a blue cardigan. Standing, hands on hips, waits Shanya. She doesn't look particularly happy nor sad to see me as I enter. But she does softly smile. She's wearing a UT hoodie.

"Thank you for coming, Jordo," Brenette says. "You of course know Shanya, but I'll let her introduce her colleague."

"It's good to see you," I say, crossing my arms. "Something I can help you with?"

"Actually, yes," says the unknown woman.

"This is Natalie," Shanya says. "She's a friend, works for the United Nations. We heard about what you did for my mother."

"I swear we aren't crazy," I reply. "Brenette saw it too! So did my parents."

"We know," Natalie says. "That's why I'm here. My official job is for the United Nations, but I'm here regarding another matter. An opportunity for you, so to speak."

"You're offering me a job?" I definitely did not expect my next interaction with Shanya, if it ever happened, to be a job interview.

"Not exactly," Shanya replies. "It's really been a long time since we've had the chance to catch up, and I wish this could have been a conversation to have under different circumstances."

"Are you sure you want to tell him the truth?" Brenette interjects. "Do you think he's ready?"

I bite my tongue, hating the way they talk as if I'm not in the room. My mind's a whirlwind of contradictions, because a few of Shanya's words send up worrying signs. "Are you in some sort of trouble?" I ask.

"Aren't we all?" Natalie says. She snaps her fingers, and on the other side of the room, a window snaps shut. With three more clunks, the other windows follow suit.

I try to hide my surprise, but I know my eyes are spread wide. "Did—" Shanya lifts her arms, and the windows slide open.

"Somehow, this is crazier than seeing an algae monster attack my parent's farm," I say. And I mean the words.

"I can understand that reaction," Natalie says. "I'll cut to the chase. I can't offer you a job. You'll need to keep your current position in Columbus. But Brenette trusts you. Shanya trusts you. They've been part of our team for a few years now. And after this past weekend, they've recommended you."

"Recommended me for what?"

"We'd like you to become the Senior Policy Advisor for the World's Revolution," Shanya says.

"The who?"

"And if you've ever heard the rumors, know they're true. We're both Awakened."

I'd be lying if I said I didn't accept their offer. I'm not sure yet if I'll ultimately regret my trip this past weekend. If I'll regret joining their organization. But at least I'll still be trying to love the river from afar, in my own way.

INTO THE BRAMBLE
CHRISTOPHER R. MUSCATO

A zoo in North America
2056 C.E.

It begins with a bribe. In fact, there is an entire section of the treasurer's ledger cataloging funds set aside specifically for that purpose. This warming of palms with charitable donations to private pensions, this inconspicuous bartering in the free markets of secrets and whispers, this is how relationships form. This is how doors open.

The dove was remarkably cooperative, but then again, it had little else to do. It also may have simply lacked the energy to fuss and jump about too much, being so near to the end of its natural lifespan. Jamie looked at the dove, then back down to the sketchpad in her hands. *Zenaida graysoni*, it read, the heading on her page written in fanciful lettering. Such a simple epithet. She had liked the font at first, but having spent a few days in the presence of the dove, the lettering now felt cold. Sterile. The placard of a museum diorama in an exhibit on species now extinct. Jamie frowned, and looked again to the bird.

A Socorro dove.

The last of its kind.

Jamie set her notepad on the bench and leaned forward with her chin on her hands as she took a few minutes to simply observe the bird. Not to study it, but to see it. Really see it. Russet feathers overlapped with patches of blue-gray, hints of pinkish purple shimmered along the nape of the neck. Beady, brilliant eyes—one slightly clouded from an eye infection—observed a world in greater motion than it was any longer capable of. Even in its advanced age, it was beautiful.

People around Jamie shuffled into the small, tented space, bore witness to the fact that this creature had existed, and were escorted out. A new batch of revenants came in. To prevent the viewing room from being crowded, none were allowed to stay long. Except Jamie. As the official illustrator hired by the zoo to complete a final portrait of the last Socorro dove, it was her privilege to be here as long as she needed.

> *Once introductions have been made, the event planners step in. After all, what is ceremony without theatricality? The décor is minimalist, somber, but looms in the background. A table is procured with linens for the holding of symbolic artifacts. The first item set on this table is a statue of a small rodent, cast in pure gold.*

Jamie yawned, closing her sketchbook. This completed a third full day in the dove's presence, and her sketchbook was full of detailed impressions, color swatches, and notes. But now, her eyes were tired. She glanced around the room at the final grouping of guests who would be admitted today, and one woman caught her eye. This woman had been through before. In fact, she had been a frequent visitor over the last few days. Jamie would likely have never noticed if not for the dashing fields of color dyed into the woman's hair, a veritable mosaic of hues molded into a bob cut.

The woman caught her looking, and Jamie quickly dropped her gaze. The woman, however, did not. After a moment observing the now blushing artist, the woman with the colorful hair eased her way over to Jamie's bench.

"Something else, isn't it? To see the last of a species. I'm Kay."

"Jamie," she responded, fidgeting a little in her seat. "Jamie Gurnay. And yeah, it's . . . it's really something."

"You're an artist," Kay observed, looking down at the open sketchpad in Jamie's lap. Jamie gulped.

"I'm a scientific illustrator. I was commissioned to do a final portrait of the dove."

"Ever seen it from the other side of the glass?" Kay nodded to the one-way mirror partitioning the resting bird from its adoring public. Jamie shook her head.

"They can't risk the contamination. As much as I would have loved the opportunity." She glanced down at her sketchpad. The details were all there, but somehow, it still felt like something was missing. Something more . . . intimate. Kay caught the look on Jamie's face and nodded to herself, but said nothing.

The ceremony occurs more frequently now than any of the participants would like. But it is not theirs to choose the time or place. They are simply there to witness. This is their sacred responsibility, their privilege, their penance. Once it is done, they disperse, anonymity incarnate, dissolving silently back into society. Yet with each ceremony, they change, a piece of it written into their spirits, a treasure and a burden they will carry forever.

The viewing room attendant signaled that it was time to go, and Kay rose, nodding her farewell. Jamie spent a few final moments observing the dove then packed her things. Before she left, she whispered against the glass.

"I'll never forget you. Go in peace."

And with that, she left the room and slowly made her way through the zoo.

"Say your goodbyes?"

Jamie spun her head as she exited the zoo's front gates to see Kay leaning against a fence, casually reading a pamphlet on the Socorro dove as if there were nothing strange about surprising someone in a parking lot. Jamie opened her mouth, surprised, but stumbled on the words. Kay straightened, folded the pamphlet, and jerked her head.

"Come on. We need to get you ready."

Jamie looked around as Kay strolled off, hands in her pockets. Jamie considered bolting for her car, but something about Kay intrigued her, something she couldn't explain, something that bubbled through her inhibitions and instinct for self-preservation. She glanced around one more time. Her anxiety bowed in resignation to curiosity, and she trotted after the mosaic-haired woman.

Through the parking lot they walked, eventually reaching a large van in the very back row. Kay started to unlock the back of the van, and Jamie froze.

"Just look," Kay rolled her eyes as she opened the doors. Not moving from where she was, Jamie craned her neck, then tilted her head. The inside of the van contained a spacious wardrobe, brightly lit, lined with black garments on two of the walls. Along the third was a magnificent dresser and vanity set.

"Lucky for you, it's my job to bring lots of options in case some of the guests forget to dress for the occasion," Kay said as she jumped into the van and started pulling things out of shelves, placing them on the dresser. She climbed back out and jerked her head.

"Up you go. Pick out anything you like, but the stuff on the dresser is mandatory."

"Kay . . . what's going on?" Jamie finally managed to ask. Kay winked.

"I think you know I can't tell you."

Minutes later, Jamie was inside the van, still unable to explain even to herself what reason she had to trust this colorful stranger. Jamie looked in the mirror. She'd found a simple black dress on the shelves that fit, shoes to match, and then black gloves and a large black cloak set on the dresser for her. There was a gold pin on the cloak—some sort of mouse, it seemed. Jamie picked up the final object from the dresser and put it on. The carnival mask was black, save for a single teardrop on the right side, a small but ornate tile mosaic laid into the mask with gilded lines between the diminutive tesserae.

"Well, look at you!" Kay clapped as Jamie emerged, and Jamie felt herself blush. Kay had changed as well, now similarly adorned in hooded black robe and mask, a matching pant-suit underneath.

Kay checked her watch and cursed, then started hurrying back towards the zoo. Jamie followed, heart pounding and skin tingling with excitement and confusion and anticipation. She had no idea what was happening, why they were returning to the zoo, why she was dressed in this unusual fashion.

Rather than approach the main gate, Kay headed to a staff entrance on the side. She knocked on the door, and it creaked open.

"Zoo's closed. Unless you have a key."

"The bramble is the key," she answered, and the door opened fully. The man at the door held out a hand, and Kay shook it. As they did, Jamie was just able to catch a glimpse of small, matching tattoos in the shape of a tiny paw print at the base of each wrist.

Kay nodded Jamie inside, then slid in after her. Through a passage of hallways they twisted, until they passed through a set of doors and walked into a room draped in black finery, candles flickering, filled with guests wearing black cloaks and black masks with ornate teardrops. At the front, a table displayed a larger candle, a glass of wine, and a statue of a gold mouse. Kay turned to Jamie.

"Welcome to the Bramble Society of the Knights of *Melomys rubicola*."

The official records do not identify the
founding members, nor the exact date
of said founding. Regardless, the ledger
contains enough names (or at the least,
aliases) to indicate that membership is

> *more expansive than most would as-*
> *sume, and growing. Members identify*
> *each other through the* Melomys ru-
> bicola *pawprint tattoo on the wrist, or*
> *the exchanging of words. Some symbols*
> *of the society have been incorporated*
> *into jewelry or other accessories, hid-*
> *den but accessible to those who know to*
> *look for them.*

"Kay, what is this?" Jamie asked, her voice hoarse.

"We're a society of conservation-minded activists," Kay replied, the casual nature of her tone and demeanor in sharp contrast to the somber theatricality of the setting. "Our mission is to try and save what's left of this world that humans have so thoroughly destroyed."

Jamie nodded, though she couldn't pretend to fully understand. A clandestine organization of masked activists who congregated in the hallways of zoos after hours. Made zero sense.

"You said something about the Bramble Society . . . of the Knights of, of what?"

"*Melomys rubicola,*" Kay gestured to the small statue of the golden rodent. "The Bramble Cay Melomys, first recorded mammal to go extinct as a direct result of human-caused climate change. This little martyr is the patron saint of our order. This is why we do this."

"And what is . . . this?" Jamie gestured around the room. For the first time, a weight settled onto Kay's shoulders, and when she spoke, the normal bravado in her voice was muted, wavering.

"Our most sacred ceremony. You'll see."

Just then, the lights dimmed. There was a rustling, and from behind a curtain came a succession of people in black, bearing candles, escorting a small cadre of veterinarians still in their zoo scrubs. Between them was a magnificently carved and lacquered box, which was set on the center table amid a laurel wreath tied with gold ribbons. The attendees in the crowd shuffled into a line. Red and white roses were distributed to each person. As Jamie accepted the flowers, she craned her neck to try and see what was in the box. Then, her eyes bulged open and her mouth went dry. She felt a hand on her shoulder.

"Jamie," Kay's voice whispered in her ear, "say hello to the last Socorro dove."

Ears ringing and hands clammy, Jamie shuffled along the line, the slow processional providing each attendee a chance to lay their roses at the base of the lacquered box and pay their respects. Once all had done so, they gathered in a circle and waited.

Time passed. Jamie had no way of knowing how much. All stood in silence, unmoving. Time itself must have ceased its progression out of respect for the moment, an instant stretching into infinity as Jamie's fingers trembled under her dark robe. Finally, a vet examined the bird and nodded. It was over. The last Socorro dove was dead, but it had died in the loving hands of its caretakers, its passing observed in awed reverence. None would forget this moment. None ever did.

A sob caught in Jame's throat, a stinging striking her eyes. Again, the gentle weight of a familiar hand pressed on her shoulder.

"It never gets easier. This is my fifth ceremony. This is the reminder of why we fight."

Jamie turned to look at Kay and the two held each other's gazes, sharing the pain of the moment. Then Jamie returned her attention to the table. She approached, observing the deceased bird, wrapped in finery and laid to rest. The candlelight flickered on its worn and tired feathers, the gilding on its box dancing in flame. Hues of russet and pink and purple and grey and blue burned with warmth. The wings shimmered under the rhythmic pulse of light and shadow, almost as if they were beating their way to glory on the speckled light of candles.

"I don't think you'll have any trouble finishing that portrait now," Kay said gently, and Jamie nodded. For the first time, she truly saw the dove. For the first time, she understood.

As the ceremony concluded, Jamie and Kay walked back to the parking lot, slowly. "Thank you for this, Kay," Jamie said, eyes tracing the pavement. "I still have a lot of questions."

"I'm sure you do," Kay laughed. She looked up. "Stars are out tonight."

"Yeah, they are," Jamie nodded, looking up from the pavement to the worlds above. "Tell me, Kay . . . Kay?'

Jamie spun around. Her mysterious escort, with the mosaic of colors in her hair, had disappeared. Jamie stood in the parking lot alone. She turned a few more times, pulled the black cloak tighter around herself, and left.

Later that night, as she emptied her bag and opened her sketchbook, anxious to complete her portrait of the last Socorro dove, a small business card tumbled out and onto her desk. Jamie picked it up. It was blank, save for a small letterpress impression of a golden rodent, and on the back, a phone number.

> *In board rooms and behind closed doors, on lonely hiking trails and in crowds of protestors, within military ranks and along corporate ladders, there are handshakes. One person notices the tattoo on the other's wrist. A look is exchanged. A nod. They know that they have come for the same reason, with the same purpose. They carry the same pain, the same experiences and marks of somber rituals carved into their hearts. They are setting themselves into place, preparing, readying the world. And when the world is ready, they will be too.*

THE BOY WHO CALLED FROM THE SEA

P.J. SKY

In a small town somewhere
2056 C.E.

I suppose you'll want to know how I ended up in that old beach house by the sea, with its two stories of weather-beaten board, seemingly only held together by sand and salt, and the corridor in the attic where I first met Benjamin Blake. This is his story after all, and I don't think I'd be telling it otherwise. But to tell it right, I gotta go back to the beginning, to when I was still at Birchwood with my folks, but after old Mrs. Simpson died.

Because that's what had happened. Old Mrs. Simpson had *died*.

That word still sticks in my throat. You know, because sometimes something happens, and it's so wrong you can't see a way it can ever be made right again. From now until the day I die, my life will be forever that little bit broken, because something happened that should never ever have happened, and worst of all, it was my fault. After everything she'd done for me, and everything she'd taught me, I'd gone and opened my big mouth and spilled it to Ma, and she'd spilled it to everyone else, and then the whole town opened its big mouth and swallowed Mrs. Simpson whole. That morning after, there weren't nothing left of Willow Way but burnt embers and that acrid stench, sticking on the back of my tongue, of kerosene.

I felt sorry for Pa. I guess he'd done what he thought he could, but in the end it weren't enough. After, he got quieter than ever, and spent long evenings staring into the fire, his right hand pulling at the loose skin on his chin, and his eyes everywhere but mine. I got the feeling something was broken inside him too. He knew the folks of the valley had done wrong, and then they'd turned their backs and pretended it weren't nothing to do with them, and I think he knew Ma was one of them.

Maybe you think that's unfair of me?

I guess Ma never set flame to the kerosene. She didn't know what'd happen any more than I did. But that night she took it to the memorial centre, and she said all those lies, spilling stuff she didn't know nothing about.

I remember that last night in Birchwood, when I'd already made up my mind to split. Ma and Pa didn't look at me once as they sat at the dinner table, sipping miserable beet soup that was more water than anything else. Ma had talked about how Mrs. Jenson thought she was better than us because they'd bought a new electric harvester, and what did she have to even harvest anyhow? And I thought about how things would be different if old Mrs. Simpson were still here. For a little while back then, things had been different, but then Ma and her big mouth had gone and made everything the same as everywhere else.

Of course, I could have done something too then, but I was too scared. So scared I went hungry rather than bring the townsfolk to Birchwood, just so they could burn it down.

After we ate, and I'd washed up our dishes, as I did every night, I was walking to the stairs when Ma called to me. I turned. In the kerosene lamplight, her hard face glowed, all chiselled angles, with the shadow of her blunt nose hiding the mole on her cheek.

"You know that night, what I said, it was for your own good. I know it's on your mind, but what I said needed to be said. I had to protect you."

But she hadn't protected me. She hadn't protected anyone, and worse, she'd got Mrs. Simpson killed, and all because I opened my big mouth about why everyone's tomato crops were blooming like never before.

"I thought," I said, "you'd always said folks should mind their own biscuits."

"Yes, well, that only goes so far. Sometimes you gotta speak up. That woman was evil, and she had it coming."

A heat rose in my chest. My right hand twitched and I wanted to slap Ma. I preferred it when she didn't talk to me. Right then, I never wanted to see her again, and in that moment, I was never more set on leaving. I wanted to get as far away from Ma as I could ever possibly go.

I wonder now if perhaps she saw it in my eyes. I'd waited at the foot of those stairs, half hoping she'd take it back, like if only she could give me one reason to stay longer, but she didn't say another word. I turned and climbed those stairs like I was climbing the gallows, for I knew I'd reached the end of something, and beyond lay only darkness. And at that time I dared not think what Ma would have thought if she'd known I too shared a little of Mrs. Simpson's powers. I didn't know it then, but that was the last time I ever saw Ma.

At midnight, I stole out of the house, turned my back on the town, and climbed over the valley edge and into the dark world beyond. That night the air was cool and crisp, and near as silent as the dead. Soon I reached the highway and followed it east. I ignored the horns of the overnight truckers, the eyes of condemned cattle we could never afford to eat glinting through the trailer slats.

At first light, I reached the bus station in Greenville, and from there I took a bus out toward the stateline. I didn't know where I was going exactly, but I knew I was heading east. The coast seemed as good a place as any, for I'd never seen the sea. From the wide bus windows, covered in a film of grey dust, I watched the dead fields pass by, with their scrawny cows, ribcages pushing through their matted fur coats, and their endless rows of failed crops, and I listened to the whine of the electric motors beneath my feet, and imagined the crash of ocean waves onto warm, sandy beaches.

I didn't have an interstate pass. There was no way I could afford one. So, from the stateline, I joined all the other migrant workers as we trudged for hours down farm tracks and across dusty fields, until my feet had blistered and my throat was as parched as a desert. I waited two days in a leaky barn, wedged in with kids and mothers and screaming babies, and living on stale bread and watery goats' milk some church brought us each morning. Finally I made it onto one of the do-gooder pickups, and that night I crossed the border.

The pickup ran all the way to the coal mines, their towers like sentinels in a monochrome world straight out of an old movie. People moved between iron shacks, their eyes hollowed out, their skin as ash-grey as the walls of the valley around them. I didn't stick there long. I walked to the highway and hitched a lift with a couple of old folks crawling along it like a snail, with all their worldly belongings packed up on the roof of their ancient station wagon. For three days they plied me with candy and soda, and they talked of the daughter they were going to stay with. They took me east, all the way to Charlotte's Cove.

I remember that first pale morning at the cove, the sea spray having covered the weather-beaten buildings in a fine, grey film. I remember the tang of salt; the way I smelt it in the air and tasted it on my lips. The main street was empty. The old folks were going north and wanted me to join them. I won't lie, for a moment I was tempted. It was the safer option. They said there was plenty of room for me there. They were good folks for sure, but something kept me from joining them. It's hard to explain now, but I just had this feeling. I was at the sea, and I didn't want to go further. So, they thrust a scribbled address between my fingers and told me if I changed my mind that's where they'd be.

Once their snail-like station wagon had crawled up the road and out of sight on the bend, I moved across the damp tarmac and down onto the heavy sand. I saw the skeletons of boats, their wooden hulls disintegrating into the sand. Ahead, the dark sea churned, sucking and hissing and gnawing on the shoreline. Jagged waves flung salt-spray into the air, their peaks lined with white surf. The sea was like a living thing, ever moving, from moment to moment never the same. Out at sea, the hazy shadow of an island, like the hump of a whale, loomed below a blanket sky of grey cloud. Scrawny gulls cried, and somewhere a little bell rang.

The cold air bit my lips. I hunched my head between my shoulders and shivered. Looking out to sea, I sensed the scale of the world, ever larger than I ever imagined. And I knew then I'd found my new beginning. Finally, I was as far away from the valley as I could ever possibly be. I had escaped.

· · · • • · • • · ·

On the main street, the red neon sign of a diner blinked. Every other store seemed boarded-up. Between the stores, the empty houses looked on with dead eyes, their doors falling off their hinges like loose teeth, and their moth-eaten curtains swinging listlessly in the sea-breeze like the discarded dresses of stood up brides. A giant plastic swordfish hung over a boarded-up restaurant. A movie-theatre signboard had so many letters missing it was impossible to read what movie it had closed on.

In the diner, an old man made his way to my table. I rubbed my hands together, trying to push out the hard cold. I wondered how many of those precious black-market coins I still had. I didn't even know if they were good here.

"You new up there, are ya?"

I didn't hardly know how to answer him. Did he mean was I new in town?

"Yeah, I guess."

The man nodded. Even though I hadn't ordered, he placed a mug in front of me and began filling it with thick, black liquid.

"Ya look like ya need something warm in ya," he said, and added, "How's Sandra holding up? Her leg still causing trouble?"

I frowned. I had no idea what he was talking about.

"I've told her before," he said, his voice as course as the sand on the beach, "she's probably better having it off. Causing her pain all the time, can't hardly get about that big, old house. No wonder she needs you kids to look after the place. Still, I reckon you lot need her more than she needs you."

He winked and hobbled off toward the kitchen. I pressed my fingers around the warm mug and smelt the rich, nutty aroma. I couldn't remember when I'd last tasted coffee.

He called back, "Don't worry about the coffee. I always look out for you beach house kids. The name's Barry. Just you holler if ya need anything. An' say howdy to Sandra from me." He looked over his shoulder, a twinkle in his eye, like the grit that forms the pearl. "I still ain't forgotten her, an' I ain't so old, neither."

He hollered a deep, gravelly laugh as he disappeared behind the door.

I was about to sip my coffee when, two booths down, a mop of purple hair appeared. I guess she was close to my age. I don't think I'd ever seen someone wearing so much makeup. Her pale skin was almost doll-like. Her eyes were like something from one of those old Japanese paintings, the corners all curled upwards, and outlined in thick red and black liner. She pursed her purple lips, as purple as her hair. She slid out of her booth, rounded the corner of the seats, and before I knew it, she'd slid into my booth opposite me. She stretched her hands across the plastic table, her purple fingernails poking through her black fingerless gloves. She rolled her jaw, split her lips, and blew a small, pink bubble. The bubble burst and she sucked in the gum.

I leant back in my seat. I didn't know what to make of her.

She grinned. "You ain't from the house."

I fingered the rim of my coffee mug. "So?"

"But you're one of us." She leant forward and lowered her voice. "It's my gift, see. I can sense it."

My heart quickened. "I don't know what you're talking about?"

She raised her pencil-line eyebrows. "I mean, I feel it. You got a gift. See, my gift is to see where others don't." She crossed her arms and leant back. "You can hide from everyone else, but not from me."

Smacking her lips, she rolled the pink gum around her mouth.

"So, fess up, what's your gift?"

"I . . . I don't know what you're talking about."

She shook her head. "Come on, you can tell me. Can you see through walls? Can you walk on ceilings? You got the strength of a thousand walruses? I'll keep guessing till you tell me?"

She narrowed her eyes and smacked her lips together around that gum until I was hungry for more of the candy the old folks had plied me with.

From somewhere toward the kitchen I heard a crash.

I jumped.

She leant forward and spread out her hands. "Relax kid, we gotta stick together. There's room for you at the house. By the by, I'm Judy—Judy Jones."

· · • • · • • · · ·

Judy took small, rapid steps, her hands thrust into her pockets and her heels crunching on the crumbling sidewalk.

"See, I'm like Professor X. You know, like the X-Men."

I held my bag close to my shoulder as I followed Judy up the hill. I still didn't know what to make of her, but it would be getting dark soon, and I didn't see so many other options.

"I can find people with powers," she continued. "I can bring them together. But you know, with more style, and without the whole Cerebro thing."

I didn't really know what she was talking about. As far as I could tell, Judy had fallen from the stars. It was like she was from another planet. But then, before now I'd never been much further than Greenville. I supposed maybe this was what big city folks were like.

On the far north of town, set away from the road, at the end of a track lined with bare weeping willows, we found the beach house. It was getting dark then, and a welcome bulb burnt in a downstairs window. Beyond the house, I heard the waves crashing ceaselessly against the shoreline.

On my arrival, Sandra appraised me with hard, cold eyes, and I feared she'd turn out to be just like Ma.

"So, Judy, you've brought me another mouth to feed."

In that moment, I wanted to run away and be no burden to anyone. And I didn't want to be around anyone who'd remind me of Ma. But then the corners of Sandra's thin lips creased upwards.

"It's all right," she said. "My bark's worse than my bite. There's always room for strays here."

Judy prodded me. "See."

Up two flights of stairs, Judy showed me to a tiny room in the attic with a bed and a small chest of drawers. Pins stuck out of the faded yellow wallpaper in the corners of square shadows of colour, like once someone had tacked up pictures and postcards. I'd wondered who'd lived in this room before me, and what pictures they might have pinned up.

On the windowsill sat a small wooden boat, with a mast, but no sail. Beyond its empty rigging, the dark sea churned.

I dropped my bag next to the drawers.

Judy pulled at a strand of pink gum. "I'll leave you to unpack. Supper's at six, and you don't wanna be late."

With the sound of food, my stomach groaned.

Judy turned into the corridor. Pausing, she looked back. "Thanks for, you know, coming here. It's real cool of you. Don't worry, you'll totally fit in. We're all a bit weird here."

She grinned, pink gum between her teeth, and closed the door.

Over the sound of crashing waves, I listened to Judy's footsteps disappear down the hall.

I suddenly felt tired, like I could sleep for a week, but the thought of food pushed me on. Instead, I moved to the chest of drawers, as if in return for Judy and Sandra's kindness, I should do as Judy had suggested and unpack.

It felt strange to be opening those stranger's drawers. The top draw was bare, but for a brown paper liner at the bottom. I don't know why now, but something caused me to lift that liner. Beneath it I found a piece of folded paper. I felt like I shouldn't read it, but I couldn't hardly help myself. The handwriting was all over the place, like it was written by a child. It didn't stay within the lines, but I could read it well enough. This ain't exactly what it said, but it's close enough:

No one believes me but I know I can prove what happened. You all think I'm just a stupid kid but I'll show you. I'll be back before dark.

Ben

The wind rattled the window frame, like the world outside knew what I'd done in reading a letter never meant for me. I refolded the paper and pressed the note back underneath the liner.

Moving to the window, the words continued to play on my mind. *I can prove what happened.* But prove what?

I watched the dark waves roll upon each other, again and again, in their endless drowning dance. Along the shoreline, the sea spray and sand spun together, like the ghostly spectres of all the dead seafarers, forever pushed back to the brine.

In the beach house no one ever had to say grace, and I tell you, that kinda took some getting used to. Sandra sat at the table's head, like a fallen queen holding exiled court, and spent her mealtimes sitting side on, her legs crossed, blowing blue vapours through her thin lips. Her fingers would toy with an electric cigarette while her pale blue eyes gazed out through the window, across the collapsed veranda, and toward the dark sea.

Judy always sat next to me. She ladled the thin vegetable soup into her bowl and broke into it chunks of the hard bread. *Croutons* she called it, like she spoke French or something.

Opposite her sat Sparks. Judy called him that, and for the longest time I never learnt his real name. Over his big hands he always wore these black kevlar gloves, and that first night, despite Judy's prods, he didn't want to talk about his power.

"He never does," said Judy, like she knew the conversation would annoy him. Her right elbow on the table, she gnawed at a crust of bread, her eyes like two pink diamonds. "But I know your little secret, Sparks."

"Judy," he said, "you're such a child."

Judy grinned. "You'll have to get used to us. This is our thing."

"It really isn't," said Sparks.

Sparks looked like one of those clean-cut football jocks, like the ones that'd always hold the door open for you, or help old ladies cross the street, like he'd be just about ready to apologise for everyone else not opening every door you ever came across before.

Sitting next to Sparks, a thin girl, her face as pale as milk, dipped bread into her soup and sucked on it. She looked down at the table, never at us, and she never spoke a word.

"That's Silent Sally," said Judy. "She never speaks. None of us really know her deal." She turned to me. "So come on, what's your gift? You have to tell us. We're your family now."

"Don't rush her," said Sandra, never taking her eyes from the sea.

"Oh," said Judy, "that's just because you don't have a power of your own."

Sandra sighed. "You know, I sorely regret the day I took you in."

"Hah," snorted Judy. "You lot would be so bored without me."

I could feel the energy seeping from Judy. She could never sit still. She fidgeted in her chair, her right leg twitching, her fingers toying with her food or her hair.

"Ignore them all," said Judy. "You know it's so good to have a girlfriend here I can finally talk to. I just know we're gonna be fast friends."

Sparks grinned. There was something boyish about his grin, all lopsided, with dimples like two moon craters, but his eyes were dark, like he was burying something, or perhaps I only saw in him my own secret sadness.

"Don't worry sweetie," said Judy, eyeing the boy across the table. "I've not forgotten you."

··•·••·•••·

That first night I must have been exhausted, for I curled up under the covers, shivering, and I went out like a light.

I dreamt I was in a small boat, its bow dipping into the chopping waves. The wind whipped through my hair and caused my eyes to sting, while the dark waters splashed up the side of the boat. Ahead, the ghostly shadow of the island loomed. Squinting, I could just make out a thin beach, and upon it stood a tiny figure.

I'd awoken sweating, my nightshirt wet. I sat and slipped my feet over the side of the bed. My toes curled with the cold. Outside the window, a thin rain sprayed the dark glass, and I could hear the ocean crashing against the shoreline, waves tumbling over themselves again and again.

In the dim light, I moved to the door. Beneath my feet, a floorboard squeaked. I paused, listening to the old house creak around me, like it was an old ship, only temporarily beached. Soon the sea would return and drag it back out among the waves.

A sudden rain hammered the window and the wind started to howl. It sounded like a storm was whipping up.

I turned the doorknob and moved into the corridor toward the bathroom. Through the skylight and down the wallpaper, the thin moonlight cried streaks of tears. The bathroom door stood ajar, beyond it a well of darkness. Just as I reached the door, a small figure slipped out.

My heart jumped. I drew my hand to my chest.

I could just make out the features of his small, round face, the shadows of raindrops streaking his cheeks.

The boy grinned. "It's okay, I won't tell."

"I reckon you near gave me a heart attack."

"Sorry," said the boy, his voice almost a whisper. He put his finger to his lips and slipped past me into the corridor. I stumbled into the bathroom and closed the door behind me. Fumbling for the light switch, once I'd found it I leant against the door, catching my breath. I wondered how many more kids I'd find hiding in this old house.

Did we all have some sort of gift?

I remembered the words of Laverna Simpson, Mrs. Simpson's daughter.

"There are more of us. Soon the whole world will know about us, and together we can really change things for the better. But we need people like you. People who can see we're not monsters."

That boy weren't a monster, any more than Judy or Mrs. Simpson . . . or me. But then I let that happen to Mrs. Simpson. It was my fault. Maybe none of us are monsters, or maybe we all are?

·····•·•····

And so it were like that for a while, with me bumping around the house, trying my best to fit in. Breakfast and supper were held at the same time each day, and it was always pretty much the same. Mostly, I was just as hungry as I was back at Birchwood, but I could hardly ask for more. I was lucky I got anything at all, seeing as I was an uninvited guest, and so I set to making it my mission to be useful. I got to peeling vegetables and baking bread, and washing dishes and sweeping paths clear of sand, and helping with laundry and house repairs. The beach house was falling apart, and with every board we repaired or replaced, we were only ever buying time. The beach was slowly consuming the town, and our house was no exception.

Sometimes we walked down into town, and we came back with boards, or doors, or windowpanes, or whatever else we needed and could take from any of the many abandoned houses slowly disintegrating into the salt. I always felt strange exploring these abandoned houses. I preferred the empty ones, already stripped of furniture and possessions, but Judy liked to explore the ones where it seemed like the folks who'd lived there had just up and left their lives and everything behind, like they'd gotten up halfway through their breakfast and just given up. She was obsessed with seeking out vinyl records, or makeup, or shoes. We had a few digital screens, but we didn't have no internet, though Judy had a record player that could play all this music old folks had left behind, like echoes from a time before.

I remember in this one house seeing on a mantelpiece a framed photograph of an old couple. I wondered why no one had taken it with them. Photographs were normally gone. But then I wondered if maybe the old couple had never left. Maybe they'd died here, in a room in the house, and no one had ever come to look. They'd sat here, between the abandoned houses, the wind whistling around the window frames, and the dark ocean crashing against the shoreline, and they'd died and been forgotten. A chill had run up my spine then, and I'd not wanted to go no further, and had persuaded Judy to leave with me.

Sometimes, on such expeditions, we'd stop by the diner and Barry would give us sodas, or bitter coffee, and he'd never expect a cent. One time he gave us slices of cheesecake. Judy had wanted to know where he'd got it but he wouldn't say, he'd just tapped his nose and winked at us. But I didn't rightly care. I devoured my slice, and it was about the best thing I ever did taste.

So, at the beach house we made our own borrowed time, and tomorrow didn't seem so important if we could only get through today. We were like beachcombers, shipwrecked, but we didn't want to think about going home, or at least I didn't. This was our rescue. And I never pushed Judy on it, but I got the feeling she felt the same. I didn't want to think about all that stuff back at the valley. Instead, I tried to keep myself busy, even if that was just sitting up late in Judy's room, listening to some old record with the sound on real low, so it didn't disturb Sandra. I don't think she liked us taking stuff from the houses, but she didn't say nothing about it either. I guess all this stuff we took once belonged to her neighbours and that must have felt kinda weird. But she was always pleased when another windowpane or board was replaced.

Sometimes at night, I dreamt of the sea and the figure on the beach. Sometimes I seemed to be getting nearer to the island, and sometimes further away. I didn't run into the boy again, and I figured he must keep himself to himself. I wanted to ask Sandra about him, but we just never had that kind of relationship. She kept herself to herself. She couldn't get around well on account of her leg, as if this one part of her were decaying with the town. Mostly she just sat and stared out to sea. And she had this way about her, like whenever I was alone with her, the words just seemed to dry up. And then she'd give me this thin smile, like she kinda pitied me, and I didn't really like that feeling. And she'd tell me something like: "You'll be all right, child. Stick with Judy. She's a survivor."

· · · ● · ● · ● · · ·

One morning, Judy and I were walking north up the beach, away from the town, when she brought up my powers again. My eyes were tearing, and I'd pretty much covered the lower half of my face with a thick scarf I'd found in a dresser and laundered. The sand blew in eddies around the carcasses of old fishing boats, their hulls rusting and the oil from their engines cutting channels in the damp sand toward the dark sea.

"I'll figure it out, you know."

"What?" I asked.

"Your power."

I rolled my eyes and pushed my hands deeper into my pockets.

"It's all right," she said, her eyes squinting into the distance. "We've all got bad secrets. I try not to think about it, you know? But most people hate what they don't understand."

I could hear the hardness in her words. "I think folks are scared."

"Yeah," she said. "Well, it's funny how the ones who claim to be scared are also the one's running after us with pitchforks, driving us out here. They should try being in the minority. They should try being the one's doing the running, instead of the ones doing the chasing. Then they'd know what it really feels like to be scared."

"Is that what happened to you?"

"I don't wanna talk about it."

No, I thought. Me neither. I'd been trying not to think about it for so long, I'd almost forgotten how. After I'd turned my back on Birchwood, I'd closed a door I still weren't sure I was ready to open.

We walked on in silence. To our right, the ocean churned, dark waves barrelling over themselves, and I thought of my dreams. I looked toward the shadow of the island, and I wondered how far it was, and how long it would take me to row there. I hadn't never been on a boat before.

"Do you think Spark's cute?"

I blinked, taken aback. I looked to Judy. She was grinning.

"I dunno," I said. "Do you?"

"Yeah, kinda. I dunno. I guess he's the only guy in twenty miles of here. I mean, you know, there's Barry at the diner, but that really doesn't count.

And you know, I think him and Sandra had a thing once, not that you'd ever get anything personal out of Miss High-and-Mighty."

"She ain't so bad."

"I know, I shouldn't bitch. Like, I know she pretends like she needs us to clean her dishes or whatever, and fix up the house, but I don't know who else would have taken me in. Honestly, if it weren't for her . . ." Her face fell dark again, like she was pushing away a difficult memory. "I just don't wanna go there."

At the end of the beach, the headland rose upwards below jagged cliffs, bolstered with heavy concrete blocks and a mountain of discarded lobster pots and fishing nets. Just off the beach stood a concrete building with a chimney, one wall collapsed inward revealing a rusty skeletal webbing. Following up the headland, toward the point, I could just make out the old lighthouse that no longer blinked.

"What happened here?"

Judy sucked at her bottom lip. "Barry says the fish all died. No one seems to know why, or if they did, they didn't stick around long enough to tell us. And with the fish, the town died too."

A chill ran down my spine.

"Judy, who's the boy in the attic?"

"What boy?"

"The boy. He can't be more than eight or nine years old I reckon. I met him in the attic on my first night at the beach house."

Judy shook her head. "You were pretty out of it that night. I reckon you must have been dreaming. You've already met everyone at the beach house."

• • • • • • • • • •

A few nights later I dreamt I was back in the rowboat, its bow dipping back and forth. I sat in the stern, the sea spraying my face. Ahead, the island loomed, ever closer. I could make out the beach now, and upon its shore stood the small boy—the one I'd met in the attic. He was pointing to the water and shouting. The wind carried his words.

"They're all dead. They're all dead."

I awoke, my heart racing. I looked toward the window. The curtains hung half-open. Outlined by the thin moonlight, the small boy sat out upon the ledge, his face toward the sea.

He did exist.

Turning his head, he grinned at me.

Pulling aside the covers, I leapt from my bed and moved to the window, ready to open it and confront him, but when I drew aside the curtains, he'd gone.

The miniature wooden boat still sat on the windowsill. Moving it, I slid up the heavy window frame. The wind stung my eyes and the dark ocean pounded the shore. The ledge sloped forward. I leant as far out of the window as I could and looked down toward the dark sand, and then to the roof of the collapsed veranda. The boy was nowhere to be seen. I slipped my legs over the sill and climbed out. My bare feet slipped against the cold surface of the ledge.

"Hey," I said, my voice barely a whisper, but it was instantly swallowed by the churn of the sea. "It's okay. I just wanna talk to you."

I inched along the ledge to the next attic window. Nailed up boards covered the window frame. I ran my fingers over the weathered boards, caked in salt and grime, like they'd been up there for years.

Beyond the second attic window, I could see the bathroom skylight, like a dark well. There was nowhere else on the roof the boy could have run to.

The cold wind stung my eyes, and I shivered and curled my bare toes. Squinting toward the beach, I could see the white froth at the edge of the sea. Beyond it lay the dark emptiness, where the island lay hidden.

I made my way back to my window, and back into my bed, where I curled up under the covers and shivered, thinking of the boy. As my mind drifted, I listened to the old house sway and creak, as lost at sea as my dreams. And I thought of the people of this house, marooned in this forgotten place, living on their borrowed time.

· · · · ●· ● · · ·

"You know," said Judy the next morning as we walked toward the town. "It sounds like you saw a ghost. Either that or you were dreaming again."

"I weren't dreaming," I said. "I climbed out on the roof. I practically pinched myself. I tell you, I saw him on the roof."

"But while you were in bed? When you got up, he was gone?"

"Yeah."

"You know, sometimes, after I wake up, it can take me a couple of minutes to realise I'm not still dreaming, and I have to tell myself this stuff in my head isn't real. Are you sure you weren't dreaming?"

"I can only tell you what I saw, and I tell you, I saw him."

Judy nodded. "There's another possibility of course."

"Which is?"

"You're nuts." Judy grinned. "Don't worry, I won't tell. You still won't be as nuts as Silent Sally."

"You shouldn't call her that, you know."

"You know, if he is a ghost, I bet he's a ghost of a boy who once died in that house."

"Yeah, too bad we can't find out who lived there before us."

Judy narrowed her eyes. "But maybe we can? This town don't have much, but it does have a library."

From the main street, Judy led me down a narrow alley between two abandoned stores. Beyond, we passed by empty houses, their vacant windows staring down on us. An entire house had collapsed forward into a dry swimming pool. Once white picket fences were now bare wood, consumed by salt and sand. Long dead lawns now rippled with the pale shapes of sand dunes, their crests lined with grey salt. One day these little dunes would grow to consume the entire town, and this place would become one vast waste of salt and sand, and the ocean would take our secrets, and there'd be nothing left to say that anyone were ever here at all.

We found ourselves on 2nd Avenue. A faded signpost leant into the sidewalk. Behind a wire fence, in the old schoolhouse, an electric bulb still burnt.

"Come on," said Judy, leading the way. She slipped through the gate and up the path to the steps and the school entrance.

Inside, faded posters still clung to the corridor walls, asking us to *Keep the Sea Plastic Free, Recycle and Reuse, Help Nature Heal the Earth, End Fossil Fuels,* and *Fight Diabetes.* I wondered what happened to all the children who once every day read these posters.

Between the posters, lockers hung open and classrooms sat empty, their desks covered in a film of dust. On a wall, a lonely clock still ticked, counting down the hours until the beach and the dark ocean finally consumed the town.

Judy's heels echoed down the corridor. I followed her through a set of double doors and into the library. Shards of thin light filtered downwards between dusty stacks. The shattered windowpanes of spider's webs crisscrossed the stacks, each shelf overloaded with the spines of long forgotten volumes.

"We can just walk in here?" I asked.

Judy shrugged. "There's still a janitor around here somewhere. The school didn't close, it just ran out of kids."

I thought of how the few remaining townsfolk seemed to maintain their daily occupations, like they were the mechanical figures of a clock, forever destined to keep doing their thing until the clock of the world finally stopped ticking. It was like everyone else had accepted the world had changed and moved on, but not them.

On a dusty windowsill sat a row of pots that must have once contained plants. Beyond the window, I listened to the whine of a jet aircraft that must have been passing far overhead. I imagined those onboard looking down at the shoreline, and seeing the little coves with their dead towns, and the beach gradually consuming them, like it was getting us back for all those years of beach erosion. But they probably didn't look down at all. They were probably too busy sipping their liquor, watching their movies, and doing whatever else it was that folks did when they're rich enough to fly through the sky. Up there in the sky they were really from another planet, and passing us all by, and seeing us as no more than maggots picking at the old carcass of the world. Or maybe not even that. I reckon they didn't think of us at all.

Judy lowered herself behind a computer terminal.

"As far as I know," she said, "here's the only place left in town where you can still get online. And they got all the town records right here too, from the time before, when people still lived here."

I lowered myself into the chair next to Judy. "You often come here then?"

Judy nodded. "When there's nothing better to do, which face it, is pretty much always. I've read a whole bunch of books in here. I dunno why, but I always return them when I'm done. Just kinda feels right, you know?"

Judy was a puzzle. She'd steal records from people's houses but borrow and return books from a library with no librarian and no kids to use it.

She tapped away at the screen, sliding from page to page. "I'm looking for stories about the beach house."

Judy slid past colourful pictures of a vibrant seaside town, with sidewalks heaving with women in pink summer dresses and men in canary-yellow shirts. People wore sunshades and licked ice-cream cones, their spectral faces like ghosts from another time.

Had they left the town, or had they simply disappeared?

There was a picture of a carnival parade, with a boy in a tuxedo, and a girl in a tiara and a silver dress, both sat atop a float. Another showed, suspended above the onlookers, a giant inflatable clown, as if laughing down upon them, a manic grin beneath its giant, drunken nose.

"Here we are," said Judy. "The Charlotte's Cove Gazette ran a story on the beach house."

I looked at the headline: "*Nine-Year-Old Boy Lost at Sea.*"

A chill ran down my spine.

Judy scrolled down to the photograph. When I saw the face, my skin prickled.

"That's him."

"Are you sure?"

"Sure, I'm sure. That's the boy."

"No way." Judy moved closer to the screen. "My god, he was her son. Look, there's a picture of Sandra, only younger: *Benjamin Blake, the only child of Joe and Sandra Blake, 4242 Ocean Drive, Charlotte's Cove.*"

Beyond the doors, in the corridor, a locker door slammed.

My heart leapt.

"Spooky," said Judy. She kept scrolling. "Here's another, look." She pointed to the screen. "Twelve months later: *Ten days ago, Joe Blake was found hanging from the rafters of his veranda. His death coincided with the twelve-month anniversary of his son's disappearance.* The guy killed himself. Okay, so I'm freaking."

I moved closer to the screen. "This was 10 years ago."

"So?"

"So, the boy I saw hadn't aged a day. I mean, the stories say he went missing at sea."

"You know, when people go missing at sea, they're basically dead. It's not the same way *we've* gone missing, or Sparks, or Silent Sally. I know we're all missing, but when you're lost at sea, you're really missing. You're not just hiding out in some beach house to escape the pitchfork brigade."

I felt a heavy lump move up my throat. "I know where he is."

"Where?"

"The island. That's where he went. We need to go there."

"Go there, how?"

"In a boat. There must be one here."

"Sure there is, but in case you missed it, the sea ain't exactly welcoming, or not in any other way but that it wants to swallow you whole. I get the feeling Benjamin here was lost at sea precisely because he went to sea. So, you're not gonna get me near a boat."

"Judy, you live by the sea. You're telling me that you live by the sea, but you'll never go near a boat?"

"Yeah, and for the same reason I live in a wooden house, but I don't see no need to go visiting a forest any time soon."

"And what'd be so bad about going to a forest?"

"I dunno. Ask Sparks. Ask him why he left the loggers up in the hills."

But I knew then, more than anything else, I had to get to that island. If I was ever going to start making things right by what I'd done back there in the valley, I owed this to Benjamin Blake. I couldn't completely explain it then, but I knew it was what I had to do. I couldn't just keep waiting it out in this egg timer, with more sand pouring down every day, and never thinking about tomorrow. If I was going to start making things right, I had to follow Benjamin Blake to that island.

"Then I'll go on my own."

"No, you won't," said Judy. "I've been sitting out here alone for far too long. I ain't having you lost at sea too."

I gotta be honest, I was a little taken aback. I weren't sure I'd ever had a friend before, except for Mrs. Simpson of course, but now I got the feeling I'd accidentally made another.

Judy's diamond eyes glistened, and for a moment I didn't know what to say. But I knew one thing she really wanted.

I looked down at my hands. "Do you wanna see my power?" I looked up and Judy was nodding. "I'll make a deal with you. I'll show you my power, if you help me get to that island."

Judy swallowed but she didn't answer. I stood, walked to the windowsill, and lifted one of the plant pots.

"Come on," I said. "We need to head for the diner."

Sitting in a booth, opposite each other, the plant pot between us on the plastic table, I asked Barry for a glass of water.

"I'll get you sodas," he said, grinning.

"No," I said. "Just a glass of water."

"And two sodas," said Judy. "With ice-cream."

Barry grinned as he returned with two ice-cream floats and a glass of water. He placed the water in front of me. "But the soda'll do ya more good." He gave the plant pot a confused look.

Once he was gone, I took the glass of water and tipped a little liquid into the plant pot. The water bubbled as it worked its way down through the pot. Muddy water seeped onto the table.

Judy folded her fingers together. That she was still with me said this weren't her first rodeo.

I placed my fingertips to the sides of the pot. Even through the clay, I could feel the water moving through the soil, creating channels of mud along which life might flow. The original plant was long dead, its carcass decomposed into the barren soil, but I sensed the tiny seeds of weeds just waiting to be awakened. My fingertips tingled. I felt those tiny pulses, like static electricity, moving through my fingers to the life still sleeping in those little seeds. Was it any coincidence that, beneath the soil, the networks of roots looked so like forked lightning?

I closed my eyes and felt the seeds split. I heard Judy gasp.

When I opened my eyes, a small stem pushed its way above the soil's surface, and from it sprung a tiny green leaf.

Judy moved her hands to her mouth.

Leaning back, I drew my fingers from the pot. I had that light, giddy feeling I remembered from my parents' tomato garden. I took my ice-cream float, and I downed half the glass and gave myself a brain freeze.

Judy lowered her hands. "That is awesome."

"Yeah, well, at home they didn't think so."

"You know Sparks can start fires? That's why he wears those kevlar gloves. He burnt down something like half a forest before they had chance to log it. Blames himself and everything, like he ruined his folks' livelihood."

"You know forests need fires?"

"What?"

"Fires," I said. I remembered all the things Mrs. Simpson had once taught me, about the cycles of life, how they can start, and how they can end. "Some seeds only open with fire. And some plants need the fires to clear away the forest, otherwise they don't never have a chance of growing."

"You should tell that to Sparks. He carries around this big guilt."

"So," I said. "You gonna help me or what?"

· · • • • • • · · ·

"I really don't like this," repeated Judy as we hauled the small rowboat down across the sand to the edge of the ocean.

"Don't worry," I said. "I'll row."

"You really think we'll find him there?"

"I do."

"You know, even if we do, he'll still be dead."

"I know," I said. I weren't under any delusions about that. "But I feel like there's something I have to do there. Like, look, this is real hard to explain, but there was something I should have done before, back home. And I didn't. I felt it but I didn't. And I let something terrible happen. Something that was really my fault. I need to at least make this right. You know?"

Judy shook her head. "But you know, you can't carry the world on your shoulders. You gotta look out for yourself. And all those folks with pitchforks—sometimes you just gotta let them go."

We waded out into the water, the boat bouncing with the waves.

"God damn it, it's freezing," cried Judy. She'd thrown her heels into the boat, and we both piled over the sides. We landed together, on our backs in the keel. Staring upwards, the blanket of grey clouds rolled, as if to mirror the ever-moving surface of the sea.

"You know," said Judy, "I really hate you right now."

I swallowed, already queasy. "Yeah, I know."

Scrambling on my backside, I slid to the bench in the centre of the boat and turned my back on the island. Judy sat up in the stern, her arms folded over her chest. Her purple hair, blowing around her pale face in a vibrant burst of colour, defied the otherwise monochrome world.

I'd never been in a boat before, let alone rowed one. I heaved the oars into place and began slapping and splashing them against the water, which only sprayed up at us, while the boat moved closer back toward the shore. And as the boat rocked, my stomach started to churn.

"Umm . . ." said Judy, "I think the island is that way." She pointed a finger in the direction behind me.

"Yeah, yeah," I said, as the boat ground against the shoreline and began to turn away from the island. With one oar, I tried to push against the beach. We started to tip sideways until we were near close to falling back out of the boat.

"Ohh, for god's sake," said Judy. "Get out of the way."

Standing and swaying with the rhythms of the waves, she ushered me to move. As she strode easily around me, I had the feeling I now understood the phrase of some folks having sea legs.

I staggered into the stern, taking Judy's place, and she sat down on the bench and took the oars. Taking deep strokes, she eased the boat back in the direction of the island. Heaving the oars back and forth, she began to row.

I raised my eyebrows. "You've done this before?"

"Yeah, yeah, I know what I said, all right, but I grew up beside a lake. We had row boats. I was still never mental enough to go out to sea though. I'm seriously mad at you right now."

I grinned. "That's okay. Right now I deserve it."

Pushing into the swollen waves, we began to make good time, and before long we were already halfway across.

"Can you swim?" asked Judy.

"No."

Judy rolled her eyes. "You're so dead, you know that?"

We were silent for a while then, the oars lapping the waters in rhythmic slurps, and I looked out to the island ahead and tried to calm my stomach. Further out, the waters seemed a little calmer at least.

"So, what do you think?" asked Judy.

"About what?"

"Sparks. You think if he took off those gloves his fingertips would burn?"

"I dunno, maybe he can control it like I can? I'm not always channelling energy into stuff."

"That's true. I've been hoping someone might have an answer. Like, can you imagine being with him, like, really with him? And then his fingertips go and burn you?"

I smirked.

"Seriously," continued Judy, "if I go there, I just don't want blisters on my ass."

I shook my head.

"You know, I'm just trying to make conversation." She eased the oars back and forth. "It's better than thinking about whatever stupid thing you've gone and made us do. Taking a boat into the ocean when you can't even swim. If I wasn't here, you really would be dead right now."

The boat inched closer to the island. I could see the pale curve of the beach, just like in my dreams. The sea sprayed my face, and the gulls swooped overhead, each one calling out, like the lost souls of a thousand fisherman lost beneath the waves. We passed a buoy covered in thick, black sludge. I dipped my fingers into the icy brine and sensed the thick death beneath the waves, and it weren't no empty death. It weren't a void. It was a thick, choking death. The water was like ink, heavy with all the terrible stories it could write—if only someone would listen.

Approaching the beach, we passed rocky outcrops thick in the shells of dead mussels.

"Come on," said Judy. She tossed the oars into the keel and slipped into the knee-deep water. I did the same and we dragged the boat up onto the beach.

Gasping, Judy moved to a rock. "You look around. I'm gonna take a break."

I still felt queasy, like I could easily return my ice-cream float to the world. My legs felt like jelly and the world trembled, like I was still balancing in the boat's stern. Looking back, the town we'd left behind was lost in the shadow of the mainland, only betrayed by the shape of the dark lighthouse sticking up on the headland.

Turning to the beach, the pale sand was littered in plastic debris and driftwood, and everything was coated in that same black sludge. I worked my way along the shoreline, picking around empty soda bottles, orphaned traffic cones, and a mangled shopping cart that had somehow made it here. Washing back and forth in the froth, a plastic sign was covered in Japanese writing I wouldn't have a hope of reading.

At the far end of the beach, I followed a narrow path across the dark rocks. I passed pools full of black sludge that must have once teamed with life. The rocks spread far out to sea, where the dark oceans churned, but on reaching the cove beyond, the water was almost still.

Something drew me to kneel at the water's edge. I can't really explain it, but it's like I just knew that was what I needed to do. I dipped my fingers into the cold, dark water, and I sensed the death of the plants that once grew here in this protected sea cove. Reaching deeper, almost to my elbow, I felt the stubs of seagrasses that once carpeted the seafloor. I closed my eyes, dug my fingers deep into the sludge, and sensed the silent seeds, waiting out the eons for life to return. I shuddered, electricity coursing, connecting me with the ground beneath the cove. Energy deep inside the earth pushed itself up toward me. My energy had never come from me. It had always come from the earth itself, from some deep, secret place, if only we all could reach it.

I heard a pop and burst. I opened my eyes, and the waters of the cove were boiling.

My head spun. I closed my eyes again, concentrating on the energy coursing through me. I was the bridge between the world above and the one below. I saw old Mrs. Simpson moving through her tomato trees, finding harmony in a world restored. Old Mrs. Simpson, and her daughter who'd given me this gift, and then left me behind in that awful place.

Old Mrs. Simpson paused and smiled at me, and my mind slipped away.

· · • • • • • · · ·

Judy shook me awake. "Hey, look what you did."

I opened my eyes.

Judy's eyes were red, her lipstick smudged, and black mascara tears worked their way down her porcelain cheeks. I sat up, my head dizzy.

"Look," said Judy, pointing to the bay.

I looked, and there before us lay a bay of crystal-clear water, and beneath its surface a fresh field of green seagrass.

My jaw dropped. Did I really do this? Is this even what I planned to do when I dipped my hand in the icy waters?

No, I didn't do this. The world did this. Nature did this. The earth reached upwards from deep in its core and drew its fingers to mine.

Judy helped me to my feet. I was shaking all over.

"Honestly," she was saying, "this is so awesome. This is so much cooler than starting fires with your fingers."

"No, it ain't."

"Honestly," continued Judy, "I knew there were people out there with powers, but for the longest time I thought the only one's I'd find would be Sparks and Silent Sally. And I don't even know what Sally does."

"You know," I said, still finding my breath, "this is why the fish went away. Because the plants died. Without the grasses, there weren't no air in the sea, and the fish couldn't lay their eggs."

"You mean, the fish will come back?"

"Maybe. I mean, not any time soon. These things take time. And there ain't nothing to stop whatever did this in the first place from just doing it again. But they might."

"Hang on," said Judy.

"What is it?"

"I sense something. This deep . . . sadness. It's like when I sense there's someone with a power, but this is different. This time it's like I'm sensing sadness, but not mine, someone else's . . ."

She moved away, further down the cove. I followed. Battered against the rocks were the remains of a small rowboat, smaller than the one we'd used to get here, its hull split open like a seedpod. Beyond was a small cave. I followed Judy to the mouth of the cave.

There, on the cave floor, lay the bleached skeletal remains of a small boy, his right leg visibly splintered below the knee.

I shuddered. I knew for sure it was Benjamin Blake.

"He had a power," said Judy. "I can sense it now. But it's like, even as I stand here, I can feel it all just slipping away. Like all this time he was just waiting for us to find him."

"He knew this was why the fish had gone."

Judy nodded. "I guess, now he's brought us here, and he's saved the cove, he can finally rest."

· · · •·•· · ·

So, I guess you want to know what happened next. Well, to cut what's turned out to be a long story short, Judy rowed us both back to the mainland. She wanted me to stay on at the beach house, but now I knew I couldn't just hide out my whole life there, living for today and pretending like there weren't no tomorrow. Too many folks had already spent their lives doing that. I told Judy she couldn't either. We had things to do. I didn't quite know what yet, but somehow, we had to use our powers for something. We all did. But all that's another story. This one was really just about the boy who called from the sea, and how I came to hear his call. I'd like to tell you all the fish returned to Charlotte's Cove, but honestly, I never did get to find out. What I can tell you though, in all I've learnt since then, is there ain't no quick fix to repairing the world, but with the time we have, and with the chances we're given, we can try to make some difference.

But I'll never forget that house by the sea, and the island, and Benjamin Blake.

THE IRON HEART OF THE FOREST
NICHOLAS HANEY

A few years earlier
2049 C.E.

1

Claire

Somewhere in Canada, Undisclosed

She had read the words a dozen times. Every time she felt the sharp knife of reality run through her chest.

"This evening, in a radical act of terrorism, several fringe environmentalists hacked and stole corporate property. The Merkos Group has vowed a full investigation to bring those responsible to justice."

Radical. Fringe. Terrorist. Thief.

The implications were present in the yellowed piece of paper. She had printed it out as a keepsake, and it had always been hard to read. That little event had been almost a year ago.

True to their word, the 'investigation' and subsequent arrests came swiftly. The number was well into the hundreds, last she had heard. Whether peaceful or not, nearly every person present at Hartwick Pines that day was considered complicit. As they say, property is nine-tenths of the law.

Connor, Harris, Yuri, Tucker. They had been arrested. Caught up in eco-terrorist charges. Serious stuff, with the full weight of dozens of corporate lawyers behind them. Full state backing, the government hand in hand with the Merkos Group.

Casey and Marti were MIA, much like herself. More accurately, she had gone into hiding. The two of them had checked out of the hospital as soon as she was able and hit the road. They felt it safer to separate, and she had no idea where he had ended up. She hadn't seen Marti since the protest. A single tear rolled down her check. She had spent plenty of time mourning her lost comrades.

As it turns out, multimillion dollar metallic moose are a pretty big deal; even though she would argue they hadn't actually been "stolen." In truth, they ran away. She had set them free, and they still lived, last she knew, in Hartwick Pines.

Several other articles were pinned to the wall of her living area. A single cot in a small room, her little dingy in the ocean of chaos. The headlines told the rest of the story

"Merkos Group to capture stolen robots . . ."

That one gave her a laugh. Turns out corporate trappers just weren't very good. They had sent in a small group to try and shut down the Moose. The result had been a lot of running and screaming, and several overturned vehicles. Go moose, go!

"Merkos Group: *We will attempt to reprogram the stolen machines*"

This one had gone about as well as the first attempt. Based on the limited information she could get these days, it turns out the Moose were not keen on surrendering their newly found freedom. The hackers had gained access to their systems, only for the Moose to use the access point to reverse hack them in turn. The way Claire heard it, an entire facility had been *rendered inoperable* as a result. She could only chuckle as she imagined laughing Moosey skulls flashing on monitors right before they all promptly caught fire. They say every machine is a smoke machine if you use it wrong enough.

Probably not strictly true, but she liked her version better.

"Merkos Group to take all steps necessary to return stolen property."

The last was by far the most serious, and the article only a little over a week old. She felt her heart rate spike, and the anxiety rising in her again. It had taken some time to clear the courts, no doubt with plenty of hand greasing by Merkos, but they had finally gotten the green light. All means necessary, which she suspected meant some version of kaboom. The Merkos Group was adamant that the technology *not fall into the wrong hands*, and that it was imperative that they *retain control of corporate property*.

The best part though? This news had been met with substantial protest, hampering the whole operation. Labor activists, environmentalists, anti-corporatists, scientists, even robots' rights protestors. The backlash had been fierce, and *that* had been unexpected. Some claimed it was a short bridge from machines as "corporate property" to workers being treated the same way. The environmentalists protested because they saw the threat to Hartwick Pines. The roboticists argued that the machines clearly had free will, and should have rights to that freedom. The last was an interesting one. Robotic personhood.

"Hey, you doing alright in here?" a woman said as the door cracked open. The answer must have been obvious, because the woman came inside.

"Thinking about your friends again." It was a statement, not a question.

"Yeah . . . I feel responsible. For their arrests . . . for . . . all of it," Claire said.

"And you'd do it all again regardless," the woman said.

Claire nodded, and then started to cry. The woman crossed to the bed and embraced her. The two held each other until Claire's sobs stopped.

"Thank you for taking me in, Kit. Kit, kitty. Kitty cat." Claire stifled a sad laugh.

"Bad humor is better than bitter depression. Plus, I've *never* heard that before." Kit smiled.

Claire sat back on the bed and looked at the articles on her wall. She had abandoned her phone long ago. Turns out tech companies and lap dog governments have no problem violating privacy rights. The EU had written that into law decades ago. The now fractured "United" States? Not so much. Americans had preferred corporations write laws for them.

Kit broke her reverie. "So . . . What happens now?"

"I have to go back. Something feels unfinished about all of this," Claire responded.

"You want to see your moose friends?"

"I want to see my moose friends. And, no insult to your hospitality, some fresh air would be nice," Claire said.

Kit smiled. "Humans aren't meant to live life in a cage. Some might say the same about robotic moose."

2
Brutus – Hartwick Pines

Brutus stood staring up at the trees. This is where it had all happened, over a year ago. Looking around at the tall pines, the needle covered forest floor, the uneven and pitted old growth soil. This is where his life had changed. The rough part of it was, he couldn't even tell there had been a protest here.

The paddock was gone, the buses were gone, the corporate security too. Hell, even his job with the security company was gone. But that was a whole other matter. He had to marvel at the resilience of this natural place. It had been the site of a large protest, and one that had changed the world in many ways. Had changed his world in all sorts of ways. And yet, here it stood as it had for probably thousands of years. Different, in a different world, but in no small way, unchanged. It was an odd thought to hold.

He couldn't help but wonder what his son might think of all this.

As to the job, he had been hit with what they called "downsizing." Everyone in his former company knew exactly what that meant though. They had been expendable from the start, especially as contractors. They had also been blacklisted. The Merkos Group hadn't liked how they'd handled the protest. Rumors said security hadn't done their jobs properly, and perhaps, even helped the protestors. So the contracts had dried up, and the contractor income with it. After that, they had all been pink slipped.

It made his brain itch, and he clenched his fists. America had really screwed up, handing so much power to corporations. You had to work to survive. Not thrive, not at those wages. Survive. Hell, you couldn't even really get healthcare, as the employers controlled that too. Even as the old US broke down, the power of corporations had grown bigger in every way. Almost every industry was controlled by a very small group of very wealthy companies. And because of one of those very massive tech firms, he was still fighting for unemployment.

Maybe he should move to Europe? He'd be better off with basic social services they all had enjoyed for decades.

He had an estranged son, Charlie, but he hadn't heard from him in years. Not since the divorce. Ten years ago? It hadn't gone well, and he sure hadn't been innocent in all that. You try to move on, but that kind of thing haunts you.

The wind whispered through the trees. Could he hear them, hear their voices if he listened hard enough? Time seemed to drop away as he watched birds flit about, and the long quiet settled over the forest. It was unreal, otherworldly. He couldn't hear a thing.

And then—A hollow rumble rose through his feet. It was rhythmic, and he knew instantly what it was. The low, heavy footfalls of a robotic moose Forester.

He wanted to catch sight of it, so he took off down the trail as it meandered through the woods. With each step he knew he was getting closer. The footfalls grew louder, and he heard other sounds as well. Whirring, and maybe the sound of a saw. His pace quickened to the point he was at a near run. His field of view was limited as the trail crested a hill. He should be able to see it as soon as he reached the other side.

He took the hill as fast as he could, nearly fainting in the process. Part of that was being a bit out of shape.

The other part was the multi-ton machine standing less than a dozen feet away, staring at him.

"Ah . . . ummmm. So . . . now what?"

3

Marti

Undisclosed Location

Marti had always been a little bit different. Took to paganism early, even with an otherwise unremarkable Catholic upbringing. Had chosen "they" as a pronoun, even though certain members of the family still insisted on "her." Marti bit their lower lip, pushing back the small frustration shooting across the mind.

Marti also hated capitalism with a passion. What had it really brought humanity other than pain and suffering? Sure, material needs had gone up, as well as the industrial means to meet them. But the water was fowl, the air choked, the planet scorching hot.

That was another difference.

Marti was a raging ecosocialist, and most of the family just didn't get that . . . or generally avoided them to sidestep the arguments. The endless arguments about how people could support an economic and political system that had left Marti, and a huge swath of several generations, an increasingly unlivable planet.

Marti continued to pound away at the computer, looking for answers to questions they would never let go. Maybe that was another difference. Perhaps it was autism, perhaps it was some form of ADHD, but hyperfocus and obsession over their passions had also been with Marti as long as they could remember. They were stuck with an incessant and anxious need *to know*. To understand, to research and deep dive so far into the rabbit hole that all they could see were stars.

There were too many browser windows to count. News articles, reports, academic journals, blogs. Also, music came from one of them, but Marti ignored it. They were on a quest after all. Another quest to find a tidbit, to find something. Chasing the next breadcrumb.

"Where are you Claire? We need you," Marti said to no one.

There had been all the reports of course. A major protest had stolen corporate property. That was a big deal, one that brought media slobbering and governments eager to help. Corporate government complex, manufactured consent, the military-industrial (Merkos had several high level defense contracts) complex. Didn't matter what you called it. Just another head of the hydra that was capitalism. Another piece of the endless growth paradigm, looking for one more way to turn a profit on human and environmental suffering.

All for the grinder. The march of progress.

It had all gotten worse of course, since the old US started to break up. The Machine had sensed an opportunity, to throw off more regulations and grab another piece of an ever-shrinking pie. Without a federal government (or the hapless remains of one); things like federal lands were up for grabs. Hell, even tribal lands enjoyed less protections now, having to now "negotiate" with alliances, States, or declare independence all together.

Marti's phone buzzed.

CASEY: Any luck?

Oh, it was good to hear from him. Another ship cast adrift.

MARTI: None so far. It's nice to hear from you. Thought you were gone.

CASEY: Not yet.

MARTI: Dare I ask where you are?

CASEY: You can, but even on an encrypted chan- nel I ain't gonna say. You know how corpora- tions and police are.

MARTI: Backdoors, ques- tionable warrants, lack of privacy.. Yeah, I know.

CASEY: Right.   Any progress on our mission?

MARTI: Quest. More romantic and daring.

CASEY: Okay, quest. Have we found thee maiden faire?

Marti snorted.

MARTI: No, she hasn't popped back up yet. But . . .

CASEY: That sounds serious?

MARTI: It's hard to explain. Seeing lots of. Anomalies. Stuff that just doesn't fit.

```
CASEY:    Stuff    like
Claire?
```

```
MARTI:   Exactly.   Odd
stones,  ICARUS, secret
societies  .  .  . It's
unusual.
```

```
CASEY: Just sounds like
another day on the in-
ternet to me.
```

Could be. Could also be more to it.

Marti's computer chimed. One of their many search bots had found something. They put their phone aside. Sorry Casey. Duty called.

A world map appeared on their screen. It was full of data points in various colors all across the globe. A map of what Marti called anomalies. Things that just didn't make sense. Wasn't just Marti's work of course, because others had noticed too. A big collaborative work. Marti had added their own work to it.

Whatever Claire had done to the moose, it had also made tracking data available. Marti could see every one of the robotic beasts on their screen, doing whatever it was motor moose do. Also, every so often, they had fed data into the system. Wireless motor moose. That is what had pinged Marti's attention. They read through the code and data streams, watching for something . . . Anything.

```
UNIT007>DATAHUB>IN-
QUIRE>GRASS
```

```
COMMAND-UNIT>NON-NA-
TIVE GRASS>INVESTIGATE
```

It wasn't a native grass, log it for later. Probably for removal. This is most of what the moose did. Played scientist, logged, and gathered data. Once in a while they would dig something out, plant seeds here, take down a diseased tree there. The live feeds were kind of fun to watch sometimes. Seven numbered units and command-unit. Eight in all. Command-unit was the big one. To Marti, that was Steve. Marti had named them all. Command-unit just seemed like a Steve. Just an everyday person doing a job. Steve.

Several more pages worth of code dumped, and Marti scrolled through it all quickly. More routine operations and then… Bingo.

```
UNIT002>INQUIRE>HUMAN
PRESENCE.
```

Not that unusual. Still a public park.

```
COMMAND-UNIT>CONFIR-
MID>CLIFFORD,BRU-
TUS>MERKOS
CONTRACTOR>SECURITY
```

```
UNIT002>THREATDE-
TECT>STANDBY>CONFIRM?
```

"Uh oh," Marti said out loud.

4
Brutus
Hartwick Pines

The robotic Forester shifted slowly from side to side, every inch of synthetic muscle and hydraulics whirring. Brutus watched as the eyes shifted from neutral blue to a green, a mode of heightened awareness. It had seen him, and was running the numbers. There were two more levels, and he hoped it wouldn't have to see yellow or red. Either of those would swiftly result in his untimely demise. A rather messy demise at that.

We are all compost in the end.

He grimaced at the thought, tamping down every instinct to run. If he ran it might chase, and this would all be over real quick. He spread his hands, raising them slightly.

"Easy there big fella . . . I don't mean any trouble," Brutus said.

The robotic moose shifted its considerable weight from the left to the right.

Brutus could almost hear the thoughts of the steel beast. "You're talking to your boss right? Trying to figure out what to do with me? Maybe you know who I am? Or . . . well who I was. What I used to do for a living?" He stepped back. The moose took one step forward, and Brutus took another instinctive step back.

Through some wizardry of mechanicals and hydraulics, the moose let out a snort. Brutus had no idea how it did it, as he didn't think they had been given that level of detail. It shook its head, and then took two heavy steps back before turning and started to walk away.

Brutus took the time to exhale.

"Okay . . . Okay. Well nice meeting you," he said as he watched the metal moose go. It took several long strides down the path away from him, before leaving the trail and entering a small patch of grass. The moose lowered its head and quickly eviscerated the small patch of grass in a dramatic whir of steel teeth, leaving only a pile of finely tooled soil and bits of organic mulch behind.

"Must not be meant for this place. I think I know the feeling," Brutus said. The moose snorted again and started to paw the ground. The sound and rumble could have easily been mistaken for an excavator unearthing a drain pipe. The moose then turned again and returned to the trail and thudded several feet away before turning back to look at Brutus. The eyes shifted from green to yellow, before settling on a tealish shade of blue. One single mechanical snort followed.

Brutus knew that look—had seen it in dogs plenty of times.

"You want me to follow you?" Brutus said. Another snort, and the machine shook its head widely. The moose continued on its way, a heavy thud thud of a gait, each and every one Brutus felt all the way up its spine. He had been a younger man once, and the throb of bass heavy speakers had nothing on this moose. Its rumble rattled his teeth and every single one of his cells, while all his adrenal glands wondered why the hell he wasn't running. As he passed the torn up patch of grass, he envisioned what his body would look like in a similar state. He shuddered.

He also noticed the moose had pawed a very precise arrow in the patch, leading the way.

His brain overrode every alarm bell in his body, and so he followed multi-tons worth of steel and synthetic as it made its way slowly through the woods.

"Here I am, just taking my pet robot for a walk." He chuckled at the thought. The moose looked back at him over its shoulder as it thundered down the path. A look of disproval? Or perhaps it had been amusement?

Was he ascribing emotions to a robot?

Leave it to humans, to look at tons of steel and death and wonder . . . friend? He chuckled again and also noticed the second set of heavy footfalls. Around the bend of the trail ahead came another robotic moose. Much larger than the first, there was no mistaking the lead machine.

There was also no mistaking the fact that it looked like it had been through war. Several parts on the back appeared damaged or bent, plus what looked a hell of a lot like bullet holes. Several news tidbits ran through his brain from the past months. He remembered now. First they tried to shut it down, then they decided to take it down.

The results had been months of protests, and several encampments throughout the park of protestors with fancy names like Robot Defenders, Friends of the Forest, and so on.

The two moose bowed to one another in only what Brutus could think of as a greeting. He awkwardly waved to them.

"Hi! Nice to meet you!" He instantly felt silly about doing it. Something passed between the two moose instantly, and he was grateful they didn't laugh at him. The boss robot led the way and the other followed shortly after. Brutus followed at a respectable difference. You don't walk up to pet wild animals, and he figured that went doubly so for autonomous sentient walking chainsaws.

A long walk later, by the end of which Brutus was sweating slightly, a protest camp came into view. Numerous tents scattered about the edge of a clearing, surrounding what looked to be several hundred people. Lots of different people, from all walks of life. Brutus stood stunned.

"Uh. Okay. Not exactly sure why you lead me here?" Brutus said. The two moose turned to look at him. They had no facial expressions, but he still got the impression that the answer to his question should be obvious.

A cheer went up from the camp.

"The machines have returned!" someone shouted.

"Mighty protectors of the forest," Another shouted.

"Oh, I see," Brutus muttered to himself.

5

Marti

En Route to Hartwick Pines

One of the old corporate security people was now at the protest camp in the Pines. Why? Marti knew infiltration into protest groups was nothing new. Hell, corporations as well as governments had a long history of it. Yet, the moose had seen and guided him in. That was a mystery in and of itself. Maybe Marti would find more answers on the ground. It was the never ending quest for the next piece of the puzzle.

Well, maybe more like several puzzles dumped into the wrong box with pieces missing. They never quite knew what they were working toward.

```
CASEY: Are you on the
way?
```

```
MARTI: Yes, you?
```

Marti typed away on their laptop as the train sped south. In this day and age, information was plentiful and easy to come by. The trick was finding reliable information, cross checking it, and seeing the larger pattern. Information was easy. Knowledge took a lot more work. It was a bit like mining gold.Take a rock and break out the gold, melt it down, and make something beautiful. It took time, it took skill, and Marti had that skill when it came to cyberspace.

```
CASEY: Going to try my
best. I'm a bit further
away. What's going on?
```

Marti sifted through dozens of protest feeds. Some people had been camped at the Pines since the Foresters got loose. It had grown into a kind of occupation, as well as . . . a spiritual experience. People came and went, but many came to see the moose. Some had come to revere and worship the moose, turning the machines into some kind of land spirit. Others had come just as a curiosity, and others still because they had felt something shift. Something in the air and the land. Another text popped in.

```
CASEY: It's going to be
great to see you!
```

```
MARTI: Getting the band
back together.
```

There were also the corporate thugs. News had started to pop in over the last few hours that indicated they had some "final solution" to the moose problem. Yes, they had called it that. Yes, Marti had shuddered with the implications. Not everyone knew their history. Not everyone knew that the 'final solution' was what the Nazis called their final genocidal campaign against the Jewish people.

Either that, or the people at the Merkos Group absolutely knew their history, and frankly didn't care. It was possible the terror was *the point*. Marti shuddered again.

> MARTI: Do you think she
> will be there?

The three dot 'meatballs' appeared at the bottom of the screen. Casey was typing his response, and Marti's heart quickened. They hadn't seen Claire since the last protest, and too many of their friends had gone to jail or disappeared. Marti knew better than most. They were the information person. They had skimmed all the arrest documents, court orders, and news sources slandering the name of anyone who resisted the corporations and the destruction they had wrought. Marti had also read the climate reports, the missed benchmarks, the failure of governments. Hope was a hard thing to come by, and they had stared over the edge into that pit of despair one too many times.

Then, there were people like Claire in the world. People who looked despair in the face and laughed. People who cracked their knuckles, and said "let's dance."

Marti wasn't that person, but they desperately hoped to see Claire again.

Meatballs appeared, disappeared, appeared again. Typing and re-typing, come on Casey.

More and more people were resisting now. Like that old Tank Girl comic meme, the world didn't have to be this way. They all had to do what they could to make the world a better place. Some planted trees, some built solar farms, others took a more direct approach. Birthing a new world was a messy process. Spilled ink, sweat, and tears.

And blood.

> CASEY: You can feel it,
> can't you?

Marti stared at the text. Felt . . . felt what? Marti shook their head. He meant the shift. That subtle . . . feeling . . . that something was different this time. Marti looked out the window. The train was coming into station, the Pines only a few miles away. A tourist destination for nature lovers, now a pilgrimage.

To Mecca? To Jerusalem? Probably more like a natural sacred site. A place of power. Maybe a Shinto Shrine. Marti smiled. She knew what Casey meant.

```
MARTI: Yeah, I can feel
it.  The  shift.  I'm
close now, and every-
thing feels different
than last time.
```

```
CASEY: More alive. It's
weird.
```

```
MARTI: Yeah. That.
```

```
CASEY: Claire can feel
it  too.  She'll  be
there. She can't not
be.
```

Marti started to type their doubts. What if Claire wasn't there? What if she had been arrested or caught . . . or . . . or . . . or. Marti forced themself to take a deep breath.

It was the despair monster, coming to chew on their brain. To take them back to the dark place.

```
MARTI:  What  if  she's
not?
```

```
CASEY: She will be. I
know it. She misses her
robo-moose too much.
```

Marti didn't share his confidence, but they smiled all the same. It would be nice to be back among friends, even if those friends were non-human.

Marti froze. The moose and the trees, the non-humans. Old rusty gears started to squeal and grind as a new thought started to take shape in their brain. An epiphany. Something Marti had missed. *Of course.*

Marti immediately cleared every screen off their laptop and started anew. New tabs, new text documents, new notes. Their fingers flared across the keyboard, as news articles and other data appeared. The truth was . . . It wasn't just Claire. More and more people with similar . . . weirdness . . . were popping up around the world. Marti knew that, but—what if there was something that connected them? Something that tied them all together. Like . . . a spider web. What if there *was* something that connected Claire and the moose?

6

Claire

Hartwick Pines

Claire had said her goodbyes to Kit, thanking her profusely. They were old acquaintances from school, and it wasn't just anyone that would put her up, given the circumstances. Hiding her had been a big risk on Kit's part, and Claire would be eternally grateful for it.

She had hopped on a train across the border, grabbed a prepaid phone at the station, and then hopped on a bus for the rest of the trip. It had taken a few hours, but she was on her way back to the park. She sat with the phone in her lap for a good part of the trip. Just a phone, a small printed article in her pocket. The only possessions she really had in the world, along with clothes on her back.

When everything changed at Hartwick, she hadn't really planned ahead. Hadn't seen much need for it. That day could have ended with her arrest, or even her death. 'What came next' was always an afterthought. A long bus ride gave her way too much time to think.

"I wonder what comes after this?" she said quietly to herself. The passenger beside her was asleep, so she didn't worry about being overheard.

She twirled the phone over in her hands. She had memorized the numbers of a few friends. Contacting them was a risk for sure. Put a target on both her and the recipient. When you were labeled "terrorist" and "radical," she couldn't trust she had any degree of privacy. Still, she loaded up an encrypted app and entered the number she knew by heart.

> CLAIRE: Hey Casey. Long
> time no text.

She was shocked to find her hands shaking as she typed out the words. She forced a long shaking breath out her mouth. Coming back on the grid had a load of anxiety along for the ride. She waited and wondered if this had been a mistake. Could be some law officer sitting on the other end of that phone when her text popped in.

Was it foolish to expect any kind of response at all? Casey could have been arrested by now. Too many of her friends were already behind bars, and judging by the news feeds, more people every day. Protests were growing, increasing pressure on governments and their corporate overlords. The result had been a predictable backlash against the freedom of protest and assembly.

Her heart skipped a beat when the three little meatballs popped up at the bottom. Someone was typing.

CASEY: HEEEEY!!!!

Was it really him? Was it someone else on the other end of the line? A thousand questions ran through her mind. She didn't even know what to say next. Her eyes felt wet, just from one simple text. Her hands continued to shake, and she wasn't even sure she could type . . .

> CASEY: A friend and I
> are taking a walk in the

```
woods, if you wanted to
meet up?
```

That was the one and only message that popped in. It wasn't exactly coded language, but she knew what he meant. Casey was at the place it all began, almost a year ago. He was at Hartwick Pines, already all around her as the bus pulled into the parking lot.

She did not expect the number of people—or the number of cops. She put up her hood before she pushed her way off the bus. Several scuffles had already broken out, and the feel in the air was that something big was going down. She pushed through the crowd and made her way into the woods on the far side. She couldn't deal with the crowd right now. All she wanted was to find her friends. Trees and metal moose fit that description as well.

As she walked deeper into the woods, the presence of the place started to press down on her. It was different than the last time she was here. She had trouble putting words to it. It was . . . more dense, heavier, as if she was in a thick fog. Even though she was past the roar of the crowd, the voices didn't ease. It was still . . . loud.

Her feet turned to lead, and she fell to her knees. She wanted to cry out, but no voice left her lips.

```
Welcome back.
```

```
We were waiting for you.
```

```
She seems to be in pain.
```

```
She will be okay.
```

It's a cognitive error.

She can't handle it.

She will be okay.

INQUIRY>CLAIRE>DETECT

*The machines are looking
for her.*

Claire looked into the canopy of trees. She coughed and tasted acid in her throat. She spat and then heaved onto the needle-covered soil. She heard the sound of running footsteps.

"Oh gods, Claire!" one voice called. Casey, her brain said. She tried to utter his name. It wouldn't come out.

"What happened?" That one was Marti. Claire tried to smile but heaved again.

Casey and Marti hugged her, and her body registered their care. Casey helped her sit up on her knees.

"She's shaking really bad. Should we take her to the hospital?" Marti said.

"She did this last time too. Passed out, I think. Let's get her out of here."

Not this time, child.

Not just yet.

```
COMMAND-UNIT.TRIANGULA
TE.CLAIRE
```

The ground rumbled as one of the moose approached. Claire's stomach lurch again, and her head spun. Something was off; the rumbling sounded wrong. Mismatched. The command unit came into view moments later, and she instantly knew why.

It was limping, its right foreleg sparking and whirring in a way that meant a serious injury. Marti ran over to the moose and tried to take a closer look. The moose gave a quick snort, and shook its head. Marti scrambled back to avoid getting hit.

The moose stopped mere feet from Claire and lowered its head to where she sat on the ground. She looked up at it through tear-filled eyes. She was pretty sure she was going to throw up again. Instead, she reached up and touched the moose on the nose and then collapsed.

"Claire!" She heard Casey yell, and then his voice trailed away.

But the darkness never came. The long sleep of unconsciousness never came.

She opened her eyes and looked around. She was still in the forest. Or at least, a version of it. This one was a lot brighter. The trees ran with what looked like veins of blue-green light. It ran across their bark and leaves like small rivers. The light ran down into the soil too, and across the ground. Even what looked like a fog of blue-green flew through the air and around the place. Claire looked down at her hands, seeing the same light glowing beneath the skin.

"What the . . . What is this?" she said out loud.

"It would take a long time to explain, time I don't think your brain has," a voice responded. It wasn't a singular voice, but maybe a chorus. Many voices talking in unison. Claire turned towards the sound and came to face with a being riding a large, robotic moose.

"I'm in the hospital dreaming," Claire said. The moose looked fairly solid, but the being on its back was more ethereal, not clearly any one thing. Misty, and not solid.

"Have I died?" Claire said.

"Not yet. But you might," the voice said. The words came from both the being and the moose simultaneously. As well as from everything around her, all at once. Like having an entire crowd trying to talk simultaneously. Whispers and broken voices spun all around, as if others were listening and commenting.

"Who are you?"

"Call me a forest spirit, because that is something your brain can handle."

"What do you want?"

"To deliver a message."

Another voice broke through, far away.

"HURRY CASEY! The ambulance is waiting!" Marti's voice.

She is fading.

"What has begun here cannot be undone. Humanity has finally started to awaken, like children first looking at the sun. Shadows will fall away, and things that stood forgotten will be remembered."

"That's all very prophetic and mysterious sounding, but if you are about to tell me I'm the chosen one . . ." Claire cut herself off.

The moose snorted, and the being . . . appeared . . . amused?

"No. You're not. You're just among the first. You won't be the last."

"Which means what, exactly?" Claire scoffed.

```
COMMAND-UNIT.bandwidth.
exceeded>COLLAPSE.DETEC
TED
```

The being patted the moose.

"I know my friend, we are out of time," the being said, and it turned and started to walk away.

"Wait! That's it! All this . . ." Claire gestured to the forest. "And you didn't tell me ANYTHING?"

The being looked at her. Sadness washed over her.

"*You* are out of time. The days ahead will be hard, and humans will face a choice. They can follow the green roads through the trees, or, they can follow the road covered in oil and blood. That is a choice you all must make. Yet, also know that those like me are also awake, and we will be watching."

The world flashed.

"CLEAR!"

The forest vanished, the lights vanished.

Time. To. Pick.

The world darkened.

"CLEAR!"

Another flash, and her eyes strained against the light.

A side.

"We've got a pulse." A man's voice.

"The girl's a fighter." A woman's voice.

The world blurred from white to red, and back to white. A light came into focus above her, and then a couple of masked faces.

"Welcome back," the doctor said.

**Epilogue
Hartwick Pines**

Iron from the ground

Gears, motors, servos

Blood in our veins

Star fire, and earthly forges

Life is but a short dream

Rust, ash, dust

We all return to the earth

When our time is done

Marti read the poem aloud one last time and then placed it on the makeshift altar. Someone had got a lucky shot in, and the largest moose had fallen. The resistance had been fierce when corporate came for the body, and they had not been able to take it.

Instead, the metallic moose had been propped up with stone, and the vines and plants had grown in. The plates had rusted, the light disappearing from its eyes. Still, the people came to the make-shift shrine after all this time. It was covered in flowers and offerings, wreaths and garlands. The moose head stood up above it all and watched over the forest, antler strung with bright strings and ribbons.

It stood watch as a guardian, protector, and sentinel.

Marti laid their hand on the shrine then turned and left.

The spirit of the forest watched them go.

"Until we meet again, child."

HIERARCHY OF NEED – PART I
ERNEST SOLAR & AE FAULKNER

SustainAble Corporate Offices, the Midwest Federation
2056 C.E.

Ainsley Rayne glared at the older gentleman sitting on the other side of the mahogany conference table. Glancing at the image on the tablet screen one more time, she flicked her wrist, the device sliding across the polished wood. Pushing away from the table, she stood. She shrugged off her blazer and tossed it onto an empty chair, moving to the north end of the conference room to gaze out the floor-to-ceiling windows. As she strode across the room, Ainsley imagined the clacking of her heels punctuating the frustration coursing through her veins. Reaching the windows, she pressed manicured fingertips to her temples and relished the prick of pain as the nails pressed into her scalp. She straightened, dropping her hands to clasp behind her back. She could feel his eyes on her. Watching her. Waiting.

Ainsley shifted her attention to the protesters across the street from the main headquarters of SustainAble Corporation. She would make him wait a moment longer. Forcing others to wait on her response gave her power and control. Then again, forcing Edward to wait never seemed to work on him. Oftentimes he would use the same tactic on her. Which always infuriated her. In truth, Edward intrigued her because she saw him as an equal, even though he worked for her.

Turning around to face Edward, Ainsley smoothly sauntered back to the seat across from the man. Edward combed a hand through his gray-streaked black hair and leaned back in the boardroom chair to cross his right ankle over his left knee. Placing both hands on the table she leaned slightly forward and motioned toward the tablet with her chin. "Who is she?"

Edward's blue eyes stared into hers. "A bounty hunter."

Ainsley barked a laugh. "A what?"

"Her name is Mikayla and she's—" Edward hesitated. "An independent contractor for Stewardship Earth. She is one of the best."

Ainsley dropped into the chair behind her. "Best at what?"

"Finding and disposing of corrupt and high-powered CEOs of organizations that are not adhering to climate agreements or any of the other supposed national or international plans," said Edward.

Ainsley's anger flared to life. "What does that have to do with me?"

Edward's eyebrow cocked, then he smiled. "Nothing, I suppose. But according to the Dark Web, Stewardship Earth and The Network are both hunting for the CEO of SustainAble Corporation for their unethical practices and mistreatment of animals."

Ainsley could feel the fire building in her green eyes as she glared at Edward. Through clenched teeth she hissed, "I am not the CEO. He's been missing for two years."

"Of course not," Edward whispered, sarcasm lacing his tongue and lips.

Ainsley stood and stomped back to the north window. She slapped her hand against the thick glass in frustration. Whirling around on Edward, she countered, "They are the monsters! Not me! Not SustainAble! If it wasn't for us, they would starve!"

"If I may?" said Edward as he stood.

"If you may what?" barked Ainsley.

"Be . . . honest."

Ainsley flicked her wrist at him and spun around to glare at the protesters. Through the reflection of the glass she watched as Edward buttoned his suit jacket and pulled his sleeves tight to straighten them under his blazer. Walking with his hands clasped behind his back, he moved to stand next to her.

"First, you hired me to acquire new resources for you. Then you asked me to gather intelligence. Now, I am tasked to protect you. My professional assessment of the situation . . ." Edward paused for a brief moment as if collecting his thoughts. "The world is changing, rapidly. Like me, you've seen the reports. Weird shit is happening. As the media says, *Gaia is fighting back*. The new generation wants to save our Earth. The Miami Accords is one attempt at punishing the old generations for their lack of effort in preventing the climate crisis we now face. As a species, humans need to place blame before they can heal. You have been a target since the disastrous press conference with your intern and frankly, I'm surprised you have lasted this long."

Ainsley stood silent as she processed Edward's words. She knew he was likewise watching her through the reflection of the glass. Many of the protesters started to disperse as the sun dipped lower in the sky. But one protester, a young man, stood like a statue, seemingly staring up at Ainsley and Edward.

"Can he see us?" she asked.

Edward looked down at the man. "No, the windows are reflective on the outside."

"The Miami Accords are barbaric," Ainsley muttered.

Edward nodded his head in agreement. "So is the looming Dark Hours Legislation sweeping the former United States."

"My cousin," started Ainsley, "In New Jersey, sacrificed his older brother during Superstorm Victor as if he was trying to appease King Neptune for the travesties brought upon the seas."

Edward's eyes found hers through the reflective pane.

She turned to face him. "Do you know why I work at SustainAble?" Before Edward could answer, she said, "I watched my father starve to death during the famine of the late twenties. He refused to eat so I could live. Even as he wasted away before my eyes, he would stand guard over me every night so the cannibals wouldn't eat the flesh from my bones. I know what it feels like to have your stomach gnaw at your insides." Her voice dropped to barely an audible whisper. "I know the taste of human flesh."

Regaining her composure, Ainsley's green eyes penetrated Edward's blues. "I provide these ungrateful fools the basic hierarchy of need! I will not let another father or little girl go hungry because of some foolhardy belief we need to sacrifice our means of food and nutrition to save *Mother freakin' Gaia!*"

"I understand." He took both her hands in his. "But you are in danger and you hired me to protect you."

Ainsley exhaled. "What do you have in mind?"

Edward smiled. "A fishing trip in the Big Thicket of Texas."

"Texas? Interesting." She gulped. Whatever she was about to say gave her pause. He nodded once, as if encouraging her to continue, fully anticipating a ridiculous demand that he would not even consider accommodating.

"I've been thinking," Ainsley said, "and this whole bounty hunter threat? I am perfectly willing to take the helm at SustainAble. The CEO, on the other hand, has completely abandoned his position. What if we . . . hand over Mr. Draven . . . to this bounty hunter. Then, together, we could expand SustainAble into the Texan Alliance. I'm guessing you have influential contacts that could expedite the process." She crossed her arms and studied Edward's features, eager for a response.

"Ms. Rayne, I fear we'd just be buying time, and likely not much." He shook his head, taking a step backward.

"This bounty hunter just wants a CEO to skewer and we've got one. We give her what she wants and we go about our business. Simple."

"Ms. Rayne—"

She cut him off before he could confirm his disinterest in her proposition.

"Think about it," she whispered, rising and stepping toward him, pressing a delicate palm to his chest. "If we teamed up, you could be a very rich man. You could have anything and everything you ever wanted."

Ainsley watched as Edward pulled his gaze from the desire of power leaking out of her green irises. She knew that she was driven by the urge to dominate a broken world in order to fix it. She just needed time and help to accomplish such a lofty objective. Watching Edward stare at her palm on his chest, she hoped he would accept her invitation.

· · · ● · ● · · · ·

Jarrett raked a hand through his long hair, pausing at his bangs for a moment before releasing them. The curtain of brown strands fell over his eyes; he gave a quick shake of his head before squinting at the mirrored windows of SustainAble's main headquarters building. He saw them on the ninth floor through the reflecting glass, Ms. Rayne. And, he assumed, Edward. The man fit Hodges's description. He stood stone still watching them. Trying to read their lips. However, even with his enhanced vision, it was hard to catch every word the two shared. He could tell from Ms. Rayne's body language that she was not happy. The older man was calm, almost jovial.

A wave of dirty water assaulted Jarrett, breaking his gaze from the corporate window. Covering his face with both hands he dropped to a crouch and groaned. He vaguely heard a little girl's voice sing out, "Sorry, Mister." Between fingers he watched a young girl peddling away on a bike.

"Damn, that sucks," said a voice behind Jarrett.

He knew it was Jack. His shadow was overarching as the man stood behind him.

"Get dirt in your eye?" Jack said.

Jarrett stood and wiped the putrid water from his skin. The smell reminded him of the night he followed Graeson into the pits of filth beneath SustainAble's Central Food Production Greenhouses. The night he literally started seeing the manure SustainAble blatantly flung in everyone's faces. He glanced back up at the ninth floor conference room window. They were gone. The last words he picked up were *Big Thicket.*

"At least you didn't get your shoes wet, friend," said Jack as he slapped Jarrett on the back.

Jarrett glanced down at his bare feet. They were covered in black, tar-like mud. He wriggled his toes in the muck. He felt the pain of Mother Gaia surge through the heels of his feet into his very essence.

"Come on bro, if we don't catch the last bus we'll be walking." Jack tugged on Jarrett's shoulder.

Turning his back on SustainAble, Jarrett propped the protest sign over his shoulder and easily caught up with Jack in two strides. As he passed his friend to the bus stop, Jarrett was lost in thought on how he needed to contact Hodges and give an updated report.

At the bus stop, Jack asked, "Why don't you wear shoes again? Emma wants to know."

Jarrett focused on Emma, whom he just realized had been in step with them the entire time. She was petite with dark hair and innocent doe eyes. She was one of the new protestors that joined last week. However, something about her made him feel uncomfortable. He squinted his eyes for a deeper look. A black swirl of dark energy emanated from Emma's aura. Jack's was more of a yellowish pink.

"Oh, that's right," said Jack with a playful smile, "You feel a deeper connection to Mother Gaia if you are barefoot."

Emma glanced at Jarrett's mud-stained feet. The bus pulled up and hissed to a stop. The supposed "clean" fumes wafted over the waiting crowd.

"Come on bro, let's go grab a bite to eat with Emma and her friends," encouraged Jack as he moved toward the bi-folding doors.

Emma's dark aura reached out toward Jarrett as if to ensnare him. He took a step back. "No thanks, I'll walk."

Before Jack could protest, Jarrett turned and walked off into the lengthening shadows of dusk.

CIVILITY POLITICS
C. D. TAVENOR

Geneva, Switzerland
2056 C.E.

To change history, to change reality, it only takes a few backspaces. A few deletes. Truth is malleable, it bends to the will of those wielding it. When the fate of the world rests in the balance, it becomes essential to amend truth.

Especially when it comes to the Awakened.

The world wasn't ready to understand the truth, to understand how the world was transforming. That day would come soon—very soon—but until then, Natalie knew it was absolutely essential to change the truth. It was one of the few reasons she remained in her position with the United Nations. After the events in Sacramento all those years ago, Sofia Huber had helped her cover up the truth of her own Awakening. The UN took her in, giving her a job doing exactly that.

A few of her colleagues knew the truth, but only a few.

And none of them, save one, knew her actual work with the World's Revolution. With people like the Bent Greens in Appalachia, or their other contacts across the planet.

Instead, for nearly a decade and a half, she was Special Agent Natalie Vorn, in the office of Special Projects for the Secretary General. She spent her time digging up narratives about supposed Awakened, traveling to where the sitings occurred, and "muddying" the waters in the news. All the while, she made connections of her own, bringing more and more Awakened into the fold.

Both jobs became more difficult with each passing day. At some point, she would need to end the double life, but not yet. There was still good to come from playing both roles, from bending truth to seek many different goals. As long as defeating the climate crisis remained at the center of it all, she could handle the pressure.

The most recent report on her desk was particularly intriguing, involving reindeer in Siberia. Nenets, indigenous people to the region, were flooding the socials with videos of reindeer herds attacking oil pads still in use by Russian National Oil. The animals would rush the wellpad, scaring away all humans, then work together to destroy the machinery. The videos themselves were grainy, often filmed from far away. The recording Nenets were often following their own herds, who deviated away from their migratory pathways to attack the facilities.

It was often easier to obfuscate the truth regarding a person than an entire species. Already dozens of biologists were talking about how out-of-character these actions were for reindeer on their own social reels, often overlaying their commentary over the hazy footage. Natalie sighed. She'd likely need to get an expert on the airwaves quickly briefed with proper talking points, but she needed something more immediate. She—

Her watch buzzed. Welcoming the momentary distraction, she checked the text on the circular screen. The message came through on Constant, the encrypted communication app used by many World's Revolution members. An invite to a mass protest in Washington, the old US capital, from Sofia of all people. She wished them well in quick response, but as much as college Natalie would have loved to attend a protest, adult Natalie couldn't risk the public exposure. Especially a protest planned in the volatile Coastal Republic.

She shuddered, remembering Ben's stories. Washington was supposed to be neutral territory for the former US nations, but it was practically owned by corporate interests all with ties to the zealous nation.

Before Natalie could return to the suddenly anti-oil reindeer, her watch buzzed again, this time with a call. It only took seeing the words "Secretary" for her to immediately answer.

"How can I help you, Secretary General?"

"Natalie, I need you upstairs right now," said Chinara Lawal. The call immediately ended.

The Nigerian woman had been in her role for a half-decade, and Natalie had gotten used to the woman's abrupt style. No words were said that didn't need to be said. And when the Secretary General summoned her, she always promptly reacted, as per protocol.

It only took a half-minute to collect her tablet and purse, and then she was out of her office, winding along the outer corridor toward the elevator bank. Out the windows, the Alps stood pristinely beautiful, almost declaring the truth of their immortality—*Natalie, if you fail to save the world, it doesn't matter to us. We will stand tall long after you're gone.*

Even after what happened last year, during the covert creation of the World's Revolution, Natalie struggled to embrace the spirituality so many others understood implicitly. It directly conflicted with everything she understood about the world. Even with her own Awakened power, she could conceptualize a scientific explanation for how she could bend air to her mental will. It had to be some genetic trait, like the old mutant comic heroes.

But no.

She'd had the same vision as everyone else. She'd heard the words of the planet, of "Gaia," as some called it. She'd responded to the planet's call to action.

What did it mean? Were all planets sentient? Were stars sentient? Were the gods of Earth's religions real, or fake, or slightly off-base?

She stepped onto an elevator heading up as these thoughts swirled. While reports of Awakened continually intensified, and her job to hide the truth complicated, more and more philosophical discussions permeated the boards and feeds of the internet. Her questions weren't unique. She simply had a more front-row seat to the conversation.

As it stood now, she'd come to the conclusion that the "truth" didn't matter. The explanation didn't matter. What mattered was how they used the powers received; what mattered was how they responded to the planet's call to action. If they wanted humanity to survive—and eventually thrive—the balance of power needed to change.

The elevator dinged, and the doors opened, revealing a small foyer. Natalie exited, nodded at the desk assistant, and headed through the double-doors to the left.

Secretary General Chinara Lawal's office: an urban jungle of plants and flowers imported from across the world. Open sky-lights and long windows allowed light inside during most parts of the day, and the lush greenhouse doubling as an office always brought a smile to Natalie's lips. Of all the Secretary Generals she'd worked under, she appreciated Lawal's office the most.

Sitting in the center at a conference table beneath two hanging ferns, Lawal and four other high-ranking UN officials sat, their fingers sliding up and down on tablets. Natalie moved to join them at the table, but Lawal held up a hand.

"There's no need to sit." The Secretary General's face looked grim. "I have some bad news, Natalie. Well, first, I need you to answer a question. Ambassador Rogers?"

One of the chairs swiveled around, revealing the UN Ambassador from the Southern States of America. "Special Agent, I have just been discussing with the Secretary General a most egregious problem with your portfolio, and with you. I have solid evidence that you have been in communication with the Bent Greens, a known alt-left terrorist organization, and that you have likely visited their compound multiple times. In the Southern States of America, we take these reports very seriously, and we expect the United Nations to hold its staff to the utmost regard. Unless you can provide us with a satisfactory explanation, we will be demanding your resignation on the floor of the Assembly tomorrow. What say you?"

Natalie swallowed, trying but failing to unclench the stress fists formed during the man's brief monologue. Her worst nightmare had occurred with no warning. She intentionally avoided making eye contact with Lawal; it would only make matters worse.

"Ambassador Rogers, I understand the worry you bring to the table," Natalie said. "I can assure you, all of my dealings with the Bent Greens have been in furtherance of the goals of my assignments and portfolio in the Special Projects Division. We are monitoring the Bent Greens for Awakened activity to ensure no word of the truth of what happened there escapes out to the public. I have managed to make contact with them and gain their trust, which allows us to monitor their work closely."

Rogers shook his head. "The UN should be providing us with this intelligence, then, under the Shared Operations Resolution of 2047. We have never received a single report from your office. I don't buy it."

"I can provide you with a full report answering any interrogatories you might have," she replied. "I—"

"That won't be necessary," interjected Lawal. "Special Agent, I will be placing you on indefinite administrative leave. Ambassador Rogers, please place a formal inquiry with my office to answer your questions, but please rest assured that my office will be taking this matter seriously and attempting to rectify any harm that may have been done to your country. We can work out the details later, please let me escort her from my office."

The words landed dully. Natalie heard them—understood them—but she couldn't believe how quickly her entire career had been smashed by one request from one Ambassador. She'd always been careful. She'd checked her corners, wiped cameras when necessary, bribed the right local officials.

But it hadn't been enough. And now their carefully constructed house of cards was tumbling to the table.

She barely noticed the Secretary General's arm loop between her own and pivot her back toward the exit. She barely registered the soft touch of Lawal's hand, the gentle whisper of her words. But she understood them as she said, "—and now you have a chance to be untethered. To use the World's Revolution to do what you must to change the world."

They reached the elevator; Lawal kissed Natalie on both cheeks. "Do me proud." The words were barely a whisper. "I know you can. The world is counting on you."

The elevator doors closed. Natalie checked her watch, anger and fear and . . . excitement simmering in her heart. Too many thoughts bounced around her mind. Instead, she needed to act. Thinking clearly would come later. She scrolled to the protest invite received truly only a few minutes prior. It was time to book a flight.

· · · ● · ● · · · ·

Natalie had flown into Reagan International many times over the past decade and a half. More often than not, it was the most convenient airport when traveling internationally to utilize if she needed to travel inland to the Bent Greens enclave. But she wasn't heading into Appalachia; she was heading right into the heart of the former home of the United States federal government.

Washington, in some ways, transcended its own history. When the five nations formed, Washington D.C. became just "Washington," an independent city-nation encompassing the former district and a few nearby counties from both Maryland and Virginia encompassing nearly five million people. While it held close political ties to the Coastal Republic of America, it maintained its independence by acting as a neutral diplomatic zone both for the five American countries and for international events. The United Nations had even moved its North American headquarters here from New York, especially following the last superstorm to strike that metropolis.

It was only natural that Natalie's mentor and friend, Sofia Huber, would find her home in Washington. And it was to her apartment Natalie headed, located in Pentagon City, right across the Potomac from central Washington. The metro ride from the airport didn't take long, and before she knew it, she was walking up the stairs of an apartment building that felt like a second home.

Natalie had already briefed everyone on her "administrative leave," and everyone meant Sofia, Laverna, and Ben. Laverna was the central organizer of the protest planned for this afternoon. She should already be across the river, leaving only Sofia and Ben at the apartment.

No, connecting with her friends was the least of her worries. She'd slept on the flight—jet lag was present but minor. But every second since the meeting in the Secretary General's office, anger simmered and threatened to smother. Her anger worried her—anger at politicians for playing political games, the same way they played them when she attended her first COP and she first Awakened.

Her therapist always reminded her—the deaths of those hundreds of people wasn't her fault. She didn't intentionally murder them. It was an accident.

But Natalie always knew part of her had wanted that outcome. As she understood her power—the power to control the air around her—it required significant intent to use. She had intended to harm them. And inside, she always justified the result because that event had changed the way the international community viewed climate action, at least nominally. Her actions had changed hearts and minds.

That was the lie she told herself. The game reared its ugly head once again when the Ambassador from the Southern States made his accusation, though. They didn't care what good the Bent Greens did for the world—they held a decades long grudge against the one community willing to stand up against tyranny in their territory. It wasn't about what benefited people or the planet—it was all about power.

Maybe it was time Natalie let power dictate her own actions, too. Maybe she needed to demonstrate the power given to her by a living, thinking planet.

As she reached the door to the apartment, she shook her head. She'd hoped for clarity while traveling, clarity from time alone with her thoughts, but only more confusion swirled in her mind.

She knocked.

The door answered almost immediately, revealing Sofia Huber smiling. "You look like a wreck," the woman said.

"Thanks?" Natalie chuckled. "Thanks for letting me crash."

"Thanks for accepting my invite." Sofia held the door but stepped back into her apartment, motioning for Natalie to enter. "Second guest bunk is all made up. You're sharing the room with Laverna, while Ben is on the couch."

Ben was also quite literally on the couch, hands typing away on a bluetooth keyboard presumably linked to the nearby tablet. "Good to see you," he said without looking up from the screen as she stepped into the main room.

"That's the only greeting I get?" Natalie set her bag against the wall and placing her hands on her hips.

"No time to talk," he said. "Coordinating spotters around the city. Lots of cop activity; they're already activating gas teams."

"Of course they are," Sofia retorted. "Don't act surprised."

"I'm not surprised," Ben said. "Just stating the truth."

"You're not heading into town?" Natalie asked.

"You know I can't," Ben said. "I'm too hot on the Coastal Republic's lists. And we all know who runs the police in Washington. Who *really* runs the police." It was true. The police chief of Washington was the younger sister of the Coastal Republic's Assembly Speaker. The ties within the political elite ran deep.

"Then it's just the two of us?" Natalie said, looking at Sofia.

"You take the time you need to rest, then off we go."

For a moment, Natalie considered whether she should share her anger. Share her thoughts, especially with two of her closest compatriots. But no. It wouldn't help. Now was the time to act. Last year, when the planet had spoken to them all at the Bent Greens, it had made clear how little time remained; it had emphasized what was at stake. The World's Revolution was all about following instinct—following the calling of "Gaia."

Maybe Gaia was guiding her here, through her anger. The planet was angry all right.

"No need for rest," Natalie said. "Let me change and I'll be ready."

· · · ● ● · ● · · · ·

"No justice, no peace!"

The shouts echoed through the Washington streets, amplified by megaphones and a network of wireless speakers scattered throughout the crowd. The staple chant of many protest movements, its words always brought infectious energy. Natalie shouted the words alongside a group of college students all wearing their American University hoodies, within a crowd positioned at the intersection of Pennsylvania Avenue and 15th. After three more chants, she briefly pulled down her mask to drink some water. Her thirst quenched, she slipped the water bottle back into her bag and readjusted the googles sitting snuggly above her forehead.

She hoped she wouldn't need them, but Ben's latest text almost guaranteed the tear gas would be coming soon.

"All right y'all," said an organizer a few meters away. "We've received reports of cops kettling on 9th. The rally is officially over, on more speeches, no more petitions. If you're staying, you need to be ready for anything."

Natalie glanced around, seeing grim eyes above multicolored masks. Protest culture hadn't changed much in two decades—from what Natalie understood, many of these tactics were utilized even further back, in the 2027 and 2020 uprisings, in the Ferguson uprisings, and beyond. It was a mostly oral tradition passed down through international networks of oppressed people groups. Above all else, it was essential to ensure fellow protesters consented to the danger they faced, especially against the cops.

The nods of Black, brown, and white people in the crowd, a multiracial crowd all fighting against the destroyers of the planet, represented a shared understanding—they knew what they faced if they remained in the streets heading into the night. And they were ready.

"Last chance, otherwise, follow me!" said the organizer. "No justice, no peace!" The shouts echoed again.

As they walked north up 15th, the US Treasury Museum to the left, Natalie checked her phone again. Laverna had sent a link to her live feed broadcasting from the steps of the Washington Monument; Natalie quickly reshared it to a half-dozen channels. A text from Ben on Constant said a curfew had been ordered for thirty minutes from now, but at least fifteen arrests had already occurred. Sirens blared in the distance as if confirming his message.

"Glad I caught up with you."

Natalie glanced to the left, finding Sofia there with her distinct pink mask.

"You sure you want to take this risk?" Sofia asked.

"I'm here to support Laverna, these organizers, and the public fight." Natalie glanced to the sidewalk where no fewer than fifteen reporters trailed their march with shoulder-mounted cameras. "The whole world is watching."

"But your job—"

"Fuck my job." Natalie scoffed. "We knew I'd need to leave eventually. The choice was made for me. You and I both know what 'Administrative Leave' really means."

"It means there's still a chance you hold the position in a few weeks," Sofia hissed, then shouted the next round of a more complicated protest song. "I'm glad you're here, but we don't need to stay the whole time."

Natalie looked around the crowd, seeing the eyes of the youth who once again had the optimism to believe the world would change if they shouted loudly enough. Protests had the power to change hearts and minds, to organize people to create new systems to fight oppression, but they also had the power to make someone feel as if nothing will ever change at all, to feel the weight of an entire oppressive power upon them as their friends are beaten at the hands of the state. She'd been fighting her entire grown life, had unique powers, and a spiritual planet mind thing who talked to her and her friends—but Natalie still felt the pull toward dispair and hopelessness. She would not be another older white woman who walked away from a protest right as the fight became dangerous.

"Sofia, if you need to leave, do so. But you've protected me for long enough." Natalie nodded at her mentor, who, to her credit, didn't step away.

The chants continued as the crowd continued its march north, reaching H Street and 15th. A group of organizers came sprinting down H Street from the east, shouting to the march leaders, but their words were lost beneath the clamor of song. The safety team must have heard, however, because the bikes guiding and blocking intersections veered west.

"We're heading to Lafayette Square!" said a voice bouncing between networked speakers.

Evening twilight accentuated the glow of LED street lamps along H and into the square. The White House, a complicated, contradictory symbol of climate complacency, denial and action stood behind the park and its statues. The crowd streamed into the center, where four blueish-gray cannons sat beneath a brown statue of a man atop a horse—relics of a rarely referenced history of a nation forever divided. Natalie shook her head. And if the climate crisis wasn't solved, it would be forgotten before long, too.

Without warning, sirens screeched into crystal clarity. She looked back toward H Street; dozens upon dozens of blue and black police vans screeched to a stop. Her watch incessantly buzzed. She went to silence it, but it was Ben, calling. She accepted it and moved her wrist close to her mask. "Yes?"

"Nat, you've got to get out. They're coming for you and your position, it's a call for mass arrest."

"No justice, no peace!"

She could barely hear him over the renewed chants.

"I'm not going anywhere, Ben."

"No, you don't understand. You! You've specifically named over the police scanners. They're mass arresting to get you! Southern State troopers are in the mix."

"Fuck." Over the past few decades, at least three protests in the Southern States had resulted in deaths from live ammunition. "They're not in charge though, right?"

"No, but they're there for you. Get out." He ended the call from his end.

Time seemed to pause as Natalie looked about the crowd. She'd traveled here from Geneva ready to express her anger alongside thousands of others oppressed by the constant capitalist exploitation of the planet and its climate. To express her anger at the politicians who used her as a pawn in their power games. But now the threat was more real. The kids around her may know they face bodily risk, but many of them likely had never tasted tear gas in their eyes, taken a wooden bullet to the knee, been corralled into an alley and handcuffed with plastic zip ties. Her first time, it had been Natalie's freshman year at a protest in Phoenix opposing a water diversion pipeline. The wounds took months to heal.

She looked at Sofia. "You should get out of here," Natalie said. "Get as many of these kids out of here and go."

"I'm not going to leave you," responded her mentor.

"Do this for me, please?"

Sofia gave a curt smile, nodded, and pulled her into a hug. "Don't do anything reckless. But fine."

"I've never been more certain about what I'm about to do."

She slipped out of the hug and turned her back on her friend. After pushing through the crowd for a few meters, she chanced a look back, but Sofia was gone. Satisfied, Natalie continued through until she reached a throng of organizers behind a perimeter of bikes designed to resist the line of encircling police.

"I'm with the TWR crew," Natalie said as someone eyed her. "I've got a direct line to our police scanner. Can I be of help?"

"We just lost connection with our police scanner," said a young white kid with grizzled blonde hair above a grey mask. "We're flying blind at the moment."

"Shit, is that why you stopped here at the park?"

"We figured they'd ignore us if we were off the streets while we regrouped. What word do you have on the cops?"

"Mass arrest order's been given." For a moment, she considered whether she should note it was intended to get her, but what good would that truth do anyone? Nothing. Even if she turned herself in, they'd likely still arrest everyone *out of principle*. "For this group specifically."

An older Black woman with straightened, red-streaked hair shook her head. "We all knew what we were signing up for. Start ensuring everyone's got the legal number on their arms." She handed markers to two guys who sprinted into the crowd.

"So how do we get out?" said the blonde kid. "What—"

"This is your order to *disperse*," said a rough voice over a megaphone. "You have been warned!"

And without actual warning, five pops in quick succession sounded, followed by the clattering of cannisters on the ground right in front of the bikes.

"Goggles down!" shouted someone—or more than one someone.

Natalie responded appropriately, sliding the plastic down above her eyes. She eyed the cloud of tear gas—she could already taste it on the air. There was no time to think, no time to consider the consequences of her actions. She needed to protect.

More importantly, she needed to be who the Earth had made her be, all those years ago, in Sacramento.

After a brief bending of the knees, she vaulted over the protective bike line, using twisting bending currents of air to defy the pull of gravity. She landed gracefully above the cannisters, sucked the spicy air from her own mouth, and swirled the gas into a cyclone. With a physical push of her arms, she sent the tear gas storming toward the line of cops and away from her fellow protesters.

The whispers immediately began behind her, the whispers she'd fought to silence for many years. *She's an Awakened. They're real. She's one of us. Will she hurt us? Will she save us?*

If only the world could be saved by one person.

If only.

"Make sure you record this," she said, turning back to the protesters. More than a few phones were already held high. "Share it far and wide. Let the world know the truth. The Awakened exist. We're here to serve the Earth, protecting it from all that threaten its future."

Natalie slowly walked toward the line of police, her hands raised high. Her fingers twitched with anticipation, and she considered the many choices before her.

She could kill them all—she knew how to do it. To suck the air from their lungs. But she would not be a killer. She would not continue that cycle of violence.

She could escape—easily, flying over their heads before they knew what hit them. But she would be painted a coward, a coward who fled a bunch of kids in their hour of need.

No, she needed to do something wholly unexpected.

As she walked, she commanded the air to swirl in a vicious vortex all around her, an impenetrable air shield of supercharged particles. She left channels for ears to hear words from outside, but otherwise, she was, in theory, protected from even live arms fire.

"Let the protesters leave unharmed," Natalie shouted, letting her targeted currents take her words to the ears of the police. She could barely see them over the bright lights of their vehicles. "Let them leave, and you can have me, Natalie Vorn, the person I know you're here to apprehend."

The words left her mouth, and she knew they were the right ones. She needed to make a statement—the planet needed her to make a statement. She was throwing herself into an unknown, uncertain future at the hands of some government or another, but first, she would say her message loud and clear.

"Stand down, Miss Vorn!" shouted an officer over a megaphone. "We will open fire."

"Let the kids go!" Natalie responded in kind. "You want me, you have me. But let them—"

The sound, sudden sound, the ear-breaking sound smacked into her ears like a freight train. She lost focus, fighting the urge to vomit on the spot. Her shield dissipated; she dropped to her knees. A momentary glance at the line of cops revealed the LRAD they'd used to disorient her. They'd been using a megaphone all day; of course it would be an LRAD.

"We told you to stand down," the cop said again.

· · · · ● · ● · · · ·

Natalie wanted to pretend she remembered the moments after the LRAD's use, but in truth, she only remembered the wounds. Rubber bullets, wooden bullets, tasers, it didn't matter in the end. They'd incapacitated her, and now she lay in a hospital bed, handcuffed to the railing, with two broken ribs, a fractured fibula, and a broken collarbone.

And the ringing. The constant ringing in her ears. She tried to summon the air to swirl before her eyes, but she could barely concentrate enough to ignore the mind-numbing pain coursing through her extremities.

Had she succeeded? Had she saved the protesters? Had her truth been revealed to the world at last? Had she inspired anyone at all?

Her vision blurred. A figure stood by the door, arms crossed, but she couldn't make out any distinguishing features.

"Where . . . where am I?" she croaked.

The man walked forward, the visage clarifying into a grey uniformed woman with at least three weapons on her belt. "Albany High Security, and you're going to be here for a long time."

THE GIRL IN THE FOREST

BRIAN SCHMIDT

In a forest near you
2056 C.E.

The tree toppled to the ground with an ear-splitting crack that echoed through the empty air. It was a sound I'd heard all day, every day, for the past week. Without any other trees around, it sounded far worse. Like I'd taken someone's finger and bent it back until it couldn't move anymore, and then kept pressing down until I tore it out of their hand. I felt just as dirty.

I looked out over the veritable sea of stumps. When I was a child, the forest extended farther than I could imagine. Now I was an adult, and I'd cut down the last tree. I climbed out of the rumbling Harvester and walked over to the fallen log, running my hand over the trunk of the now dead tree. I wasn't happy cutting down my old home. Just because we were evicted didn't mean we had anywhere else to go. Jobs were few and far between, and the pay wasn't much better. I'd worked twelve, fourteen, even eighteen hour days just to scrape by. It sucked that the best paying job was cutting down the forest. Unfortunately, food and water were more important.

"You're sure it'll all grow back by tomorrow?"

I'd only been hired a week ago. Balmer had been cutting down this forest since almost the moment my mother and I had been forced out. As I was growing up, I'd built him up in my mind as a monster who'd eaten my home and my forest. A being of indescribable evil who I could blame for all my life's hardships. It was easy to hate someone you'd never known. Now I worked with him, and I'd learned he was just some guy trying to feed his family, who wore the same faded denim overalls and wide brim bucket hat every day because his pay barely covered the cost of food and water, same as me.

Well, not exactly the same. Between the two of us, you'd think I would be the one enamored with the forest. I spent my formative years running through the shaded valley floor, crunching every decade-old red oak leaf under foot because mom told me they were magic, and if I crushed a thousand I would get a wish. I must have crushed thousands that last summer, but it didn't make our eviction notice go away. Balmer took it a step further though. He seemed to think the forest had some sort of magic to it that mom and I never found.

"Boy, I don't know how many times I need to tell you." Balmer patted the dead tree and let out a booming laugh that echoed through the empty valley. "It'll grow back alright. Just you wait, you'll look away for a minute and find the whole damn forest replaced when you weren't looking."

"The whole forest is going to just spring back up. You've actually seen that happen?" I wiped beads of sweat from my brow and resisted licking the salty droplets off my hand. I was parched. The droplets shimmered in the orange evening light, looking ever so tempting, but I knew I'd regret it if I lapped them up. I dug my hand into the log's bark and let the pain distract me.

Balmer's laughter echoed back at us from the other side of the valley, but Balmer himself looked at me seriously over the small, round glasses continuously sliding down his nose. "I've been harvesting trees here for almost two decades. The valley might be big, but even with the best planting technology around you can't grow a full tree in a year."

I couldn't help but scoff at that. "Seventeen years isn't two decades Balmer."

He waved his hand dismissively. "It's close enough. The point is, this isn't the first time I've seen the last tree in this valley cut down, and I doubt it will be the last. You'll see it for yourself tomorrow morning boy." He pointed out at the sea of stumps. "All of this will be back the way it was, and you and I"—he slapped my back—"you and I will still have a job. Now, let's get this one loaded up."

The seat of the Harvester was twenty feet off the ground. I moved the log to the transport truck and Balmer pulled the ratchet strap tight.. He wrangled the night's water rations out of the driver before he sped away, but my attention was on the valley. The mountains around us lay bare of any trees, and the treads of the Harvester had ripped up and destroyed the vegetation within the valley. Most of it had been done before this week. The number of trees I'd cut down was only a fraction of what I saw, but I couldn't help the sense of responsibility taking hold of me as I watched the sun set on the other side of the valley. This was my forest. I'd grown up in it, been fed and sheltered by it, loved it as dearly as my own mom. Even if it grew back to full height tomorrow, I shouldn't have let this happen.

As the sun fully slipped away and shadows overtook the valley, I turned off the Harvester and met up with Balmer at the campsite he'd picked out. I sat on an oak stump and watched Balmer gather logs and twigs for the fire. He tied them up in a teepee and ringed them with the shredded remains of last week's newspaper before lighting it. He passed me my dinner, a prepackaged meal provided by Central Logging, and stuck a nutrient bar from his own dinner on a sharp stick.

"The smoke adds flavor," he'd say every night. I tried it my first night here, but I couldn't stomach it after that. He was right—the fire added a smoky texture that reminded me too much of the nights mom and I used to roast berries and squash on an open fire.

Without the sun, the temperature plummeted and goosebumps rose wherever the cool, dry air touched. I scooted as close to the fire as I could on my stump. "Have you ever seen the trees grow back?" I asked him. "I don't mean, did you see the end result. I mean, have you actually seen it. In the process of growing back."

Balmer carefully chewed on his smoky nutrient bar and swallowed. "The way I see it, it's not my place to look." He poked the fire and a spindly twig fell into the ashes, sending cinders spiraling into the sky. "We fucked this planet up good. If she wants to do something about it, well, I figure the least we can do is give her some privacy."

"You think it's the planet?" I couldn't keep the surprise out of my voice. "Why not one of those Gaia spiritual people who can supposedly absorb battery acid, or turn plastic back into something worms and fungus can degrade? Seems more realistic to me."

Balmer leaned back on his stump, his sun weathered skin crinkling and his wispy white mustache glowing orange in the campfire's light. He said, "I think whoever it is, has been doing this for almost two decades, and I ain't seen them once." He shrugged. "Might as well be the planet." He chuckled. "Course, I haven't exactly been looking. No point in looking a gift horse in the mouth, ya know?"

"Yeah," I absently agreed. I'd been too caught up in the idea that it would grow back to think about the how of it. Forests didn't just grow back on their own, and especially not with how little water there was to go around. And they especially didn't grow back overnight. Balmer thought it was magic, but I'd long since realized there was no magic in this valley. There must be someone working on this, one of those people that showed up in the news cleaning up oil spills or purifying unusable lakes to save their town. Whether they had "powers" or not, they were doing *something*.

Balmer retired to his camper for the night to get some rest, but I couldn't calm my nerves. The idea bounced around in my mind. There was someone coming to the valley to restore my forest and I had to . . .

The thought stalled in my head. What exactly did I need to do about that? I wasn't going to stop them, that was for sure, but it wasn't like I could help them in any way. Still, a part of me called to find them, this unknown, unseen helper in the night. Insisted on it. To thank them, I finally settled on. It didn't feel like the right answer, but I decided that must be it, because there was nothing else I could really do for them.

With the idea fully nestled into my mind, I settled in for a night of watching stumps. I tried to keep the fire going, but there were only so many twigs nearby. It fizzled out into smoldering coals after barely half an hour. The night grew cold, colder still when my sweat grew cool against my skin, but I was too afraid of missing the forest to grab my old blanket from the camper. Hours passed, and my eyes burned when I became too scared to blink regularly, fearing the forest might pop up between one blink and the next just the way Balmer described it. My lips cracked under my dry tongue. I wanted to sip my water rations, but Balmer had left them on the other side of the fire, and I couldn't make myself move.

It was well after midnight, my eyes crusted and my mind very excited at the prospect of sleep, when I saw a speck of green in the distance. I had to rub my eyes open and slap myself awake to make sure I wasn't imagining it.

I wasn't.

There, before my eyes, the valley filled in with green. Like someone had taken a crayon to a coloring book and filled it in. It took my breath away to see it, and I was overcome with both guilt and relief. I had killed the forest, and the forest had come back.

My legs were running before I even knew what I was doing. All I knew was that I needed to be there, to see the trees spring up one by one. That I was being called to see it. I tore past the Harvester and down a gentle sloping hill. Stumps flew past me, and as I entered the valley's dip I could see the trees approaching. Not just the trees, but the tall grasses and blue and orange and yellow flowers, and bushes and moss. The spent dirt beneath my feet became black, fertile soil and eventually I met the tree line, crossing into it and feeling the branches of new leaves whip me as I ran past them.

There, a clearing. I ran into it and found three tree stumps surrounded by towering oak trunks. Panting, I sat down on one of the stumps, recoiling slightly at the now unfamiliar feeling of the thick moss growing on it.

I waited there for hours, breathing in the forest air, somehow knowing this was what I needed. Where I was needed.

There was a rustling behind me—I turned. A girl in a green dress walked out of the tree line. She looked very young, maybe ten or eleven, but she carried herself with confidence, and her brown eyes held a deep pool of empathy. She smiled at me and sat down on one of the remaining stumps.

"Thank you for waiting for me. I'm glad you could come." The little girl kicked her legs back and forth as she looked around us. "I think I did a good job this time. What about you?"

I looked at the wild greenery that had sprouted from nothing. This was something you didn't find anymore. There was no such thing as a forest, not really. Land was too precious for the government to let it be used for something so uncontrollable as an old growth forest. After our eviction, the only large groupings of trees I'd seen until returning here had been the oxygen gardens in the city, but those were carefully maintained, and I hadn't been allowed to walk through them. They held none of the beauty of a wild forest.

"Yeah," I breathed, "you did an amazing job."

The little girl tilted her head, her long black hair falling to the side. "I know I did a good job. I wasn't asking about that; I was asking about you. If you thought you'd done a good job today."

In an instant my heartbeat must have tripled because it sounded like the roar of the Harvester in my ears. Viscous blood welled from my cracked lips when I pursed them, and I wished I'd sipped at my water ration with dinner. When I swallowed, no saliva wet the back of my throat. I knew exactly what she was asking me. "It always comes back, doesn't it?"

The little girl didn't stop smiling at me, but it didn't make me feel like I'd said the right thing. "I mean, you brought it back, right?" I was standing and spreading my arms, taking in the sights she had made. Not just the trees and moss that I had noticed, but bird song filled the air where none had been only hours ago,insects crawled across the ground, mushrooms decomposed one of the stumps which I knew had only been cut this morning. I walked around the clearing, circling it. I swatted at a mosquito as it landed on my bare arm. "You even brought back the mosquitos, you brought it all back." I wasn't looking at her and she didn't say anything. "It's not like it matters that I cut down the last tree, right? It's not the last tree anymore. And when they're gone, you'll bring them back again, and again, right?" There was still no answer. "Right!" I yelled, but the valley wasn't empty anymore, and the wind rustling the trees whispered back to me like a demented parrot.

It's okay, right? It'll all come back, it'll all come back, so it's okay, right?

The little girl's voice cut through my swirling mass of justification and doubt like rain through a city. "It sounds like you don't think you did very good today."

I didn't know what to say to that. It was true. I leaned against a tree, letting the moss running up its trunk cushion me like it used to, back when I would argue with mom and run into the forest because I'd been an angry fool who thought he was too good to listen to his mother. "I lived here," I told her. "I grew up here, and I've personally cut it down to nothing for barely more than minimum wage." The grass behind me rustled and the little girl's hand wrapped around mine. "I can't make up for that." She pulled me back to the stumps and sat down. I followed her lead.

The girl reached down into the grass and let a caterpillar crawl across her finger. She giggled. "You're so serious. You're so stuck on the how and the why, you've paralyzed yourself into inaction. Don't worry about making it up to the forest." She pointedly looked behind me and there was a scream. I just turned in time to see a bloody rabbit pulled behind a bush. "Death and rebirth are nothing new to a forest. It just needs you to do what you can to help it."

I shook my head. "That's it though. I can't. My job is to cut it down and I need that money. My mom isn't doing too well and if I don't bring in the money . . ." I didn't know how to explain it to a little girl. "The hospital isn't going to help a woman with dehydration."

The girl laughed hysterically, her hair flying wildly as she threw her head back. In the moonlight it looked green, then silver, then a thousand colors, then black. "Are you trying to say you can't care for the forest because you need food and water?"

I tapped my foot angrily. I was arguing with a ten-year-old girl. "Yes!" I cried. "If I lose this job, then I can't buy the food and water my mom needs."

The girl fell off the log and rolled around in the grass, gasping between giggles. I wanted to grab her and shake her back and forth and tell her to stop laughing because it wasn't funny that I couldn't provide for my mom. But I didn't let myself act on the impulse. I'd cut down the forest, but I was at least better than that.

The girl leapt up and ran off into the trees, disappearing from my sight in seconds. She returned just as quick with something in her hands. "You told me you grew up here, so I thought you'd be a forest boy. But it looks to me that you're acting more like a city boy." She smugly presented the branch to me like a fox who'd snuck past all my traps, and I realized it was a fat pear, the kind I hadn't seen since I was a boy. "Fruits and vegetables." She laughed again. "You can get everything you need. The forest will provide."

I took the pear from her and bit into it. Juice—water—flooded my mouth, and I greedily gulped it down. I took another bite, and then another, and another until the pear was gone. I licked my lips, already feeling the moisture pouring into them. This was the most hydrated I could remember being in the last two decades, but the girl had probably only found any fruit because her abilities created it. "I'm not like you," I said to her. "I can't just snap my fingers and make a pear tree sprout, or make a vine of grapes appear."

But the girl wasn't upset at my dismissal of her solution. Instead, she put her hands on her hips and beamed up at me. "Sure you can. You just don't know how yet. Come on, I'll show you." She grabbed my hand and pressed it against the trunk of one of the stumps. She was surprisingly strong, forcing me to kneel next to her. The girl's fingers traced the tree rings on the stump, slowly working her way toward the edge until her finger slipped off and she placed her hand on top of mine, her fingers slotting between my own to touch the stump.

"Listen to it," she murmured. "Trace its history, find the image, and then pull on it."

I listened, and I heard. The stump told me its story. The seedling it had been. The storm that buried it in the ground. How its roots took hold and its first leaves sprouted. It soaked in the sun, letting the years pass by it like the wind. "That's it," the girl murmured. The sprout grew and grew, its trunk thickening and growing by the foot, its branches splitting and splitting again like a lightning bolt until it had a million tiny twigs that each had their own leaf. It stood tall and proud in the forest, one among its kin, but a beast unto itself.

"Now hold the image."

I could tell there was more, feel how its life after that splintered as it was cut down again and again. Everytime, the little girl pressed her hands against its stump and raised it back to its glory, always rising again and again to her call, willing to endure the pain of death for the call of life. Every time it stood tall, and I held onto that image.

"A bit shaky, but good. Now, pull on that image. Pull it toward you and onto the stump."

I wasn't sure how to do that, but I reached my free hand into the air and grasped the image. It hurt. Fire ran through my arms, and someone screamed—but it wasn't the little girl. My fingers dug into the tree's bark, both the stump and the image, and I pulled with all my might. I pulled on the two of them longer and harder than I had ever done anything. The image dragged in my mind, rooted, not wanting to come to reality, but I forced it to actualize. I pulled its ghost over the stump and pressed them together.

I expected a flash of light, or a pop, or a loud noise when the tree reappeared, but one moment it was a stump, and the next its branches swayed in the wind. I collapsed onto the grass; my shirt soaked through with sweat while the little girl squealed with glee.

"You did it! You did it!" She pointed at me with a triumphant expression across her face. "I told you! I knew you could do it, forest boy." She cartwheeled past me. "Now you don't have any more excuses not to help."

I sucked in breaths so I could laugh with her. "That was incredible." I sat up, propping myself against the restored tree's trunk. I looked up at the tree's canopy, and it dawned on me what exactly we'd done. That wasn't possible. "How did we do that?" I asked her. "That's not natural. There's no way something like that could just happen." And then I remembered the feeling from earlier. I hadn't just wanted to be here to see if there was someone restoring the forest. I'd known there was someone here, and I'd felt compelled to come meet them.

I studied the little girl, and truly looked at her for the first time with a clear mind. Her green dress was made of leaves. When her hair caught the moonlight it flashed earthy reds and leafy silvers. When her cartwheeling took her out of the moonlight, she seemed to be ten, but also twenty, and fifty, and nothing, and everything.

"What are you?" I asked.

"Does it really matter?" The little girl turned her cartwheel into a handstand and smiled back at me. "If I said I was the planet, would you believe me?" Thoughts of Balmer flashed through my mind and I almost said yes, but between one breath and the next the little girl tipped back a bit too far and let out a startled yelp of surprise, looking for all the world like an ordinary little girl. Any thoughts of her being the planet seemed ridiculous. The girl laughed. "Of course I'm not the planet. I'm just a girl, doing her part, just like it's time for you to do yours."

She knelt next to me. "I've spent a lot of time helping this forest, but I can't stay here any longer. There are still so many more people I need to meet with, and places I need to protect for them." I wanted to ask questions, but I knew it was time for me to listen. "So, I'll leave this place to you, forest boy. And I'll have to trust you'll do the right thing with your power and protect this place as best you can."

"It was nice to meet you," I told the little girl. "And thank you for waiting for me."

She gave me a silent smile and then skipped off into the woods.

I stood up and brushed the dirt off my pants. There were two more stumps in the clearing I needed to fix before sunrise. Then, I needed to have a long talk with Balmer and figure out how I was going to stop people from harvesting the forest. And I needed to find a way to get mom out here. I could rebuild the old house, and we could live off the land again.

My fingers traced the tree rings on one of the stumps, slowly circling outward until they slipped off onto the stump and my hand came to rest against the trunk. There was a lot of work to be done. I'd just have to do my part.

THE AMULETS AND THE MIST

JASON A. BARTLES

Appalachia
2056 C.E.

Clive poured a satchel of gemstones on the dining room table mere hours before he was abducted. He separated them by size and raised them, one at a time, reciting their names. He held up peridot, tourmaline, and moldavite, but to me they looked like a pile of rocks scratching the newly refinished bamboo—a bunch of emeralds at best.

"Are you kidding me, Landon? Come closer." He drew me to his side, handing me a magnifying glass. "This is eastonite. It's local, from Easton, Pennsylvania, where it was first discovered." His hands remained steady, but a childish glee crackled behind his voice.

I could always tell when he was on the verge of a breakthrough. He liked to clue me in on the basic concepts and the hurdles so I could understand later just how big of a deal his discovery was. I humored him, leaning in to inspect the mold-colored crystals. He rambled on about how it splits the light, its chemical composition, and its purported healing properties.

Clive was a trove of information. When he became obsessed with a new topic, he devoured every book and article on the subject until he could recite not just facts and figures, but entire narratives. He could tell the history of the vacuum as a story of class divisions. A fact about doorbells would spin out into a dystopian treatise on surveillance states.

Had he been born a century earlier, he might have been a reporter for public radio; instead, he played amateur sleuth between long hours at the SustainAble bioengineering labs.

I had no idea where this new obsession with gemstones had begun. First a few glitzy rocks appeared as bookends in my reading nook. Then, they popped up beside lamps and picture frames on side tables before spreading to every flat surface in our little home. They were a bit new age for my tastes, but I assumed they'd be replaced by his next obsession in a few short months.

I turned the magnifying glass toward the sparkle in his deep brown eyes. "To the initiate," I said in my best narrator-of-a-documentary voice, "the surface appears taught, but if we look closer, subtle creasing, commonly known as 'crow's feet,' demonstrates the specimen's true age."

"Hey, now!" He snatched the lens from my hand. "You're not one to talk, mister salt-and-pepper." He tousled my hair, and as I tried to push him away, he grabbed me by the waist and kissed my forehead.

Had I known he was about to be taken from me, I would have lingered in his embrace. I would have drawn him tighter and begged him to stop his investigation with Douglas. I would have packed a small bag and dragged him to the car and driven as fast and as far as possible without giving a second thought to everything we would leave behind.

"Ok, keep your hands to yourself, sir," I said with a smirk.

"We're going to do a lot of good one day," he said. He gathered up his rocks and squeezed my shoulder on his way to the garage.

"Did you eat?" I asked, but he didn't hear me, already tunnel-visioned on the experiments that kept him tinkering away the rest of the evening.

· · · • · • · · ·

After dinner, I scooped strawberry ice cream. I stood over the sink and watched as the backyard faded into night. The house was quiet, except for the tinkling of the spoon in the ceramic bowl. Fog poured out of the freezer when I went back for more. I had promised myself to ration this carton, because even with Clive's privileges, we could only get one pint a month. The assistants working in his lab didn't have freezers in their apartments, so I tried not to complain, but I couldn't get enough.

I was savoring the melted dregs from the bottom of my second bowl when the lights flickered and the floorboards rattled under my feet. I heard a bunch of banging in the garage; it sounded like a shelf crashing down, and for a few seconds, the smoke alarm pierced the air. Then Clive burst into the kitchen.

"You ok?"

He was frazzled and flushed. He tugged at a gold chain around his neck, one I hadn't seen before. It was unlike him to wear jewelry, and I wondered if it had been a present from Douglas. "I've got to go out for a bit," he said without looking at me.

He could get like this—distracted, turned inward, buzzing with a million thoughts. But that night I sensed an uncharacteristic hesitation. I told myself he must have hit an unexpected roadblock.

"What's going on?"

"I need to talk something through with Douglas."

"Does it have to be tonight?"

"Yeah," he mumbled and grabbed his keys.

I crossed the empty room between us and grabbed his hand. "Clive, what are you not telling me?" His skin was warm to the touch, though not quite feverish.

He pulled away and scratched his head, unwilling to face me. "Nothing. You know how I get. I'll be back in an hour. Promise."

The door shut behind him. I stood there, holding my empty bowl, unsure what had just happened. The car screeched out of the driveway.

I paced in little circles, running through scenarios in my head, telling myself not to catastrophize. Douglas was the lead electrical engineer at SustainAble and Clive's best friend. His only friend, really, besides me. They had bonded during nerdy nights of concocting engineering solutions to the climate crisis, from soil that doesn't dry out to carbon-collecting nets, though none of their outlandish designs had ever come to fruition. Douglas was a good guy. Handsome, too, I had to admit. He'd calm Clive down. He was better at that than me, which I usually appreciated, but that night I felt suddenly jealous. I needed to shift my focus. To trust Clive's behavior was nothing more than an overreaction to a minor setback.

· · · **·** · **·** · · ·

About an hour and a half later, I messaged Clive to say I was going to bed soon. I started one more episode of *Survivor's Guild*. When the credits rolled and he still hadn't responded, my worst instincts overcame me. I never liked going into the garage. That was his space, his refuge from work and the world. The garden and the reading nook were mine. We both cherished our alone time as much as we loved being together, so barging in on his room felt like an intrusion. But I couldn't distract myself any longer. I needed to know what was going on.

Clive had left the fluorescent lights on, and the garage smelled of burnt plastic. Industrial shelving lined the far wall to hold metal boxes for his tools and trinkets and whatever else he collected. Two of them had spilled across the cement floor leaving a pile of gemstones, wires, and jewelry-making tools strewn everywhere.

On the back wall, Clive had affixed a map of the world above his work bench. He had drawn red circles at a hundred different locations, and near many of them he had tacked clippings of strange stories from the past few years.

In the Appalachian Mountains, the quote read: "2045: Soldiers from the Southern States of America rushed to a military hospital to be treated for burns after reports of a tire fire at the Bent Greens."

In the Pacific Northwest: "2046: Impenetrable wall of flora, fifty feet high."

Somewhere in Illinois: "2049: Home video of a tornado barreling down on a man, but moments before it crushed him the funnel disappeared. Reporters on the scene found no trace of the man, only a white powder coating the surrounding fields."

Elsewhere, in green circles, Clive had pasted photos of various gemstones alongside other stories. Emeralds in Australia, related to the end of a drought. An Argentine city in the Pampas Negras appeared overnight, built entirely of Inca Rose. Another mentioned Iceland Spar being used to cool the air over farmland by controlling the passage of clouds. The reports, copied from social media threads, imagined a planet full of fantastic events: people with elemental powers, sometimes boosted by curative stones, who could embody animals, heal polluted fields, and cause explosions at SustainAble plants. Some stories waved away the impossible with journalistic incredulity that spoke over the witnesses, but that did not invalidate them. Certainty was only a tone of voice after all. The more popular ones, however, were written with a mystical awe in the face of the unexplainable, like fairy tales for a world in crisis.

Elsewhere, I noticed the letters "SA" written in blue at four locations in North America. Around each one, Clive had drawn a precise circle. When I checked the map for scale, they corresponded to a one-hundred-mile radius. One of the circles was drawn nearby, centered on the SustainAble labs in Easton. The other three overlapped with some of the peculiar events narrated in the clippings, but there were no stories of magical powers happening here. If I took all of this at face value, our normality seemed to be the anomaly, the outlier.

My head spun from the whirlwind tour of cities and nations and natural wonders I would never visit. None of it made any sense to me. It was too hard to picture such unreachable locations, not to mention the strange and improbable events said to have taken place there. I worried that Clive was losing his grip on reality.

I took a deep breath to hold at bay the panic settling across my chest. It didn't work, but I forced myself to search for other clues. Clive's workbench was covered in drafting tools and sharpies. A glass paperweight, filled with tiny air bubbles, sat on top of his notebook. I tried reading it. His handprint was practically illegible, but among the scrawl and mathematical formulas and charts projecting seismic activity, he had sketched a device, or maybe a chamber. Whatever it was, it appeared to channel electricity through the human body. Near the end of the notebook, he had drawn a series of gemstone necklaces. Each was a subtle variation of the one that preceded it, gradually moving from densely coiled metal bands that hid the stone to the finest, gravity-defying designs. The final three or four pages had been ripped from the book. I dug through the trash, looking for those pages, but I only found scraps from the printouts of the stories on the map. He had hidden or destroyed the final plans.

I looked back at the mess of stones and tools on the floor and bent over to sort them, to reconstruct what was missing by tracing the contours of its absence. That's what Clive would have done.

Someone pounded on the garage door, and I about pissed myself.

"Clive?" I shouted.

"It's Douglas. Open up!"

"What's going on?" I asked as I raised the door.

Douglas ducked inside and lowered it immediately. Sweat beaded his forehead, and stains spread from his armpits. His gaze darted around the garage, as distracted as Clive had been. He gave off a panicky odor.

"What's going on with you two?" I could barely choke out the words because I knew this was bad.

"They took him. I've got to find the amulet."

"Took him! Who?" I shouted. I thought I might black out. I braced myself against the workbench.

"Have you seen a little—" He ignored my question and made circles with his forefinger as he flipped through the notebook and opened every drawer within sight. "It looks like a coil of gold and silver."

"No. There's just his jewelry-making tools." I pointed to the floor.

"Damnit!" Douglas balled up his fists and pounded the work bench, knocking the paperweight onto the floor. It smashed into a thousand shards. "We can't let them have it." He headed for the garage door.

I ran over and stopped him from raising it. "What do you mean they took him?"

"Look, Clive asked to meet me tonight, but he said it had to be somewhere we wouldn't be seen." He noticed the look on my face and waved his hands. "No, nothing like that. He knew our work wasn't safe. I suggested we meet at the gas station, but as I pulled up, security personnel from SustainAble dragged him into a black van. This has all gotten way out of hand."

"What have you two done?"

"I'll explain on the way to the lab. Come with me."

I tried to tell myself it was all a misunderstanding while I wiped tears from my eyes. Clive wouldn't be caught up in a dangerous discovery. He and Douglas were just dicking around with things they'd never be able to build. This couldn't be real. Denial was easy and comforting, but it could not change the reality we were about to face.

• • • • • • • • • •

As we drove along the empty highway, Douglas told me the story of their newest project.

"The Earth began granting powers to a select group of people, called the Awakened, a few years ago. Most of the time, these powers come to the aid of those fighting to save the planet from further climate collapse, though there have been reports of Gaia swelling up in rage and attacking humans indiscriminately."

"The stories on Clive's map are real?"

"Completely. The problem is that the Earth has been pretty fickle. For most of the Awakened, their powers faded as soon as immediate danger passed."

"What's this got to do with you and Clive?"

"SustainAble charged our labs with researching the anomalies. We've been working on a way to tap into that power and keep it flowing, regardless of the Earth's intentions. Clive hypothesized that we could force a connection with the Earth, using local stones in the amulets he designed, and tap into a source of renewable energy. My contribution was to build a chamber that would connect this limitless power source into the electric grid."

Douglas paused as he turned onto a gravel road that wound into the woods. Flood lights from the quarry glowed above the canopy.

"That sounds like the technology of the century. What's the problem?"

"At first, we thought we were researching this great new tech. But tonight Clive realized SustainAble does not want to make a renewable grid. They don't care about that. It would cut into their profits and threaten the power they've accumulated since the collapse. All they want is to expand globally, but the Awakened keep meddling in their plans. They used us to develop a technology that could counter the Awakened, block their powers within a given radius. By the time we realized their true intentions, it was too late. We had already shown them our preliminary results with the amulet and the chamber that required a human body. It was never supposed to be real. It was just one possible engineering solution. Clive wanted me to smuggle everything out of the area tonight and get it to, well, let's just say to an organization. But SustainAble was one step ahead of us."

"We've got to save him!"

"No, Landon, we've got to get his amulet back. In SustainAble's hands, the tech could—I don't even want to think about how they might use it. This is the biggest mistake of my life. And of Clive's, too. I need you to understand that. We've been living in a fucking bubble, pretending not to notice all the shit SustainAble has been up to, and I'll never forgive myself if they use my work to cause even more destruction."

I opened my mouth to argue, but Douglas jerked the car to the right, turning onto the road that rimmed the deep quarry. We wound around the edge and pulled up to their lab, a windowless, brick building. We got out and walked to the side entrance. Machines scraped and grinded in the distance. I felt the hairs on my arm prickle in the night air as he swiped his security pass. This all felt too easy.

· · · · ● · ● · · · ·

The lab looked like a generic office building from the outside. When I had used the front entrance as a visitor, it opened onto a reception desk in a lounge with free pastries. Turns out that was a ruse to hide the true nature of the building.

Douglas and I stepped into a twisting maze of corridors. The walls and ceiling were coated in the same rubber lining that compressed beneath our feet. At signs pointing left, Douglas led us to the right. Where there was no sign, we first turned left; the second time we walked straight ahead. When Douglas made us backtrack, I could have sworn the walls shifted before I spun around. After countless turns designed to trap unwanted visitors, we arrived at double doors that opened onto a mining shaft. I felt weak in the knees peering over the ledge.

Douglas called the elevator—if the metal frame with a grate for a floor can be called that. I had to look straight ahead to be able to take that first step while steadying myself on Douglas's shoulder. I did not need to know right then how deep the shaft plummeted below us. The elevator shook and dropped an inch that felt like ten feet, before locking into a rickety rhythm toward the underground lab.

"When we get there, I need your help looking for the amulet."

"Then we find Clive," I insisted.

"Yes, after we get the amulet."

I nodded and reminded myself to trust Douglas. He would not simply throw Clive to the wolves. If what he said was true, then SustainAble would be on the cusp of acquiring a power that would be impossible to stop.

I wasn't dumb. I knew SustainAble wasn't a benevolent company. I turned a blind eye, because it was easier to get lost in the little luxuries and daily comforts that came with Clive's clout. I told myself we deserved it, because of all the good Clive was doing, because of the time I spent hosting charity events. In theory, we were working to make the world better, but at some point, there was no getting around the fact that nothing developed in a SustainAble lab would ever go on to benefit humanity, that no event they sponsored would ever threaten their chokehold on the populations they controlled. It would only ever be sucked into the corporation's gaping maw to drain the Earth of every possible resource, including whatever these new powers were.

Now our complacency was coming back to bite us. Now I understood Douglas's insistence that what mattered most here was preventing SustainAble from acquiring this amulet. If something happened to any of us, that would be a small price to pay. I pulled myself together for the battle ahead.

The elevator came to an abrupt stop at the bottom of the shaft, and we walked along a corridor saturated in dark blue light. I had no idea which direction we were headed, but my gut told me we were now underneath the quarry's basin, hundreds of feet below the surface.

Douglas used his security card. The wall parted in the middle, interlocking rods rotated and withdrew, and two thick panels retreated into the bedrock. I had never imagined they worked in a fortified lab. We stepped inside, and the lights responded to our presence.

"Open every drawer you can find. I'm going to search Clive's computer."

The sprawling lab was filled with unassuming gray cabinets and workbenches. There was a large mirror on one wall and another door that must lead further inside. The counters were covered with microscopes, beakers, test tubes, various devices I could not identify, and so many monitors. There were no signs of gemstones or jewelry to be found in any of the cabinets. In fact, most of them were empty.

"They must have taken everything," I said.

"Give me a second."

I watched Douglas answer riddles and solve complex mathematical formulas to unlock Clive's hidden files. It seemed like a test designed so only Douglas could pass. I couldn't help but feel a pang of jealousy toward the level of access Douglas had, an intimacy I would never receive.

"I'm in," he shouted.

A compressed hiss let out behind me, and the door on the mirrored wall slid open. Out walked a man dressed in olive trousers and a tan, short sleeve button-down shirt. "Agent Townsend" was stitched in blue lettering on his chest. He had a gun on his hip, but he appeared to be so confident of his power over us that he did not reach for it.

"Thank you very much, Douglas. Now back away from the computer."

Douglas turned around. He reached for something in his jacket, but before he retrieved it, I saw his mouth gape in horror. I turned back to the security officer. He had lit up the room behind the mirror, and inside I saw my worst nightmare. It was Clive, shirtless and suspended from the ceiling by a harness. He was unconscious, and electrodes were attached to his chest, wrists, temples, and ankles. This had all been a trap to lure in Douglas. My presence was negligible, an error that could be easily erased.

Still, some buried instinct took over. I rushed the security officer, shouting from deep inside my gut, and I swung at his face. He dodged at superhuman speed and, using my momentum against me, pushed my shoulder to throw me into the mirrored wall. My nose and cheek made contact with the glass. I fell to the ground. My brain threatened to burst through my skull, and my shoulder prickled as if sunburnt.

"I wouldn't try anything like that again," said the officer. He pointed to a fob attached to his hip. "One press of this button, and old Clive over there gets quite the jolt. Now back away from the computer, Douglas."

"You'll never understand our data."

"See, that's where you're wrong. You and Clive aren't that special. We've got three other labs working on the same little mystery. The only difference is your optimism drove you to work out a solution faster than the others. I knew it would come to this in the end—you and Clive, trying to steal the tech, running off together in the night. That's the risk of working with idealist faggots. Then again, it'll be fun to pry the secrets from your cold, dead hands."

At that moment, Townsend unbuttoned his collar to reveal a stone dangling from a chain around his neck. I was still reeling, but I was close enough to recognize the big green stone as the mold-like eastonite Clive had shown me at home.

Townsend yanked the chain off his neck and held the amulet in his closed fist. The test tubes rattled in their holders as the lab began to shake and the lights flickered. Townsend's skin blistered, and the light around his body waved like heat rising from the pavement. He was not on fire, not exactly; he was more like the smoldering remains of a fire pit—ashen, unassuming, but capable of igniting an entire forest if the wind blew just right. He walked toward Douglas in a smoky blur, and the scent of sulfur trailed in his wake.

I stood up and braced myself against the shaking wall. I shouted with impotence as a last resort, too distant to help Douglas. I was certain Townsend would smash into him and singe his skin wherever they made contact.

Meanwhile, Douglas pulled a second amulet from his jacket pocket. Clive must have made one for each of them. Maybe there were more. I checked my own pockets, hoping Clive had snuck an amulet to me before he left. But my hands came out empty.

Douglas's body began to glisten with sweat. He suddenly soaked through, and a sparkling foam rose from his pores. Instead of being sideswiped by Townsend, Douglas lifted off the ground. His chest pushed forward with his arms behind him as if ascending in mystical awe, and his cells vaporized, forming a Douglas-shaped mist in the air.

Townsend sizzled as he passed through Douglas like the dregs of coffee poured on a campfire. I struggled to believe my eyes as Douglas's mist cloud dodged Townsend's feverish lunges. Douglas swirled around him, dissipating to avoid contact, and taunted him. Townsend barreled toward him again, missed, and grabbed the counter to slow himself, burning handprints into the linoleum. When he turned to re-engage, Douglas had condensed into a soupy mist. Even across the room, I felt the air turn damp, and the glass behind me felt slick. Douglas appeared to be everywhere. The mist blew toward Townsend. It spun around him in a tight funnel, and Townsend's body steamed and curled inward.

Douglas's hand materialized, yanked the fob from Townsend's waistband and threw it toward me. I grabbed it and stumbled over the shaking floor toward Clive. I ripped the electrodes from his bare skin and begged him to wake up. He was breathing, but he did not regain consciousness. I unscrewed the harness clips suspending him from the ceiling, and he slumped onto the ground. I ducked my pounding head under his armpit and dragged him toward the door.

When we crossed the threshold into the lab, Townsend was back on his feet, he and Douglas tangled in a violent dance that was wrecking the lab. Fire engulfed the cabinets; black smoke flooded the ceiling. My progress was too slow, and I wasn't sure how I'd get past Townsend.

I had no other choice but to try.

Douglas's face materialized in the mist, noticing me dragging Clive, and Townsend took advantage of the distraction to sear his fist into the back of Douglas's fleshy neck. Douglas's human body fell out of the mist and to the ground. I lowered Clive and reached for the hose attachment on one of the lab sinks. I aimed it at Townsend and sprayed him. The water pressure was low, but it slowed him as he backed out of range, allowing Douglas to regroup.

To my surprise, Douglas did not continue his fight against Townsend. Instead, he ran toward us and drenched his arms around Clive and me. We immediately became weightless, liquid atmosphere. I was myself yet indistinguishable from Douglas and Clive. I felt each of them, an affection toward them both, but also the strong bond between the two of them that stretched beyond mere friendship. I had tried so hard to ignore it, but with the boundaries between us dissolved, it was undeniable. The three of us, a sodden bundle of unresolved emotions, had become a million harmonious particles suspended in unison.

We rose from the floor as one, and we drifted toward the air vents that sucked the black smoke from the room. We flew upward, bending around corners in the clattering ductwork, gaining speed against the toxic fumes, until we passed through the industrial air filters on our way to the open skies.

Douglas directed us above the canopy and into the moonlit clouds. We picked up speed in the shape of a comet and streamed southwest, following the peaks of the Appalachian Mountains. The cool, flowing rush overwhelmed my senses and my insecurities, until we slowed and lost altitude, becoming cloud, then fog, then morning mist.

A pang of regret hit my gut as Douglas pulled away and our three, material bodies strained and cleaved. I felt heavier than lead, yet fractured, severed, torn into shreds, and deeply alone on the dewy ground.

I sat up, shivering, and turned toward Clive. Douglas and I leaned over him, avoiding each others' eyes. I rested my ear against Clive's chest, and I heard his heart beating. I wanted to remain there, hugging him forever, when I felt Douglas's arm wrap around my burnt shoulder. It stung, and I recoiled. I was still caught in a tangle of gratitude and envy, unsure if I could straighten things out. Then Clive coughed, and Douglas helped him sit up against a wall of old tires. They held hands, but Clive's eyes, sparkling in the moonlight, turned toward me.

"You need a towel," Clive said with a smirk and ran his fingers through my damp hair.

I laughed as a tear ran down my cheek. "Are you ok?"

"I think so. Just groggy. Townsend's guys knocked me out with chloroform or something. How'd you find me?"

"Landon can fill you in on the details," said Douglas. "I've got to get back. Townsend still has the other amulet. I can't let him keep it. You'll be safe here."

Before Clive could protest, Douglas released his hand and dissipated in the night air. It happened too fast, before either of us could protest. We owed him our lives. He helped us escape and made sure we stayed together. Yet, ashamed as I am to admit it, in the moment, I was relieved to see him go.

Eventually, Clive stood, and we slowly followed the strange wall of tires some distance, drawn to voices echoing in the woods. Around the bend, the bright light of a bonfire greeted us through an opening in the tire wall. Douglas had brought us to the Bent Greens, one of the locations on Clive's map in the garage. Clive told me about the battle fought here, the community who held together during the fight against the Southern Army, merging with and drawing from the tire fire to defend their home. Now, the inhabitants of the Bent Greens enjoyed the relative safety provided by the valley and the Awakened, and they welcomed us to dry off.

· · · ●· ● · ·

Clive and I tried for months to make contact with Douglas or with anyone who might know what happened to him or the amulets. But the area around the lab and the quarry has become a dead zone. No radio transmissions. No secret messages smuggled out. Only the rumor of a massive construction project in a nearby valley. If Douglas escaped, he did so without the amulet, or he would have returned to us immediately. We can only hope he managed to get out alive, but I'll never forget the recurrence of loss I felt in the days after he flew away. The lost potential for reconnection, for resolution. It was a repeat of that pain I felt as we separated from the mist, only amplified by the sadness behind Clive's eyes. Whenever it resurfaces, sometimes as a fleeting image, others as an all-consuming emptiness, I try to tell myself Douglas could still be alive. That he's in hiding. That he hasn't made contact in order to protect us, in case someone were to discover our location.

But I fear the worst has happened, and not even Clive, the master storyteller, can come up with a compelling explanation for his prolonged absence.

Clive is always being tasked with jobs to repair machines or configure used parts into something new. I spend most of my time in the fields tending to the crops. I dig my hands into the soil to distract myself from replaying that horrible night, from imagining what SustainAble will do with those amulets and chambers. For now, we do our work here. We focus on what is within our control to care for and to improve. We brace our relationship around his absence.

On mornings like today, when the mist rises off the valley floor at sunrise, I squeeze Clive's hand while he tells me stories about Douglas. It is not always enough to bury the guilt, but the memories are all Clive and I have, together with those who also survive here shrouded by the loved ones we have lost along the way.

THE BRAMBLE SHAKES
CHRISTOPHER R. MUSCATO

An office in North America
2057 C.E.

Borders are of no relevance to a ghost. This is a lesson that is included in the earliest stages of instruction among inductees. It is an important one because the same powers that seek to impose limitations on the less powerful often see themselves above such restrictions. Much of this impunity is purchased through incalculable wealth, but there are also other shadows that cannot be contained, other ghosts that haunt the halls of the privileged.

Darnall flipped through the portfolio, eyes scanning over charts and arrows and numbers organized into columns of black and red. He scratched the thick hair on his chin, rolled his sleeves up to his elbows, and loosened his tie even more than it already was. Finally, he nodded.

"I think this might be our candidate," he announced.

"Who, the lawyer?" A bespectacled head popped out from behind the large monitors shielding the desk opposite Darnall's. "You think he's ready to take charge of a corporation this size?"

Darnall stroked his chin again.

"He's a senior partner at his firm, and his consulting work with FirmaTech probably saved them millions in litigation. They'll accept his nomination. He can handle it. Plus, he's been on our list for years."

"Then say hello to FirmaTech's new CEO." The man across the desk adjusted his large, circular glasses and disappeared back behind his screens. The sharp rapping of a keyboard pushed to its limits echoed throughout the cramped office. Darnall rolled his eyes then leaned forward.

"Wasn't actually talking to Berto. I wanted you to know we are taking over the corporation that bulldozed your home."

"I can hear you." Berto's voice rose over the clacking of his keyboard. "It's weird enough that you named that lizard after yourself, let alone how much you talk to it."

Darnall looked at Darnall Jr. and shrugged. The anole tipped his head to the side but said nothing.

> *Bureaucracy, while far less flashy than costumes and candlelight, is a remarkable tool when wielded by masters of the trade, craftspeople in the art of secret influence. A map denotes the basic regional units, but within those are systems of hierarchy, councils and secretaries, that coordinate the unison of the Society from the macro to the micro. Few known organizations or institutions can share resources on a global scale with such efficiency or effect.*

"After FirmaTech accepts Johanson's nomination, we can begin replacing minor secretaries in a few weeks. At six months we'll force out a board member. Sounds like nobody in that room is too fond of their

CFO so that should be an easy play. By that point, our investors will be starting to see returns—and if the FirmaTech old guard aren't fighting too much, we should be able to buy out whatever remaining portion of the company we need. I give it eighteen months, and the corporation will be a very different institution."

There was a round of applause in the small conference hall. Darnall and Berto took a bow then fielded a few questions, Darnall loosening the tie specifically tightened for the sake of the presentation.

"Nice work you two." A woman stepped forward as the pair started to pack their things. She gestured to her companion. "May I introduce Jamie Gurnay, of Bramble Cay. Berto, a word?"

Berto shrugged and followed their PR director towards a group of people dressed in dark suits and crisp white shirts, edges of tattoos visible around wrists and collars. Investors, likely. Darnall and Jaimie watched Berto leave, and then Darnall extended a hand.

"A handshake is a bramble."

"The bramble is the key," Jamie responded. She jerked her head in Berto's direction. "He doesn't know?"

"Not yet." Darnall shook his head. "But he's a great candidate."

Jamie chuckled softly and glanced around the room.

"When I heard about your operation, I assumed everyone here must be members of the Society. Gathering investors to buy enough stocks in corporations to gain seats on the boards, and then filling those seats with climate activists who change the direction of the company. Inspired work, Mr. Couvert."

"Darnall, please. And no, there's only three Knights here. Myself, Patrice in accounting, and Ms. Furtiv." He nodded toward the woman still escorting Berto through the fields of potential investors. "So, what can I do for you Jamie? I get the sense you didn't actually come here to see our investment firm."

Jamie bit her lip, glanced over her shoulder, and pulled a tablet from her bag. She retreated a little deeper into the wall. Darnall noted several paintings flashing across her screen as she turned on the tablet.

"These are incredible. Yours?"

"Yes," Jamie nodded. "But not why I'm here. I came to see you because you're the regional chapter head for San Antonio, and I thought that if anybody had heard the rumors, it would be you."

"Rumors?" One of Darnall's eyebrows lifted. Jamie tapped her tablet, and across the screen appeared a parade of reports, instant messages, social media posts, some grainy photographs and videos. Darnall took the tablet, eyes wide.

"Jamie, what am I looking at?"

"The future, I hope."

Thus began a long conversation Darnall had never expected to have. Retreating to his office for want of better privacy, Darnall asked Jamie to elaborate. At first he had wondered if this was some sort of code, a bit of Society messaging he hadn't learned yet, but Jamie did not seem to be speaking in metaphors. Every word dripped with sincerity.

As you can see"—Jamie flipped through the screen—"these reports are coming from all over the world. But they're so infrequent, and information sharing across borders has become so difficult, that nothing has been confirmed. The only reason I have even this amount of data is because of my contacts with Knights across the continent. Even in the Bramble Society, though, there are only whispers. But two of these reports have been in your chapter's jurisdiction, which is the only case I've found with multiple accounts so close together. So, have you heard anything?"

Darnall ran a hand over his thinning hair. "Have I heard anything? About . . . superpowers? This is . . . no, no of course not. What did you call them?"

"Awakened." Jaimie bit her lip, focused on a report on the screen. "A witness I spoke with who knew one of these people said that the individual described a sensation, like feeling something in the Earth come alive, which awoke that same something in them as well."

"I'm sorry, I'm just having a hard time seeing this as anything but a joke," Darnall confessed.

"I understand," Jaimie responded. "But I wouldn't be here if there wasn't a lot of evidence that something incredible is happening. Let me walk you through it."

From there Darnall and Jaimie examined stories of many fantastical people doing what he knew should have been impossible. Curiously, a good number of the reports were redacted corporate files, many with SustainAble letterhead. There were videos of a woman at a protest supposedly throwing air at cops, while counter videos claimed it was all just an elaborate prank, going as far as to invalidate the eye witnesses. Others were clearly corrupted webpages—probably from conspiracy crackpots—printed in an attempt to salvage the record. A report of a woman devastating a polluting factory with an earthquake. Corporate espionage, via a person—or group of persons—who turned into steam? And anthropomorphic wolves?

They inspected photographs and testimonies, listed commonalities and differences between each incident. Finally, the shadows outside grew longer, the reader on the wall indicated that the heat/humidity index was lowering to safe levels, and ambient sounds of mass transit increased as the nightly commute began. Darnall promised to reach out to Jaimie if he heard anything.

"One last question," he said as she packed her bag.

"Yes?"

"These . . . Awakened. If any of this is true, such powers could mean a lot of different things to different people. Some people might get ideas, dangerous ones. What are you going to do if you confirm their existence, if you find one?"

Jaimie paused, eyes going unfocused for a moment, a hint of melancholy crossing her face.

"I've spent years painting the last of things. Flora. Fauna, as they become extinct. I'd love to be able to capture the first of something."

> *Those who work in the bureaucracy of clandestine relations are aware of the power they wield. It is not something they take lightly, nor should they. It is a great burden, a sacred mandate they honor as those who defy the law, subvert restrictions, and rebel against the apocalypse. Because of this, they are cautious of any who wield power, for they know the ways that power can reshape the world.*

If anyone were to be honest in their opinion of Darnall Couvert, they would note his empathy towards those who suffered, his inclination towards justice, or his sharp mind. They would not list organizational skills among his finest traits. And yet, even by Darnall's standards, his office and appearance had become particularly untidy. This did not go unnoticed by others at the firm, although few chose to comment. They knew Darnall was often busy, occasionally on projects he did not choose to share with them, and his work had not diminished in quality.

One person who did feel a stronger sense of inconvenience, however, was Darnall's officemate, whose workspace was disappearing under piles of papers. In the month since the strange woman's arrival, Berto and Darnall's office had become infested with scientific studies, newspaper reports on unexplained occurrences, maps with small towns circled, and reams of data on climate conditions. Only Darnall Jr.'s tank remained safe from the encroaching web of oddities, and when the little lizard ventured from his glass-lined oasis, he didn't mind slipping between piles of papers.

Berto mostly kept his opinions to himself, offering little more than a narrow-eyed glance through his round glasses from day to day. Today, however, even the distracted Darnall noticed that his officemate and friend seemed unusually anxious, restless, irate. Berto had spent the morning mumbling under his breath in short, punctuated bursts of obscenities. Darnall wondered if the heat was getting to him; despite the air conditioning, it was very warm and very humid, a dangerous combination in San Antonio. The heat index reader on the wall flashed a foreboding burnt orange.

"Berto, can I get the quarterly analysis for FirmaTech?" Darnall asked, neck stretched slightly so he could try and gauge Berto's mood. The elusive officemate remained obscured behind a wall of screens, but the sharp rapping of fingers against a keyboard indicated that the request was heard, and within moments the reports appeared on Darnall's screen.

Darnall leaned back in his seat. Rotating slowly between his fingers was a business card, white, with nothing on the front but the image of a small rodent in gold. On the back was a phone number, one that Darnall had been planning to share with Berto. When the time was right. But that did not seem to be today.

Darnall flipped a finger and the card disappeared. He refocused on his screen, ready to work. He'd been a little preoccupied himself lately, chasing leads from Jamie's files to determine if this was something he needed to worry about, and needed to devote some time to his clients. He sighed, pulled his keyboard close, but then his ear perked up. The sound started softly, almost like sand in an hourglass, but by the time Darnall realized what it was, the pile of papers perched atop a filing cabinet was already in freefall. The entire stack cascaded off the cabinet like an avalanche, hitting the ground and exploding with equal ferocity.

"I cannot work like this!" Berto shouted, jumping suddenly from behind his desk. Darnall, shocked at the outburst from his friend and still wincing from the paper-slide, was also surprised to see Berto drenched in sweat.

"I need some air." Berto grumbled, taking off his glasses to wipe his brow and aiming a kick at the scattered papers as he stomped towards the door. Darnall glanced at the heat index reader, now flashing red.

"Berto, wait!" Cussing, Darnall snatched a water from the fridge and bolted after him.

The sun was merciless as it beat down, but crueler still was the humidity, a shroud of moisture that clung to the ground like an invisible fog, suffocating and dense. Darnall coughed as he felt it in his lungs, his brow instantly thickening with sweat. He glanced around. The few people out here were scurrying short distances from cars to shops, offices to cafes. And then he saw Berto.

Standing in the middle of the least-covered part of the sidewalk, directly in the sunlight, Berto was motionless. He had removed his glasses, his arms were outstretched, his eyes closed as he faced the sun. As Darnall approached, he could see a broad smile stretched across Berto's face.

"Berto, what are you doing?"

"Do you feel it, Darnall?" Berto sighed, shoulders relaxed, as if he had never been more content.

"The humidity? Yeah, and it's killing me. Let's get inside Berto. We can talk about the office."

"Office?" Berto seemed confused. "No, the AC stifles the air, the moisture. It wants to move. It's stirring, like it's just woken up."

"What did you say?" Darnall froze, skin turning clammy despite the heat. "Berto we need to get you inside, you're not feeling well."

Berto opened his eyes, pupils wide, glasses dangling limp in one hand.

"I feel fine, Darnall. I feel . . . awake."

Darnall rubbed his eyes, wincing at the sting of salt. Something wasn't right. If Berto had been dripping before, he was now positively drenched.

Darnall rubbed his eyes again. Berto wasn't just sweating, he was . . . melting.

Evaporating.

Berto closed his eyes and sighed as he became translucent, a mirage of himself, fading slowly.

"Berto? Berto!" Darnall lunged as Berto vanished, his hand passing through the space where Berto had stood. Shaking, Darnall reached down and picked up the only thing left on the sidewalk, a set of round glasses, beads of water rolling down the lenses.

"Berto? Ber-Ber . . ." Still reaching for his friend, Darnall began to cough. The moisture in his lungs was suddenly much worse, the pressure of the humidity and the heat constricting, smothering him. He tried to call out again, but he couldn't form the words. Gasping for air, Darnall fell to the ground.

The air around him, somehow thicker, stickier, was moving. It brushed against him, heavy against his chest as he collapsed. Darnall wheezed, ears pounding, vision darkening. Then, as if by a miracle, the weight lifted. None of the trees shook with the indication of wind, no discarded papers rustled along the street. But around Darnall, the air was alive, the moisture gathering itself until it suddenly lifted, flitting away in a spontaneous gale.

"Berto?"

The last thing Darnall felt before he passed out was a rush of cool, dry air.

> *Do ghosts move with the wind? Are they subject to shifts in the breeze? It is a question relevant to the invisibly influential. When there is a change in the wind, the choice is to let it pass through, or to let themselves be caught in it and taken wherever it may blow.*

HIERARCHY OF NEED – PART II
ERNEST SOLAR & AE FAULKNER

The Dark Divide, Washington, the Western Republic of America
2056 C.E.

Franklin sat on the handcrafted wooden stool with his bare feet in the dirt. The fire blazed warm in the stone circle, the flames licking the bottom of the brewing coffee pot hanging from a wooden tripod. Franklin breathed through his impatience of having to wait for the brew to be finished. But he knew the jitteriness was rooted in the anxiety he felt toward the upcoming Council meeting. Trying to distract his obsessed mind, he glanced around the forest village Hodges had built deep in the Dark Divide in western Washington of the Western Republic of America.

The village contained a half-dozen triangle shaped lean-tos covered with Ponderosa and Lodgepole pine branches. Franklin considered them shanties—Hodges referred to them as huts. The huts were spread out among the towering forest, and the pine branches helped to keep the shanties dry, as well as camouflaged. Franklin had to admit, a casual hiker would be hard pressed to find their village, and he suspected it would be impossible for any surveillance drones to pinpoint their location. Even the various stone fire pits were hidden from a bird's eye view with similar pine branch roofs. As long as the smoke was kept to a minimum, they were safe from prying government eyes.

A few trusted members of Franklin's merry rebel band considered the forest village their home. He and Hodges were forced to relocate after the slaughter of his ecovillage by the *police* force of the Coastal Republic. He closed his eyes and took a calming breath to try and suppress the anger and pain of that horrific day. So many good people were lost.

Hearing the coffee pot finish the song of percolation, he opened his eyes. Grabbing a dirty cloth, he gripped the metal handle and poured a steaming cup of java into the mug. The dark liquid mirrored Franklin's mood and skin color. Taking a cautious sip, silently in his mind he thanked Hodges for his bushcraft skills. During the hasty flight from the destroyed village, Franklin had learned how deep Hodges's knowledge was about living in the wild. When he saw the white man whittling wood after community dinners or building wood forts for the children, Franklin assumed the man had a hobby in woodcraft. Franklin never took the time to inquire deeper; he hadn't seen the need. However, Franklin became keenly aware of Hodges's skills the night the Coastal Republic swept through their community like a horde of locusts. As hired, Hodges protected him with his life. At the same time, Hodges saved both of their lives by vanishing into the surrounding forest. The days that followed were horrendous when they learned how many lives had been lost, including his own family.

Hodges was his anchor. The man took charge of the surviving community members. He gave them a choice to follow or blaze their own path. Many left. A few followed. Hodges led them in secret across the old Land of Opportunity to the Dark Divide in western Washington state. In particular, Hodges set-up camp near the Big Lava Bed. Through Hodges's father, an old cryptozoologist and the man that taught him bushcraft skills, the old lava tubes in the area distorted the magnetic field on compasses and tracking devices. Therefore, Hodges believed the Divide would be an excellent place to hide from peering eyes.

Franklin assumed the Dark Divide was aptly named due to the dense forest, black basalt, and eerie feeling of constantly being watched by inhuman eyes. Again, Hodges educated Franklin that the remote forest was named after the gold prospector, John Dark, over two hundreds ago.

Taking a long drink from the now lukewarm coffee, Franklin stood and stretched his back and legs like a lazy mountain lion. For the hundredth time, he noticed the drying skull of a black-tail deer hanging from a tree.

The skin of the deer was stretched on a wooden drying rack, constructed by Hodges, near his lean-to. Being a vegetarian, Franklin didn't want to know where the meat was. Taking another long drag of the dark liquid, he wished to be back in the city. Any city. He had willingly admitted to Hodges that, on average, African-Americans were city folk, not mountain folk. Hodges had laughed and tossed a deerskin to Franklin and reminded him that their old community was not located in the city. Franklin countered that the ecovillage was simply located in glorified suburbia.

Franklin pushed the uncomfortable thoughts away and leaned into the shelter to retrieve the portable satellite and laptop computer. When he straightened, Hodges was standing next to him with a rucksack in hand.

Franklin visibly jumped in surprise. "Damn it, don't do that!"

"Then don't send me into the city," Hodges grunted.

The pale-skinned, broad man dropped the rucksack and shrugged off the deerskin poncho. Moving over to the fire, he poured himself a cup of coffee in a carved wooden cup. Hodges brought the rim to his lips through his salt and pepper beard and drained the steaming liquid as if it was ice water. He lowered himself onto a log and grabbed a cloth submerged in a bucket of ice water. After ringing out the extra liquid, he wiped his muddy bare feet clean. Angling the soles of his feet toward the warmth, he tossed the rag back in the bucket. Franklin refilled his friend's cup and sat across the blaze.

Tentatively, Franklin asked, "How did your meeting go with Mikayla?"

Hodges's eyes flicked up from the flames to meet Franklin's. He smiled, "Easy on the eyes." He glanced back toward the hot embers at the base of the fire. "Her hair was the color of hot embers, black streaked with red and orange tones."

Franklin nodded his head. From his intelligence, the bounty hunter from Stewardship Earth was notorious for changing her hair color.

"We met at a café. I found her reading a book," said Hodges as he peered toward Franklin across the fire as if waiting for the man to ask a follow-up question.

No question came.

Hodges continued. "A real paperback book."

Franklin smiled at the memory of when Hodges accepted the invitation to join his community. The only thing the man brought with him were boxes of paperback books. When the raid was over, Hodges was beyond pissed that all of his books got burned by the police force. For weeks he believed, and probably still believed, the raid was staged to burn his books like in *Fahrenheit 451*, rather than to silence Franklin and his movement.

"Did you offer a trade for the book?" asked Franklin.

Hodges chuckled and sipped at the cooling coffee. "No," he paused in thought, then smiled, "But I did ask if I could fan the pages to get a whiff of the book."

"Of course you did!" Franklin laughed.

The two men sat in companionable silence for a time, listening to the sounds of camp and nature. Franklin broke the stillness by glancing at his watch to check the time. Hodges picked up on the hint and sat up. He dug his bare toes into the soft needle soil of camp.

"She's been contacted by our *friend* Edward Blackstone," started Hodges with an edge of sarcasm to his voice. "Apparently, Ms. Rayne of SustainAble wishes for Mr. Draven to be removed from his lofty position of CEO."

Franklin stood and started to pace. A sure sign he was processing the implications of what he just heard. "Interesting." Looking back toward Hodges, he asked "Did Mikayla give a reason why?"

Hodges grabbed a piece of wood from the nearby pile and started to whittle a point. He shook his head no in response. "A power play, I would guess."

Franklin grunted a nonverbal response as he continued to pace. He paused for a moment and watched a young man using an auger to bore a hole into a log. He closed his eyes and listened to the hustle and bustle of camp. The subtle wind blew across his bare arms and the whistle of birds carried through the trees. Voices drifted in and out of his awareness, stirring memories that he did not want disturbed. Taking a slow, deep breath he pushed the images of his baby girl and wife deeper into the shadows of his heart.

Turning to Hodges, he asked, "Do we know where Draven is?"

Hodges skinned the bark from the branch in his hands. Concentrating on the wood, "Our network believes he is in California somewhere." He paused and almost as an afterthought, he added, "In hiding for the last two years."

Franklin nodded his head in understanding. "Makes sense, considering how many different organizations have been targeting CEOs of major corporations. I'm mildly surprised he has lasted as long as he has."

"Alive, you mean?"

"Intact, more or less," amended Franklin. "You know how some of those organizations are not kind when they *re-educate* those in the wrong."

Hodges grunted in dissatisfaction and tossed the branch into the embers of the fire. "Ms. Rayne must mean business if she wants to hire Mikayla to end him."

Franklin picked up his cold cup of coffee and drained the liquid. "Perhaps."

Hodges held up the pot to offer more. Franklin shook his head no. "Did you share with her our intel?"

"Of course," smiled Hodges, "It was how I got a whiff of the book."

"Seriously?"

Hodges leaned back against the log with a smile and laced his fingers behind his head. "Yes."

Franklin wasn't surprised. Sharing information between those with a common purpose was an understood rule in this ever-changing landscape. He asked, "Did you share our intel with Mikayla on Ms. Rayne's whereabouts?"

Hodges sat forward and then stood to stretch. "No, I haven't heard from Jarrett yet to confirm the location." He moved to grab his rucksack. "The kid believes they are heading to the Big Thicket in Texas, once he confirms I'll share."

Franklin grabbed his own leather satchel. "Interesting, isn't Texas the only hold out against SustainAble?"

"Yep."

The two men walked through camp on their way out. They nodded to a couple of the residents as they passed, exchanging short words or instructions. The camp was always on alert and ready to move at a moment's notice. Maneuvering through a single-track game trail, the two men climbed a gradual slope to the summit of Jumbo Peak. As they trekked, the Juniper and old growth forest thinned until there was only a smattering of trees in a green meadow dotted with bellflowers, mariposa lilies, and bear grass. The two men paused and took in the breathless sight of the shoulder of Jumbo Peak and Mt. Rainier haloed by white clouds in the far distance.

The sight left Franklin motionless as he soaked in the immense beauty of Gaia. In his stillness he felt a moment of pain for all those humans trespassing on Mother Gaia that had not experienced her majesty. If only more people took the time to walk through the multi-century-old trees of the Lewis River drainage valley or stood at the base of Jumbo Peak, maybe they would do more to save Mother Earth. Franklin closed his eyes and slowly shook his head. No, it was the companies that needed to change in order to make a difference.

"The hook-up is ready," announced Hodges as he pointed the portable satellite toward the skyline to the west.

Franklin opened his eyes and strode to his friend. Hodges held out the USB cable. Franklin pulled out his laptop from the leather satchel and inserted the cable. Opening the laptop, he placed it on a boulder and sat cross-legged, waiting for the computer to boot up. After a few keystrokes his image appeared on the screen next to eight other images on a video call. Of the nine participants, including himself, only four members' faces were visible. The other five council members were silhouettes. Franklin made a quick glance to Hodges, who stood far enough away to hear, but not be seen. Per the regulations of the Council, only the designated Nine were allowed to participate or hear the proceedings of the meetings. But Franklin knew that each member of the Nine had someone in the shadows listening. Usually, it was his or her successor. For Franklin, his successor was dead. For Dr. Stover, her successor was unknown to the other Nine. Hodges nodded in understanding. He knew to stay out of sight and to absorb all he heard.

"Franklin, it is wonderful to see you, my friend," blasted Dr. Stover's voice through the computer speakers.

Franklin leaned forward and lowered the volume.

"I see you are still bushwhacking it through the great outdoors," she stated, a sardonic grin spreading across her face.

Franklin smiled. "Yes, Dr. Stover, I am still in hiding."

"Of course you are," interjected a computerized male voice from Silhouette One. "Your work on the Dark Hours Legislation has made you a target of many governmental agencies."

Franklin closed his eyes and bowed his head in acknowledgment.

One continued, "It is a tragedy that the Coastal Republic responded in such a dramatic fashion."

Franklin's eyes snapped open. "Dramatic fashion?" He blurted out. "They murdered my family!" Repressed anger and adrenaline surged through his body.

"Yes, they did," conceded One.

Silhouette Four interjected with a soft feminine whisper. "Yes, they did, and we all know what you lost." She paused. "All of our hearts go out to you."

Franklin stared at the silhouette of Four saying nothing. His lineage of six generations had lost their seat on the Council of Nine with the death of his daughter. When he was dead, the remaining eight would pick another lineage to replace his legacy.

A male Pacific-Islander with tribal facial tattoos was the first to break the uncomfortable silence. "Franklin, if I may say, the Dark Hours Legislation is brilliant. You have initiated the first real change in helping to restore the balance of Mother Gaia with the requirement that all businesses and homes shut down power from eleven at night until seven in the morning."

Dr. Stover, an older woman with short gray hair, leaned closer to the video camera. "Are you serious, Daniel? Shutting the lights off for eight hours a night makes a difference? I understand the value of the conservation effort, but I do not believe it is worth jeopardizing more important initiatives. Especially those related to the Awakened and capitalizing on their strengths."

"Of course it does Stover!" shot Daniel. Franklin picked up that he dropped her title in retaliation. "What is the point of lights being on when no one is in the buildings? That is simply a waste of power generated either by wind, solar, water, or fossil fuel."

Four chimed in. "More importantly it is putting the onus on corporations to take responsibility for the health of Mother Gaia. For generations corporations have been putting the guilt and burden on the consumer to recycle or protect the environment. When it has always been the corporations who have been poisoning, defacing, and killing Mother Gaia! With this new legislation, corporations are forced to make a change or be shut down permanently if they are found in violation."

Dr. Stover threw her hands up in exasperation. "I suppose you'll support Franklin's next outrageous proposal, #OurEarth Initiative."

"Perhaps," offered Daniel.

"What is this new initiative, Franklin?" questioned Silhouette Five in broken English.

"Please Franklin, share with everyone your love of Dr. Diamond," spat Dr. Stover.

Franklin ignored Dr. Stover's verbal jab. "Dr. Jared Diamond was a scientist in the mid to late twentieth century. He believed the Agricultural Revolution was the worst mistake in human history. Dr. Diamond believed the Agricultural Revolution created the rise of infectious disease by creating environments that allowed bacteria and germs to breed and mutate, attracting rats, mice, and insects to easily transmit these new germs. Lastly, the stagnation of large groups of humans centered on farming communities allowed for close contact for infectious diseases to jump from animals to humans."

"That makes sense," encouraged Daniel.

One broke in. "And what is a possible solution to a lifestyle that has been embedded in our society for hundreds of generations?"

"Do tell, Franklin," snipped Dr. Stover.

"We go back to becoming hunter-gathers."

"Preposterous!" snapped One.

"Ridiculous!" agreed Five.

"Please explain," encouraged Three.

Franklin inhaled. "Hunter-gather cultures leave their waste behind with a nomadic lifestyle, which eliminates viruses or infectious diseases from developing and mutating to infect humans. In addition, with a nomadic lifestyle, Mother Gaia is able to replenish the land and nature more quickly without the obstruction of permanent structures."

"What? You expect us to wander through the woods barefoot like you and your ludicrous warriors?" snapped Dr. Stover.

Franklin smiled. "Please come join us, Dr. Stover."

"Pft!" she spat into the video screen. "Such an initiative would create an uncontrollable famine from coast to coast. Millions would die."

Franklin struck. "Maybe you are a little sensitive to this initiative because of the unresolved trauma you are harboring?"

"What trauma?"

"The death of your husband during the famine of the late 20s."

A flash of burning hatred flashed through Dr. Stover's green eyes. It triggered a memory Franklin couldn't quite pinpoint.

Silence permeated the meeting for a long moment.

In a harsh whisper, the older woman snarled. "My husband was an idealistic fool."

Three cautiously interjected. "Is that why you are always partial to SustainAble?"

"What?" snapped Dr. Stover, turning her venom on Three.

"In every meeting, you vote to negate any attempt of Stewardship Earth and The Network from going after the CEO or Director of Marketing of SustainAble," pressed Three.

An image of Ainsley Rayne shot through Franklin's mind. While the other council members argued, Franklin quickly pulled up an image of Ms. Rayne, isolating Dr. Stover's video image and comparing Ms. Rayne's. He immediately saw the resemblance in their mutual green eyes.

Not caring if he interrupted, Franklin broke into the conversation. "Ms. Rayne is your daughter."

All chatter ceased.

"Excuse me, Franklin?" said Daniel.

Dr. Stover glared at Franklin, daring him to continue.

"Dr. Stover, is Ms. Rayne, of SustainAble, your daughter?"

Her glare shifted to scorn and hatred.

"Yes, she is," confirmed Dr. Stover.

The other seven council members were silent for a long time.

One broke the silence first. "This is a problem, Rebecca."

Franklin blinked at the use of Dr. Stover's first name.

"This is not a problem, Michael," shot Dr. Stover. One's video call immediately disconnected. "Fool," she mumbled under her breath. "My goal remains the same regardless of who my daughter is and what she does! Yes, I am aware of the illegal practices of SustainAble. Yes, I am aware that our purpose is to defend Mother Gaia. That has been our mandate for over ten generations, and to support the Awakened for the past decade! And yes, I have been protecting my daughter because I know she can bring SustainAble into the light and be a force for good. For Mother Gaia and the human race."

No one spoke.

Hodges moved to stand in front of Franklin. He had heard the entire conversation.

"We need to think about this," said Three. Then her image faded away.

One by one, each council member of the Nine terminated their connection. Franklin and Rebecca Stover were the last two before Franklin ended the video call. The red anger of hatred in her verdant eyes haunted him.

"That means—" started Hodges.

"That Ms. Rayner is the successor to Dr. Stover on the Council of Nine," confirmed Franklin.

"Well, that's a problem."

"Yes, yes it is, Hodges," agreed Franklin.

WHERE THERE IS BRAMBLE, THERE MAY ALSO BE THORNS

CHRISTOPHER R. MUSCATO

An art gallery in North America
2056 C.E.

It requires little effort to make a mark in the ledger. A flip of the wrist or the click of a button is all, depending on the secretaries' preferred methods of transcription. But within that simple act, an entire world can be set into motion. The change in the ledger, if significant enough to merit attention, will be relayed to officers who then delegate the task of disseminating all relevant information to members within their jurisdiction. Filtering through regional and local chapters, that inconspicuous mark in the ledger has quickly and efficiently been translated into a call to action, a request for aid, or a sharing of news.

Darnall rocked on his heels, hands clasped behind his back as he observed the paintings. The linework was fluid, the colors radiant, the impact regal. If he were ever to be canonized, Darnall thought, this is what he would want his official portrait of sainthood to look like.

"Beautiful, aren't they? All extinct species, immortalized in pigment and canvas."

Darnall shifted his stance to acknowledge the woman next to him. "Indeed. Majestic."

"I'm Ruby," the woman said, extending her hand. "The gallery manager. I was told you had some questions."

Darnall shook the hand, smiling warmly, if not with overt enthusiasm. For just a second, his eyes glanced at her wrist. She instinctively did the same, noting the odd pawprint tattoo.

"It's remarkable work, obsessive in its scientific accuracy but free in its sense of line and form. And yet . . ." Darnall gestured to a small detail in a portrait of *Bolitoglossa carri*. "The cloud forest salamander was native to Central America. But here it appears nested within a bed of purslane, a variety found in Oceania. Considering the otherwise incredible commitment to detail, it's an interesting choice."

The manager tipped her head and shrugged.

"Can't say I know much about that," she admitted. "But if you'd like to speak to the artist, she maintains an office on the premises. I'd be happy to escort you."

"That would be wonderful," Darnall smiled.

Newton's third law describes a game of chess as well as the mechanical principles of celestial bodies. Every action creates an equal and opposite reaction, which means that even unassuming actions can provoke unexpected consequences. The game may be set into motion before one—or either player—is fully aware that a competition has begun.

Jamie glanced over her tea at Darnall. He seemed to be enjoying himself, head bobbing as he took in the cityscape. By his own admission he'd rarely been outside the Texan Alliance. Of course, it wasn't that strange to never leave; border restrictions made travel difficult, although not impossible if one possessed the requisite resources or connections. Darnall closed his eyes as a cool breeze drifted over the café patio, and Jamie narrowed hers. Outwardly, Darnall neither said nor did anything that seemed out of place, and yet, there was something . . . something that didn't feel right. She couldn't quite place her finger on it.

"I'm glad you were able to get time off from your firm to make it out here," she said at last. Darnall lifted his glass.

"One of the benefits of being the boss. Of course, there was no way I would pass this up." He leaned in closer. "You think you found Berto?"

"Maybe," Jamie responded. "We uncovered another report suggesting an Awakened, and from what you told me I think it could be Berto. You haven't seen him since the day he disappeared?"

Darnall shook his head. "Honestly, I didn't know if he was still alive. The man melted right before my eyes. But then I was overwhelmed with this pressure, like all the heat and humidity in the air was compressing around me, and suddenly it released. It's hard to explain, but when the air moved it felt almost . . . familiar. I don't know. I thought I was delirious for days after that, I couldn't describe what happened to police when they started investigating Berto as a missing person. You were the only one I thought might understand."

"I'm so sorry, Darnall." Jamie offered a soft smile. "That must have been difficult. But if these reports are correct, Berto might be okay. We're chasing some accounts of a ghost, a mirage, of what looked like an adult male materializing from thin air on especially humid days. Some say that he brings cooler, drier air with him, while others say the humidity follows him almost like he's a herald of doom. My leading theory is that Berto's body is evaporating, and he somehow controls moisture in the air while he's a part of it. We're not really sure yet. But we do know where he is. Or, rather, where he's been. If we can find him, he could be the proof we need to convince the Society that the Awakened are real."

"So, you've got a whole team on this?" Darnall set down his cup, and Jamie felt a tingle in her skin. There was something probing in his tone.

"Just me and a few friends, really. But we're a resourceful group. I'm still too new to the Society to have the clout for a task force. My fiancée is much higher-ranking, but this isn't her department. She's in event planning."

Darnall leaned back in his chair, arms crossed as he scanned the skies. "Devil's Hole pupfish."

"What?"

"It was a fish from Nevada. My first ceremony. Yours?"

Jamie fidgeted with her tea. "Socorro dove."

"That was, what, just under three years ago? Never forget your first ceremony." Darnall nodded.

For several minutes they swapped stories of their experiences as Knights of *Melomys rubicola*, their ceremonies, their visions for the future of the Bramble Society. They shared a meal, plus dessert and coffee. It was, for all intent and purposes, a pleasant afternoon. Then Jamie caught something out of the corner of her eye. A woman passing by. Jamie registered this because she had noticed the same woman about an hour earlier, and was struck then by the sense that she had met this person before. Now, upon seeing her again, something clicked in Jamie's brain.

"Hey, isn't that the PR exec from your firm? Ms. . . . Fortof, Furtiv. Did she come with—"

The thought froze in her throat as she turned back around to find Darnall setting his napkin on the table, tucking his wallet into his jeans as he stood. He nodded at a small stack of cash on the table.

"Lunch is on me. Least I can do."

And with that, he left.

> *Factions happen. To argue that they are anything short of human nature is to ignore a history of cataloging and organizing as deep as written history, and arguably deeper. There have always been cliques in which the like-minded find welcome company, networks that foster these relationships. But rarely, if ever—in this Society—have nebulous factions been*

> *asked to align with clear sides. It is*
> *more in the nature of the Society to be*
> *the wave that erases lines in the sand,*
> *not the rod that draws them.*

Jamie ran her hand through her hair and circled her office. It was tidy, almost more so than she had left it. At least the thieves had been considerate in that regard.

"No, they didn't take any money, none of my paintings. Yes, I'm sure. Just the reports on an Awakened individual, plus all the data from my computer. Yeah, they wiped it. I'll be home soon. Okay. Love you."

She hung up, and chewed her lip. Then she picked up her phone again and made some calls.

The next day, Jamie was in a hurry, shoes clicking against the pavement. She leapt aboard the train just as the bell chimed and the doors began to close, and slumped against the wall, panting. She took a moment to straighten her hair and her skirt, to slow her breathing and wipe the sweat from her forehead. This was not, after all, an occasion on which she wanted to look in any way frazzled.

Giving her skirt one final tug, she slowly worked her way into the business-class car, the world outside a blur as the high-speed rail shot toward the border. Seeing an empty seat, Jamie sat down, which was quite the surprise to the man across from her.

"Imagine if we'd had high-speeds back when this was all one country," she said. "It would have been easier to get home, wouldn't it, Darnall?"

The genuine surprise that had flashed across Darnall's face was now gone, and what Jamie saw instead was something almost akin to amusement.

"Why do I get the feeling that my passport isn't going to clear the border check?" he asked, leaning back in his seat with arms crossed. "How'd you find me?"

"I may be relatively new to the Bramble Society," Jamie responded, "but this is my district. I know some people who know some people. My colleagues are having this same conversation with Ms. Furtiv on her bus."

Darnall nodded. "Then I'm sure you know I can get our border clearances reinstated in a week or so."

"It will only take a few minutes if you give me back the data drive you stole from my office." Jamie tried her best to sound intimidating, although she was uncertain as to how exactly she should sound. It wasn't her normal *modus operandum.*

Darnall chuckled—not the response Jamie had hoped for—but the fact remained. She had the upper hand.

"Why'd you do it?" she asked after a moment's silence, unable to contain the question any longer. "If your goal is to find Berto, to help him, we can do that together. Why erase all the information I'd gathered on him, on any of the Awakened?"

At this, the casual half-smile on Darnall's face faded, and a certain weight settled on his brow. He glanced out the window and loosened his tie, watching the mingled hues of the blurred landscape beyond. "I do want to find him, Jamie, if it's true he's out there. But the Society isn't ready for this. The world isn't ready for this."

"For what? The truth?"

"Truth." Darnall scoffed. "Jamie, we're members of a secret society. Truth is not our business. Our business is deception with a noble cause, lies and secrets guiding the fate of humanity toward a better future, and you know why? Because when faced with a truth they can't comprehend, most people react by turning their focus inward. They don't think about the greater good, they think about themselves, either their self-preservation or their own power. The Bramble Society exists because humans couldn't face the truth of our own catastrophic consequences and work together toward a common good."

"But the emergence of a new pathway in our evolutionary lineage, Darnall!" Jamie protested. "Superpowers! Think of what that could mean. A new start, something to unite us. You don't think something of this magnitude would bring people together?"

"Jamie, the climate collapsed on a global scale and we couldn't even agree that it was happening as it was happening."

Shoulders drooping, Jamie felt less and less as if she held the upper hand in this conversation. But there was one question Darnall still hadn't answered.

"Why not trust the Society with it?" she asked. "If you believe the Bramble Society is working toward good, then let me present this information, this data to a general assembly. We can be there to guide this new stage of humanity, our future. To protect it."

Darnall leaned forward, still watching the world outside the window. "The Society does good. But its mission is protecting the natural world from humanity's greed, healing it from our neglect. A new mission could derail us. Even among Knights, no one is infallible. There will be those who believe the cause is righteous, elevating the Awakened as heroes and saviors, but what they will really worship is their power. The power to unite factions, to lead armies. To bring the Society out of the shadows. A lust for power in the general populace is a dangerous thing. A lust for power in a transnational secret society, Jamie, that does not bear imagining. Train's slowing down."

Jamie followed his line of sight out the window. The pastiche of hues separated into discernable shapes, and soon a station came into view. Jamie was out of time.

And out of patience with Darnall's pessimism.

"Last stop before the border, Darnall. Give me the data drive and your passport will clear."

"I don't have it. And neither does Ms. Furtiv."

"Wha—you're lying. Of course you do," Jamie stuttered.

But the look of tired victory on Darnall's face told her the truth. A memory flashed into her mind, a vague recollection of Darnall mentioning once that there were three Knights who worked in his investment firm. Jamie pursed her lips. "I'll call your office and make sure someone feeds Darnall Jr. Since you won't be back for a while."

"Kind of you." Darnall smiled. He was quiet a minute, and the train came to a stop with a subtle jolt. People around them jostled in their seats.

"Looks like the wind is picking up." He nodded toward the window behind Jamie. She glanced over her shoulder, following his line of sight, but when she turned back around, the seat across from her was empty. Her mouth fell open and she jumped up, but she was caught in the furious tussle of the late-afternoon commuter rush. Accepting defeat, she slumped back into her seat, arms crossed. As the train started to move again, she looked outside the window to see Darnall offering a goodbye wave from the platform. Jamie scowled, wondering at what point in her time in the Society someone would finally teach her that trick.

> *There is nothing unusual about the fact that there are whispers. By the very nature of the society, whispers have always been a vital element of its existence, a piece of its DNA, winding and twisting throughout its history and identity. They are the foundations upon which the temple of secrecy is built, the prayers of its revenants. What is notable are the contents of those whispers, because never in the society's history have these words been whispered before.*

"You spend a lot of time looking at that one."

Jamie smiled at the familiar voice, one comforting enough to make her look away from the portrait. Of all the paintings in her gallery, this was the only one not for sale. The only one that never would be.

"It helps me focus." She took her fiancée's hand and kissed it. Kay grinned.

"You have more passion for this Society, for this cause, than almost anyone I've ever met. And I meet a lot of people."

Jamie sighed and bit her lip. She may have lost the data on Berto, but he wasn't the only Awakened out there. She still had stacks of paper evidence she had printed and stored, most of it rumors, but it might be enough to turn some heads. Her fiancée placed a hand on her shoulder.

"I did some digging on Darnall Couvert, he's a decent guy. Loyal to the Society, working to levy corporate power for good. But that means he's got a good deal of influence, and from what I've gathered he's already recruiting people to his side. He knows the Bramble Society, Jamie, and he'll use whatever resources he must in order to keep this buried."

"Do you think he's right?" Jamie's voice was soft. "Would it be a mistake to make the Bramble Society aware of proof that the Awakened are real? Would it bring out the worst in us to even imagine that kind of power?"

"We're a secret society, we already wield power, enough to subvert borders and enough to let us dare dream of a better future. I don't know that there's anyone I would trust more with this information. But really, there's only one question that matters now."

Jamie turned. "What?"

Her fiancée smiled. "What are you going to do?"

Jamie chuckled. All her life, she had seen so much destruction. She glanced at her portrait of the Socorro dove. So many endings. After all of that, to see the start of something . . .

"For now, I'm going to bed," she decided. "And tomorrow, do you think you can use your connections to help me call for a general assembly of the local chapters? It's time for the Knights of *Melomys rubicola* to honor the living as much as the dead."

As Jamie turned to leave her studio, she turned off the lights one-by-one until finally she flipped the last switch, and the portrait of the Socorro dove faded into darkness.

An irony of a secret society is that, to its members, the existence of said society eventually becomes so normal as to seem mundane. The mission is sacred, but there is nothing fantastical or mystic about the organization itself. Perhaps that is why many members believe the whispers to represent some sort of loyalty test, or a prank, or a light bit of hazing. After all, how could something so incredulous be true? Even among the clandestine, some things are just too marvelous to believe. And if there were to be a register of such impossibly fantastical things, securely included on that list would surely be the word now whispered openly throughout the ranks: Awakened.

MICROCYSTIN ABOLITION

C. D. TAVENOR

Albany High Security, Central New York, the Coastal Republic of America
2057 C.E.

Days turned to weeks. Weeks turned to months. The months might have turned into years, but Natalie had no way of knowing.

Her cell, cold and solitary. The food, stale and cheap and lacking nutrition. The work, endless. Monotonous. In service to an unknown corporation profiting off the Coastal Republic's brutal prison industrial complex.

Each day followed the same routine. She awoke at 7am, when the LED lights blazed on from above. A man walked down the hallway, sliding bowls of protein porridge through a tiny gap in the cell door onto the receiving table. The barely sweetened breakfast felt like sugary glue in her mouth.

At 9am sharp, every door opened, and every prisoner walked silently to the work floor. Natalie stood at a conveyer belt laying thin, transparent filaments upon photovoltaic solar shingles. Not the solar revolution imagined at the beginning of the century. She couldn't take solace in the act of creating renewable energy for someone's home; the ends simply didn't justify the means.

Lunch came on the clock—a piece of fruit arrived on a plate with a peanut butter sandwich. But the work continued.

The work shift ended at 6pm. For one hour, the prison floor opened for socialization, but Natalie rarely talked to anyone. More aptly, no one took the time to talk to her. She didn't seek out conversation, and others were more than willing to do likewise.

At 7pm, dinner was served back in the cell as a piece of unseasoned chicken and a bland salad. Lights turned off promptly at 9pm, and Natalie welcomed the darkness. With each twilight, she once again attempted to use her power.

And as stars shone through her tiny window each night, her attempt to control the air failed.

She didn't understand how. How had the Coastal Republic learned a way to neutralize her ability? It was a question she pondered every day as she slaved away upon the assembly line. She suspected it was the food—but she'd attempted to starve herself for a week without any change to her circumstances. They could be pushing some sort of neural inhibitor into the air she breathed—a silently, easily regulated method.

But the ultimate mechanism didn't truly matter. They had found a way to neuter her power, and she had no way to fight against the supreme will of the oppressive state. Fear and hopelessness, they overwhelmed. She could feel it in her bones, in her soul, in her lungs with every breath.

She would never escape Albany High Security.

· · · • · • · · ·

One solace came each week—her weekly phone call with Jordan, operating as her legal counsel from his office in Columbus. Natalie was technically a citizen of the Western Republic, and Jordan had managed to involve the country's state department in the legal battle. Her status as "technically still employed" by the United Nations helped with negotiations. But in the Coastal Republic, people were imprisoned until guilty, even if the court still nominally considered them innocent prior to trial, a trial that often took years to reach.

Jordan had ideas, though. Good ideas. Whether they would work was a different question entirely, especially when every call was likely recorded and transmitted to the prosecution for analysis.

"I spoke with Secretary General Lawal yesterday," he said. "She wants to be helpful."

Natalie sighed. "I don't think she can be helpful. If she draws attention to me, she'll only put a target on her back."

The phone line went silent for a moment, though Jordan's own sigh came through loud and clear as the moment ended. "Lawal believes there's hope though, around the river bend. She could make headway with the Coastal Republic's representative to the United Nations. Seek a pardon."

Today, Jordan was being more explicit with his ideas. As if he wanted them to hear what he was saying. "I don't like it," Natalie retorted. "I don't like it all."

"The river bends toward justice, even when it's filled with pond scum and algae blooms," he replied.

With that line, alarm bells rang in Natalie's mind. Jordan was saying something else entirely.

"No need to get philosophical on me," she said. "But I think I understand what you're saying about rivers and bends."

"A public narrative is flowing," he replied. "The feeds are filled with people applauding your power. Sure, plenty of pundits claim you used giant fans, or advanced special effects, or a jet pack, or something, but it's working. You're gumming up the works, People can't ignore what you said, at least. You're breaking down walls, and people are letting the message flow through. Following its currents. Changing their perspectives. People are ready for action."

He was spewing nonsense. Well, not total nonsense, it just didn't include specifics. And she was pretty certain that was the point. "So the river is bending?"

"The river is bending," he replied.

· · ● · ● · ● · · ·

His cryptic words made her expect something significant, either in one of their upcoming legal meetings or something else entirely. Jordan's words had been so subtle, yet he'd emphasized the river bending multiple times.

What did it mean?

The porridge continued to taste like glue—though one day, they gave an extra packet of stevia. The solar shingles now looked like little black mirrors, reflecting the darkened world forming her tomb. She'd always heard rumors about the horrific conditions of Coastal Republic prisons. Ben had talked briefly about his experiences as part of the Coast Guard, of course. The nation's purity culture had embraced a brutalist approach to adaptive survival. A few of their World's Revolution members spoke of work camps, but the high security facilities? No one had ever escaped one of those.

If Natalie ever made it out, she'd find a way to spread the word about the Coastal Republic's human rights violations.

If she made it out.

But as the porridge continued to taste like dust, the assembly line continued to harden her hands, and social hours continued to lack anything social at all, Natalie wondered if she'd imagined Jordan's words. Maybe she was looking for a signal where there'd been none. Maybe she was seeking hope where no hope existed.

Maybe she'd made a mistake, standing up against the police attempting to crack down on protests fighting for a safer planet.

One evening many weeks after her conversation with Jordan, she lay on her bed, staring at the sterile ceiling. She imagined a world where instead of hiding who she'd been for the past fifteen years, she'd declared her power to the world from the very beginning. Had they—her and other Awakened—squandered the Earth's gifts? What if she'd spent her hours showing the truth of her power, rather than working to hide every strange event worldwide? She'd believed hiding the truth would allow the truth to work its magic in secret.

Instead, she'd smothered it with silence.

That was the first night she cried herself to sleep. She'd heard others crying throughout the nights, and during her first weeks, Natalie had vowed to never break. Yet when the tears flowed, she realized she hadn't been broken by the prison.

She'd broken herself. Or, she'd realized she'd already been broken. She'd been working within a system at the United Nations still fundamentally designed to prop up a world order resistant to fixing its mistakes. She had believed she could change the system from within. And maybe that was still possible. Or maybe it had been possible. But she been destined for a different purpose, a purpose she'd fundamentally ignored.

Earth had given her a gift to demonstrate its message, not to waste years preparing for others to act.

······•··•····

A loud *thunk* awoke her from a slumber she didn't remember entering. She immediately sat up and looked toward the sound's origin, apparently near the small window high upon the back wall of her cell. Lightning illuminated the darkness outside, revealing rain drops splattered against the glass, followed by a distant boom.

The first sound must have been thunder from another lightning strike. She shook her head and fell back against the hard mattress.

Another thunk arrived, and hearing it while awake confirmed it as a hit against her cell. She rose again and looked at the window, frowning and stifling a yawn.

Lightning struck once more, followed by an actual thunder clap. Then . . .

Barely visible against the glass, illuminated only by some distant prison light, another thunk hit the window—specifically, a wave of water splashed, forming a blue-green face.

No, that couldn't be right. Natalie had truly lost her mind, imagining faces amidst storms. She was wishing for a god of thunder to come rescue her from prison.

But with another thunk, and the face's appearance yet again, she recalled Jordan's words. *The river bends toward justice, even when it's filled with pond scum and algae blooms.*

His words were literal. The face, a blob of algae with a subtle grin, stared straight at her. She nodded. It nodded. She nodded again. It disappeared.

For a moment, silence arose from the darkness. The rain stopped—completely ending its soft pitterpatter on a roof far above her head. The eery lack of noise brought calm to her cell, and from out her door and down the hall, she heard the breathing of others locked in Albany High Security.

You're breaking down walls, Jordan had said. She'd thought he meant figurative walls with those words—her actions had likely forced the truth of the Awakened into the open, at least more so than ever before. But "breaking down walls" sounded a bit more literal as she stared at her cell wall.

She stepped forward, placing her ear against cold stone. A faint creak echoed through the wall followed by a hiss, then a distant torrent, like a waterfall beyond a nearby hill.

Unlike a waterfall, the torrent rushed toward her until it felt as if it were inside the wall itself, inside the stone, inside the—inside the pipes.

Natalie stepped away from the wall and pulled the chain to illuminate the private ceiling LED for her room. It wasn't much light, only there for a prisoner to use if they needed the toilet in the middle of the night. But it was enough to cause the droplets of water forming on the stone to glow.

Water, water everywhere. It condensated on the floor, on the metal frame of her bed, on the walls and ceiling. Her toilet overflowed, water spilling toward the wall. All of it moved with purpose, bending toward the wall in hostility. For a moment, she imagined the water in the form of a human, but its form was more grotesque, more abstract than bipedal. It vibrated with a power reminiscent of Natalie's own control of air. Whomever had the power of water here, though, had not lost their abilities upon entering Albany High Security.

All she could do was stand and watch. The now immense blob of crystal-clear fluid pressed itself against the wall, its molecules fitting into tiny gaps too small for the human eye to perceive. The water slid into these tiny spaces freely, their location only revealed by tiny air bubbles escaping toward the ceiling.

"Are you ready?" said a quiet, gurgled voice. A water creature's form of a whisper, Natalie supposed.

"I'm as ready as I'll ever be," she replied softly. "But what about everyone else here? Why me, and not everyone else?"

"If only we had the time," said the voice. "If you are ready, then let us leave this place. Please prepare to hold your breath."

Natalie grimaced but nodded. "Thank you."

She breathed deeply.

The water finished immersing itself in stone. No liquid remained within her cell. She glanced up at the window, frowning—there was no face there, nor could she see light beyond. Only inky blackness remained.

She exhaled, pulling in a second deep breath.

A sharp crack pinged from within the wall—followed by a hollow groan. Natalie bent her knees.

And the stones shattered.

The wall fell outward, crumbling beneath the immense power of water fracturing it at its seams. Pipes hissed and sprayed water everywhere. Natalie now comprehended why she no longer heard rain or saw the night sky through her window; an immense tidal wave loomed vertically above her, blocking any sight of what lay between her and freedom.

Still, she understood why she needed to hold her breath. Somewhere, maybe behind her, a prison alarm blared. But the river had come for her, and she would welcome it with open arms. She took another deep breath then leaped through the now shattered wall. The water enveloped her body, and instead of sinking, a power kept her buoyantly floating within the wave. For a moment, she could shift her position, and she turned to face her former prison. The cell's private light still illuminated the bed she'd called "home" for the past months.

She would not miss it.

But she also might not regret the time used to reformulate herself.

No warning came as the tidal wave pulled here away from the prison wall. Its strength and power pulled her along, and she let its strange, warm currents throw her at their whimsy. She only focused upon her lungs, holding back the water from entering her mouth while exhaling slowly over time. She pretended she knew the route the wave was taking, but there was no true way to know in the utter darkness. At some point, she was flung down a slope then up again—likely over the prison's outer wall.

Her lungs threatened to explode, and she wished once again for her power so she could bring herself the air needed to survive. But just as they nearly burst in fiery pain, the wave thrust her onto a muddy slope in a heap.

She gasped for air and fell onto her back, facing the starless sky.

"Thank you," she mouthed.

"Catch your breath," the bubbly voice said. "We have more of a journey ahead of us."

She nodded, gulping down air. "I'm ready."

Water enveloped her, pulling her into a river she couldn't even see. The waters would take her where she needed to go.

· · · ● · ● · · · ·

Hours upon hours later, with the sun now high in the sky, the wave threw her onto to land one last time. There she sat, hands on her knees, tired from the endless bouts of holding her breath. But they'd traveled miles upon miles by water. If she remembered her New York geography properly, they'd likely traveled west along the Mohawk River.

"Well will you look at you," said a voice she recognized, and it wasn't the bubbly voice of her watery rescuer. It was Ben's voice.

"I probably look a mess," she said between pants.

He laughed. "Yes, yes you do."

She glanced around and found him sitting on a stump to her left. Behind him, forested mountains rose. Looking to the right, she saw the sun rising over other hilltops. But right in front of her, a mass of water stood waiting, buttressed by two swampy algae creatures. They matched the description of the creatures Jordan found in the Maumee River before he'd joined the World's Revolution.

Rising in front of both the water and the creatures, though, hovered a misty, vaguely humanoid figure. She hadn't heard of an Awakened of this sort before, but she'd come to understand and recognize the inherent weirdness of many phenomenon stirred by Earth's own awakening. Talking trees, giant snakes, people with powers, spiritual visions—none of it really fazed her anymore.

"You must be my savior," she said.

The misty being nodded.

"Thank you, Berto," Ben said. "Your choice to help us . . . it means the world."

"Until we meet again," said the gargled voice. With that, his figure dissipated into the wind, and the wave of water slumped back into the Mohawk River. The algae creatures, however, remained.

Natalie stared at them, confused. "Why are they still here?"

"Not sure," Ben replied. "Jordan and I used their help to develop this plan—and they brought Berto to us. It took me awhile to crack how to communicate with them, but once I did . . . they have a fascinating view of the world. We have a lot to learn from them."

"I'm excited to learn." She took a step forward. "Do you want something from me?"

Their amorphousness bobbed sideways, like they were shaking their green heads to say no.

"Hmm," Ben said. "I think they have something for you, actually."

The creatures shuffled forward, holding out long, mossy appendages.

"Are they safe?" she asked.

"Safe as they could be. I trust them."

She held out her arms, and the two creatures embraced her hands with their swampy mass. A harsh burning sensation ran through her limbs, followed by a cold numbness. She shivered, but warmth returned moments later.

"Ben?"

He approached the creatures and spoke quietly to them. Rough, gutteral noises gargled in response.

"They say you'd been poisoned by tiny machines," Ben said. "They say they've cured you."

Natalie smiled. So it had been the food. Or maybe the water. But through water, she'd also found her cure. Reaching out with her mind, she once again sensed the solace of her power. A faint breeze swirled in the air around them, the two humans and the two creatures. "Thank you," she said.

"It's truly something, isn't it?" Ben said.

"What do you mean?" Natalie replied, furrowing her brow.

"Algae, a substance once feared for its literal toxins, now working to save the planet alongside us."

"I suppose its not the algae's fault that it poisons us."

Ben snorted. "And to be fair, we're poisoning their ecosystems quite a bit more than they poison us. If anything, they deserve to kill us."

"Thankfully, they've saved me instead."

· · · ● · ● · ● · · ·

The sign read "Now begins the Allegheny Trail."

Ben and Natalie still had many more weeks of travel ahead of them, but at least the end was in sight. From its northern terminus on Pennsylvania's border, they could take it south for many miles before heading west near Neola toward the Bent Greens.

"I still can't believe Jordan agreed to a prison break," Natalie said as they walked past the sign.

"It was his idea," Ben replied.

"I owe him a massive thank you then." Natalie readjusted the bag on her back and tightened their straps, all in stride. "Not going to lie, this hike has been hard, but I've appreciated the opportunity to just walk through nature for weeks. And you're good company."

"I doubt that," Ben retorted.

"You are!"

"I'm an endless pessimist with loads of trauma."

"You're the most dedicated person I know, beneath your facade."

Ben laughed. "That brings up a question, though. I've been waiting to ask until I was fairly certain we'd blended into the trail completely, and I think we have. The Coastal Republic probably thinks we're in Canada by now. What's next? For you, I mean."

Natalie smiled. "We could continue having our vague conversations about esoteric philosophies and theories of change, if you'd like, but I don't think that's what you're asking." The path sloped downward, and they stopped talking momentarily as they passed two hikers heading in the opposite direction. When she knew they were out of earshot, she added, "We have a monumental task before us."

"We've always had a monumental task before us," Ben said. "Protests are failing, mass movements are splintering, I'm even hearing the Council of Nine is in turmoil."

"I never particularly liked them," she said. "But that's not my point. Well, actually, I guess it is? Nature is fighting back—we've known that for years, as it manifests itself worldwide time and time again, both through us as humans and through nature, like our algae friends. But the world fights back against nature's message. And I think, even after two years ago, when we heard the planet's soul talk to us, we—I—still didn't fully understand its message."

"And now you have?"

"Ha! No. I don't think so, not yet. But I heard its message and *went straight back to my old job*. I didn't let it change me. But now, I see the world differently."

Ben chuckled again. "Prison will do that to you, I suppose."

"The immense wealth and power accumulated in the hands of the few is limitless," Natalie said. "We keep trying to take people down one at a time, but it will not be enough. The UN always spoke of catching 'catching climate criminals,' but it never held countries accountable or created real, long-lasting change. For every criminal turned in, there's another ultra-wealthy person doing the 'bare minimum' in the eyes of the UN. And I'm done with it."

"I think I like the sound of that," he said. "It's time to take true action, then?"

"It's time for me to return to how this all started, at least for my story," she said. "But perhaps with a bit more control over what happens."

"I'll be right by your side," he said. "Abolish the old to create something new?"

"Precisely."

Only a few more weeks of hiking separated them from returning to their friends at the Bent Greens. She looked forward to the walk, bounding up and down Appalachian ridges and embracing the ecosystems barely recovering from the region's ravaging history. Those weeks would give them plenty of time to develop a plan worthy of the task set before them by Earth.

Or, she supposed, maybe it was time for her to embrace the name used by so many of her friends.

It was time to develop a plan worthy of Gaia. She would spread its message to all who would hear it.

She smiled, finding hope once again. Natalie only had one fear left in her heart— what if they had waited too long to act?

WATER, WOLVES, AND SALT
LAUREL BECKLEY

Oregon, the Western Republic of America
2057 C.E.

"So tell me again. What kind of *wicked smaht* things did you do in *Bahston?*"

Liv rolled her eyes, glad she was half under one of the generators for the water treatment system. It was pointless to comment that no one actually talked like that in Boston—and that she hadn't actually been in Boston, but in Cambridge.

"She got an environmental engineering degree from MIT," Rhea said, the pride in her voice unmistakable. "Graduated summa cum laude, too."

"Mom," Liv groaned, hating the whine erupting from her throat. Her cheeks flushed.

"What, hon? I'm just saying, not bad for a hick from rural Oregon."

Liv tightened the screw she was turning a touch harder than she should have. The metal squealed, but the screw wasn't stripped and the panel covering the generator's interior wasn't compromised. If it had been one her wolf family getting upset . . . Liv took a deep breath.

Leaving her family to travel across the continent to one of the most politically unstable countries in the former United States had not been easy. And spending three years at a school where she was belittled for being a country kid, where she felt like a minnow fighting upstream in the deluge of information pouring on top of her—it had been a lot. She hadn't fit in at Boston, not at all. But she had survived. And she had learned.

She'd been back less than a month, and her nerves were still shot from the road trip home, from dodging bandits and shanty towns and roadblocks and procuring her Western Republic ID and travel visas and vaccination cards at each checkpoint. She'd traveled with a handful of recent graduates in a convoy—two cars packed to the brim with essentials. They'd split in Hermiston: one car heading toward Seattle, the other to Portland.

Liv had reported in to Outreach Aid's Portland headquarters, where she'd been sent on to the supply depot in Salem. A smug little manager had tried to assign her to one of the outreach teams servicing the dam rebuilds in the Columbia River Gorge—a mistake quickly rectified when the deputy of personnel whispered that Liv was a *Team Wolf* member. Liv had been assigned as security for the convoy heading to the Roseburg depot, and at that point, she'd lacked the spoons to tell them she wasn't one of the *hairy* members of Team Wolf.

There'd been tears upon her reunion—of course there'd been tears. Liv never had a chance to go *home* since she left. She'd missed her family, and was disappointed when Team Wolf only had a week of downtime before the western route. She'd had two days at the ranch to greet the family who weren't part of the team, and then it was back to work.

She thought returning would feel like slipping back into her old self and skin.

But the team had changed since she'd been gone.

Of the team Liv was used to, only Rhea and Ella still did the routes. She knew the new members—they were all cousins—but they'd been *babies* when she'd left for school and now they were suddenly grown-up and packed with confidence.

She'd changed, too. She wasn't a half-trained nurse slash firefighter slash human pollinator slash whatever Team Wolf needed anymore. She was their environmental engineer—which was why it had been such a fight to get her down to Roseburg and back on Team Wolf, and why she hadn't corrected the deputy of personnel on their mistake. The Columbia Dams project—rebuilds that were taking the input of the Yakima, Umatilla, and Warm Springs tribes this time around—needed engineers.

But southern Oregon needed her more. Even if she felt like a stranger in her own family.

Liv pulled herself from underneath the generator and met the weathered face of Coquille's water treatment plant manager. Coquille wasn't their first stop on this trip, but Harry was the first person with a background in water treatment and an extensive lived knowledge of working to reclaim fertile farmlands from flooded flatland. He'd planned the system of dikes and canals along the Coquille River, set up the power grid and water systems and everything else to rebuild after the earthquake that had destroyed so much of Oregon in the twenties, and fought the ocean's rise in the time since. If Liv had to deal with the man's horrible sense of humor, well. She'd dealt with worse.

She gave her suggestions and listened to Harry, trying not to hide the constant surprise that he was so open to her ideas. He countered with his own, and she countered back, fighting back the rising clog in her throat and the tightness in her chest telling her she wasn't *good* enough. She didn't *know* enough. She wasn't enough.

Not yet.

······●·●····

After dinner, Liv needed a breath of fresh air.

The wildfires weren't bad this summer, and the ocean breeze was a wonderful respite after being trapped under generators and inside the water treatment facility all day. They were only six miles from the ocean and the coastline—a distance shortened by the earthquake years ago and rising sea levels—and the way the valley dipped meant the ocean pushed that much further upstream at high tide.

Harry had warned her about going too far from the town's borders. Coquille was surrounded by a chain link fence, with all of its citizens living inside the boundaries, leaving only to tend to the land and fish the river or for other parts of their lives. There was a second fence surrounding the water treatment plant and docks and stables, all patrolled by the Coquille militia, who were also the volunteer fire department. Further out, where the treatment relays and dikes lay, there was a roving patrol.

The amount of security surprised Liv. The last time she was here—three years ago, right after surviving a wildfire—there hadn't been any fences.

But Coquille's rising prosperity and the growing extremism in the rural areas had changed things since she'd been gone. Southern Oregon was a different place. Where the people had greeted Team Wolf with open arms and parties, they were now eyed with suspicion from folk who had only heard the rumors of the great big scary world out there.

Something weird was happening. Something that affected people and the planet. Something was fighting back, trying to reclaim and rebuild and regrow after humanity had nearly killed it, and that bigger *sense* trickled through the information networks, growing and distorting until fear took the place of news—and even when the news did report on any of it, they rarely based their stories in fact. That something had already infected Team Wolf, whose name wasn't just a cute moniker, which made Liv's family more of an *other* than an outsider.

And some communities just didn't want the other among them. Liv had experienced that as a child—there had always been groups who didn't want the rumors of Team Wolf to touch them in case whatever affected her hairier family was contagious—but it felt *worse* this time around. Perhaps she'd been away for so long. What had once seemed normal was now strange.

To the south, smoke rose beyond the hills. Her heart sped up, beating against her chest before she realized it was just a single spiral of gray instead of a roiling wall of death. Someone's cooking fire, or a burn pile, maybe.

"I see you've spotted Josiah's campgrounds."

Liv yelped and turned, almost bumping into Harry. He'd come up beside her and put up his hands. "Whoa, sorry, didn't mean to scare you."

"I'm a little jumpy," Liv admitted. She couldn't believe she hadn't heard him approach. She didn't have the hearing of her hairier cousins, but she was still road-twitchy. She pointed at the smoke column. "Who's Josiah? I thought everyone lived in town?"

Harry grunted. "Not everyone. Josiah is the *patriarch*"—the word was thick with disdain—"of a sect—whatever you do, *don't* call them a cult—of religious woo-woo heads who came up north from California two summers ago."

Liv raised an eyebrow. There were a lot of religious woo-woo heads in this part of the country. "Is he the gentle love-everyone-isolationist kind or the fire-and-brimstone-prepare-for-the-rapture isolationist kind?" she asked.

"The latter," Harry said. "He worked his way into the town's church when he first got here, but he didn't like the way we did things. Didn't agree with our system of time banking and community, so about a year ago he split. Took his people and some members of the town with him and has caused nothing but trouble since."

"He didn't go very far," Liv observed.

"No," Harry agreed. "He's not going anywhere. Josiah believes his divine right is to shepherd the peoples of the Coquille valley and the Coos Bay area to salvation."

"What?" Liv asked. All this had *not* been in the mission brief. She'd only heard there had been heightened activity from bandits in the area.

"They've been stealing from the town to survive. They started with tools and food, and now they're on to cattle and sheep."

"You haven't tried to drive them off? Or report them?"

"No, because at the heart of it, most of us have family in that group. One of my daughters went with him in the split. I haven't heard from her in over a year." Harry sighed. "I'm not happy with her choices, but I want her to live long enough to come home."

Liv didn't know what to say to that.

"Enough depressing shit," Harry said, breaking their silence. "While we're out here, let me tell you about the drainage system we've got to reduce flooding."

They walked along the edge of the fence line, watching the sun set over the broad swatch of the Coquille River. It was wide and flat here, stretching nearly all the way across the valley. Even the dike systems hadn't reclaimed this portion of the river, and Liv could smell the salt and fish from here as the ocean pushed its way inland. She could also smell wood smoke.

She shivered, grateful her people would be moving on at the end of the week.

· · · ● · ● · · · ·

The next morning was hot and dry. Liv eased out from underneath the 7-ton, where she'd cuddled with a pack of cousins, and stretched. Sweat beaded against her forehead. This weather wasn't the oppressive humidity of the northeast, but it was still *hot*.

She pulled her backpack from underneath a cousin, who'd claimed it as their pillow, and packed her supplies for the day.

Harry pulled up in a battered Ford pickup that had been refitted to solar power right as Liv finished bringing breakfast plates to her cousin Ella in the med tent. There were four people in the back—all carrying rifles. Liv gulped, but she climbed into the passenger seat beside Harry for the ride out to the dikes. She didn't twist around as the truck pulled out of the town's fence. For the first time on a mission, she'd be apart from Team Wolf.

The drive to the first dike took ten minutes, mostly because Harry kept stopping the truck to point out bits of infrastructure they'd put in since last summer—an osprey nest in one of the old power lines, a clump of reeds that they'd chased a beaver out of last year, a spot in the road that caved in each winter.

By the time they made it to the dike, Liv was socially exhausted, the day was only just beginning. She stared out the window, her eyes unfocused at the hills to the north, as Harry chattered on about his grandchild and their first loose tooth.

Someone thumped on the cab's roof and the truck skidded to a stop on the gravel road.

Liv jolted upright, her hand flying to the pistol at her hip. "What's going on?" she asked.

Harry leaned out the window, listening as one of his team gave a quick sitrep. Liv, unable to hear him over the thrum of the truck's engine, wished she had the sharp hearing of her hairy cousins. Harry leaned back into the cab, a frown marring his face. "Looks like someone's at the dike," he said. "There's a truck parked behind the relay station."

"One of your people?" Liv asked.

Harry shook his head. "Doubt it."

Liv leaned forward, trying to make out any details. The Coquille river stretched before them, broken by a stretch of wall that funneled the water into a channel. The river here was brown and brackish at high tide, with a stream turning from the main river toward the water treatment plant to be used for farming and consumption after processing. A long, narrow road stretched along the river bank. Trees with thick underbrush lined the other side, beginning a steep climb from the flats to the hills. Liv couldn't see a truck further down the road, or even past the wall, but she wasn't standing in the truck bed.

A crack of gunfire. Liv ducked down in the dashboard instinctively. Harry shouted, and the truck jolted forward, jerking around as Harry maneuvered the truck around on the narrow road, trying to turn them around. Return gunfire exploded from ahead, and Liv pulled her pistol, knowing they were too far away for her to make any difference. She heard nothing but the *crack crack crack* of gunfire against the sound of her pulse pounding in her ears, and she turned around just in time to see someone in the back crumple forward.

But there was someone standing on the dike wall—and they were carrying something heavy and bending down and—*oh shit.*

"Go faster!" Liv yelled.

The person on the dike leapt down. The gunfire trailed off, leaving only dust rising in the distance as the truck on the other side of the dike sped off.

The dike and relay station erupted in a ball of flame and dirt and smoke. The sound and energy wave hit next, slamming Liv forward as the truck skidded into the ditch by the tree line. Her head hit the dashboard with a thump, and she thanked Harry for disabling the air bags because she was able to pull herself forward just in time to see the wall of brown water cascading toward them as the Coquille River burst free.

"Get out!" Harry yelled, grunting as he struggled to release his seat belt. It was caught. The people in the back were already out, pulling the injured person up into the trees toward safety. They'd have no way of knowing Harry was stuck. Liv dropped her gun and pulled out her knife, cutting through the waist strap just as the water tackled the trunk, slamming them forward once again.

Ice cold water tumbled into the cab, and Liv had just enough time to suck in a breath before the truck rolled over and over, tumbling along with the force of a newly freed river. Salt burned up her nose as she fought to free herself from the truck as they turned. What felt like a boulder slammed into her chest, and she gasped, sucking in more and more saltwater.

Her vision blazed red, her eyes burning, and the world was salt and salt and salt and she was—she was gone.

········

She dreamed of floating atop the water, buoyed in a raft made of salt.

Salt, her mind supplied unhelpfully, was a prized mineral in the ancient times. Valued for its healing properties, for its ability to preserve and season food, for the way it revolutionized humanity. In many places in the world, it was difficult to obtain. More difficult than fresh water, for salt was hard to separate from the ocean. Perfect conditions were needed. Coquille was not one of those places. It was too brackish, too wet, save for a brief month or two in the winter.

Each particle of salt infiltrated in her body, each grain sifting through her veins, grating as it traveled throughout her. A small thought drifted, reminding her that it wasn't salt but *sodium*, but she felt the collisions between sodium and chloride, twitching her muscles and nerves and sending spikes of pain down her limbs.

She couldn't see anything.

Was this death?

She'd thought death would be more filled with *nothing*.

Shuffling brought to her semi-awareness. Were those footsteps? Thoughts fled her mind as something hard drove into her side, the force so strong she rolled. Liv reached out to catch herself, but her arms were behind her back and she couldn't see and—the cloth covering her head was wrenched off, along with strands of her hair.

Liv squinted. There was a human-sized mountain before her, blocking out the sun with their body. Bright rays radiated around them, transforming them into a saintly being, and Liv opened her mouth to ask if they were a god when something hit her leg and everything was stars and darkness and salt once again.

· · · ● · · ● · · ·

Liv woke to smoke-tinged darkness. The world smelled of meat and fire and salt and sweat. She wasn't wearing a blindfold this time, but she had no idea where she was, or what was happening. She was inside, she thought, but where, she didn't know. The last thing she remembered was drowning.

"Liv, is that you?" someone whispered in the darkness.

The voice was familiar. "Ella?" Liv asked, startled. She struggled to sit up, trying to figure out how the hell her cousin was . . . wherever they were. "Where are we?"

"Quiet," Ella hissed. "I think we're in that compound place."

"What happened?" Liv asked.

"Bandits attacked," Ella said. "I'm not sure what happened, since I was in the med tent, but we heard gunshots right after you left, and then there was an explosion and the Coquille flooded. Knocked the fucking tent over and into the river. I was picked up by a boat full of these assholes, along with a couple other people—they're in one of the other smokehouses, I think—and taken to someplace in the woods."

Liv's head hurt. "Wait. We're *captured*?"

"We're not tied up for shits and giggles," Ella snapped. She took a deep breath, clearly trying to calm herself. "I don't know if anyone else was taken. There were only three other people tied up on the boat I was on. They were going to put me in with the other women, but they saw my Team Wolf arm patch and pulled me aside."

"Shit," Liv whispered.

"Shit is right." Ella scooted over until her boot tapped against Liv's leg. Liv bit back down on the pain—something was *not* right with her right knee—and welcomed her cousin's touch.

"What do you think they want?" Liv asked.

"I don't know," Ella replied. "But I think I overhead one of them call me an abomination. They shot me up with something and now I can't change."

Liv said nothing. The silent *shit* she could have whispered reverberated between them anyway, hanging in the darkness. She had a strong inkling she knew who these people were: the isolationist cult Harry warned her about. She wished she'd learned more about them, but aside from the mission briefings warning about various dangers in the local areas, she hadn't paid more attention than that. She should have, and she was kicking herself now, but what good would it have done her to know more and be terrified of the unknown?

The door opened. Light stabbed into her eyes, and she squinted, trying to make out how many and who and what—

Someone kicked her in the side. Pain spiked across her ribs, and she cried out. A knot in her stomach released, and she tasted salt—salt in her mouth, salt in her nose, salt bubbling up her throat. Liv tilted her head just in time to throw up. The vomit felt like gravel.

The person who'd kicked her hissed in disgust and jumped away.

"Damn it, Richard, get your fucking act together," someone snapped. "It's just puke."

"Looks like she's ODing," the man who must be Richard mumbled, but he bent over Liv, so close she felt his breath against her neck, and grabbed her arms. With a sharp motion that wrenched her left shoulder, she was hauled to her feet and dragged out of the building.

Ella shouted behind her, but Liv's head swam too hard to make out much more than building, building, dirt, trees—fuck, puking again—another building, and then she was dumped onto a wide swath of hard-packed dirt. She landed on her knees, screaming as her right knee contracted. Richard smacked her across the back of the head, and she heaved several breaths, trying to *focus*, to get her bearings even as her body weight pressed down on her knee and she could barely breathe and—someone spoke.

Blood roared in her ears, preventing her from hearing whatever was being said, and she couldn't really look up because Richard's meaty fist cupped her head, bending her neck until her chin touched her chest. But through her eyelashes, she could make out the tips of shoes, the hems of what must be dresses and not curtains since she was outside and who put curtains *outside* and oh fuck she must be going into shock or something because—she took a deep breath. Then another.

The blood still roared and lightning arced from her knee, but she could make out the cadences of the words spoken to this crowd. It *was* a crowd. She couldn't make out numbers, but there were enough to make it impossible to fight, even if she could fight. She wasn't a wolf. She was just Liv. Weak, human Liv.

Her hands tightened into fists. The rope binding her wrists together bit into her skin, grounding her with the sense of manageable pain. She could *control* that pain, even if she could control nothing else in the situation. All she could do at this point was to try to keep Ella and herself alive until the rest of Team Wolf rescued them. Because Team Wolf *was* coming. She had to tell herself that.

Individual words emerged. *Abomination. Witch. Fire. Hell. Salvation.* The words repeated, rising out of the slurry of speech sluicing from the speaker's mouth. He had a great voice—rich and commanding, both friend and leader—and while Liv was having a hard time figuring out just *what* he was saying because it was laced with religious speech and she'd always had a hard time wrapping her head around that, she had a pretty strong feeling he was condemning her and her family.

She could not focus on the words, no matter how hard she tried.

The world's beauty kept her attention instead. The sun scalded her eyes. The susurration of leaves and needles, blending together in the low-tangled mess of Oregonian coastal forest, drowned the speaker's words. The sound grew from a whisper to an all-consuming roar, blotting out all sound but leaves and greenery and the rush of salt-laced wind swirling around her, rustling her damp hair and drying the brine caking her skin.

Liv's vision swam. She felt pulled between ground and wind, drifting in between the sensation of flight and earth. Rocks and sticks dug into her knees and shins, and her bare toes dug into the sandy loam until she felt the pulse of the ocean.

Something trickled from her nose. It felt . . . *solid.* Not the quick-flowing sensation of water or snot, or the sticky cloying of blood, but like . . . *salt?* That was weird. She felt so light-headed and her vision started turning gray at the edges as the roar of wind became all of her senses, as the ocean came to her in an endless wave of sound.

A hand clamped down on her shoulder, pinning her in place.

Liv didn't quite know what happened.

One moment, the hand was on her shoulder. The next, she was on the ground and there were shouts and screams rising above the wind and the ocean's pounding. Someone else touched her, and another scream wrenched from a throat that was not hers, and Liv was hunching in on herself as guns cocked and—she smelled salt all around her.

She felt salt. Each granule and grain, so close. If she just stretched with her mind—Liv pulled, wanting the salt to stuff her ears and her hurts and turn everything to white nothing and to just stop the *noise* and—her vision went white as something inside her *heaved*.

· · • • · • · · · ·

Silence.

Liv opened her eyes, blinking to remove the crusties. She had to snort to blow out the dried snot in her nose, and the snorting made her nostrils burn, like she'd swallowed several gallons of saltwater and needed to rebalance her electrolytes. Her throat burned, too.

She tried to sit up, but her hands were tied from behind her back.

Liv groaned and managed to roll over. The ground crunched and shifted beneath her, and for a moment she thought she'd been taken to the beach and was in the loose sand among the dunes, but then she opened her eyes fully and saw the trees looming protectively over her and heard the wind through their strong limbs.

She tilted her head from side to side, trying to take in where she was. She was in a clearing, perhaps the same one from earlier, except there was no one with her. And her captors would certainly not leave her alone, right? The ground was coated in a fine, white sand that glittered from the rays of sun filtering through the tree crowns, and she didn't remember the sand from earlier.

There were also odd piles of fabric, and shoes next to each pile, and the sand was mounded into little anthills near each fabric and shoe grouping, which was really weird but also oddly familiar, as if she'd heard a story of people disappearing and leaving all their clothes behind from somewhere.

With a groan, she sat up, running her tongue along her cracked lips and tasting nothing but salt. The taste made her feel better, less thirsty than before. The taste also made something inside her waken, and suddenly she was aware of a sense she'd lacked before: an awareness of salt.

The awareness brought a realization: the white sand was not sand after all, and the building wrongness intensified, because who the hell left piles of clothes and shoes and a fortune's worth of salt just laying around in the middle of the woods?

Trying to think about a religious fanatic's idea of a prank was too much for her aching head. She needed to find Ella and whoever else from Team Wolf and Coquille were here in this hell hole, hoping she didn't run into her captors, wherever they were.

Liv staggered to her feet, her right leg buckling. There were three paths leading out of the clearing, but only one of them had piles of boots and clothes and salt laying along it, so she took that one and limped her way into a deserted compound.

There was a cluster of buildings built into a semi-circle, made from cedar shingles stained dark brown. Most of the buildings were open on one side, with bunks built into the walls and small gatherings of clothes, with two larger buildings for communal activities, a couple sheds, and a separate building with signs saying it was a restroom. All showed heavy decay and a sense of cobbled together-ness and age, and Liv suspected they dated from before the Big One, which meant they'd probably been rebuilt from the rubble of an abandoned campground. Because it *was* a campground that was being lived in long-term, with salvaged chain-link fences and ropes with tin cans and sound-makers strung between the trees to warn of intruders. The roaring in her ears had faded to a low growl, although it took a minute to realize the sharp squeals she was hearing were shouts for *help*.

Liv went to the nearest shed. The door was locked, but the wood was aged and salt-riddled, and she did that thing where she *pulled* and white trickled from its woody grains and she just leaned her shoulder into the door and it crumpled beneath her.

Ella was in the shed, her blonde hair mussed and her face red from screaming. Her eyes widened at the sight of Liv, but her cousin kept it together as they awkwardly untied each other from their bindings. Once freed, Ella sprang up, ready to take down the world.

"Where are they?" Ella demanded, barging past Liv and twirling in a circle, taking in the sight of the compound. Her shoulders were raised, her hands bunched into almost-fists, her fingers too swollen to curl properly. "What happened, Liv? I heard screams and then—"

"I don't know," Liv repeated. Speaking felt like forming words through a mouth full of cotton.

Ella whirled, catching Liv by her shoulders before her legs gave out and she collapsed to the ground. Exhaustion sagged her, and Ella eased her down until the ground bumped against her bottom and her back was massaged by the sharp ridges of bark from a nearby tree. Liv smiled up at her cousin, relief flooding through her now that they were free. Ella would know what to do. Ella would save them, now.

"Damn it, Liv," Ella swore. She tensed, and looked up, alerting to a sound Liv couldn't hear. Ella patted her shoulder, roughly, and hissed. "Someone else is here. Stay down and stay quiet. I'm going to check it out."

"You got it, boss," Liv slurred, her head lolling against the tree. It was a *good* tree. Solid and firm and able to hold her up. It smelled like cedar and salt, a familiar mix of the Oregon coast she'd missed so much when she was in Cambridge.

Ella made a strange noise and was gone. Liv saw her flitting up the hill toward the larger of the two main buildings before she lost consciousness again.

········•·····

Liv woke to the familiar scent combination of hot plastic, metal and the particular funk of old military-grade fiberglass cases. Everything around her was a drag olive green, which made sense, as she was in the back of Team Wolf's 7-ton truck. Nothing rumbled or shifted, so she was pretty certain the only thing moving was her head and the throbbing headache taking up residence inside her skull.

Someone leaned over her, their shape coalescing from fuzzy shadow into her wolf-mom's comfortable form. Liv squinted, wondering just when Rhea's hair had gone so gray in the temples. "How're you feeling?" Rhea asked.

Liv sat up, wincing. She pressed a hand to her forehead. "I feel like I was hit by a truck," she said. "What happened?"

"What do you remember?" Rhea asked, her tone guarded.

Alarm bells rang in Liv's head, in time to the pulse pounding at her temple. "Ella was leaving me to figure out what was going on? We'd been captured, and the dike blew and—" Her eyes widened. "Harry! His team!"

Rhea winced. "Harry didn't make it," she said. "But the others in the truck were able to get uphill to safety." She paused. When she continued, her words were careful, as if she was considering everything she said. "Do you feel all right, honey?"

"My head is killing me and my right knee feels like a balloon," Liv said.

"Nothing . . . out of balance?" Rhea asked. Liv shook her head. "Or . . . like you can sense something inside you that might not have been there before?"

"Mom, you're starting to worry me," Liv said. "What happened at the compound?"

Rhea patted Liv's forearm, a smile stretched tight across her teeth. "Don't worry about that just now," she said. Her tone was *not* assuring. "Just rest up. We'll be headed out this afternoon."

"What happened at the compound?" Liv repeated.

Rhea paused half-way to sitting up, and stared at Liv for a long moment. Liv wondered what her mother was thinking. She had never seen this particular expression on her mother's face: a mix of worry and determination and . . . fear? And it felt directed at *her*. "I'm not sure," Rhea said, slowly. "It looks like there was a gathering in one of the clearings at the compound, and then . . . something happened. A couple of the townsfolk here are calling in a mini-rapture, but I've never heard of people turning to salt being good in any biblical sense."

"They turned to . . . salt?" Liv asked.

"There were a couple members of the group who weren't at the gathering, and they've been convinced to come down to the valley and join the community here. The rest of the town is rebuilding after that flood," Rhea said. "We're helping out, but we lost a lot of supplies, and Tea was hurt, along with Ella. They'll be okay. We're cutting this mission short though, and headed back to the ranch."

"To the ranch?" Liv asked. "With the trucks?" Team Wolf never took the trucks to the ranch—they always dropped them off at the depot in Roseburg and headed home in their own van. Something was really wrong.

Rhea nodded, and leaned forward, gently pressing a kiss against Liv's forehead. "We can't risk them seeing you," she said.

Before Liv could ask her who *them* was, and, more importantly, what they might *see* in her, her wolf-mom was gone, hopping out of the back of the truck and letting the flap flop back into place. Liv felt sealed in more than she had captured in that shed with Ella.

Her head pounded, and she picked up the water bottle her mom had left behind and chugged the entire thing in one go. She felt a little better, but still out of sorts. Tired, but also feeling like she needed something else.

She leaned back onto the bundle of blankets—a sleeping bag and iso mat. Thankfully she hadn't been tucked in them because it was too hot for sleeping under covers in the back of the covered truck. She lifted her hands. Her sun-tanned skin was flecked with splotches of white that fell off in grainy flecks when she scratched them.

Salt.

Each speck sang silvery threads to her. Liv stretched her hand out in front of her face, splaying her fingers wide. With a little *pull*, the particles traveled up her forearm, tickling along her fingertips and then dancing in the air between her fingers like physical static. Her mouth flooded with the taste of salt and saliva, and she stared in wonder at the new sensation running through her.

The truck shifted, and Ella joined her in the back, sinking next to her and stinking of sweat and dirt. The truck rumbled, its engine starting. Liv lifted her hand, showing her cousin the salt collecting around her skin in an impossible swarm.

"Something weird happened to me," she said, twisting to look at Ella's face, scanning it for any sign of fear or alarm. Ella just looked tired. "I think I killed all those people, Els."

Ella reached forward and gripped Liv's hand tightly in her own, crushing the salt into the webbing between their fingers. "They were going to kill us," she replied.

Guilt tightened Liv's chest. "I don't—am I a monster?" she whispered.

Ella's grip tightened, clenching their skin together. "No," she said. "No more than me or any of the others of our family."

Liv knew those deaths were going to haunt her for a long, long time. How was everyone else going to look at her, knowing what she had done? "My mom—"

"She's not scared *of* you, she's scared *for* you," Ella said. "Everyone else is worried, too. It's one thing to go wolfy, it's another to be able to reduce someone down to a singular element."

"Salt is an ionic compound," Liv corrected.

Ella groaned. "You're impossible."

The truck rolled forward, sending Ella crashing into Liv before she righted herself. As they bumped down the road toward home, Liv focused on their intertwined hands. She could sense the salt in the sweat beading on Ella's forearms, and with a little effort, Liv separated the elements from each other, drawing particles of salt toward her own hand. It was hard, moving the salt from just the sweat and not Ella's body, but she did it, and looked up to see her cousin watching her with a slight smile.

"That's amazing," Ella whispered.

Liv held the newly formed crystals in the palm of her hand. They glittered, singing to her in a way nothing else ever had. "With a little more practice," Liv said quietly, "I think I could figure out a better method of desalination."

Ella groaned, and smacked Liv's shoulder. Salt scattered about them.

"Stop thinking of implications for process improvement or whatever smart shit your brain does," Ella said. "Just enjoy it. Just for a minute."

"Okay."

And, just for a minute, before the exertion sent her tumbling back into sleep, Liv delighted in the ability to separate salt from the world.

It was wicked awesome.

HIDING OUT IN OREGON
BRANDON CRILLY

Oregon, the Western Republic of America
2057 C.E.

On her knees in the dirt, forehead brushing a cracked wooden plank so she could see her target, Mikayla contemplated violence for the first time in days. Five meters of the storage shed's underside separated her from the criminal—the *thief*—she'd been hunting for days. Who just sat there, eyeing her without remorse.

"Leave him be. The damage is done."

Her target flinched at the voice behind her left shoulder but didn't run.

"That's no lesson, Dad." Mikayla shifted her baton to a two-handed grip. Her target only twitched his nose as though to taunt her. "Besides, I caught him this time."

"Have you?" her father asked mildly. She heard the smile as he shifted his feet.

That drew the target's attention, his breath visibly quickening. Mikayla tensed.

"You're also on vacation." Her father crouched low enough to see under the shed without dirtying his pants. "And he's a rabbit."

"I know he's a—"

Mikayla snapped a little too loud—or it was the slight jerk of her head that turned her cornered nemesis into a lightning bolt of thundercloud-colored fur. Old wooden lattice bordered the shed's under-side except for the one-meter gap Mikayla blocked—and a loose panel she hadn't noticed, which gave enough for him to wriggle through. She cursed and sprinted around the shed, rustling bushes the only sign of the rabbit's flight.

"Well," her father said behind her. "One can hope he's learned his lesson."

"Tell that to the half-dozen radishes he ruined today." Mikayla pushed the tops of the bushes aside with her baton, even though she knew it was futile.

"We still have plenty. Rabbits need to eat, too, you know."

She knew better than to grumble in his presence, so she settled for marching away, wondering if more cayenne in the vegetable gardens would deter her nemesis. Except she only made it three steps before finding her father standing directly in her path.

In his casual, button-down shirt—one of her favorites, in soft aquamarine—dark brown pants, and well-worn walking shoes, Leonard McNair often looked like the most unassuming college professor left on Earth. Except when he leveled his trademark look—somehow piercing and gentle simultaneously—it was almost impossible to move past until he spoke his mind. Which served him well when negotiating on behalf of one of Oregon's most successful regenerative farms, or in his genuine side gig *as* a professor.

"It's never about the rabbit, sweetheart," he said softly. "This little break of yours is starting to get to you."

"Wasn't that supposed to be the point?" Mikayla asked. "You didn't think I was going to last two days."

"I said four, and to be fair, you started noticing that rabbit's tracks on day three." Leonard pivoted on one foot, his unspoken way of letting her know she could end the conversation whenever she wished without judgment.

She held her ground instead. "Chasing one rabbit doesn't mean I'm not relaxed."

"Says the bounty hunter."

He said it wryly, but Mikayla felt her cheeks redden all the same. She'd come home to Oregon specifically to escape the never-ending nature of her job: still too many names on the UN's eco-criminal watchlists. She'd felt how one too many chases—maybe seven too many—was leaving her hollow and sore, unable to appreciate the colors of the world she fought for. Except without a target on her plate, she found one instead, since apparently turning off that part of her brain wasn't as simple as coming home.

One of her father's well-worn hands squeezed her shoulder. "Your mother and I love having you here. But we would understand—"

Mikayla shook her head and leaned into him, letting the coarseness of his hand-sewn shirt comfort her like when she was little, wanting to be an ocean diver and swim with whales. "A little more time might do me good."

Leonard grunted and gave her a quick, one-armed hug. "Perfect. There's plenty more work to keep you occupied."

·········

Even before droughts and the rising Pacific forced thousands to move further inland, Mikayla's parents planned for the inevitable influx of refugees. Not by closing off the land that had been in her mother's family for generations, but by readying it to support as many people as it sustainably could. What started as a handful of families living in a small collection of cabins expanded by hundreds of acres through grants and careful negotiation, becoming a community of homes, regenerative farmland, and everything they needed to be practically independent from the Western Republic.

Despite Mikayla's doubts, there had been almost no issues in the seven years since they formally founded the Harbor. As she walked back to her parents' house to wash up before dinner, all she saw were people grateful for somewhere to call home, who didn't balk at the expectation that they pitch in, either at the greenhouses or the river or wherever they could be most useful. She wished she could imagine the whole world like this, but unfortunately, she knew better.

The house was quiet as she went upstairs. Her childhood bedroom was much more adult and utilitarian now, the twin bed offered to someone in the first wave of arrivals and replaced with a basic single, and only a dresser and shelves for what she brought along when she visited, plus the mementos she didn't move to her quarters in Geneva. Space being at a premium, there was a standing offer for anyone to use her room when they needed, given how rarely she came home. But she knew almost no one did, out of respect for her parents.

Before changing out of her field clothes, she crossed to the closet where her equipment pack lay open. She dropped her baton inside with a sigh, wondering when a job became a habit. Her father would probably have a long treatise on that.

Shut it now and don't open it again, she told herself.

As she swung the lid shut, she noticed the orange light blinking on her comm.

She snatched it out on instinct, only to stop. *You can read it, then turn it off, right?* Except the message wasn't from Stewardship Earth. The sender used a coded account, with the subject line, *Someone dangerous in your midst*:

Ms. Ando,

We believe this man is at the Harbor. Thought the information might be of interest.

Below that was a corporate still of a grinning, tawny-skinned man with high cheekbones, green eyes glittering behind the sort of thick-framed glasses Gen Z corporate geniuses used to wear. His thick mop of curly, black hair had been styled to look casual, but the three-piece suit and glittering watch made it clear this was someone who put thought into presentation.

"No way."

SustainAble might have become notorious worldwide, but within her circles, its founder Alex Draven was almost royalty. She'd been contacted both by SustainAble execs and environmental radicals to find him over the past year. Possibly the best-known ex-CEO to totally disappear before someone could drag him in front of the UN. The idea that he could be hiding in the Harbor made absolutely no sense.

Except that in the early days, she'd caught a lot of people in transit, either between third-party safe houses or to a permanent hiding place. SustainAble's headquarters had been on this continent, meaning Draven could make it to the Harbor in one short trip. He would've had the money to disguise himself and forge an identity. And living as a refugee was a far cry from the comforts someone of his standing typically craved, even on the run.

She didn't reply to the anonymous sender. Stewardship's operations people needed to attempt a trace before she sent even a thumbs-up back. Besides, she knew it was likely one of Hodges's people, anyway.

But a confirmation trace would have to wait. If she had been on vacation anywhere else, she might have set it aside, regardless of what her dad thought about her ability to relax. But not here.

This was her home, after all.

········

The Harbor didn't have a citizenry database like a nation would. Any rejected applications for refuge were deleted, and the successful ones were stored on a single server in the Harbor's squat, octagonal utilities building. Accessing one required two permissions: one of her parents' and the person whose information was being called up.

That didn't stop Mikayla from lingering outside, patting the turnkey in her pocket. The palm-sized tech could override the server's security in a heartbeat. If she didn't find anything to back up the anonymous tip, her parents would never need to be concerned.

Unless they sense a spy in their midst, which is what I'd be.

She swore and marched off, only to see her mother six meters away.

Jaye Ando was about equal height with her husband, but whereas Leonard was stoop-shouldered and casual, she held herself straight-backed and firm like the trees she cared for. And while he couldn't shake the obvious tells of his career in academia, her jet-black hair was tied under a floral-patterned shawl that clashed beautifully with the chestnut and smoke-colored coveralls she wore in the orchard.

"The talk with your father went that badly?" she asked, adjusting the tool bucket against her hip.

"What? No." Mikayla tried to roll the uncertainty out of her shoulders. "Having a hard time relaxing today, apparently."

"Did he give you the stare?" Jaye mimicked her husband's gently piercing look so closely that Mikayla had to suppress a giggle. "I keep telling him that's a cheap move."

"Not like it's intentional." Guilt replaced the giggle, as she remembered she'd been about to break her parents' trust. Admittedly because she didn't want them to worry—but the Harbor was theirs to worry about.

"You mind looking at something for me?" She cast her comm's holographic display and swiped to a facial reconstruction she'd run before leaving the house. Her targets could usually pay for high-quality disguises, so she had the Stewardship server generate a dozen potential likenesses of Draven. "Recognize any of these guys?"

Jaye set down the bucket, eyes narrowed with the same focus she showed to a plant's biorhythms or the thrum of one of her bee colonies. "These are all the same person," she said matter-of-factly. "What's this about, Kay?"

"Hopefully nothing. Thoughts?"

"You need to spend more time meeting people." She pointed at Image Seven. "That's Alex Cardinal. He's lived here for two years."

"You're sure."

"The nose isn't exact, but close enough." Jaye's piercing stare could give Leonard's a run for his money any day. She repeated: "What's this about?"

Mikayla sighed. "The sort of thing I need to check on my own."

· · · ● ● · ● ● · · ·

According to her mom, "Alex Cardinal" came to the Harbor with a botany degree and experience, so she set him to work in the greenhouses. In the two years since, he'd done nothing except coax even healthier cucumber and zucchini to life, and then switched to tomatoes.

Mikayla waited across from Greenhouse Five as people wandered inside, starting their shift after the Sun passed its zenith. It didn't take long to spot her target, chatting with a waifish Filipino man Mikayla recognized as an early refugee but couldn't put a name to. He favored her with a nod and smile as she stepped into their path, offering her most disarming smile back.

"Mind if I borrow you for a second, Alex? Got a tree question I think you can answer."

Draven had changed his appearance less than Mikayla expected. The beard was new, naturally scruffy without a publicity team's care. The early crow's feet had likely been there before he went into hiding but masked by makeup. If one didn't expect to be standing next to one of Earth's richest men, it would be easy to not make the connection.

To his credit, he didn't try to run—but the wariness in those green eyes told her he knew exactly what this was about. "Maybe somewhere private?"

Mikayla led him around the corner to the narrow alley made between Greenhouses Five and Six, currently bathed in shadow as the Sun started to set. She half-expected Draven to try to hit her and run, but all he did was lean against the side of Five and let out a long sigh.

"You know, I've been here long enough that I thought people would stop looking. So who sent you? The enviros? Or my own people finally give me up?"

"Patting yourself on the back? Not a great idea." Mikayla stood against the other greenhouse, out of his reach, intentionally ignoring his questions. "This is my home you decided to infest, Draven."

"What, I don't even get points for ingenuity?" He flashed a charming, magazine-cover smile that made Mikayla want to gag, but he dropped it when her scowl didn't shift. "Sorry. Old habits. Listen, I know what your impulse is going to be here—"

"Impulse? Try job and training. Diminishing people isn't nice."

"I'm not here to cause any harm."

Mikayla rolled her eyes. "I read the stories about SustainAble's *meat-free enterprise.*"

Draven sagged a little further against the wall, hands on his knees. "I used to be proud of that. No, pride isn't the right word. I thought we were being ingenious, hiding the true source of our income while we tried to push environmental practices. I mean, it worked for governments buying pipelines while they passed EV subsidies."

"Save it. I'm on vacation."

As soon as Mikayla unclipped the zip ties from her belt and grabbed his wrist, Draven yelped. She twirled him around, but before she could press his wrists together and finish snapping the ties, Draven had wriggled out of her grasp. He dropped into a stance that looked vaguely like Krav Maga but then relaxed out of it, palms raised toward her.

"Just listen! I'm trying to convince you I'm not the bad guy here."

"Says half the people I bring in." Mikayla snorted. "The other half actually don't think they ever did anything wrong. Which one are you exactly?"

Draven sighed. "The kind that knows he's been a douchebag. It's not that I've *never* been a bad guy. But . . . look, just let me show you."

He marched past her, keeping a wide berth, and only her desire not to make a scene made Mikayla pocket her zip tie and follow. Inside the greenhouse, Draven led her down the furthest row of raised beds, waving and smiling to people who only gave Mikayla a polite nod. At the end of the row, he gestured at twin rows of tomato seedlings, which looked unremarkable to her other than a deeper vermilion in their stems and a rouge in their leaves that bordered on violet.

"They looked stunted."

"I know." To her surprise, Draven beamed. "Before I founded . . ." He glanced around, but there was no one in earshot. "Well, before, I worked in a food lab. Admittedly, to learn things for my—"

"Evil empire."

He acknowledged the jab with a dip of his head. "Anyway, GMOs were the focus, but we worked on how to grow in difficult climates. I've been nurturing tomatoes to grow with less water, without producing inferior fruit. These tomatoes? Four inches taller than the previous generation."

Mikayla raised her hand. "Better practices. Using your smarts for the good of humanity. 'Part of a long project that needs more time, trust me, I want to do better.' I've heard it enough times."

"But it's true. For me." When she rolled her eyes, he added, "Two years. Why would I spend two *years* working on tomatoes, if I had some ulterior plan? In what world does that make sense?"

"Hey, you're the one who raised secret cows underground."

"Look," Draven said, finally looking impatient. "I deserve whatever punishment the UN wants to throw at me. But . . ." He gestured half-heartedly at the tomatoes, as though that alone was justification for not hauling him away that instant.

To Mikayla's surprise, it made her hesitate.

In the silence, his eyebrows quirked hopefully, only to fall when her comm chirped again. This time it was from a number she recognized:

Got a good tip there's a rodent in your backyard. Eyes open. Be there soon.

"Shit," she grumbled. Tamati was another hunter contracted by Stewardship Earth. She flicked back to the tip she received, cursing herself for not checking the time stamp more closely. It arrived shortly after she reached the Harbor, and her anonymous source must not have been content waiting.

"Lie low. Someone else knows you're here."

Draven paled so noticeably his slicked hair looked jet instead of charcoal. "The UN?"

"Another hunter." Mikayla glanced around, but no one was paying them any attention. "Go home."

"Wait, why not claim my bounty first?" Draven genuinely looked puzzled. "That's the smart business move."

"I . . ." At first, she couldn't explain the hesitation. Except that with every protest Draven made, she'd noticed his desperation, and not from being caught or going to prison. As though what he was doing at the Harbor mattered to him.

Like he'd changed.

"Go home," she repeated. "Make an excuse. Until I figure things out."

He looked even more bemused hearing that, but Mikayla didn't wait around to explain.

She paused at the edge of the greenhouses, not liking the question swirling in her mind. The one that started by pointing out that she felt more like herself now than at any point since she came home. And then asked: *if* someone like Alex Draven could change, what did it mean if she couldn't?

Which was why her gut didn't want him dragged away. Yet.

• • • • • • • • • •

It took a little convincing—begging, if she was honest—to get Stewardship to activate Tamati's agency transponder and figure out how close he was. To her surprise, it pinged within kilometers of the Harbor. It didn't take long to realize what he'd done.

The sun was almost completely set when the refugees' EV caravan pulled up outside the Harbor. Long-time community members welcomed them into a ring of solar lamps, and Mikayla lurked on the edge of the courtyard until a stocky figure in a massive overcoat wandered her way.

"Glad you got my message," she said as she led Tamati between two grain silos.

"Surprised you sent it." Tamati shuffled along like he was on his way to a drug deal, broad shoulders hunched to make him seem even shorter. He'd told her once he couldn't help but present a smaller target, like he couldn't keep from glancing in every direction as he walked, trying to constantly take in three hundred-sixty degrees. "And that you didn't notice this scum first."

Mikayla coughed a fake chuckle and steered him toward the orchard—in the opposite direction of the cabin where Draven lived. "Maybe there's a reason I'm on vacation."

"Can't let the bottom feeders sap your energy." Tamati never seemed to run out of creative ways to describe his targets; being Maori, he had more reason than most to dislike them. "You look into him since you got my message?"

"Well, that's the thing." Mikayla finally stopped where the space between two storage sheds opened onto the orchard. "He isn't here."

"Beg pardon?"

Mikayla shrugged. "Your tip was wrong. Draven's not here."

Tamati's eyes narrowed, the grimace stretching his aged, ochre features. "He's not hiding under your floorboards or something?"

"Tam." She gave him a look. "You think I want to keep him for myself."

He chewed the inside of his cheek, one shoulder twitching as he likely tapped the stunner strapped to his hip. "No, you're better than that. Makes me wonder why you're lying."

"Hold on—"

"Remember when we ended up on that snipe hunt? You lined up every piece of proof you had—for yourself. With colored tabs, too, if I remember correctly." Tamati straightened, which only reminded her that he was half-again her width in pure muscle. "Where's your spreadsheet this time, Kay?"

"Can't show you what isn't here. That's like, I don't know, trying to show you a ghost."

"Maybe Draven is a ghost. Came and went, and you're embarrassed."

"That's just insulting."

Tamati took a step, grimacing when she blocked his path. "I'll be looking around, Kay. Just to be safe."

Before she could protest, someone spoke up behind her.

"Actually, I'd rather you didn't."

Her father stepped out from behind one of the apple trees. Casual as ever, hands in the pockets of the plaid jacket he wore when the nights got cool. She'd bought it for him because it had three shades each of red and gold.

"You wandered away before roll call," Leonard said mildly, as he came to a stop less than two meters from Tamati. Within striking distance, which made Mikayla's hackles shoot up.

"Dad, I can—"

"Tamati Valen D'Souza," her father said, reading from his tablet. "Fifty-one years of age. Formerly of Akaroa. Retired sergeant with the New Zealand Defense Force. Now freelancing with Stewardship Earth, specializing in the apprehension of ecological criminals and the armed and dangerous." He smirked as he looked up. "And you've fulfilled almost as many contracts as my daughter."

"Who never mentioned how well informed you are, Mister Mc-Nair," Tamati said. Mikayla noticed his right shoulder slump, as his hand fell away from his stunner.

"We like to know who enters the Harbor," Leonard replied. "Especially when certain details don't line up with our passenger manifests." He held up the tablet. "But I think we can overlook that as an honest mistake. You wanted proof?"

He tossed the tablet to Tamati, who caught it in both hands with a grunt.

"Access to our full registry. Names and photographs of every resident of the Harbor, past and present. You won't find a single person matching Alex Draven's description."

As Tamati scrolled, Leonard added, "And you can imagine that, in a place this size, a new stranger tends to stand out."

Mikayla stifled a snort, which turned into clearing her throat when Tamati glanced her way. His scowl deepened as he finished looking through the registry. "Disappointing," he muttered.

Leonard shrugged and stepped forward with one hand extended. When Tamati slapped the tablet into his palm, he leaned in a little further, and the look he gave was only a fraction more piercing than gentle.

"Transport heads back shortly," Leonard said quietly. "Sorry you came all this way for nothing."

When Tamati glanced at Mikayla, she gave him her best *told you so* look. And held it, until Tamati's slouched form disappeared between the storage buildings.

When she was sure he wasn't lurking around a corner listening, she whirled on her father. "How did you . . . ?"

"You act like I don't notice anything you're up to around here." Leonard shook his head ruefully. "But if you mean this," he added, waving the tablet, "I wiped the file. Or rather, Alex and I did."

The eco-criminal himself peeked out from behind a distant tree, stepping forward cautiously when it was clear they were alone.

Mikayla threw her hands up as he approached, hissing, "I told you to go home."

"I couldn't." Draven looked sheepishly at her father. "What if someone accused the Harbor of hiding me? That's not worth the risk."

"Surprising, who decided to be honest today," Leonard murmured.

Mikayla bit back a retort, knowing that he was right. That she owed him an apology, and more, for insisting her mother not say anything until she investigated. For not being a better daughter, who could relax and truly enjoy their company without twitching the further she got from her work.

Her father must have seen some of that on her face. "Kay," he said softly. "Not that you have anything to atone for, but if you feel like you do . . . you're welcome to when you get back."

"Get back?"

"I can't stay here." Draven shrugged. "Someone else will come. Or someone here will figure out who I am. Two years was more luck than I deserved." He straightened into the sort of firm expression she'd expect at a SustainAble board meeting. "You'd better take me in."

Mikayla looked to her father, who offered nothing back but acceptance and understanding. More than *she* deserved. Decision made, she told him, "There and back. I'll be chasing that rabbit again before you know it."

She hoped keeping that promise would mean she had changed as much as an eco-criminal could.

"So," she said to Draven, "why'd Ainsley Rayne turn on you, anyway?"

HIERARCHY OF NEED – PART III
ERNEST SOLAR & AE FAULKNER

SustainAble Corporate Offices, the Midwest Federation
2057 C.E.

"The Big Thicket?" She spat each word as if the mere syllables scorched her tongue. Ainsley crossed her slender arms. "Do I even want to know what that is?"

Edward brushed a palm over his chin, concealing the smug smirk threatening to tug at his cheeks. "It's an isolated area of the Texan Alliance. Not many people even know about it. And that's exactly the sort of cloak we want to wear right now."

"The Texan Alliance . . ." Something flashed behind her green eyes. If not excitement, perhaps challenge. "So if not many others know about this place, does that mean you have . . . connections there?"

"Ms. Rayne, that really isn't the point," Edward started, pausing as he read her reaction. A manipulative smile spread across her crimson lips, and he was determined to erase it with a quick brush of reality. "Your life is on the line. The only opportunity you should be considering right now is one that keeps your heart pumping."

"Yes, of course. We'll talk more on our little excursion." She tilted her head, unamused. "I assume we won't exactly be short on time."

"Yes, and the sooner we leave, the better. I was able to speak with Stewardship Earth last week. I explained that Mr. Draven is the acting

CEO and that's where their focus should lie. While I believe I've held them off from seeking you out, it's likely only short-term. Mikayla, or any of her cohorts, could be anywhere, including tracking your movement right now."

For just a moment, Ainsley's back stiffened. Maybe the unseen threat of being hunted breached that arrogant exterior, injecting a shot of sobriety. She smoothed her raven hair back, as if even one strand could ever be out of place.

"Fine." She blew out a frustrated sigh, waving a hand in the air as if this was some great concession on her part. "I just need an hour to run home, gather some necessities and meet you back here."

"Meet me back here?" Edward questioned, dipping his chin and raising his eyebrows. "That's not your safest bet right now. Ms. Rayne, I have been retained to protect you and that is exactly what I will do until the threat has been neutralized or eliminated."

She attempted to fold her hands in a demure manner, but Edward noticed the pinched creases in her forehead. The skin stretched thin across her white knuckles. She was holding back, anger and frustration kindling just below the surface. Edward couldn't resist having a little fun, tamping down a smile as he baited her for a snarky retort.

"Besides, Ms. Rayne, I believe my assistance would greatly benefit you as you're choosing what, and how much, to pack. For instance, I suggest you change into some practical shoes." he nodded toward her sky-high heels. "This isn't going to be an elegant stroll down the sidewalk." Edward raised his eyebrows again, awaiting the challenge that was sure to come.

Her lips pressed into a thin line, Ainsley muttered, "I am well aware of what I need to pack." When her nostrils flared, he nearly chuckled, catching the audible exhale just in time. He'd pushed enough. It was time to get her out of here.

"Speaking of packing, we should go. It will save time if I accompany you. I can wait outside your door, after I check to make sure no one's already waiting for you inside, of course." Forceful demands would never work with Ainsley. Edward knew that. Subtle suggestions were his only ally when it came to convincing her to do anything.

"Fine," she huffed. Without looking back, she marched to the conference room door and paused, a delicate hand hovering just over the handle. She turned her head and closed her eyes, sucking in a breath, as if she was bracing to say something. Pushing out a sigh, she shook her head slightly and tugged the door open.

· · · · • · • · · · ·

Edward stood at attention, impatiently tapping a foot on the black tiled floor. After sweeping Ainsley's apartment for any intruders, she promptly escorted him to the hallway to wait while she gathered her belongings.

Though he only briefly scanned each room, the many instances of unnecessary extravagance were not lost on him. An elephant figure carved from what he presumed was ivory. A teal armoire, its satin-lined door hanging open, revealing beaded bracelets, dangling necklaces and sparkling earrings.

He counted no less than five crystal vases, in varying heights, each one bursting with a colorful bouquet of fresh flowers. *Fresh flowers.*

In a time when a severe water shortage triggered world wars and the continued assault on the environment deteriorated nature's many resources, Ainsley Rayne felt a need to snip the life from precious blooms that most others would only see in artwork or aesthetic images from the past.

Edward shook his head. *No wonder she needs protection.* After what felt like half an hour, she pushed through the front door, two bags slung over each shoulder. Instinctively, he reached out, relieving her of half the weight. Without a word, he led them to the ground floor, through the concrete maze of the parking garage to the waiting car.

· · · · • · • · · · ·

"So how long of a ride will this be?" Ainsley asked, staring out the window. She didn't even wait for Edward to respond before she blurted out what she really wanted to know. "How long exactly do we have to stay in hiding? A ship can't steer itself, you know?"

"Ms. Rayne, we will stay in hiding until it is safe for you to return to the SustainAble spotlight. They'll just have to make do without you for the time being. I'm sure there are others who can take the reins in your absence."

Though she remained facing the window, Edward sensed her scowl. She radiated impatience and annoyance, hints of the fiery ball of fury sparking beneath the poised exterior. An odd urge tugged at him, to inhale the charged air her attitude ignited.

While most others might avoid even speaking to this woman unnecessarily, he was drawn to push her limits, almost craving the reaction he could trigger. It was more fun to ask what was brewing in her mind rather than letting her simmer in silence.

"Ms. Rayne, if I may ask, you've obviously risen in the organization to a leadership role. If the CEO vanished, who appointed you the acting leader in his place?"

And that did it.

Her face snapped toward Edward, a condescending sneer sliding into place. She turned a perfectly manicured finger toward her chest. "I appointed myself! I didn't climb my way to the top, I clawed my way there. And I earned every ounce of it! I'm better than all of them!"

Edward fixed his eyes on the road ahead, uninterested in scrutinizing her temporary loss of control. He'd let her marinate in any regret or embarrassment for as long as needed. After a few moments, she shifted in her seat, sitting up straighter. Inhaling a deep breath, Ainsley smoothed her hair. Restoring her usual professional demeanor, she turned to Edward, flashing him a cunning smile.

"If you'll excuse my little outburst, I'm just very . . . passionate . . . about my work."

"And that's exactly why we've got to keep you safe, Ms. Rayne. So you can return to SustainAble and get back to business." He didn't add that when she could safely step back into her life, she'd finally be out of his.

* * * * * * * * *

The seven-hour drive was mostly silent. After their initial conversation, Ainsley slumped toward the window. Edward wasn't sure at what point her eyes closed, but a faint snoring confirmed she let sleep overtake her.

The hum of the engine and churn of the tires relaxed him. For this time, at least, he had complete control of the situation without dissent—and his charge was safe. All too soon, that would come to an end.

With a sharp turn, the wheels rolled from smooth concrete to a jarring rutted path. Ainsley stirred, blinking and stretching away the grogginess. As Edward maneuvered the vehicle along the narrow route, branches clawed the doors. A few even dipped low enough to tap the roof. After a short distance, the engine slowed to a stop.

"Well, Ms. Rayne, we're almost there."

"Almost there? You stopped the car. I'd say we *are* there."

Edward shook his head slightly. Of course. She'd trust her own instincts rather than a factual statement someone else provided. He pushed the car door open and rose from his seat, eager to stretch his legs. She may be unaccustomed to following someone else, but he was in charge out here. He leaned down, meeting her eyes.

"We'll gather our bags and head to the cabins."

Without a word, she swung the door open and climbed out. Edward noticed she took no time to admire her surroundings. Singly-focused, she marched to the trunk and removed two of her bags, slinging one over each arm. Edward loaded the remaining belongings, his and hers, onto his shoulders and arms. He lowered them to the ground at her feet. She cocked an eyebrow as if daring him to challenge her to carry it all.

"I've got to hide the car. Wait here for a moment." He started the engine and slowly rolled toward a cluster of large trees with drooping branches. Within minutes the foliage seemed to swallow the metal box on wheels. He emerged, brushing stray leaves and any multi-legged stowaways from his clothing.

"So, on to the cabins." Ainsley stated, glancing around, likely in search of their destination. Unless she had some sort of extraordinary visual acuity, Edward knew she wouldn't see the basic structures from here.

"It's only a two-hour hike." Edward struggled to keep his tone even. She wouldn't appreciate the smirk behind his words.

She didn't respond, but her incredulity was as thick as the humid air hanging between them. Perhaps it was time for Ms. Rayne to learn that the world did not, in fact, bend to her every expectation or desire.

Edward maneuvered through the dense foliage effortlessly, in contrast to Ainsley's uneven trampling steps. His attempts to deflect branches from their path were futile. With each lash, her sighs grew louder, her frustration boiling over. Planting her hands on her hips, she stomped once in place.

"I shouldn't be here . . . in this overgrown jungle!" Ainsley huffed. "SustainAble needs me. Who knows where Draven is. Someone's got to take charge or everything will fall apart."

"Ms. Rayne, that's the whole point. Everyone knows Draven's disappeared. Right now it appears as though *you* are the acting CEO. If that were not the case, we wouldn't be here right now."

Pursing her lips together, she waved a hand through the air, encouraging him to continue on the path. Though she didn't initiate any further conversation, Ainsley's distaste was evident. Her random sighs and grumbles carried on the slight breeze, barely audible above the cawing birds and buzzing insects. They were in the heart of nature, embracing its honest beauty. At least he was.

Edward let his mind explore questions he would never ask. *How does one lose the innate compassion we're all born with? Why is she so laser-focused on the corporation? Doesn't she have anything else in her life?* He knew her father died when she was young, that much she shared. *But what about her mother?* Trying to slide imaginary puzzle pieces into place left him with more questions and a gnawing ache behind his temples.

Two hours felt more like four as they traversed the uneven ground. He could have reached the cabins in just over one hour if he hustled, but her clumsy pace slowed him greatly.

Finally, they reached a clearing. Sunlight poured onto the forest floor as the trees spread into an opening that led to four rustic cabins. They formed a box, each facing the one directly across from it. Edward's chest swelled as he inhaled a deep breath. No matter where his usual bed was, this was home. The isolation called to him. As long as he had the basic creature comforts, he didn't need anything else. And he wasn't going to let anyone else's attitude taint his mood.

· · · · · · · · · ·

"So what do we do here all day and all night?" She crossed her arms as if eagerly awaiting what was sure to be an inadequate response. It didn't much matter; there wasn't anything she could do to change it.

"We fish," Edward stated simply, unzipping his duffel bag. He could feel Ainsley's eyes narrowing on him. Unperturbed, he continued unpacking, sliding a stack of clothes into the wobbly dresser's drawer.

"Fish? That's it?"

"Yes, we fish and we lay low. This is a chance for you to embrace nature, Ms. Rayne. Forget about the concrete and glass for a few days and enjoy the simple wonders of fresh air and blue skies."

Reluctantly, she stacked her bags on the flimsy mattress, making no move to unpack anything.

"I'd like you to stay here while I check the other cabins, Ms. Rayne, just to be sure we don't have any unwelcome visitors. After that, I'm going to catch our dinner. It would be best if you joined me. I'd like to keep you in my sights at all times, for your own safety."

"Do you really think anyone followed us out here? Or knew we were coming and set a trap in one of these run-down shacks?"

For just a moment, he wondered if the bounty hunter was right. Maybe he should be doing the world, what was left of it, a favor by turning her in for a mental reconditioning. She narrowed those green eyes at him as the thought tickled his mind.

No. He had a job to do, and his personal feelings would not change the course.

· · • • · • · · ·

Dangling her legs over the dock, Ainsley watched Edward cast a line and slowly drag it back. His fluid movement was mesmerizing. After a few more tries, the line pulled taut. He rose to his feet, spinning the reel, drawing his prize closer.

Without turning his head, he reached back and grasped the handle of a large net. Ainsley watched with great interest as the man single-handedly raised the line and scooped the striped fish into the net. Pride washed over Edward's features as he turned to her.

"How does grilled bass sound for dinner?" he asked, though it was more of a statement.

She smirked, running her eyes up and down the flailing fish.

"Well, that might do for an appetizer. But how about I catch us a meal?" Her green eyes glinted with challenge. She couldn't resist a competition. Even if it was one she created.

Edward chuckled. "Why, Ms. Rayne, is that a genuine smile crossing your face?"

"Call me Ainsley."

"Well, Ainsley, I'll take you up on your offer," he conceded. "I'll get a fire started while you catch us a sufficient dinner. I assume you've never fished before?" He thought it was best to ease into an offer of help rather than dive into a lesson.

"No, but I'm a fast learner. And I've been watching you long enough that I can handle it."

"Alright, I'll be just across the way." He pointed to a small circle of rocks with a mound of powdery ash in the center. "If you need anything, give me a sign. I'll be able to see you." *And I will be watching,* he didn't add.

·· • • • • · · •

The next day, they awoke to a stunning sunrise and warm breeze. Edward set to work clearing away the ash from last night's fire while Ainsley organized the clothes she'd packed but not yet worn. He guessed she needed to have control over *something,* and at least the menial task kept her quiet.

As Edward turned to gather some downed branches for the morning's cooking fire, he heard a distinct snap. *We have visitors.* His adrenaline spiked as he silently cursed himself for not conducting a full perimeter check as soon as he woke up. With the speed and stealth of a deer, he dashed to the cabin while removing the pistol from the holster he always wore.

Opening the door without warning, he commanded through a hiss, "Ms. Rayne, we have company. You need to hide." Her eyes widened in fear, but she remained standing before the bed, bundles of shirts and pants piled in small stacks.

"Go as quietly as you can. Walk right into the water and hide under the dock."

Her features twisted with disgust and disbelief.

"Ms. Rayne, whoever is out there *will* find you if you stay here. Stay low and keep your face horizontal, just out of the water enough to breathe. I'll get you as soon as everything is . . . taken care of."

He grabbed her hand roughly and escorted her out the door, pressing a finger to his lips as a reminder to stay quiet. His tone and actions finally motivated her to comply. When they were a few yards from the dock, he released his grasp, nodding for her to continue. He watched for a moment to make sure she would comply with his directive. Seeing her emerge into the water, Edward darted toward the army of trees surrounding the cabins. His goal was to head off whoever was attempting to infiltrate their safe haven.

Faint, clearly human sounds drifted on the breeze. The low murmur of hushed voices. A rock shifting from an unsteady footfall. Edward fought his instincts, instead waiting and watching rather than approaching the unseen threat. Crouching behind the nearest cabin, he watched two figures emerge from the cover of foliage. They weren't even trying to hide their arrival.

Squinting past the sun's glare, Edward studied the pair: a middle-aged man with blazing red hair and a scruffy beard and a thin, gray-haired woman. Not much of a threat even though he was outnumbered. Noticing no weapons on them, Edward stepped into the open as he slipped the pistol into the belt around the small of his back. The visitors stopped in their tracks, inquisitive gazes landing on him.

· · · ● · ● · · · ·

Edward stalked to the dock, his mind reeling in shock and trepidation. Retrieving Ainsley from the water, he assured her that the threat was neutralized. He shushed the river of questions she released and simply shook his head, shuffling back to the cabin.

"I demand to know what's going on right now!" She paced, ready to erupt into a full tantrum, but he ignored it and kept going. After a moment of seething disbelief, she stomped after him.

One of the travelers stood at attention outside the cabin. He nodded toward Edward before momentarily gawking at Ainsley's drenched frame. She shot him a scathing glare.

Pausing, Edward knew she was already formulating an offensive retort. With seconds to spare before she offended the man, Edward offered a generic introduction.

"Ms. Rayne, you have a visitor, and this gentleman was kind enough to escort her here. They came a long way to speak with you. My only condition was that I remain in the room so that I can ensure your safety at all times." He hesitated before adding, "I believe this is a conversation you want to have."

As her green eyes narrowed on him and her lips quirked, readying to fire another barrage of questions, he swung the door open. Pushing past him, Ainsley strode inside impatiently. Waiting was not one of her strengths. She stopped mid-step when she recognized the older woman standing before her expectantly.

"No smile for me, dear?" Dr. Stover raised her shoulders innocently, as if the question she asked was warranted. Although her eyes landed on Ainsley's dripping hair and soaked clothes, she did not acknowledge the younger woman's current state. She casually dropped onto the flimsy mattress Edward slept on last night.

Smoothing out the wet shirt clinging to all of her curves, Ainsley cooly responded, "I have no affection for those who stand in my way or take away the only person I ever cared about."

"Still blaming me for your father's death, I see. I'd rather hoped you'd moved beyond that by now." Dr. Stover lowered her chin and raised her eyebrows in expectation of an adequate response. Ainsley crossed her arms and shifted her focus to the notched walls.

Dr. Stover rose, linking her fingers behind her back as she slowly paced.

"We've been over this a dozen times. Your father chose his fate. He had the best intentions in mind, his love for both of us. But what you want, dear, is the opposite."

Ainsley stepped forward, running furious green eyes over her mother.

"I want exactly what Daddy wanted! To take care of others. SustainAble can do that, if all of your radical followers would just back off and let us do our job!"

"SustainAble takes the easiest route for economic gain. Your father could have stolen food, but he chose an honorable path instead. An honorable path for SustainAble would be to work with nature, not against it, depleting it in the process of providing temporary solutions."

Taking Ainsley's hands within her own, Dr. Stover leaned forward, resting her forehead against her daughter's. Edward narrowed his eyes, surprised by what he considered to be a confident move. Based on what he'd witnessed thus far, he wondered how likely it was that Ainsely and Dr. Stover could bridge the gap of their severed relationship.

"Ainsley, you knew your father for eight years, and most of that was during the blur of childhood. All of the good . . . but then the bad. And I know the bad is what stuck. But I knew your father for twenty-six years. I know what he would want. And it isn't what you're doing." She shook her head, sadness radiating within her watery eyes.

"You don't know me! You don't know what I've done to make sure no one has to starve!" Ainsley hissed through clenched teeth, backing away. Edward fought the urge to rush to her. To comfort her.

"Ainsley, just think about it," Dr. Stover pleaded, pressing her palms together as if in prayer. "The world has gone to hell and it's going to take a hell of an effort if we're going to save what's left of Mother Gaia. You, my daughter, and I would be a team to be reckoned with. Together, we could make your father proud."

A single tear rolled down Ainsley's cheek. She swiped it away, pinching her eyes closed. Brushing a lock of hair behind her ear, Dr. Stover continued.

"Ain, let me in. Let *us* in. We can help you set SustainAble up to feed everyone, but in a truly sustainable way. I don't want to get rid of you. Hell, you're one of the only ones smart enough to actually pull this off. We need you."

Edward saw the moment Ainsley's will shattered. That sound of that one syllable—Ain—softened her features and slouched her shoulders. He wondered if it was a nickname from her childhood. Perhaps a reminder of the family she once had, the love she once shared.

Before Edward could reach her, Ainsley collapsed in her mother's arms, her body racking with sobs. He continued watching this intensely private moment even as Dr. Stover's voice dropped to a whisper.

"I have connections, Ainsley, to a whole network of people who can help us gain support for SustainAble and their new mission. If you're willing to lead it." The younger woman's back straightened, pride radiating in her stance.

After a few minutes, she raked fingers through her damp hair and smoothed her puffy cheeks and eyes, seemingly collecting herself.

"We can talk. I'll hear what you have to say. But the first thing I need to do is officially gain control of the corporation. I need to talk with Edward to develop a plan to contact Mr. Draven."

Dr. Stover nodded, curiosity lining her features. Did she know what her daughter was capable of? Was this a lie to further Ainsley's agenda, or was she truly willing to drive a powerhouse in the right direction—finally?

· · · · ● · ● · · · ·

Edward remained stoically silent during the discussion, but as soon as Dr. Stover excused herself, he moved to Ainsley's side.

"Did you mean what you said?" He tried to hide the distrust creeping into his thoughts.

She licked her lips and drew in a breath, uncharacteristically contemplating her response rather than just blurting it out. "I did, Edward. I did."

Their eyes met and, for the first time, a sense of genuine trust passed between them.

"Ms. Rayne, I have a call to make and I believe you should witness it. May I?" He retrieved a phone from his pocket and raised his eyebrows.

"Of course."

· · · · ● · ● · · · ·

"Well, Mother, we've got some news." A small smile crept over Ainsley's lips before she turned to her colleague. Edward stood beside her, ready to explain.

"I was able to confirm that Mr. Draven has officially resigned his position as CEO," he stated.

"Following SustainAble's organizational chart, and based on the other recent executive . . . disappearances . . . Ainsley is next in line to lead operations."

Unable to suppress her eagerness, Ainsley burst into the conversation. "Based on this new development, it's critical that we return to the office as soon as possible. As another integral employee of the corporation,

Edward can vouch for my appointment and procure official documentation."

"Ms. Rayne." Edward defaulted to the formality she tried to dissuade at one time. "Just because Mr. Draven is . . . no longer interested in his former role . . . does not make you any safer to return to work."

"But there's much work to be done, and I have a feeling if this bounty hunter learns about the direction SustainAble will be taking, she and all of her comrades will want to see me remain in my new position."

Ainsley turned toward her mother, extending a hand. Edward watched, calculating if this was truly a promise-binding handshake. The action was automatic, a fluid motion she'd probably made, mindlessly, hundreds of times in the corporate world. He was surprised when the touch didn't end with a simple release. Ainsley retracted her hand and spread her arms, inviting her mother into an embrace. As the older woman reciprocated, Ainsley spoke.

"We will be talking very soon. As soon as I'm back at the helm, negotiations will begin, and I expect you to be an integral part of them."

Emotions overtook the older woman as tears spilled down her cheeks freely. Ainsley whispered in her mother's ear, hugging her tighter. Edward turned away to allow the two women to have their moment, but he did indeed see a new side of his charge. Stepping away from the embrace, Ainsley turned to him.

"You know, this would be an ideal time for a change that may help . . . cloak my identity." She glanced toward her mother and then squared her shoulders to Edward. "From now on, I'd like to be addressed as Ainsley Stover."

Pride mirrored both women's features. With a final nod, Ainsley motioned toward the door.

"Let's gather our belongings. We leave in one hour."

· · • • · • · · · ·

Jarrett crested the slope of the ridge on the single-track game trail as he summited Jumbo Peak with Hodges. Conscious of the burn in his thighs and the quickness of his breath, he used the spectacular view of Mt. Rainier shrouded in clouds as an excuse to rest. Hodges respected his need and continued along the trail with ease. Jarrett wriggled his bare toes in the humus dirt of the forest floor. He could feel the subtle beat of ease and comfort from Gaia in such a peaceful and beautiful space. Using his enhanced vision, Jarrett took his time to enjoy the vibrant array of colors from the bellflowers and lilies that dotted the meadow.

Hodges broke the moment. "Hey kid, let's go!"

Just ahead Jarrett saw Hodges standing next to Franklin, who was sitting on a boulder facing Mt. Rainer. He took a deep breath and exhaled deeply to calm his nerves. Jarrett had never met Franklin, only heard stories of his intensity and passion for wanting to save Gaia. He believed he had the same passion, that's why he sought Hodges to join their cause. As the leader of the Barefoot Warriors and Franklin's personal bodyguard, Hodges was intimidating in his own right.

Jarrett hesitated, second thoughts invading his mind as he silently compared his own passion to that of the two men just yards away. He closed his eyes and remembered the night he spent in the filth pits below SustainAble's Central Food Production Greenhouses and the atrocity the organization was causing Gaia. His bare feet tingled as he felt the pulse of the earth. Confidently he strode toward the two advocates.

As Jarrett approached, Franklin spun around on the boulder to face him. The man looked tired. But he forced a smile that curved his lips and extended his hand. "Thank you young man for making the trek."

Jarrett returned the firm shake. "It's my pleasure to help."

Hodges clapped Jarrett's shoulder. "Franklin, Jarrett was contacted by Mikayla and was given some important information that we may need to act on quickly."

Franklin wrinkled his eyebrows in momentary confusion. He glanced at Jarrett. "Do you know Mikayla?"

"No sir."

"Then how did she know to contact you?" said Franklin.

Jarrett dropped his gaze to his dirty toes and smiled. "Because I was bare footed." He made eye contact with Franklin. "She said I must be one of those crazy Barefoot Warriors that belonged to Hodges and I could be trusted to pass on the information she had."

Hodges squeezed his shoulder.

Franklin smiled in pleasure. "What did she pass along?"

Movement over Franklin's left shoulder caught Jarrett's attention. He squinted, but couldn't recognize what he saw in the distant sky. Hodges and Franklin both turned and looked as well. They looked back at him. "Son?"

"Sorry, I thought I saw something. Maybe a bird?"

Hodges pulled out a pair of binocs and held them by his side.

"Anyway," continued Jarrett, "She said that Mr. Draven is no longer a problem. He had a change of heart and has relinquished control of SustainAble."

"Hmpf," grunted Franklin.

Hodges scanned the skyline with the binoculars. "Who's in charge of SustainAble now?"

"Ainsley Stover."

"What?" snapped Franklin.

Hodges lowered the binoculars and turned toward Franklin. "We knew she was making a play."

"But why change her name?"

Jarrett continued. "Mikayla said she is turning over a new *leaf* and changing the ways of SustainAble with the help of her mother, Dr. Rebecca Stover."

"Bullshit!" barked Franklin as he spun away from the other two men.

Jarrett raked a hand through his long brown hair and saw the object in the distant sky again. It was not a bird.

Hodges and Jarrett both waited as Franklin paced for several long moments in deep contemplation. At one point the man dropped to his knees and curled his fingers in the soil of Gaia. When he rose, Jarrett could see a sense of resignation on the leader's face.

"Hodges, they need to be eliminated."

"They?"

"Mother and daughter." Franklin looked down at his hands as if he could see the blood on them already. "They are becoming too powerful and dangerous."

Hodges nodded his head in agreement. "But Franklin, a council member removing another council member is a violation. If the Council of Nine find out, you will be removed, punishable by death."

Franklin grabbed Hodges's shoulder and whispered. "My friend, my place was lost when my daughter perished. This must be done to protect Gaia."

Hodges took a step closer and bowed his head in a whisper. "But you're a pacifist."

Franklin stood mute.

"Um," broke in Jarrett, "There's a drone monitoring us. Several, actually."

Both men spun to look out toward Mt. Rainer. Hodges brought the binocs to his eyes. "Damn, we've been compromised."

Franklin stood for a long moment in silence staring out at the horizon of Mt. Rainer. Jarrett could feel the anxiety and worry pulsating off of the man's aura. Hodges stood confidently as he awaited orders.

"Gaia help me," whispered Franklin. After a moment, he faced Hodges with a new air of confidence. "Time to relocate again," he said with a smile.

Turning to Jarrett, "Thank you Jarrett for your loyalty to Gaia and our cause. I would like for you to stay with us for a bit."

"Of course," nodded Jarrett.

The drones started to drift closer to their position.

"Hodges, after we're settled, we'll eliminate the Stovers," Franklin said, glancing at the sky, "Time to go, my friends."

Together, with Hodges and Franklin, Jarrett descended the far slope, out of sight of the drones. With each step he felt the gratitude of Gaia pulsate through the soles of his feet. At least he hoped it was gratitude. It very well could be sadness, sadness in knowing cycles of violence were about to continue.

BONE SEEDS

ERNEST SOLAR

Whidbey Island, Washington, Western Republic of America
2057 C.E.

What the hell?

The thought hung in the ether of Xylon's mind as his brain registered what lay among the debris of the forest floor. The stark white bones were a contrast to the wet, vivid, green of the bracken. Even from a distance he could tell the animal had been large. The rib cage was still intact with the spine and pelvis. He slowed his advance toward the bones, as the remains of the torso oddly resembled human remains. He paused a step away from the skeleton and soaked in the magnitude of his discovery.

Momentarily fearful of being watched, Xylon glanced around the dense forest half expecting a pair of eyes to be watching him from the branches. There were no peepers, but unseen critters and birds chirped and skittered nearby. But he couldn't shake the feeling that something was watching him. Peering up the trunks of the ancient trees reaching for the sky, he listened to them moan and rustle in the wind. The consistent and monotonous dripping of raindrops trickling from the leaves to the underbrush reminded him of the consistent moisture of the rainforest.

Confident he was alone, far from any humans, he squatted next to the skeletal remains. The rib cage was massive. Xylon was not considered a small man at six feet tall, with broad shoulders and a muscular build.

But whoever this rib cage belonged to had to be a professional wrestler or linebacker. Even the spinal cord was longer than he was tall, and the pelvis could have supported a giant of a man. The clavicle and sternum were still in place, but the limbs and skull were missing.

Xylon's gaze followed the trunk of the tree next to the remains, searching for a branch with a noose. He found none. He shook his head out of frustration. Looking for a noose felt pointless, but at the moment seemed logical. Upon closer inspection of the skeleton, he found no broken bones to indicate trauma. It was as if this human torso was dumped in the middle of the forest. However, *human* didn't seem to classify what Xylon had found. The word *giant* kept leaping to the forefront of his thoughts. Tentatively, he reached out a hand to touch the bones.

CRACK!

His hand froze over the remains.

Deer.

It was just a deer.

Xylon knew deer rarely stepped on twigs when grazing. Only in flight did the timid animal care if a twig broke under its hoof. But it wasn't a twig. It was a branch—and a loud crack. He closed his eyes in a combination of fear and concentration. His senses tingled with anticipation as he stretched himself to perceive anything. His tongue silently brushed the back of his teeth as his nose twitched for an aroma. But he only heard the patter of raindrops dripping on the leaves; even the critters and birds had gone quiet.

When in the forest, Xylon's internal clock seemed to stop. He always lost track of how long he sat among the trees or walked under the canopy. Seconds became minutes or hours became a blink. And in this moment, time ceased.

Three more breaths, then I'll move, he thought.

Inhale. Exhale.

The raindrops trickling over the leaves permeated his sense of awareness.

Inhale. Exhale.

The mold and decay of the underbrush enveloped him. His mouth opened slightly and he felt the moisture of the earth on his tongue.

Inhale.

A piercing shriek just beyond his vision shattered the silence of the forest.

Maybe out of fear or a sense of survival, Xylon was never sure, he threw himself down the wet slope of the small rise where he had found the skeletal remains. He let his body tumble through the damp decay of the earth, hoping to put as much distance between himself and the source of the shriek. He struck a massive fallen fir tree and came to an abrupt stop. He rolled over the moss-covered trunk and firmly pressed his back against the jagged surface. He stared at the bark-strewn forest floor and forced himself to exhale.

Crack!

Xylon's exhale caught in his throat.

Snap!

His lungs burned with the sensation to release the stale oxygen held captive. A moment passed. Maybe merely a handful of seconds. The forest remained eerily quiet. Xylon strained to hear a bird or even a raindrop falling from the canopy. Nothing. It was as if all the world had been muted. Slowly, he forced himself to exhale and inhale through his nostrils. The sound of his breath screamed in the silence of the forest. The acrid smell of body odor tinged the wet air passing through his nostrils. His eyebrows squinted in confusion.

Something grunted behind him.

Xylon froze. He pressed himself tighter to the fallen tree. His breath caught in his throat once again. His lungs protested. Consciously, he exhaled as softly as he could. He drew in another breath. Seconds—or minutes—passed.

A myriad of thoughts bombarded his mind as he consciously focused on the anchor of his breath. As the moments passed, Xylon steeled himself to peek over the massive deadfall.

This is why you wander the woods, he thought. *You want to see the mysteries of Mother Gaia. Be brave, dammit!*

Every rustle of a leaf or scrape of a rock sounded like a screech of heavy metal music at a rock concert as Xylon positioned himself to steal a glance over the fallen tree.

Long seconds ticked away until his forehead rested against the cold, wet moss blanketing everything in the forest, including the fallen trunk masking his location. With his fingers grasping the hair-like moss on the trunk, Xylon slowly peeked over the edge of the wood. Incomprehension struck him like a lightning bolt.

Quicker than a squirrel, he retreated. His chest constricted his lungs out of fear. His vision blurred and the forest shrunk around him. His pulse quickened; he suffocated under sensory overload in his defenseless hiding spot.

Xylon firmly pressed his eyes and forehead into the cold moss. He used the pain of the rugged bark digging into his eyelids to focus the fear shaking his body. He chanted in what he thought was a whisper.

"Whatthehell! Whatthehell! Whatthehell! Whatthehell!"

He pressed his closed eyes deeper into the moss trying to get his mind to understand. The dead bark of the tree bit deeper into his eyelids and face. His clenched fingers dug into the moss until nails started to lift from the nailbeds.

"Whatthehell. Whatthehell. Whatthehell," he continued to whisper.

Not real.

Not real.

Not real.

Tears or moss water seeped from Xylon's eyes. His stomach clenched and convulsed in protest. He squeezed his buttocks like a vice.

THUMP!

The ground shook.

"Please go . . . please go . . . please—"

Something akin to a metal vice seized Xylon's head. The pressure in his skull was unbearable. He screamed into the moss of the fallen tree. He grabbed whatever was crushing his scalp with both hands.

"Oh God no!" He moaned and vomited against the dead tree.

The acidic smell of his vomit assaulted his nose and stung his eyes. The massive hand palming Xylon's head lifted him off the ground as if he was a pebble. He clawed at it in a vain attempt to escape. The creature holding him grasped both ankles and flung him over its shoulder like a sack of potatoes. His head struck the rump of the giant creature, which felt solid as petrified wood. Stars and blackness swirled before him. In his fading view, a spindle-legged creature picked up the skeletal torso he had found only moments before. Cradling the bones, the creature turned and gracefully climbed the forested mountain slope beside the one carrying him.

On the shoulder of the creature, Xylon saw a young man with green tinted-skin and long dark hair watching him. Within a few strides through the dense forest, his world went black.

· · · ● · ● · · ·

Xylon awoke with a throb in his head, his face downturned in the damp soil. He could feel the fir needles digging into his forehead, cheeks, and chin. Memories of how he came to be face-first in a bed of damp needles flashed through his mind. Afraid to move, he squeezed his eyes shut tight, trying to block out the thoughts racing through his brain.

Was that a man riding on the shoulders of that creature?
Impossible!

He compressed his eyes tighter in thought.

But the creature was massive. Big enough for a man to ride.

Xylon pressed his forehead deeper into the fir needles and pebbles on the ground. The images of the young man astride the creature peering at him with vivid green eyes kept flashing through his mind like a film caught in a loop.

In the void above his prone body came cracks, snaps, creaks, and thuds. The sounds reminded him of towering trees sweeping against each other in the wind. Xylon always thought of those sounds as the trees communicating with one another. As he listened to the echoes, he recognized a cadence between the creaks, snaps, and screeches. With each passing moment he distinguished two variations to the cadence of sounds. The snaps, cracks, and thuds were deeper in tone. The creaks and screeches were a higher tone. Together, it made him wonder if he was listening to a conversation.

Sliding his forehead along the ground, the jagged pebbles and pine needles dug into his skin. He squinted his eyes to the pinprick of pain. He wanted to maneuver just enough, without being noticed, to catch a glimpse of whatever grabbed him. A flash of the creatures and then the man's green eyes and tinted green skin skipped through his mind. He grinded his teeth together and tightened his jaw muscles to keep the memory and myriad of questions from overwhelming his thoughts.

Were they even creatures? Is that the right term? Animals? Beings? They weren't human. The green man was, but . . . the other things were creatures. What scared him more? The man? Or the creatures?

The questions overwhelmed Xylon. He needed to pull himself from his panicked thoughts and focus on the present moment. He breathed in through his nose and smelled the damp leaves and mold of the forest. He scraped the ground with his fingertips to feel the earth beneath him. The snaps and creaks of the trees punctuated the chirps of the birds. His mouth tasted dry, with flakes of bark on his tongue. He needed to open his eyes.

No!

Fear consumed him.

RUN!

The word exploded in Xylon's brain. All he needed to do was get up and run as fast as he could. It would take his captors, the creatures, by surprise. He pictured throwing himself into the thickness of the forest. Barreling through the underbrush like a warthog. Bouncing off trees like a monkey. Rolling down the slope like a runaway avalanche. Throwing himself over objects. He wouldn't care about the pain. He could heal later. Escape was a must.

Escape?

Doubt overwhelmed him as images of the creatures flashed through his mind. The way the second creature gracefully moved through the underbrush before he passed out. Then he remembered the man sitting on the creature's shoulder watching him with abject curiosity, as if he was a repulsive beetle or an inexplicable oddity. He squinted his eyes tighter to force the thought and doubts from his racing mind.

Yes. I'll just run!

He pressed the palm of his hands into the cool, damp earth. He tilted his forehead slightly against the rough edges of the pebbles to use his head as extra leverage as he propelled himself forward.

On the third exhale I'll run!

Inhale. Exhale.

Crack. Crick. Snap.

Inhale. Exhale.

Creak. Creak. Screech. Creak. Squeak.

Inhale.

Exhale.

Xylon shot off the ground like a rocket from earth trying to reach Mars. His fingers dug into the earth, throwing clumps behind him like a bull. He felt the tiny pebbles of stone bite into his forehead, protesting his escape plan as the extra leverage propelled his momentum forward. His left knee bent and the corresponding foot struck the ground. He brought his right leg up; something tightened around his ankle and calf like a boa constrictor preparing his meal.

"GAH!"

The force of the hold on his ankle brought him down hard. Open-mouthed, he crashed back to the earth. His teeth dug into the mixture of moss, pebbles, and dirt. He twisted his body and saw a rooted vine wrapped around his lower leg. He tried to jerk his leg free, but it was frozen, as if superglued to the earth.

Behind him, came a deep *crack crack crack crack*.

Just below the deep repetitive cracks, he heard the distinct laugher of a human. He arched his head back and stared at a canopy of trees. Among the branches of one tree sat the green-skinned man, laughing.

Xylon collapsed in resignation.

Moments passed before he pushed himself to his elbows and then a sitting position. He rubbed a hand over his face to brush away the debris of the ground. He spat out the mud and moss invading his mouth when he struck the ground on his failed flight attempt. He glanced at the vine wrapped around his lower leg. With each attempt at movement, the vine twitched and tightened. After a few moments of stillness the vine loosened its grip. Nearby leaves rustled slightly.

A second vine creeped toward Xylon. He jerked his free leg away, but the vine attached to his leg cinched tighter. The invading vine stopped. He eyed it. He was pretty sure the second vine would shoot out like a viper if he made another sudden move.

Then a thought popped into his mind.

The forest was alive.

Mother Gaia was real!

Resigned to his situation, Xylon sat with his eyes closed for a long time, assessing his feelings. The silence of the forest was deafening, but it allowed his inner thoughts to settle. Slowly his situational awareness returned. The chirp of a bird drifted to his ears. A rustle of a branch. A squeak of a chipmunk. It was the crack of a branch that brought him back to his current reality. He intentionally twitched his bound leg and felt the root tighten in response.

Gaia is real, he thought. *Gaia has awakened.*

The thought filled him with a sense of joy and wonder. He hadn't wasted his time, like everyone believed.

If the forest was 'alive,' then there really must be Awakened.

All the hours of research, news feeds, and podcasts rushed through his mind like a runaway train. The Awakened, Gaia, Earth fighting back against the humans polluting her world. He'd seen the most recent stories of a woman throwing air at a protest, but that video had certainly been faked. Or maybe not. The story about metal moose protecting the forests of Michigan in the Midwestern Federation, the religious zealot controlling flowers, the woman that could control twisters, the other woman who could convince the Earth to grow food . . .

And the werewolves! They were all real.

With renewed energy and purpose, Xylon leaned forward and massaged his legs. He reached for his toes. The guarding root twitched when he peeked at it. He sat up in a dignified posture and breathed.

Inhale. Exhale.

With courage he was unaware he possessed and with an attempt to act unconcerned, he turned to peer at the creatures he knew were behind him.

Not creatures.

Trees.

Battle of the Trees. He remembered reading something about a company trying to claim fresh water at a memorial park in Oregon, but they'd been repelled by trees. In the lore developed over the years around the Awakened, it became known as the *Battle of the Trees* because it was believed the trees came alive and defended themselves. Most people called him crazy for believing because "these events are never caught on camera, how could they be real?" But he'd always felt the truth in his bones.

Xylon blinked once. Then twice. Then squinted. Then he saw them. Three of them, staring at him in silence. Two trees and the green man. He held his gaze and breath as his brain comprehended what was before him.

The taller of the two creatures tilted its head with a slight groan of wood. The dark eyes soaked Xylon in from under thick, pale-green mossy eyebrows. Its equally shaggy, mossy-gray beard wriggled as a smile stretched across thin lips. Xylon had no way of knowing if the creature was male, but it exuded traditional caricatures of masculinity. His arms were as thick as mature boughs of a birch, which tapered to hands with three twig-like appendages. The torso was hard to distinguish due to the amount of foliage wrapped around the creature. His legs were no more than spindles of knotted wood ending in claw-like protrusions of roots. Xylon must have been staring because the creature waggled his root toes at him. The second creature laughed with the sound of rustling leaves.

The second creature was beautiful and regal. Compared to her "male" counterpart—for lack of a better way to differentiate them—she was the size of a lean, young mountain rhododendron. Her large, kind eyes were a triangle shape of fuchsia. Her lips, thin and delicate as gossamer wings. Her limbs were lithe and supple. Outside of her striking eyes the leaves on her back rose behind her almond-shaped head like a pair of wings. For a flash, he imagined her gliding through the moonlit forest watching over her kind.

The green man was gone. Xylon scanned the branches but found no trace of him.

The male tree broke the silence of the forest with the sound of a small twig snapping. On the forest floor, between Xylon and the trees, waited a pile of nuts and berries on a flat stone. The tree nodded its moss-covered head to the edible offering. Xylon's stomach growled in acceptance with a hand drifting to his midsection.

How could I be hungry? he thought. *I just ate an hour ago, didn't I?*

He peered at the sky. The sun was further along toward the horizon than he expected.

How long was I out?

Another twig snapped.

Xylon peered at the creatures, realizing they weren't actually breaking twigs, rather communicating in their own language. He glanced at the root wrapped around his leg. It slowly untangled itself and slipped away. But the second root coiled like a viper, waiting to strike.

Conscious of the audience, Xylon shifted closer to the nourishment. Taking one at a time, he savored the texture and nutrients of the small gifts. He ate in silence as they watched him chew. Together, Xylon and the trees sat in a clearing ringed by mature trees of such varieties that he couldn't even begin to describe each of the species. Near the center of the meadow were three half-rotten stumps, two of them jagged and splintered with fresh wood as if the long-vanished trunks were snapped from their foundation. The third trunk was cut smooth from a saw. On top of the smooth stump lay the skeletal remains Xylon discovered earlier that morning.

Savoring the last berry, he stood. The viper root struck. The smooth bark bit into his ankle and calf, viciously yanking him to the ground. He caught himself in a push-up position before his face struck a large oblong, rounded stone.

"Come on!" Xylon barked at the ground—partly in fear, but mostly in frustration.

He violently tugged his leg away from the viper root. The root just as aggressively dragged Xylon several feet across the clearing. The rocks and roots in the earth dug into his palms and fingertips as he clutched at the dry clumps of grass. Fire lanced his forehead and cheeks as the dry ground tore at his face.

Reacting to the stinging pain, he shot a look at the larger tree with the gray beard. "I'm curious. I just wanted to stand and look around."

Graybeard—Xylon had decided to call him that—blinked in silence.

Xylon pressed his forehead to the ground until the granulated dirt dug deeper into his skin. He audibly exhaled. He pushed back to a kneeling position. He forcefully sighed. "Can you call off your pit viper?"

The viper root squeezed Xylon's leg tighter. He looked toward the thick gray clouds drifting by with little care to his circumstances. For a prolonged moment, he watched the heavy rain-laden clouds slowly float toward the eastern horizon. He was sure it was going to rain soon. He could taste the moisture on his dirt-covered lips. As soon as the thought crossed his mind, sprinkles of mist peppered his upturned face. He closed his eyes and slowly exhaled as he let the ground beneath him support his weight. With each drop of rain a wave of acceptance baptized him in the moment.

Speaking to the clouds, he conceded. "I know I can't escape." Looking at Graybeard, Xylon all but whispered, "And I don't want to escape. I'm curious."

Graybeard stared at him for a long time. The drops of rain periodically fell on Xylon and the leaves of the trees as he waited for a response in measured silence.

The creature groaned like a tree swaying in the wind. The viper root released Xylon's leg and shrunk back into the underbrush.

Xylon stood. "Thank you."

A thin curve of what Xylon thought was a smile stretched across the smaller tree-creature's face. Tulip. She reminded him of a tulip.

Graybeard unfolded spindle legs and gracefully stood. The creature extended to his full height. Xylon leaned back slightly with his head tilted all the way back. He estimated the creature was at least four times taller than his six-foot frame. Tulip stood as well. She was only twice his height. But it amazed Xylon how both creatures were able to compress themselves while sitting. Actually, they weren't that tall when he first saw them. Almost as if the creatures could understand his thoughts, they both shrunk to his height with the sound of rustling leaves.

Graybeard strode off toward the tree line of the meadow. Xylon watched as the creature moved among the trees with a graceful, fluid movement. It was as if he melded and mingled with each tree he encountered. Xylon would momentarily lose recognition of Graybeard amongst each individual tree. Then the creature would step back into the meadow with its bough-like arms tussling the branches of the trees as if he was rustling the hair of a small child.

Snap. Crack. Pop.

Xylon spun on his heels toward the cracking sound. Tulip was by the stump with the bones. She was breaking the bones of the skeleton he had found. With more confidence than expected, he moved over to the creature. She paused momentarily to make eye contact with him before cracking another rib in half.

If that thing starts to suck the marrow from the bones, I'm outta here.

Behind him came the soft sounds of swaying grass. He looked over his shoulder, finding the viper root a few feet away and ready to strike. The realization dawned on him.

In a whisper he uttered, "They can understand my thoughts."

The viper root shook as if it was indicating "No." Then it relaxed and submerged its striking end into the soil.

"What?"

He turned back to Tulip. Her hand rested over her chest where Xylon's heart would be. He mimicked the motion and thought for a moment while the two mirrored each other.

"You feel my heart?"

Tulip tilted her head at an angle and smirked.

"Love?"

She tilted her head to the other side.

Xylon continued to stare at her as the words *heart* and *love* ricocheted through his mind.

Sounds almost treehuggish.

Tulip's smile stretched slightly more. Then it came to him.

"Intention."

Tulip straightened her head with a large smile and nodded in agreement.

"You can feel my intention."

A shiver coursed through his body at the acknowledgment of his statement, coalescing and humming at the base of his throat. He swallowed several times as his heart rate increased in anticipation.

Tulip groaned and nodded toward Graybeard. He half-turned, barely recognizing the creature in the tree line. His heart eased and the tickle in his throat passed through the cells of his body as Graybeard moved off to visit another tree. Understanding blossomed within Xylon.

Turning back to Tulip, he whispered, "And I can feel your intention."

Tulip smiled. She glanced back down at the bones and cracked another. Then the dainty creature brushed away the moss and leaves hanging from her torso to reveal a layer of bark. Along the flank, a chunk of bark was missing. In the missing space was a rib bone. Instinctually, Xylon leaned forward, his mind comprehending what he was witnessing. When recognition dawned, he straightened in shock. His eyes shifted back and forth from the rib bone underneath Tulip's bark and the bones on the stump. An unbelievable thought flowered in his mind.

Moving toward the bones on the stump with excited curiosity, he questioned, "This is from one of your kind?"

Tulip nodded yes.

Stepping back toward Tulip he stretched out his hand. His fingers twitched in anticipation. Tentatively, Xylon touched the bark near the rent in Tulip's side.

"You have bones just like me?"

Tulip nodded again with a rustle of leaves.

Reaching out to touch the rough texture against his fingertips, Xylon soaked in the bark, moss, leaves, and branches covering Tulip's body. More to himself than Tulip, he whispered. "You're a tree-based entity. A Tree-Folk. An Elemental. A type of faerie folk."

The tickle of sensation at the base of his throat burst for a moment and then faded.

"Are all trees creatures like you?" asked Xylon.

Tulip cracked another rib from the sternum laying on the stump. Her delicate mouth frowned.

"I suppose not," answered Xylon. "If all trees were like yourself and your friend, we, I mean humans, would already know about your kind."

He glanced toward the tree line to find Graybeard. It took him a few moments to distinguish the creature from the other trees. Keeping his eyes on Graybeard, he commented, "It must be pretty easy to remain elusive to humans."

He turned back to Tulip as she cracked another bone.

"At least in this modern world. So many of us are distracted by technology or lost in our own thoughts." Xylon's throat tingled with a sense of confirmation. "Or hardly ever walk through the few remaining forests anymore."

A sadness from the tree line rippled over his body. He considered the trees, but could not find Graybeard. He turned back to Tulip and watched as her delicate twig-like fingers snapped the pelvic bone in half.

"Why me?"

Tulip peered at Xylon with her lime-green eyes. They closed. A handful of silent breaths passed as he waited for some type of response. Then, a loud rustle of leaves blowing in a gale wind shattered the quiet stillness of the forest. He turned to see Graybeard stepping from a clump of saplings with the green man.

Striding across the meadow, he only wore old tattered jeans too short for his long legs. Dark green hair shrouded the man's face in shadow. As he moved closer, Xylon realized the man was closer in age to a teenager than an adult, but his lean, muscular frame hinted at a long life of physical activity.

"Welcome," said the green man, "In your world, my name would be Sage. I am the reason why."

"I'm Xylon," he responded as he stared at the man.

Snap. Creak. Rustle.

Crack!

The tree sounds and snapping of bone pulled Xylon from his dumbfounded stare. He glanced at Tulip. Her lime-green eyes crinkled at the corners in a smile.

"Who are you?" Xylon asked Sage.

Sage peered into the canopy of trees surrounding the meadow and then toward Tulip. "We are the trees."

A warm shiver fluttered in Xylon's heart and throat. He stood in silent contemplation as Sage moved to assist Tulip in separating the bones of their kin. Graybeard weaved in and out of the forest with the grace of a mountain lion.

Then Graybeard appeared in front of him as sudden as a hummingbird. The tree reached out its long branch-like fingers to take Xylon's hand. He followed the graceful tree to the sawed-off stump. Sage joined them as silent as a moth.

Graybeard gently brushed bone chips off the smooth surface. He watched the small chips flutter to the ground like snowflakes. The tree pointed to the bones Tulip cradled in her branches and then back to the sawed-off stump. Graybeard motioned to one of the splintered, jagged stumps and then to himself.

Xylon gently touched the stump with reverence as if he was touching a friend's deceased body at a funeral. Then he understood—the torso bones Tulip and Graybeard recovered belonged to the stump. A sense of validation rippled through his throat.

He looked at Sage. "The bones are from this tree?"

Sage solemnly nodded his head in acknowledgement.

"When we are cut with a saw, we can never re-attach," said Sage.

Graybeard moved toward a jagged stump, carefully and methodically situating himself on its base. For a moment, he rested. Xylon watched as roots, bark, and branches curled themselves around Graybeard's torso until he was as indistinguishable as any other mature tree in the forest.

In awe, Xylon moved to Graybeard's side and gently placed his hands upon the rough bark of the weathered creature.

"If we are not cut, we can detach and re-attach at will," said Sage.

The pronoun *we* burst into Xylon's mind. He spun to face Sage. "Are you an evolved species of this type of tree?"

Sage peered at Graybeard. "No, I am not a tree. I am only human like you, but I was raised by them. They are my family."

"How?" asked Xylon.

Sage's dark emerald eyes peered into Xylon's. "As my Uncle Peat told me, my mother was pregnant with me when she passed. She was buried in a seed pod. The trees sensed my life force through the soil and nourished me in her womb through the roots of the forest."

In awe disbelief Xylon whispered, "You're an Awakened."

Sage barked out a laugh. "No, I am just a part of Gaia's forest. The 'Awakened' label is created by humans; it means nothing to Earth itself."

Graybeard's leaves and branches rustled with an intensity that mimicked a vicious wind storm. Sage placed a hand upon Graybeard's bark in an effort to soothe the creature. A leaf floated down past the two men, landing on the mutilated, sawed-off tree stump. Xylon noticed the bone chips Graybeard had swept off the trunk had sunk into the moist soil. He squatted down and watched as small, green shoots of growth broke through the surface of the earth.

"The bone chips?" Xylon said, pausing to look for the right word. "Are seeds."

"Yes," confirmed Sage.

In the clearing, Tulip squatted with her branch-like legs sticking out in various directions like an overgrown rose bush. With her delicate branch fingers she dug a trench in the earth and shook the cracked bones from the skeleton over the shallow trench. Small white flakes from the marrow of the bone drifted to the surface of the soil like falling flower petals. Then Tulip covered the shallow trench with soil and foliage.

Tulip glanced at the sky. Her lime-green eyes crinkled at the corners into a smile. Thick black clouds blew in from the west. Tulip scurried on her two legs like a spider to another bare spot. Hurriedly, she dug another trench, repeated the process, and then moved on to another spot.

Xylon felt the urgency in Tulip's actions. She wanted the bone seeds planted before the rain came. He recalled many occasions when he and Chi would anxiously race to plant new trees and flowers in their yard before a rainstorm. He moved beside her and offered to help. She hesitated and looked toward Sage. Sage moved to join them. Then, with the creaks and snaps of broken twigs and the rustle of leaves, Tulip indicated the burial pattern.

Xylon smiled and nodded in understanding. Tulip gave both men a third of the bones. Together they finished burying the seeds throughout the barren field as the sun dipped below the horizon and small drops of rain fell to the ground like tears.

Just before the last rays of the day's sun vanished, Tulip moved to the second jagged trunk near Graybeard. Graybeard's massive body gently swayed in the winds of the growing storm. The branches and leaves rustled a calming melody, tingling Xylon's throat fluttering his heart. Tulip reached out and gently stroked both Xylon's and Sage's faces with her delicate twig fingers. Then she motioned for Xylon to rest against her trunk.

"I will," whispered Xylon. "I want to watch you first."

Tulip's reddish purple eyes shifted toward a soft pink and slowly blinked in acquiescence. Then she climbed onto the stump. Roots, vines, bark, branches, and leaves immediately swarmed over her delicate body as she settled on the stump. In moments Tulip's body was synonymous to any other tree in the forest. But he could still see her beautiful lime-green eyes peering through the foliage. They crinkled as a large canopy of branches formed over his head, shielding him from the steady drops of rain.

Sage skillfully ascended Graybeard's branches as Xylon settled against Tulip's trunk. A layer of moss wiggled over him like a blanket. The viper root curled up on his lap like a sleeping kitten, and a lavender flower stretched down from the canopy to rest on his shoulder, its fragrance intoxicating. The muscles in his body relaxed, his eyes grew heavy, and his breathing slowed.

Sleep enveloped him.

"Thank you," he whispered to the rustling trees singing him to sleep.

Xylon felt a soft shake and blinked his eyes into awareness. Sage squatted in front of him with a broad grin stretched across his green-tinted face.

"It is time for us to leave."

Xylon smiled and sat up from his reclined position against the tree. "Leave?"

"Yes, I want to show you my home forest," said Sage.

"You do?"

Sage stood. "Yes. The trees and my uncle both think it would be a good idea for me to learn from a contemporary in age."

Xylon laughed. "How old are you?"

Sage shrugged with a smile. "Not sure, but trees age slower than humans."

Sage stuck out his hand to help Xylon up. "Come, see what you helped to create."

Tulip's branches creaked, and Graybeard's leaves rustled. Xylon peered into both canopies and smiled. He then gently picked up the tangle of roots from his lap and placed it on a bed of leaves as if it was a sleeping pet. Grasping Sage's hand, he rose from the ground as he casually rested a hand on Tulip's trunk. Bark vibrated; leaves shivered. Sage glanced at the shaking tree and seemed to shiver himself before walking off. Knowing Sage would understand, Xylon pressed his forehead to the bark and breathed. He then moved to Graybeard and lightly brushed the bark. The tree groaned and moaned as it swayed. Behind Xylon, Sage encouragingly said, "Come on, tree-hugger."

Xylon smiled and turned away from the two Elementals and froze in his tracks at the sight of hundreds of new saplings peppering the once-barren meadow. Tears stung his eyes as they welled under the rims.

"It's nice to see a new growth of trees in this meadow," Sage commented with a smile.

In a reverent whisper as to not wake a baby, Xylon added, "Mother Gaia is amazing."

"Hmmm," agreed Sage.

Xylon squatted to the ground and touched the delicate trunk of one of the saplings and whispered to it. "Trees are immortal, they never really die naturally. But you aren't just a tree. You are all Elementals."

Both Xylon's and Sage's chests and throats thrummed in pleasure. The future was uncertain, but Xylon was ready for it, by Sage's side. Whatever the green man was, Awakened or not, stirrings inside himself made Xylon feel as if he were now the same.

Human, but not.

Tree, but not.

Their bones were made of different stuff, but together they would plant the same seeds.

THE DECAY OF ROSES

S.E. MACCREADY

Appalachia
2058 C.E.

Moss tickled Briar's ankles as she crept along the forest floor.

She didn't know why she was sneaking, and she didn't know why she was doing it *now*, when the sun was about to set. But she did know she had a feeling there was someone . . . or some*thing* . . . she needed to see.

So here she was, crawling along the dirt floor, letting moss guide her, illuminated only by the setting sun.

She wasn't used to the way plants acted around her. Years ago in Georgia, she discovered she had an ability to bring them back to life. Vegetables, flowers, fruit—anything with roots. She even summoned a field of wildflowers. At the time, she didn't question it. She was *starving*. But once she got some food in her stomach, and once she looked around and noticed she hadn't dreamed it all, she realized it was more than a little bit odd.

Disorientation will do that to someone. The questions always come later.

Perched on a cliff face, Briar unslung her pack and nestled it between her knees. She dug out a jar of water, sipping from it carefully as she gazed down in the valley.

Moss, again, tickled her ankle.

She brushed away the sensation with a dirty hand.

Deep in the valley loomed a mining town. It was a ramshackle collection of buildings reclaimed by nature, most charred beyond recognition. She raised a hand, blocking the sun, squinting through the haze. Whatever happened to this town, there wasn't much left. She took another sip of water, letting it sit in her mouth before she swallowed.

The tolling of a bell carried across the valley.

The center building was mostly untouched. But from this distance, she couldn't make out many details. It was made of white wood, with a tall steeple in the front—that much she was sure of.

Carefully, she wrapped a spare shirt around the jar of water, nestling it between two others. Glass was easy to keep clean, easy to fill and, in a pinch, you could use it to cook.

Problem was, it was fragile. She'd lost a lot of glass jars over the years.

From the front pocket of her pack, she pulled out her black holotape. Its plastic coating was scratched and faded, mostly due to her trek north.

She lightly brushed her thumb over the power button—there was only enough battery for a few more plays of the recorded conversation with her sister.

Pressing the button, she said, "Tell me what you're thinking, Rosie."

"You always know what I'm thinking," the recorded voice answered. Then, "That one looks like a snake."

"They all look like snakes." Briar leaned forward, staring down the cliff face. Deep in the valley, smoke rose, thick black plumes reaching toward the sky.

Moss tickled her ankle.

She swallowed. "Do you remember what mom used to tell us?"

Rosie's projection shook her head, a grin twisted onto her lips.

She had been so innocent.

"She always told us we were flowers," Briar said. "Pretty as pictures. I always thought we were more like weeds."

"*Weeds?* We're not weeds."

"We can grow anywhere. Do anything. And when they stomp us out, we come back with a vengeance."

Smoke trailed higher into the sky. The bell continued to ring.

Sighing, Rosie stretched her fingers toward the sky, as if outlining the smoke. "It's been so long since I've seen a flower. Do you think they're out there somewhere?"

Briar didn't answer; she knew the recorded conversation was over. She'd replayed it hundreds of times over the years. Rosie's lines never changed. Sometimes Briar played along, sometimes she didn't.

Most days, she didn't play it at all.

After powering off the holotape, Briar shoved it back into the small front pocket of her pack.

She let the moss guide her.

·· · ·•·•·· ·· ·

Fresh tire tracks edged the town on its western border. Briar picked her way over them, stepping carefully through loose soil and rock. They were settled deep, as if by something large and heavy. If she had to guess, maybe a construction vehicle of some sort.

But why would there be construction in a decommissioned mining town?

Leaving the tracks behind her, she crept further along the road.

As she'd noticed from the cliff, the outer buildings were husks.

For a moment, she imagined what this place may have looked like. A small town, nestled between the mountains, with a sheet of fog hovering above. She could *almost* see white picket fences, enclosing yards where children played.

But she also knew this town had a secret.

She felt it as she stepped around fence posts and ducked under collapsing awnings. The closer she drew to the center of the town, the less damage there was, as if whatever ate at this city never made it far enough to destroy it entirely.

She stopped behind the old church.

Even though the bell no longer tolled, she felt the echoes of it through the trees. The harshness in the way it cut the air, disturbed the silence, commanded the mountains. It needed to be heard. Obeyed.

But something fought back.

Briar rolled her shoulders, squeezing her eyes closed.

Fought back against what?

Then she smelled the smoke, and remembered.

Something here was burning.

A glance around confirmed it wasn't any of the buildings—that damage was old. Whatever fire ate through this town, it happened a long time ago—maybe even while she was still down south. She trailed her fingers over the burnt wood. It was smooth, almost glassy. The fire had burned hot.

But this was a *mining* town.

And somewhere, coal burned.

Creeping around the church, she stopped beside a window. It was propped open with an old hymnal, spine holding the weight of the glass. The cover was dusty and sun-bleached, but fresh fingerprints smeared the grime.

A strong gust of wind rattled the window. A leaf landed on the windowsill.

Was she supposed to go inside?

Standing on her tiptoes, she peered into the church. Someone had to be around, the tolling bell told her as much. But as she glanced around, she discovered only crooked pews and a deteriorating pulpit.

There wasn't a soul to be seen.

She eyed the opening; was it wide enough for both her and her pack? She wasn't willing to leave behind the few jars she had left. What if she had to run, and couldn't circle back? She slipped her pack from her shoulders, dangled it through the window, and carefully dropped it to the church floor.

She hoped her jars were wrapped well enough.

Pausing, she made sure nobody heard her pack land. All was quiet.

She pulled herself up, hands finding purchase on the rough wood. She knew she'd have splinters. But in only a few moments, she was dropping to the church floor, landing next to her pack. She slid it back onto her shoulders, reclipping the extra belt across her chest.

Now what?

Aside from those pews and the pulpit, there wasn't much here. A few tattered bibles were scattered across the floor, mixed with old announcements and molded communion wafers. At the back of the church was what used to be an office, but the door was barely hanging on the hinges, and the room's contents were gone. Stopping in the small foyer, she spied the cord dangling from the ceiling, directly under where the steeple would be. She didn't see any stairs, or a ladder, or *any* way to get up there, if it were even meant to be accessible.

But if whomever rang the bell is the same person who propped the window open, where were they now?

She was called to the church, meant to find something. Problem was, she didn't have a clue what that was.

She was about to give up and leave when she saw it.

Writing, ever so faint, on the wall behind the pulpit, etched below the remains of a crumbling wooden cross.

A shiver ran along her spine.

Was this what she was supposed to find?

Another leaf blew in through the open window. Caught in the wind it drifted to the back of the church, landing just below the writing.

Briar quirked an eyebrow. But over the years, she'd learned to just go with it.

She walked forward.

The writing was faded; it was nothing more than barely discernible scratches in the walls. But in the right light, and at the right angle, she could still make them out.

The Bramble Society knows what you did here.

She had no idea what that meant.

Was it referencing the fire? Or, was this society *responsible* for the fire? Either way, she didn't know how she was meant to find out.

Because when nobody's around to talk about them, secrets tend to remain hidden.

• • • • • • • • • •

Briar remained in the church well past dark, wrapped in a tattered sweater and the smell of smoke.

In one hand, she toyed with the holotape, rubbing her fingers along the cracked surface, absently wondering how many plays she had left. In her other hand, she held a handful of nuts she'd scavenged from the forest on the way here. They didn't taste like much, but they quelled her hunger pangs well enough. She supposed that was all she could hope for—when something edible was found, in the *wild*, of all places, it was best not to be picky.

If it came to it, she knew the location of the closest greenhouses. Or, she could bring new life to an abandoned family garden. Problem was, there weren't many of those left, and she hadn't earned a meal voucher in years.

She dropped the rest of the nuts into her pack and stared at the holotape for only a moment before zipping it into the front pocket.

Over the years, she'd honed her rules. Travel at night—unless in immediate danger. Don't stray too far into cities—except for the promise of food. Don't answer any questions—but she learned information can also be currency. And the last rule? Keep moving.

That one hadn't changed much.

She pulled herself to her feet, tugging her pack with her. It was lighter than usual, reminding her she still needed to refill her jars. Unfortunately for her, they didn't last long when full, and every few days she was searching for a trustworthy stream. Telling which ones were safe was easy—safe water drew animals, and the plants that grew along them always seemed brighter than others.

She usually found mushrooms nearby, too.

After glancing once more around the church, she silently dropped her pack out the window, waited a moment, and then slipped out after it.

Because of her rules, she was most comfortable traveling at night, with the moon and stars as her guide. She drifted through the town without fear of being spotted, using shadows for concealment, and knowing how easily her silhouette could be concealed, if it ever came to it. The human outline was the most recognizable shape. But at night, with enough background noise, she could be just another tree, or fence post, or crumbling remains of a front door.

At night, she became anything she wanted.

So she crept away from the church, past dilapidated houses, under crumbling roofs, and through the remains of streets, heading toward where the smoke smelled the strongest.

What she discovered was the opening of a mineshaft.

Her brow twisted in confusion—were the mines on fire? But as she stepped through the opening, she realized the truth of it.

The coal underneath the town was burning, and the smoke escaped through any opening it could find. Each step further was dangerous, but she needed to be sure. How long had it been burning? Was there any way to stop it?

What did this mean for the people who lived here?

Then she froze, catching herself with a hand on the tunnel wall.

Would a fire spreading from the town be enough to ignite the mines?

She wanted to shake the thought away. No, she didn't think it was possible. The town was a surface fire; the mines were hundreds of feet below the surface. But there was a lot she didn't understand, and nature always found a way to surprise her.

After removing the scrap of fabric securing her hair, she draped it over her mouth and nose, tucking it behind her ears.

She walked forward.

· · • • · • • · · ·

As she walked, Briar lost track of time. There was something here to discover, just as she was sure something directed her to this place. She descended into the mines, careful of her footing, searching for any sign of explanation.

Around the next corner, she found it.

A man's body was slumped against the wall, mining helmet carelessly tossed to the side. She approached him, already knowing he was gone.

What was he doing so deep in the mine?

Why was he alone?

She knew his death wasn't recent. Had he lived here?

Clasped in his bony hand, she noticed the holotape.

She instantly thought of her own, tucked safely in her pack. But she knew she wouldn't find Rosie on this recording.

Was this what she was meant to find?

She hesitated for only a second before prying the holotape from the man's hand.

A surge of anticipation rushed through her. This was it. This was what she was meant to find.

But why?

She dropped the tape into the pocket with Rosie's, turned away from the body, and rushed back to the surface, leaving all smells of smoke and decay lingering behind her.

· · • • · • • · ·

Briar returned to the church, the place where she felt safest, content that whoever propped the window open wasn't around.

She didn't plan on staying long enough to be sure.

Rule four: keep moving.

She removed her makeshift mask, retying the coils of her red hair out of her face.

After nestling her pack on the remains of a pew, she lifted the new holotape from its hiding place. It wasn't as damaged as Rosie's. In fact, it barely even looked used. Its black paint was smooth and unblemished. The writing on the buttons was legible. She wondered, once she played the message, if she would be able to transfer the battery pack to her own holotape—then she wouldn't worry about the looming end to Rosie's conversation.

But she already knew attempting to switch the batteries meant risking destroying both.

It was nice to have the option, though. If she ever grew desperate enough.

She perched on the edge of an overturned pew, sat the new holotape beside her, and pressed play.

The man from the tunnel flickered to life in front of her.

He leaned against an unpictured wall, staring at the helmet he held in his hands. With a sigh, he threw the helmet away from him. Once out of his hand, it disappeared from the recording.

"If you found this," he murmured, "then that means I failed, and I'm dead." He brushed a hand through his hair, smearing soot across his forehead. Then, he chased away sweat with the back of the same hand. He sighed again. "This wasn't supposed to happen. It was a perfect plan, meticulously calculated, supposed to buy just a little more time." He seemed to stare right through Briar as he spoke, focused on whatever he faced as he recorded. "They burned the town, when we . . . when we fought back. When we realized we were getting sick. It was the water, I think. Contaminated with their runoff. They were only supposed to take a little coal, but they worked faster and faster, until it was too late to stop them."

A shattering cough worked from his chest. He bent over, cradling his head in his hands.

"Sorry," he said, waving a hand in Briar's direction. Then he snorted, saying, "I don't even know who I'm apologizing to. Guess it doesn't matter."

With a deep, shaky breath, he collected himself. "They burned our town," he repeated, "so I burned their coal. In hindsight, it wasn't my smartest decision." He smirked. "Suppose anger does that to a person. It was only supposed to be a little bit, to send a message." He gestured vaguely around himself. "But it got out of hand. Obviously."

He rested his head on the invisible wall. "I left them a message in the church, to let them know what they did won't go unpunished. The sickness has me, though. I won't be able to see it through. Maybe *you* can," he said, pointing in Briar's direction. "Whoever you are. I've heard of some special people. If you made it all the way down here to me, well, maybe you're one of them. So at least I have that right now. Hope. Or at least a semblance of it."

The holotape cut out.

She knew recorded messages weren't long—the little tapes could only store so much information. But she found herself wishing the man had said more; she didn't even know his name, couldn't provide a proper burial.

Now, removing the battery didn't feel right. This was all that was left of him. His last words. Removing it felt a lot like destroying him.

Even knowing what was on the tape, she was still confused why she was directed here. She discovered the cause of the fire, discovered why the mines burned.

What was she supposed to *do*?

She had no way to stop the mines from burning. And the man was vague in his message—she didn't know who was responsible for the town's destruction.

Wind rustled leaves outside the church window.

She searched the tree line, looking for anything out of place.

Her eyes fell on one shape, and it looked strangely human.

......·..··

By the time Briar collected her pack and strapped it to her back, the shape was gone.

She still hadn't found any trace of whomever propped the window open; the prints on the hymnal were too recent for it to be the man from the holotape. Someone else had been here recently, but they hadn't ventured into the mines, hadn't discovered the holotape. She did a lap around the church, looking for anything she may have missed earlier. Aside from a few hymnal pages—one of which was titled *Amazing Grace*—she didn't find anything of note.

Picking her way past charred buildings, she knew whoever peered from the trees was already gone. But as she reached the spot where she'd seen the shadow, she found no trace of them. No footprints. No broken branches. No disturbed vegetation.

It was as if nobody had been there at all.

Wind rustled the leaves above her; they tore free of their branches and drifted away from the town, deeper into the forest.

Moss tickled her ankles.

Without a second thought, she took a step forward, following the trail of floating leaves.

......·..··

The sun was rising by the time Briar stumbled upon the city.

Golden light filtered through the treetops, glittering off the dewy forest floor. She snuck to the edge of the tree line, lifting branches out of her way to get a better look. Unlike the mining town, this city was in great shape. It was a collection of newly constructed buildings—lumber was piled sporadically throughout the city—all nestled along freshly paved streets, baking under the early morning sun. These streets were jet black, shiny, and they washed out the green world surrounding them.

At the far edge of the city was a factory, spewing black smoke high into the sky. Were these the plumes she'd seen from the cliff? She carefully lowered the branch, escaping behind the curtain of trees.

Venturing into the city would break two of her rules: only travel at night, and don't stray too far into cities.

But even as she made that realization, she knew she was going to ignore her rules. There was something in the city she needed to find, needed to see, needed to *stop*.

Why? She didn't know.

What? She had no clue.

When? Now.

Making note of the nearby landscape, she stepped over the edge of the forest, eyes trained on the city.

As she drew closer, she smelled the asphalt first. Chemical and acrid, the harshness of it had her securing her makeshift mask into place. Her hair tumbled over her shoulders, occasionally drifting on wayward breezes. Red hair, like Rosie's. Pretty as pictures, their mother used to say.

Briar shook away the memory.

When she reached the buildings, she noted their emptiness. While they'd been fully constructed, as far as she could tell, they were empty. Many of the doors still leaned against the houses, as if the final step was securing them in place. She paused, glancing at one house, then across the street at another. They looked exactly the same. Same white siding, same black roof, same metal mailbox along the street.

Then she spotted the billboard, rising ahead of her. She squinted through the bright sun, reading: "SustainAble Housing, at No Cost to You."

There's always a cost, Briar thought bitterly.

She passed the same house at least ten more times as she walked toward the factory. Its smoke blew away from the city, but the smell was still strong, mixing with asphalt and mud.

At an intersection in the road, she looked left, then right, finding the same houses dotting each street. Ahead was a bridge, and a freshly paved road leading toward the factory. A light gust of wind nudged her back.

Forward, then. Whatever.

She paused halfway over the bridge, glancing below her. The banks of the river were higher than necessary for the water cutting through it. Leaning over the railing, she stared at the shallow water. Each bank was empty, made entirely of mud and smooth rock.

Weird.

She stepped to the other side of the bridge, finding the same scene below her. Weak river, no vegetation.

Very weird.

Rivers were ecosystems, harboring many freshwater fish and wetland plants. Many wild grasses claimed riverbanks as their homes, providing havens for insects.

But here, there was nothing. A sterile river, and no sign of life. There *used* to be life, judging from the smooth rock. It wasn't a new river, dug out when the development was built.

Something killed it.

Continuing along the bridge, she edged toward the factory. It towered in front of her, made of new red brick, surrounded by tall iron link fencing. The gate was open. In the lot were three black SUVs, construction vehicles, and another sign advertising SustainAble.

She paused at the gate, stomach knotting.

A destroyed mining town. Coal, burning hundreds of feet below her. The promise of free housing. Contaminated water.

She didn't like where this was going.

But where were the people who owned these vehicles?

Picking her way slowly through the lot, she peered into each SUV before passing it. Each was as empty as the rest of the town. The factory door loomed ahead; two panels of black glass, edged with metal.

She hesitated.

Wind, again, brushed her back.

The door was unlocked. She carefully pulled it open, then gently nudged it closed behind her.

A deep breath settled her nerves.

Voices carried down the long, wide hallway. She followed the sound, worn shoes barely making a noise against the concrete floor.

"And when will they be done?" A woman asked.

"This time next month," a man answered. "Still rerouting the water."

"I saw water on the way in. Use *that*."

"No, ma'am," the man said. "Contaminated, from the fires. Violates safety codes."

"Only if we know about it."

"Pardon?"

"Only if we know about it," the woman repeated. "You're already a month behind schedule. I was supposed to have families move in last week. You want to push it another month because of *water*?"

A pause. "I can't sign off until clean water is routed. I know someone who can draw up plans for treatment, I'll give him a call this afternoon."

"Do you have any idea how much water treatment costs? How long it will *take*? There isn't room in the budget to invest in *another* new plant, nor do I have the time to wait for it."

"You would willingly poison people just to make a deadline?" the man asked slowly.

"They're living here for free, their payment for working in the factory. *Living* here, not *drinking* here. Water isn't part of the deal, nor am I obligated to give it to them."

"They'd drink it and die. Who'd work your factory then?"

The woman chuckled. "Lots of people need a place to live. Either you do it, or I'll hire someone else. Either way, that's how it's going to happen."

Briar's stomach churned as understanding rushed her. All the people preparing to move here were going to die. The contaminated water from the ablaze mines would poison them, and it'd be the mining town all over again. A town rampant with sickness, until there was nobody left.

This was what she was meant to discover. History, repeating itself.

·· • • · • • • · ·

Rage.

As Briar picked her way back to the forest, she felt only rage. It collected in the tall tree trunks, spread through spindly branches, and plummeted to the ground as leaves. Moss clawed her ankles as she broke through the trees; birdsong halted as she spun back toward the city; that distant river seemed to freeze, suspended in the second it took for her to make her decision.

They would never learn.

She would make them understand.

Burning coal fueled her as she knelt, pressing her fingers deep into the bracken. Heat climbed. Her breaths slowed.

And in the center of the city, the earth split.

Vines and leaves erupted from the sinkhole, darting toward houses and crashing through windows. The asphalt streets sank into the earth, swallowed by the burning mine below.

It was not enough.

But nature was done bargaining.

She dug her hands deeper, reaching for roots. Vines tore the siding from the houses, pulled walls from their supports. When the houses were nothing but shells, she destroyed those, too. Nature consumed the city, overtook the streets, and burned what fell.

New growth sprouted where houses once stood. Fields of wildflowers were the new streets. Wild rose bushes, stems thick with thorns, were the fences. Saplings crawled toward the sky, each second, to them, a new year.

Still, it was not enough.

In the distance, two people ran from the factory. The man and woman stared around them in shock.

Then vines consumed the billboard, dropping the remains into the earth.

Fire consumed. And when it was done burning, new life grew.

She understood. A necessary sacrifice.

The crack webbed toward the factory. Inside the building, an alarm rang. The man and woman ran toward an SUV. Silently, she hoped the man chose another.

She hoped.

She hoped.

But sometimes hope wasn't enough.

As they climbed into the same vehicle, racing at the promise of salvation, the ground beneath split, spilling them into the burning mine.

She watched them fall. She watched the factory crumble. And when all was gone, she watched as nature reclaimed.

· · · ● · ● · · · ·

Peace.

With the sun high in the sky, Briar felt peace.

She reclined against a tree trunk, pack at her side, jar of water in her hand. She sipped leisurely but carefully, knowing water took time to heal.

Any nearby sources of water were contaminated. In time, they would support life again. But she had a choice to make.

Where to go now?

She dug out Rosie's holotape, thumb hovering over the play button.

"Tell me what you're thinking, Rosie."

She pressed the button.

Her sister came to life, projected from the holotape. "You always know what I'm thinking." She pointed in the distance at the remains of the city. "That one looks like a snake."

Briar smiled. "They all look like snakes. Do you remember what mom used to tell us?"

Rosie shook her head, but a grin twisted her lips. A small, content grin. Innocent.

"She used to tell us we were like flowers. You the rose, and me, the thorn, there to look after you. I'm sorry I couldn't save you."

Rosie chuckled. Not in response to what Briar said, but because that was all the recording knew to do.

"I should have been with you," Briar murmured, then remembered where the conversation was going. "But we were always more like weeds."

"*Weeds*? We're not weeds."

"We grow anywhere. And when they try to get rid of us, we fight back."

Rosie sighed, stretching her narrow fingers toward the clear blue sky. "It's been so long since I've seen a flower. Do you think—"

The holotape cut out.

Briar expected as much, knew there wasn't much battery left. She stared where her sister had been only a second before.

She knew it was goodbye.

It was always going to be goodbye.

And like the water, Briar knew that, in time, she too would heal.

She tucked the holotape in her pack, then zipped the pocket shut, securing the two tapes inside.

Her fingers froze on the zipper.

Two lives. She'd taken two lives.

She glanced over her shoulder, back the way she'd came, remembering rows upon rows of empty houses.

Houses waiting to be filled.

Was taking two lives worth saving hundreds? Who decided when a sacrifice was worth it?

Who decided when a sacrifice was necessary?

Nobody, she realized. It was no longer up to humanity. It wasn't her decision to make. And in the moment, she hadn't realized a decision was being made.

It was nature, claiming its toll, demanding its price.

She released the zipper, then splayed her fingers on the forest floor. They trembled on the dirt.

Two lives. She chased away the thought. *Not up to her.*

Rosie would have known what to say, what to do. She'd tried to say so much, when she could. Attended the conferences. Picketed the dig sites, the mines, the empty forests. But this world wasn't made by people like her sister, and she wasn't convinced it was made *for* people like herself.

People like she *used* to be. The ones on the sidelines, looking away while humanity ripped and tore.

Were those two lives her penance?

Her price to pay?

Briar knew there would be more, and she knew it was too late to stop it. Maybe if she'd been more like Rosie, she wouldn't be in this position at all.

Her penance. Her payment.

Her punishment.

She slung her pack over her shoulder, clipped the extra belt across her chest, and started walking. She didn't know where, or for what, but had a feeling she would get where she needed to go.

To where she was needed most. A few weeks ago, in a rare moment of checking one of her secure chat internet apps at a library, she'd received word of a protest up in Columbus. Maybe she'd join for good trouble.

Along the forest floor, moss bowed out of her way.

GAIA'S EXALTATION

C. D. TAVENOR

Columbus, Ohio, the Midwest Federation
2058 C.E.

Months upon months of planning, all culminating in the next forty-eight hours.

It had taken thousands of emails. Hundreds of phone calls, both video and audio. Dozens of in-person meetings, at the Bent Greens and in other places.

Their goal locally—mass disruption and protest of the North American Summit on Carbon Management. Their goal internationally—mass protest and demonstration of Awakened powers worldwide.

For that was the action Natalie knew was necessary. She had first felt the need to showcase the gift given to her by Gaia on the streets of Washington D.C., but she had lacked focus then. She'd lacked strategy. But her time in Albany High Security crystalized the need for concerted, coordinated action between everyone they could muster.

And they had mustered quite a few friends to join them.

Her phone buzzed with message after message as hundreds of organizers, many of them Awakened, confirmed their plans were ready to execute. Stories would unfold across the planet, consistently revealing the truth spoken of in hushed whispers for far too long. Natalie's role was one part amongst many, alongside the many others joining her in Columbus and those acting worldwide.

Three others, in particular, joined her in the small coffee shop in Franklinton, the Columbus neighborhood across the Scioto River from downtown proper. Only a few hours remained before thousands of people would descend upon the Summit's expo at the Columbus Convention Center and its treaty meeting at the Ohio Statehouse. Only a few hours remained to mentally prepare for what came next.

"I can't believe we're finally here," Claire said. "When I got your call last year, I didn't know what to expect. But here we are."

Natalie smiled. "It's been a long road. For all of us. On our separate paths, on our separate journeys."

Ben's face was grim. "I simply wish at least one delegate, or politician, or someone would have joined us. To have someone in power on our side."

"The truth is, I think your message is stronger without a politician's fingerprints on it." Jordan leaned back in his chair and sipped the steaming mug in his hands. "You all did this. Not some politician. You did. Everyone's stories, including my own, they've led to a moment like this. To the next two days. What comes next is a question for after."

"Future politicians might be in this crowd," Natalie said. "Future visionaries, future leaders ready to overtake the mistakes of past generations."

"And that was what people have said for decades about each generation engaged in mass movements," Ben mused. "What will make this group different?"

Claire shrugged. "Maybe things won't change. But if we don't try, they certainly won't."

Ben nodded. "You all know I'm in agreement here, my pessimistic heart is just slipping out as we reach the end of all this. I'm excited to see if we finally hit the mark."

"If things go as planned," Jordan said, "I think we'll be surprised. Our legal observer team is ready for anything, though. Ready for it all."

"That's great to—" A call to Natalie's watch interrupted her thought. She looked down at the caller ID, and her eyebrows raised involuntarily. "It's . . . no, that can't be. It says its Ainsley Rayne."

"Excuse me, but what the fuck?" Claire exclaimed. "This has to be a trap. Her press conference last year was a bunch of propaganda nonsense. All greenwashing."

"I think you should take it," Ben said, barely above a whisper. "Can't hurt to hear what she has to say."

Natalie nodded. She understood Claire's feelings about SustainAble, especially given the company's ties to some of the groups who'd hurt the other woman and her friends. Regardless, she clicked the green answer button on her watch, sending the call to her bluetooth earpiece. "Natalie Vorn speaking. To whom am I speaking?"

"Natalie Vorn, head of the World's Revolution?"

"To whom am I speaking?"

Claire stifled a chuckle from across the table—Natalie raised an eyebrow at her but didn't say a word.

"Apologies, yes. My name is Ainsley Stover, CEO of SustainAble."

Oh right. Natalie had forgotten about the woman's public name change, also discussed in last year's press conference.

"Let's not waste any time here," continued Ainsley. "I have an offer for you that I think you'll want to consider. Here's the short of it—I'd like to meet you in person. I'd like to offer you and your organization the support and resources of SustainAble. I can explain more face to face."

There were many words Natalie might have predicted the CEO of SustainAble would string together, but those particular words were not on the list. "Excuse my skepticism, but why should I trust you at all? Why should I take this offer seriously in any way whatsoever?"

"It would be easier to explain in person," Ainsley replied. "It's too impersonal over the phone right now."

"I'm a bit busy at the moment."

"I'm not far. I know you're in Columbus. Everyone of importance on this continent is in Columbus this week. Your planned protest has been shared far and wide on the feeds. This meeting will take an hour of your time."

"Can you hold for a moment?" Natalie asked.

"Yes, that's fine, but it is imperative that we have this conversation. "

"Thank you." Natalie muted her watch. "She wants me to meet her in person. Today, I think. Which seems crazy, but . . . part of me thinks I should take it. This is too insane of a coincidence, for this call to be made on this day."

"You finally turning spiritual on us?" Claire asked.

"A few people have been rubbing off on me," Natalie said.

"Regardless, I'm skeptical, as you said right off the bat." Claire shook her head. "Jordan, tell me this smells sus to you as well."

"It does, but . . ." Jordan frowned.

"But I think I agree with Nat here," said Ben. "We should take the meeting. We'll record it and live stream it to a private feed in case something goes wrong. Does this sound too good to be true? Yes. Is it probably too good to be true? Yes. But if it's not . . ."

"We can't pass it up, I get it," said Claire. "All right, I agree."

"As do I," said Jordan.

Natalie pursed her lips then nodded. "All right, here goes nothing."

Her next words were either going to spell doom for their plans this week—or potentially change the work cut out for them entirely in too many good ways. After a deep breath, Natalie unmuted her watch. "I will meet with you on two conditions: I can bring a partner, and we can record the meeting."

"Deal." Ainsley's response came more quickly than Natalie anticipated. Too quick seemed the wrong way to describe it—more desperate than calculated.

"Then where should we meet you?"

• • • • • • • • • •

The sign into the museum exhibit read "Oceans," its white paint worn and faded, revealing the seafoam blue beneath. Found inside Columbus's Center of Science and Industry, the rendezvous location was oddly poetic. Why not meet within an exhibit devoted to educating families about the ocean?

If only it had succeeded in convincing enough people to go beyond learning.

The science center closed at 5pm, but SustainAble was having a special event after hours in the building's massive event space, and with their event came the perk of a few exhibits being open to event attendees. Thus, Natalie and Ben found themselves walking into the exhibit in fancy dress clothes, masquerading as important dignitaries attending the corporate gala. They'd small talked with a few non-profit execs who believed they were in the business of saving the world before escaping away to meet Ainsley.

Inside the exhibit, dim lights revealed fantastic sculptures of famous ocean imagery, including a giant relief of Poseidon. Plaques on the wall spouted ocean facts. Fish tanks in a back room featured aquatic life from across the world. The exhibit even featured a live research station maintained by local university doctorate candidates.

Their destination was in the back of the exhibit, where a miniature submarine hung above a tank of water. When the exhibit was fully live, visitors could squeeze into the sub to see its inner complexity, but right now, the room was dark save for a single emergency exit light in the corner. There, leaning against the wall, stood a woman, a woman who could be none other than Ainsley Stover.

The wordless walk across the room felt like hours, but eventually Natalie felt close enough. Ainsley looked less intimidating in person than she sounded on the phone or appeared on feeds. Something about her demeanor had shifted. Her eyes looked more certain in their conviction, but somehow softer. A few meters away, Natalie stopped and said, "We're here. We're ready to hear your offer."

"First, I'd like to make sure you know I'm serious," Ainsley said. "To make sure you know I'm trustworthy."

The exit door opened; a person in a dark, hooded coat stepped inside. Once the door closed, the figure slid back the hood, revealing someone Natalie had not expected to be here.

Natalie couldn't hold back her gasp. "Doctor Stover?"

"It's good to see you, Natalie. And you, Ben." Rebecca Stover smiled grimly. "Perhaps you never put the pieces together, but yes, Ainsley is my daughter."

Anger immediately burned in her heart, but Natalie pushed the emotions down. She could process hidden secrets later. For now, she needed to understand the implications of having a member of the Council of Nine in the room. The World's Revolution network had coordinated tangentially with the organization, but they rarely saw eye to eye on theories of change. But she did trust Doctor Stover, and her research . . .

"I feel like this is some sort of trick," Ben said. "Why bring us here? Why the subterfuge?"

"My board is always watching," Ainsley said. "They are hell-bent on opposing the changes I'm trying to institute. I am fully committed to a new path. This was the only way. The only way to make my proposal."

"And I am here to verify the authenticity of her offer," said Rebecca. "We've been working on it together for months."

"Then out with it," Natalie said. "We're here. We have no reason to trust you. So tell us what it is you intend."

"I have mulled it over for far too long—what needs to be done to right the wrongs, both of my company, and of so many others," Ainsley said. "I want SustainAble to be fully turned over to the people. No conditions. Transformed into a democratically operated company, owned by its workers and regulated by a board elected by the people like your World's Revolution. Something needs to change. This is my idea."

"You're kidding," Ben said.

Natalie glanced at him, his deadpan face likely matching her own stunned expression.

"She is definitely not kidding," said Rebecca. "We have copious contracts for you to consider, policies to explore supporting, a host of other communications strategies tailor-made to hand the world's largest sustainability corporation over to the people who deserve to decide its fate."

"What's in it for you?" Natalie asked. "What do you get out of it? No corporate executive has ever done something like this out of the goodness of their heart. What is it you want? A future presidential bid? Your own private foundation? What are you gunning for?"

The CEO sniffled. "I get it. I would be lying if I said the former Ainsley wouldn't question this offer too. I get it. What I'm proposing here is unprecedented. But it's real."

Ben eyed Natalie, as if asking for permission to say more. She was too stunned to say more than her chain of questions, so she nodded.

He nodded in reply. "All right, let's say we're interested. What is your ask of us? What is it you want of us?"

"I want you and your Awakened fighting to ensure this vision becomes a reality."

"We aren't an army." Natalie crossed her arms. "We can't just order a bunch of people to become soldiers for a corporation that's truly destroyed their lives for decades."

"Think of the signal it would send the world," Rebecca retorted. "Awakened, part of a never-before-seen corporate revolution. It would—"

Two quick pops sliced the conversation in two, followed by a cloud of red mist forming in the air. Both Ainsley and her mother crumpled against the wall and slid to ground, blood seeping from their chests.

"What the fuck!" Ben exclaimed. He whipped around, and Natalie followed suit. Far across the exhibit, A sniper fled.

Natalie quickly looked back at the two women—both appeared completely lifeless, as lifeless as Ainsley's dreams now were, shattered by an assassin.

An assassin.

Natalie didn't hesitate a moment longer; she sprinted out of the exhibit after the fleeing armed assailant.

"No! We should leave now," Ben exclaimed, running a few steps behind. "We are in incredible danger just being here."

"We must know who targeted them," Natalie said. "Who is our enemy here?"

"Isn't it obvious? They told us. It's their board."

"Then what if they try to pin it on us? We need those weapons as proof."

Ben didn't say another word, and she took that as acquiescence. Using a burst of air, she flew herself across the exhibit, turned around, and pulled Ben quickly along. She looked to the side quickly enough to see the sniper pushing open a door into a stairwell a few dozen feet away.

"Let's go," she said. "We can catch them, easy."

"I'm not of much use in this fight," he said. "Lack of water and all."

"Hopefully it doesn't come down to much of a fight." She slammed into the door and leapt five steps downward at a time. It was a staff stairwell, with signs pointing toward the Center's underground garage. A metallic clang a few flights below signaled the shooters slipping into the garage itself. Two more leaps down flights of stairs brought Natalie to the same doorway, just as the door closed.

She pushed it open with a burst of air, revealing the foe fleeing on foot through a mostly empty lot. Stepping into the garage, she reached out with her mind to sense the billions upon billions of air molecules in the room, down to the air embracing the two cowards. She visualized their gun ripping from the straps holding it to the sniper's back; with a clatter, the weapon fell to the cement.

The figure skidded to a stop and turned around, moving to pick up the weapon, and a second figure ran out from behind a van. Instead, Natalie grabbed both of them in the air and pulled them across the parking lot. She flung them to the ground a few meters away as Ben jogged up from behind.

"You're truly terrifying sometimes, you know that right?" he said.

"Don't remind me," she replied. And she meant it. Whenever someone said that sort of comment, she remembered Sacramento.

The duo on the ground said nothing; she thought they were trembling. It didn't matter—she pulled back their hoods with a simple breeze.

The revelation startled her more than Rebecca Stover's presence earlier.

"Hodges?" He'd been the sniper. "Franklin?" She threw her hands upward in exasperation. "No. What is this nonsense? Are the two of you working with SustainAble?"

"Seriously, what the *fuck* is happening?" Ben's anger bellowed through his words.

"We didn't know it was you they were meeting with, we swear!" Franklin kept his hands on the concrete.

"We invited you to this city for a protest, and you used it as cover for an assassination?" Natalie couldn't help it. She started to prepare to suck the air from their lungs. Franklin gasped.

"Don't," Ben said, resting a hand on her shoulder. "Don't."

She released her anger, and Franklin breathed deeply again. "Thank you," she whispered to Ben. His hand fell from her shoulder.

"I feel like you should be proud of us," Franklin said. "We were listening to Gaia, like we were supposed to. The Stovers had too much power. They had to be taken out."

"That sounds like you were substituting your own opinion in for the will of this movement," Natalie snapped. "Assassinating her here? In *this* moment? With everything we have planned? Do you know what this means?"

Truth be told, Natalie had no idea what it meant. How would it impact security surrounding the protest tomorrow? Would they be seen as linked at all? That remained to be seen.

"It was worth it," Franklin said. Hodges remained silent, staring at the ground.

"I'm surprised to hear those words from you, of all people," Ben said. "How was this a peaceful act?"

"Necessary act. For the future."

"Bullshit." Ben spat. "You—you know what, it doesn't even matter. I don't care what happens to the two of you. But know I'll be making sure every organizer knows to shut you out. You're black listed. No more. You've put *everyone's* lives at risk. Here in Columbus, and across the world. You think they won't want revenge? You think they won't hesitate to take it out on protestors tomorrow?"

Natlie's watch chimed—a note from Claire asking how it was going.

"We should leave," Ben said. "These two aren't worth our time."

She wanted to say more. She wanted to learn why they'd done it, but now that her feelings had settled even a tiny bit, she realized it didn't matter. They'd taken action on their own, ignoring the possibilities of what Ainsley's conversion might represent. The duo were connected with the Council of Nine—they must have known what the Stovers were considering. And they'd let their doubt push them too far.

"Your fate from this act is yours alone to resolve," Natalie said. "We won't help you. May this murder be a stain on your souls."

Just as the deaths in Sacramento were a stain upon her own.

· · • • · • • • ·

Walking the streets of the city, the next morning, it felt surreal. Bicycle cops silently patrolled alleyways. Spotters already patrolled the roofs of buildings, including the statehouse and nearby city hall. Patrol cars slowly prowled, and barricades already blocked the steps of both buildings.

Normally the seat of Ohio's General Assembly—and periodically the Midwest Federation's Senate—for the week the statehouse welcomed the delegations from across North America while other events occurred at the Convention Center a mile to the north. Different organizers coordinated different actions at both locations at different times in an effort to spread police resources thin. Another march was already launching from the Scioto Mile. For now, the statehouse was quiet, but the crowds would arrive eventually. The marches would converge and diverge at random moments in an intentionally chaotic spiderweb of mass uprising.

Amidst it all, Natalie waited, sitting in a coffee shop located across High Street from the white-domed building. She absent-mindedly scrolled her news feed, briefly pausing to read articles discussing the "enhanced security measures" employed following the mysterious killing of Ainsley Stover. There'd been talk of canceling the summit entirely, but the Midwest Federation's Senate President had made clear that "the Summit was still to continue" and that "police would be ready to respond to any violence instigated by outside agitators but would respect the right of free speech." It was the same classic rhetoric that said nothing at all—and of course never criticized cops for instigating violence. But Natalie didn't expect anything else from a political leader of the Midwest Federation.

A text from Jordan confirmed their worst suspicions—military units sat in reserve inside the parking garage beneath the statehouse. Today's action had the potential to go wildly wrong wildly fast.

But they had to try.

Natalie had to try.

Minutes of waiting turned to hours as she continued mulling over her role—and continued contemplating Hodges's actions. It had been a profoundly rash, idiotic choice—but she understood their instinct to act. They acted out of fear. Fear that things could have been different. And Natalie had felt the same fear—she had been close to accepting Stover's offer while fully believing it to be a farce. She would have accepted because she ultimately believed their actions today were doomed to fail.

Yet they were fighting back nevertheless, their voices joining millions worldwide. Still, Natalie could imagine a world where she'd pursued action similar to Franklin and Hodges. She couldn't fully blame them for their choice, but she could hold them responsible for its impact.

Anyone hurt today because of cops now more jumpy as a result of the murder . . . their blood would be on the hands of Franklin et al.

She heard them before she saw them—a march shuffled by, thousands strong, its chants brimming with power. It headed south, likely looping down to Main before heading north again toward the statehouse up Third or Fourth. Another smaller march walked by a few minutes later, turning off Broad.

Natalie continued reading; she continued typing and deleting, typing and deleting, eventually closing her notes app entirely.

Perhaps speaking from the heart would be the better approach.

It's time. The text came from Ben.

After draining her coffee and throwing the cup in the recycling bin, she exited the cafe and headed to the crosswalk. She waited for a bus to pass, then the signal switched to "walk," a rhythmic beeping echoing the message. She crossed High Street and took the first path heading into the Ohio Statehouse's main plaza, where a throng of a few hundred now gathered with signs. Ben stood near the front with a microphone and amplifier, all while a dozen cops stood a few meters behind him on the other side of the aluminum barricades.

"You ready?" Ben said as she approached. He handed her a wireless clip mic, and she attached to her collar. From a bag, he pulled a belt of bluetooth speakers, and she looped it around her waist.

"We don't really have a choice, do we?" Natalie replied.

"I suppose not. We're past the point of no return."

· · ● · ● · · · ·

"Who are we?"

"We are the Revolution!"

"No justice, no peace!"

"Give us a future, or give us death!"

"For the climate, for our future, for our children, for our planet!"

The chants echoed and bounced throughout downtown Columbus. They'd continued for hours. Natalie had given speeches large and small, as had dozens of activists.

Not a single politician had stepped outside the building to speak with the protesters.

The cops had largely ignored the protest, as it remained "peaceful" by their definition of the word.

Dozens of media crews had covered most of the day, but only a few remained.

All of it was to be expected, but now was the time to consider their next step. The big step. The one they'd planned for months.

The politicians weren't listening; it was time to make them listen.

"Everything is in position," Claire said. She rested her hands on Ben and Natalie's shoulders. "It's—" She paused, her eyes shifting to the left.

Natalie followed her line of sight to see a group of young teenagers—possibly not even teens—walking toward them. All wore forest-green leafy garments, as if they'd walked right out of a fantasy novel. They were led by an older character, their age range a little more . . . ambiguous, with green skin. She didn't recognize them, though she'd heard the stories. Except for one—Joshua. Mike's nephew, the one who'd spoken as Gaia at the Bent Greens meeting three years ago.

"Hello Claire," said the youngest-looking child. "A moose sends its regards."

Claire shook her head. "I'm sure it does."

"Joshua," Natalie said, "Who are your friends?"

"This is Sage," Joshua said, pointing to the green-skinned young adult. "And these two . . . they don't have names. They just are."

"We are spirits, you could say," said the one who knew Claire. "Manifestations. We are here, and we are also elsewhere. You are one story, and we are part of others worldwide, from Mumbai to London to Shanghai to Lima."

"I've heard of you," Natalie said, pointing at Sage. "I've heard your story."

"I am here as their protector, as is Joshua," said Sage. "They are here with a message, here at the end. Well, *an end*."

"We are tired," said the manifestation, both speaking in unison. "We speak for a tired earth, one that cannot continue giving as it has been giving. Its gifts are nearly spent. Its power will subside. That moment arrives, maybe sooner than you think. So we are here to say—it's time to fight. Truly fight. For soon the fight will end, and only survival will remain."

"But how do we truly fight?" Natalie asked. "Is that not what we're about to do?"

"Before you act, right now," Sage said, "Take a moment to truly listen." He held out a hand.

Confused and intrigued, Natalie took the outstretched hand. Sage guided her toward the grass nearby.

"Lay down," he said. He flopped onto the grass.

She did likewise.

"Breathe slowly. Quietly. Imagine the Earth, imagine Gaia. Everything, interconnected, a beating heart of one superorganism. We are all Gaia. What hurts the planet hurts us, and vice versa."

She closed her eyes and breathed, allowing the protest chants to become white noise. She imagined Earth from space, but immediately realized her mistake. That was too zoomed out. No, instead, she focused on herself. Her systems. Her relationship to the air all around, the molecules that she breathed, that the grass breathed, that the trees breathed. That the politicians inside breathed.

All of it, all of it was Gaia.

And its voice spoke.

> *You are ready. We are ready. Let us*
> *begin.*

Natalie opened her eyes to find herself already flying. She floated high above the Ohio Statehouse, the air swirling and lifting her with ease. She expected fear, but instead she only found peace. And something else.

The feelings, the feelings and thoughts of hundreds. No, thousands. Thousands of Awakened, here in Columbus and across the world, all connected together. In unison, demonstrating the gifts given to them by the planet they called home.

> A woman—no, dozens of women—stand on the statehouse lawn, guiding the growing of a vibrant forest. Its branches whistle in the wind.

Near the river, algae creatures
emerge, sliding up Broad Street toward the protest. Their bulk soaks
up the wooden bullets fired upon
them by cops outside city hall.

Animals of all shapes and sizes
rush the streets. Wolves from Oregon, snakes from the Amazon,
geese from Canada, and beyond.

Trees spring to life, standing
above the crowd and rushing the
walls of the statehouse. They release ear-piercing cries.

Natalie sensed all these things, simultaneously. She didn't know for
certain whether they were all occurring here in Columbus, or if she
just felt as if they all were here, in her spatial presence. But they were
happening somewhere. Here. Everywhere.

The cops didn't stand a chance—they rushed out of their hiding
places only to have nature swarms mixed with Awakened and protesters hasten them away. The natural world erupted upon the streets of
Columbus.

And, Natalie knew, nature erupted across the world.

She can barely register her world shifting and blurring as a tornado
thrusted forth from her soul. For a moment, her limbs burned; then,
all went silent.

Her vision cleared.

Looking up, she found the statehouse's dome cracked open. Around
her stared a crowd of stunned politicians and corporate elites.

Natalie clicked the button to activate the volume of the bluetooth
speakers at her waist. She didn't know how much time she'd have before

security descended upon her, but it didn't matter. Perhaps she was about to die, but she would say her piece.

Or, more accurately, she'd say Gaia's message for the world.

"The world has no more time," Natalie said, her speakers amplifying her voice. In her peripherals, she registered a reporter raising a small camera, and she shifted to face it. "We have always put off the time to truly, truly act to protect future generations from climate change. Not now, but later. But now is the time because *there is no more time. It is either now, or never. It is either now, or death for us all.*" For a moment, she considered threatening precisely what she'd done all those years ago in Sacramento, but Gaia's voice stayed the thought. Instead, she breathed inwardly, breathed outwardly, and simply sent a strong breeze emanating away from her body, rustling the clothes and hair of the politicos in the room. "We Awakened have made our message clear, speaking on behalf of the planet. We can do nothing else."

"What would you have us do?" someone shouted. "You think you can do better?"

"Just listen," Natalie said. "Truly listen."

She walked toward the steps leading to the doors exiting back into the statehouse's large plaza. No one stopped her, the crowd parting like a river parts for a boulder. Giant trees have already pulled back the doors, crushing the security checkpoint. The guards were nowhere to be seen.

As she approached the doors, Ben and Claire rushed inside, stopping upon seeing her.

"It won't be enough," Natalie said. "They won't listen, and even if they do, they're only one group of world leaders among many."

"I wouldn't be so sure."

Natalie turned around to see Jordan holding up a tablet. He must have been in the crowd inside the dome.

"What do you mean?" she asked.

"Your words are already spreading like wildfire across the world," said Jordan. "But not just you. Hundreds of Awakened, everywhere, saying the exact same words in dozens of languages." He lifted the tablet to eye level.

She watched the multiple feeds pinned on the screen. Cairo. Rome. Geneva. New York. Tokyo. The big cities, but also the small ones. Villages in rural Russia whose names she didn't recognize. Small towns in Nigeria. One man, standing before a county courthouse in rural Kansas.

Everyone spoke the same words.

Ben shook his head. "Perhaps I'm finally convinced by this Gaia nonsense."

"Oh?" Natalie said. "I thought you beat me to belief."

"I've wanted to believe, but you can't really deny this." He shrugged. "But I think it's clear. The planet has spoken."

"I have a feeling our stories are about to change." Natalie sighed. "Gaia said the fight would soon end."

"I think this is *an ending*, if not the end," Claire replied.

"The planet is finishing its song," said Sage. The green-skinned young man had appeared out of nowhere. "As I said earlier, this is *an end*. You are correct, Claire. Now humanity either listens or not. But it must meet its fate head on."

MOMENTS FROM A COFFEE SHOP
ADAM BASSETT

Town of Chatteris, United Kingdom
2113 C.E.

I. Monday

It's hard to imagine a time before the fens flooded. The world has changed too much and my memory of what came before feels too distant and muddled to be real. As I approach the coffee shop, I see ten wind turbines—and an empty base for another—behind it. The narrow blades spin, the air filled with their gentle humming. I hardly notice it anymore.

Some cunning people have been suggesting solar panels now as well, constructed along hypothetical bridges that might reconnect the Fen Islands to the new shores of Great Britain. Not to mention the flood tour groups; or the hotels and tourist traps erected along the new coastlines already. Everyone has big plans for the land we lost, as well as the coasts we gained.

I took my usual spot by the window, where I could watch the turbines spin endlessly above the shallow sea. The coffee's warmth. The cup in my hands. Refuge on a Monday. A reassurance that everything will be okay, despite my restless hands and a knowledge that this week would suck.

II. Tuesday

Paul's daughter began her speech
with: "I called Dad a *retroactivist*

because he always fought to fix broken
things: turbines, watches, and he composted

fucking everything," which
got her a little laugh from

those in attendance at his
funeral. I think the term suited Paul

well. He was a social media
warrior, imparting life lessons

like a bold new politician in training,
always racing to make something

of himself before the leukemia
beat him to it. His daughter concluded:

"Dad had a heart of gold, but
not enough money to polish it."

III. Wednesday

I used my lens to snap a photo of the shallow sea. You can see the sky in this one, and how the sun turns the water a bright shade of amber, though it's still snowing. Somehow, nature finds a way to dust the island despite the cutting golden light.

Most of the ten turbines are in frame, gently spinning above the water, causing ripples in the sea as their bases shift from the motion of the blades above. The ripples crash into one another, breaking and dissipating and overwhelmed by a ferry's wake but the boat is just out of sight.

The seagulls aren't, though. They fly overhead, gliding in the light. I'd seen them eat just about everything. Paul used to call them *sky rats* and said he once caught sight of one trying to lodge a plastic can from the last century down its throat.

I posted the photo online for all to see and took a sip of my coffee—and set it back down. The barista fetched me a cup of ice water for the newest burn on my impatient tongue, and I took a moment to indulge in it at my seat.

In the distance, a group of people wearing grey and blue uniforms used a special hovercraft to bring a new turbine out into the sea. I sipped my water while I watched the crane lower the tower into the empty base, and piece by piece the crew assembled the eleventh turbine.

IV. Thursday

The Californians started posting videos of fires again. A blaze is tearing across the coast. Somehow it takes me by surprise every year, when it happens every year. They post their stories en masse and we're all just watching that fractal of red and orange, each survivor lost apparitions cloaked in fear like it's a new chronic condition. It keeps me awake at night, but baby Jack's been crying so I'm up anyhow. Even after I decide to stop looking, there's just one more video about a person who lost their home, displaying it all as part of the international exhibition.

On Thursday morning I donated £50 to the Western Republic Red Cross and I've been trying to ignore the thread of notifications on my lens while I get an extra large cup of coffee before work.

V. Friday

A woman took a seat at my table and introduced herself as Anna. I recognized her from the funeral and the words she offered there about her retroactivist father.

Anna explained that she found something for me when cleaning out the old house on East Park Street. She pulled an old cloth from her bag. It was wrapped into a ball, tied off at the top.

I untied it and all sorts of pieces dropped onto the table. Bits of glass and wire and petite gears and springs and a wide leather strap worn to tatters. It was my husband's watch. I'd recognize it anywhere. I'd given it to Paul for repairs, but he told us it was too badly damaged. Anna said it was on his workbench when she finally made it into the house. It was the last thing he'd been working on.

Paul was always fixing broken things.

VI. Saturday

Her name was Jaqueline Aitken, but she goes by *Jait*. She plucks her six-string acoustic, taps a pedal with her foot. Each incremental loop brings another layer into the track, grouping it with each one that came before. After several minutes Jait takes the microphone for the chorus. By then the sound has blurred together into a solo orchestra and the words—Norwegian—sound like a rite to some forgotten God.

My husband is here with me tonight.

He brought Jack and our boy is (apparently) mesmerised by the sight. It's the first time he's heard real music. Usually the coffee shop has something playing, but never anything live. Much less from real wooden instruments. These sounds have a weight to them.

Listening to Jait makes annual memories suddenly in-season. It's evident in the way everyone records and takes photos of the musician like she's a sculpture at the Louvre and we're all just trying to prove that people and moments like this still exist in the world.

I wonder what Jack will think of music when he's our age.

After the performance, I brought Jack to meet her. I prod him to say hi, but he's shy. She shows him her guitar, tells him in English about the rosewood and nylon and mother-of-pearl, then switches to Norwegian just to make him smile.

Jack's fingers curled around a nylon string and she tells him, "Look at you, you're a musician too."

And he laughs.

VII. Sunday

Morning brew in my hands and the grounds fill the air.

Thirty-three blades spinning in prayer.

Adam Bassett

Adam Bassett is a UX/UI designer and former Editor-in-Chief of Worldbuilding Magazine. He was born in northern New York, wrote these stories in Tennessee, and might be somewhere else entirely by the time you're reading this. He's an avid writer, but currently spends most of his time helping other writers improve their work with the team at Campfire Technology.

He can be found on Twitter @adamcbassett.

AE Faulkner

A. E. Faulkner was born and raised in Pennsylvania. When she's not lost in a book, she loves spending time with her husband and two sons, especially while hiking, biking, or exploring nature. She loves almost everything about nature—ticks excluded, and one of her biggest fears is the repercussions we will face when nature can no longer tolerate human destruction. As such, she never tires of reading dystopian-themed tales. Stories about the end of the world absolutely fascinate her.

Visit her website: http://authoraefaulkner.com

Brandon Crilly

Brandon Crilly has been published by Daily Science Fiction, Apex Magazine, Fusion Fragment, Haven Spec, and other markets. He's also an Aurora Award-winning podcaster, reviewer, conference organizer, and

Dungeon Master for a bunch of other writers. His debut novel Catalyst was published by Atthis Arts in 2022. Visit his website: https://brandon crilly.com.

Brian Schmidt

Brian Schmidt is a 2023 graduate of University of Dayton. He enjoys games, and novels, and writes in his free time.

C.D. Tavenor

C. D. Tavenor is a science fiction and fantasy author based in Columbus, Ohio. Their published works include The Chronicles of Theren Trilogy and The War of Light, as well as Shattered Worlds: A SciFi & Fantasy Story Collection. They're excited to tell stories that engage readers beyond a desire for entertainment, whether through philosophical inspiration or social inquiry. And they're a firm believer in connecting every piece of fiction to reality, whether through their themes or their settings.

Learn more about C. D. Tavenor at https://www.twodoctorsmedia.com.

Christopher R. Muscato

Christopher R. Muscato is a writer, dad of twins, and adjunct history instructor from Colorado. He is the former writer-in-residence of the High Plains Library District and a winner of the inaugural XR Wordsmith Solarpunk Storytelling Showcase.

Learn more about Christopher's work at https://www.solarpunkstorytelling.com/.

Ernest Solar

Ernest Solar is an author and a professor at Mount St. Mary's University in Maryland. He's written several paranormal themed short stories and books, as well as education-related articles on mindfulness and motivation to write. His books can be found on any of the major bookseller websites.

Isha G. K.

Isha G. K. (she/her) is a civil engineer by education, climate finance researcher by training, and fiction writer by choice. Her stories champion humanity in narratives about post-colonial India, climate change, and technological advancement. Born in Mumbai, Isha has lived in the US and in the UK and currently calls New Delhi home. Most frequently, though, she can be found traveling the multiverse exploring its public transport systems, live music venues, and many plant-based dishes.

Find Isha G. K. on Twitter & Instagram: @ishagkwrites!

Jason A. Bartles

Jason A. Bartles, originally from West Virginia, now calls Philadelphia home. He lives with his husband and two dogs, a blue-eyed husky and a pit-mix who will lick your face off. He teaches Latin American literature and Spanish at a regional university.

Learn more about Jason's work on his website: https://jasonabartles.wordpress.com!

Laurel Beckley

Laurel Beckley is a writer, Marine Corps veteran and librarian. She is from Oregon, and currently lives in northern Virginia with her wife, fur creatures and a collection of gently neglected houseplants.

Learn more about Laurel at https://thesuspectedbibliophile.home.blog/

Nicholas Haney

Nicholas Haney turned to writing to stay sane in a world that seemed increasingly less so. Or perhaps it was the other way around. To date, he has published six novels, technicals works, countless blogs, and several short stories including one in the first Gaia Awakens. He calls the Great Lakes home, along with his wife and several furry quadrupeds.

P. J. Sky

P. J. Sky is a writer of short stories and novels, mostly in the post-apocalyptic and dystopian genre, for YA and adult readers. Born and raised in the UK, P. J. Sky wrote from a young age. Their first novel, A Girl Called Ari, was released in 2020 and won the Drunken Druid Book of the Year 2020. The sequel, Ari Goes To War, was released in 2021, followed in 2022 by the third and final book in there series, Ari Between Worlds.

S.E. MacCready

S.E. MacCready lives in Pennsylvania with her daughter and their four cats. When she's not writing, she can be found reading or playing video games.

Learn more about S.E. MacCready's work at semaccready.com!

Thank you for reading *Nature Erupts* and *The World's Revolution!*

For more great stories published by Two Doctors Media Collaborative, visit https://www.twodoctorsmedia.com.